# GOD AIN'T THROUGH YET

## Other books by Mary Monroe

*God Ain't Blind*

*The Company We Keep*

*She Had It Coming*

*Deliver Me From Evil*

*God Don't Play*

*In Sheep's Clothing*

*Red Light Wives*

*God Still Don't Like Ugly*

*Gonna Lay Down My Burdens*

*God Don't Like Ugly*

*The Upper Room*

"Nightmare in Paradise" in *Borrow Trouble*

# GOD AIN'T THROUGH YET

# MARY MONROE

KENSINGTON BOOKS

http://www.kensingtonbooks.com

Dafina Books are published by

Kensington Publishing Corp.
119 West 40th Street
New York, NY 10018

All Kensington titles, imprints, and distributed lines are available at special
quantity discounts for bulk purchases for sales promotion, premiums, fund-
raising, educational, or institutional use.

Special book excerpts or customized printings can also be created to fit spe-
cific needs. For details, write or phone the office of the Kensington Special
Sales Manager: Attn. Special Sales Department. Kensington Publishing Corp.,
119 West 40th Street, New York, NY 10018. Phone: 1-800-221-2647.

Dafina and the Dafina logo Reg. U.S. Pat. & TM Off.

Library of Congress Card Catalogue Number: 2010921528
ISBN-13: 978-0-7582-3859-7
ISBN-10: 0-7582-3859-2

First Printing: June 2010
10 9 8 7 6 5 4 3 2 1

Printed in the United States of America

*This book is dedicated to four of the most special people on the planet: Meredith Riley, Mitzi Dunn, Sandra "Diane" Ridgeway, and Tara Worthy.*

# ACKNOWLEDGMENTS

One of my biggest fans was a fellow author who was loved by so many folks: E. Lynn Harris. I didn't get to meet him in person and it is one of my biggest regrets. It was during one of my first public events that I realized how special he was. The host at the bookstore where I was signing handed me a stack of books to sign for people who had not been able to attend the event. One of those people was E. Lynn Harris. Later, he e-mailed me out of the blue to congratulate me and wish me luck with *God Don't Like Ugly*. I will miss him.

I am sincerely grateful for the massive support I receive from my other fans, the booksellers, book clubs, radio and TV stations, libraries, my media escorts who take such good care of me on my book tours, the staff at the Ivy restaurant in Beverly Hills, and my hosts at the Venetian, the Wynn, and Bellagio in Las Vegas. I especially appreciate the support of my fans who live outside of the United States and who go out of their way to get copies of my books in a timely manner.

I can't thank my Kensington family enough for treating me so special! My editor, Selena James, is always available when I need her. Adeola Saul and Karen Auerbach, my current publicists, and Maureen Cuddy and Joan Schulhafer, the publicists who took such good care of me in the beginning—I love you all. To the "honchos" Walter Zacharius, Steven Zacharius, and Laurie Parkin—I love you all, too! I sincerely appreciate and thank the folks in the sales department for doing so many wonderful things for me. And to everyone else at Kensington, thank you from the bottom of my heart.

Andrew Stuart, my agent, continues to guide me in the right direction. Thank you, Andrew.

Lauretta Pierce, thank you for keeping my Web site maintained.

To everyone else, as long as you keep reading, I will keep writing.

Please continue to share your thoughts, comments, suggestions, and opinions (even the mean ones . . . ha ha) by e-mailing me at

*Authorauthor5409@aol.com* or by visiting my Web site *www.Marymonroe. org* as often as possible.

All the best,

Mary Monroe
June 2010

# CHAPTER 1

*Richland, Ohio, 1997*

My husband was the *last* man in town that the people in our close-knit circle of friends expected to have an affair. Why he didn't cheat was as much of a mystery to me as it was to them. When I mentioned to one of my female friends that I was married to a man who didn't cheat, her only question was, "What's wrong with him?"

It saddened me to hear that some people thought that there was something wrong with a man who didn't cheat on his wife.

"There is nothing wrong with my husband. He's as normal as any other man," I told that friend.

"Ha! If that's the case, he's *not* normal," that friend told me.

Maybe she was right. If it was normal for a man to cheat, then Pee Wee was not normal.

Despite the fact that I had cheated on my husband just a few months ago (yes, *I'd* cheated, but I'll get to that later) and had accused him of being unfaithful on numerous occasions, I knew in my heart that he had not slept with another woman since he married me. However, one of my concerns was the other women who were dying to get their hands on him.

"If you ever break up with Pee Wee, send him to me," another female friend had jokingly suggested. "He's perfect."

When I told my mother what my friend had said, she told me,

"Girl, as brazen and desperate as women are these days, I'd be worried if I were you."

Even after my mother's comment, I didn't worry or complain because I felt secure and comfortable. Looking back on it now, I realize I was too comfortable. That was my first mistake. I had a ringside seat in the eye of a major hurricane, but I was so comfortable I didn't realize that until it was too late.

The day that Pee Wee, my "perfect" husband, abruptly and cruelly left me for another woman had started out like any other day. It was the middle of March, and still a little too cold for my tastes. I'd been a resident of Ohio for over forty years by this time, and I still hadn't adjusted to the weather. When I was a child growing up in Florida, I used to run around naked in our front yard in March. Kids doing such a thing in Ohio, in March, was unheard of.

I had crawled out of bed during the night and turned up the thermostat. When the weather was nice enough, Pee Wee slept in the nude, and I usually slept in something very skimpy. Right after dinner the night before, he had slid into a pair of flannel pajamas. I'd wiggled into a pair of purple thong panties, a matching Wonderbra, and a snug cotton nightgown. I'd slid my freshly pedicured feet into a pair of nylon socks. Large pink sponge rollers covered every inch of my head, individually wrapped around my thick, recently dyed black hair. A rose-scented, wrinkle-busting, white gel, one of the many weapons that I used to fight Father Time, covered my face. We looked like we were made up for a Halloween party, but it had been a night of raw passion. I had peeled off my socks and that snug gown like a stripper. He'd helped me remove everything else. Within minutes I had his handprints on parts of my body that hadn't been touched since my last physical exam. And I had assumed positions that I hadn't been in since I gave birth to my daughter. Afterward, I fell asleep in his arms. But when I opened my eyes the next morning, I was in bed alone.

Pee Wee had already left the house by the time I got up and made it downstairs to the kitchen. That was odd, but it wasn't that big of a deal because he didn't do it that often. He usually waited for me to fix his favorite breakfast: grits, biscuits, scrambled eggs with green bell peppers mixed in, and beef bacon. And when I didn't get up in time to cook, he strapped on an apron and did it. The last time he had prepared breakfast, he had served it to me in bed.

For some reason, Pee Wee had not made breakfast this particular morning. He'd left the small clock radio on the kitchen counter on to some rap station (how many people listened to rap music this early in the morning?) and a mess on the kitchen table, which included the morning newspaper folded with the pages out of order, his empty coffee cup, a Krispy Kreme donut box, and an ashtray with the remnants of a thick marijuana cigarette piled up in it. I made a mental note to scold him about leaving a roach in plain view. It was hard enough trying to hide certain things and activities from our inquisitive eleven-year-old daughter, Charlotte, not to mention nosy relatives and friends who dropped in at the most inconvenient times. One day my mother went snooping through my bedroom closet and stumbled across an XXX-rated VHS tape that I often watched with Pee Wee when our sex life needed a shot in the arm. She took me aside and quoted Scripture nonstop for twenty minutes. By the time she got through with me, I felt like I knew every harlot in the Bible personally. She'd "excused" Pee Wee and "reminded" me that men were too weak, stupid, and horny to know better.

Pee Wee and I had shared a good laugh over that. Our life together was so idyllic at times that my meddlesome mother's antics and crude comments didn't bother us. I had the best of both worlds. He was not just my husband; he was also my best friend.

In spite of all my shortcomings and flaws, I looked at matters of the heart from a realistic point of view. I knew that no man, or woman, was perfect, and that anybody could make a mistake. Me jumping into bed with that low-down, funky, black devil that I got involved with last year was one of the biggest mistakes I'd ever made in my entire life. It had been such an intense and passionate affair that it had me acting like a fool. I had done things for him that I had never done to please a man. I'd told lies to be with him. And I'd given him money. It had begun gradually, but when I realized I was "paying" for some dick, I got real concerned because that went against everything I believed in. When I refused to continue paying for my pleasure, the relationship ended in a violent confrontation. Luckily, I had escaped uninjured—at least physically. But I had "paid" a very high price for my mistake. I was so disgusted with myself that for a long time it was hard for me to look in a mirror without flinching.

My husband had reluctantly forgiven me, and we had moved on. "Annette, you ain't the first woman to cheat, and you won't be the last. I'll get over what you done . . . I guess," he told me, cracking a weak smile to hide some of the pain that I'd caused.

I could not have been more repentant and humble if they'd revised the Bible and included a psalm in my honor. "Honey, I swear to God, something like this will never happen again," I assured him, with reconstructive ideas about how I was going to repair my marriage swimming around in my head.

Once that was behind us, I began to focus on the only intimate relationship that mattered to me now. But I was no fool. I knew that if *I* could fall into the deep black hole of infidelity, anybody could. However, since it was usually the man who acted a fool and got involved in an affair, it was more important for me to focus on what my husband might or might not do. I believed that if he ever did cheat on me, I had to look at the situation from an overall point of view: Would I be better off without this man? Does he no longer love me? Is he worth fighting for? Is this marriage dead? Has he become such a slimy devil that he is no longer good enough for me anyway?

Had any of that been the case, the bombshell that my husband dropped in my lap this morning wouldn't have caused so much damage. Because when he informed me that he was having an affair, I could not have been more stunned if somebody had told me that the Easter Bunny was a pimp.

He had committed the granddaddy of indiscretions: a torrid, ongoing, "I'd rather be with her than you," sexual relationship with a woman whom I had called my friend. To me, that was the worst kind of affair. If I couldn't trust my husband and a woman I called my friend, who could I trust?

To make matters even worse, I was probably the last person in our circle to hear about his affair!

# CHAPTER 2

Pee Wee was self-employed, and he took advantage of his position. He usually moseyed on over to the barbershop he owned, which was located a couple of miles from our house, whenever he felt like it. Some days he didn't go in at all. He had dependable people working for him, so it wasn't necessary for him to be on the premises all the time.

He spent his time away from work fishing in some of the many lakes and rivers in the northern Ohio area or just hanging around the house enjoying the lifestyle of a successful, self-made man. Lately, he'd been taking off days so that he could do special things for me. One day last week he took off so he could shampoo our carpets and prepare dinner. Now that might not sound so romantic to most people, but when he did that, it was because he wanted me to be extra nice to him. That was one of my easiest jobs. Pee Wee didn't have to do much to get me to be nice to him. I never told him that, but it was a win-win situation. The more he pampered me, the more I pampered him.

I didn't think anything about him going in early that Friday morning and then coming back home about an hour later, until I heard the red Firebird he drove pull up and stop in our driveway. I knew it was his car without even looking out the window. He had done one of those stupid things that men do to the motors of their cars so that it now had such a distinctive sound I'd know that Firebird was in the vicinity immediately, even without seeing it.

Right away I assumed he had forgotten something, or that maybe he had decided to take the day off so he could do something special for me. Since we had been trying to repair the damage to our marriage that my affair had caused, he initiated sexy little activities like calling me at my job and ordering me to meet him at a nearby motel for a quickie.

One day last month he'd sent a stretch limo to my job to bring me to a romantic hotel suite that he'd reserved for the night. By the time I got there, he had already ordered a candlelit filet mignon dinner and a dozen red roses. The last time he'd called me at work—interrupting my weekly staff meeting—it was to tell me to meet him in an alley behind the Grab and Go convenience store so I could give him a blow job in his car.

I was the one who had cheated, but he was the one who was bending over backward to keep our marriage alive. That was the kind of man he was.

Just thinking about my passionate relationship with my husband generated a wicked smile that spread across my face like a knife wound. There was just no telling what he had up his sleeves, or in his pants, for me this time.

I turned off the radio. Now I was so turned on, I practically collapsed back into my seat at the table, settling into it like a jaybird claiming its nest. I spread my legs open as I waited for Pee Wee to come in the house. It got so hot between my legs I had to spread my thighs so I could cool off my crotch.

I was anxious and curious to see what he was up to. I hoped that it was something that we could do quickly, because I had a lot of work on my desk at the office and I wanted to get there at a reasonable hour, hopefully before noon. That was mainly because I had plans to do lunch with a sister friend from the Baptist church that I attended from time to time. That poor woman—she had just found out that her husband was fucking his ex, so she needed some advice. Advice on what, I didn't know. I was surprised that a woman with a cheating husband would want advice from a woman with a man like mine. What in the world did she think I could tell her? I certainly could not tell her what to do to keep her man from cheating. It was too late for that. But I was also known as a good listener, and I had two very nice shoulders for people to cry on. I was pretty sure that those were some of the things that made me so appealing to my husband.

My office hours were from nine to five; but as a senior manager for Mizelle's Collection Agency, I had a lot of flexibility. Some days I went in an hour or so earlier than I was supposed to, some days I stayed an hour or so late, and some days I worked from home. I didn't even have to get out of bed or my nightgown on those days. I just propped up a few pillows in my bed, kicked back with my legs crossed at the ankles, and perused a few files. I even enjoyed a few glasses of wine while doing it. It seemed like I was literally getting paid to "kick back." What more could I ask for? But since I loved my job and I loved getting out of the house, I preferred going to work to staying home.

Glancing at my watch, I saw that it was a few minutes past eight. I was already dressed and my office was only a short drive from my house. I figured I'd get there early enough to finish most of the work on my desk and address any issues that required my attention before I went to lunch with Sister Scruggs. Since it was casual Friday, I wore a fairly short denim skirt and a yellow Bob Marley T-shirt. It was a "youthful" outfit, but I was a youthful middle-aged woman. It was also one of my favorite outfits. I had been a fool for Bob Nesta Marley since his "I Shot the Sheriff" days. Before my recent 100-pound weight loss, wearing T-shirts or skirts or dresses with hems above my ankles was something that I could do only in my dreams.

The bathroom scale was still my worst enemy. When I stepped on it this morning, it claimed I had gained eight pounds back, and here I was smacking on my third Krispy Kreme glazed donut in the last twenty minutes! I laughed out loud; then I glared at the donut, hating it for what it represented. Just thinking about all the compliments I received about my drastic weight loss, and the proud way my husband looked when we went out in public, brought me back down to earth. I put the rest of that third donut back into the box and brushed the crumbs off my hands. "Now," I said with a mighty belch, proud that I still had some self-control and discipline.

I had sent my daughter off to Reed Street Elementary School, which was only a few blocks away. I still had time to have a couple of cups of coffee before I left the house. And if Pee Wee had something else in mind for me to do, there was time for that, too.

Despite all the problems that we had encountered in our eleven-year marriage, Pee Wee and I still had it good.

Life was so good to me.

I was happy. My husband was happy. I had everything I wanted. My proverbial cup was not just running over, it was falling over.

I never would have guessed in a million years that I was about to lose that cup and everything in it.

I looked at my watch again. I listened and waited. The longer I listened and waited, the more anxious I felt. The wind was howling like a wounded animal. Normally, it was one of the sorriest sounds in the world as far as I was concerned. It didn't bother me much this time, though. The wind was also blowing hard. It made the tree branches on the cherry tree that leaned toward the side of my kitchen rattle the window above my sink like a clumsy burglar. It seemed to be taking a long time for Pee Wee to get out of the car and into the house. But then he was not as spry as he used to be. Like with me and most of our friends, intruders such as arthritis, gout, excessive gas, incontinence, and other ailments associated with age had become some of his most frequent visitors. He was still in good shape for a man his age, but he had slowed down considerably over the years. However, he wasn't *that* slow. Several minutes had passed since he pulled up in our driveway!

I rose from my seat at the table and was about to trot over to the window above the sink so I could look out into our driveway on the side of our house. I wanted to check and make sure he had not stumbled on a rock, or stepped on a pop top and landed faceup on the ground like old man Kelsy next door did from time to time. Before I could reach the window, I heard his car door slam. A second later, I heard a second car door slam. That was odd, but I didn't go to the window to investigate. I scrambled back to the table and sat back down, trying not to look too excited.

As soon as Pee Wee opened our back door and entered the kitchen, I knew that something serious was about to unravel.

# CHAPTER 3

Even though I read Pee Wee like a book, there were times when I had no idea what was on his mind. He kept secrets from me, but that didn't bother me because I kept a few secrets from him, too. But I could usually tell when something was wrong. This was one of those times. Something was definitely wrong. For one thing, he didn't look directly at me, and he was not alone. Elizabeth Stovall, the manicurist who worked in his barbershop, was with him.

"Annette, we all need to talk. We need to talk right now. It's real important," Pee Wee blurted, his eyes darting around the room as he shuffled across the floor. He stopped in front of the table and finally looked at me. His face was so stiff it looked like he had turned to stone. When he coughed to clear his throat, his lips didn't even move. Then he glanced at the Krispy Kreme donut box, frowning at it like it was a dirty diaper. He was the one who had coaxed me into eating those damn things on a regular basis. But by the way he was wringing his hands and glaring at the box, you would have thought that he was looking at a hand grenade. He nudged Lizzie with his elbow.

"Uh, yeah, we all need to talk," Lizzie said.

Now, this was an interesting turn of events. I had told Pee Wee just yesterday to tell Lizzie that I wanted her to help us plan our next backyard cookout. I decided that she must have been anxious to share some ideas with me for her to come to the house so soon.

I liked Elizabeth. We had all attended junior and high school together, and I had been one of the few classmates who had not teased or made fun of her. And even though she liked me, too, back then we didn't have enough in common for me to consider cultivating a friendship with her. But she was a friend now because I had handpicked her to work for my husband when she lost her job. One reason that I'd encouraged Pee Wee to hire her was because I pitied her. Poor woman. She was so socially isolated and awkward. She was the kind of wallflower whom other wallflowers felt sorry for. I knew that for a fact, because all through my teens I'd been a wallflower and I'd felt sorry for her. She was also so shy and withdrawn that she didn't have a lot of friends other than her staid parents and the elderly people at her church whom she played bingo with one night every week. *Bingo!* And on the most popular night in the week: Saturday. If that was not the last refuge for the truly desperate, I didn't know what was.

It was my nature to do things for other people that I thought would make them happy. However, my willingness to do "good deeds" sometimes backfired. I'd been betrayed and abused by more than one person over the years. But I had survived my trials and tribulations intact, and learned a few important lessons because of them.

At the end of the day, I felt blessed. However, I was now more alert, and not as trustworthy. I was so busy trying to avoid all of the wolves with sheep's clothing in their closets that I didn't even consider the fact that there were a lot of sheep who owned a few wolf outfits as well.

In the meantime, it was refreshing to have a friend like Lizzie in my life now. Life had not been too kind to her either.

Unfortunately, because of a bout with polio, one of Elizabeth's legs was noticeably thinner than the other. People called her Little Leg Lizzie. She admitted that she liked her cute nickname, and she encouraged people to call her that. She said it made her feel "special." But she didn't like it when people stared at her leg or made fun of her because of it. "It makes me feel like a freak," she had complained to me one day in Miss Krayling's gym class in tenth grade. Feeling like a freak was one of the things that she and I had in common all through school. That and the fact that none of our male classmates wanted to date us.

She had come such a long way. Now here she was in my kitchen for the first time (that I knew of), with my husband.

*Why?*

Pee Wee moved a few steps closer to me. Lizzie walked behind him, dragging the foot on her skinny leg like she was dragging a mop. This was the first time I'd seen her in running shoes. She was very fair skinned and she had sharp European features. As a matter of fact, people who didn't know her thought she was a full-blooded white woman because she had not inherited any of her black Jamaican father's features. Her straight, jet black hair was covered under a black scarf. She wore a yellow and brown tweed dress with the hem halfway down her legs and a long beige trench coat with a thin belt around the waist. And it must have been colder outside than I thought because her ears and nose were red.

I glanced at Lizzie's leg, the thinner one. I gave it, and her, a confused look. What I didn't understand about Lizzie's handicap was that it was not always that noticeable. When she wore pants or long skirts, you couldn't see the difference in her legs, and she didn't walk like there was a difference. However, I did notice that she walked with a mild limp when she got upset or nervous. Well, whatever it was now, she had entered my house walking like she had two club feet. And her eyes were on the floor.

"I hope you don't take things the wrong way," Pee Wee told me, blinking so hard his nostrils flared.

"I hope you don't either," Lizzie added, talking to me but looking at him.

I suddenly got the feeling that they had not come to talk to me about a backyard cookout. They didn't look too happy or comfortable to be in the same room with me. And what they had just said sounded ominous. My eyes darted back and forth from him to her. Then I fixed my gaze on my husband's face. He couldn't look me in the eyes. The way his eyes rolled up, he was looking more at the top of my head than he was my face.

"Pee Wee, talk to me," I ordered. "Look at me!" I hollered. He did, but he took his time doing it.

It felt like the air had been sucked out of my lungs by a gigantic vacuum cleaner. My left leg was shaking so hard against the table leg, the top of my pantyhose suddenly split open with a run that reached from my knee to my ankle. "What's going on?" I asked, finally rising. I had to grab the back of the chair to steady myself so I wouldn't fall. "Pee Wee, Lizzie, what's going on?" I asked again. I looked from his face to hers some more. He looked at her; then they both looked at me. My words stuck in my throat like a fish bone. I had to clear my throat before I could speak again. Bile and a large lump had begun to rise from somewhere within the pit of my insides. "What . . . is . . . wrong?" I demanded, sweat forming on my face.

"Wrong? Um, nothin' is *wrong*," Pee Wee managed, looking like a condemned man.

"The hell it isn't! Why else are you both standing here looking like pallbearers?" I hollered.

Something was definitely wrong. I could tell that just by the way my husband and my friend looked. If Pee Wee's face got any longer, it would be on the floor. There was sweat on his face, too. He was obviously nervous about something.

Lizzie looked guilty.

But guilty of what?

# CHAPTER 4

"**A**nnette, I want you to know that you are the last woman in the world I ever wanted to hurt," Lizzie mumbled, choking on a sob. "You've always been good to me. . . ." She removed a wrinkled white handkerchief from the small denim purse in her hand. She honked into her handkerchief; then she blinked real hard a few times. The next thing I knew, she grabbed my husband's arm—which was shaking like one of those branches outside on my cherry tree—with both of her hands. "I was glad when we all became friends."

*Friend?*

She didn't look like a friend of mine now. And the way she was holding on to my husband's arm, she looked more like his nurse than his friend. What she said next stung my ears like a wasp. "Baby, you tell her."

*Baby?* Had all of that sugar from those Krispy Kreme donuts dulled my mind to where I couldn't hear right? Had I just heard this woman address my husband as "baby" right in front of me? Yes, that was exactly how this woman had addressed my husband.

When I cleared my throat it sounded more like I was growling. "Well, *baby*, you or *somebody* better tell me something before I turn this damn house inside out!" I yelled. My voice was loud, dark, and deep, like thunder rolling out of a black hole in the sky. I had to press my lips together to keep the bile from oozing out.

"I'm gettin' to that," Pee Wee replied in a shaky voice with a shaky hand in the air. There was so much sweat on his face now that it looked like he'd just climbed out of the shower.

"Will somebody tell me what the hell is going on here? And you'd better tell me *now!*" I ordered, fists clenched. "What the fuck have you done to hurt me?" I looked so hard at Lizzie's hands on my husband that she released him. But the look that suddenly appeared on her face angered me even more. She looked like she had just swallowed Big Bird.

"I'm in love," Lizzie announced, dabbing at her eyes with the same handkerchief that she'd just used to blow her nose.

I don't remember what my first thought was when I heard that bitch croak that line because several thoughts danced around inside my head at the same time. In addition to those thoughts, there was a buzzing noise going back and forth, gnawing on my brain like a shark's teeth. The bile in my throat and mouth had turned into the worst kind of slush. I wanted to vomit, and the only reason I didn't was because I didn't want to soil my favorite T-shirt. But something told me that there was going to be a lot more than bile for me to deal with.

Lizzie had once been the plainest Jane in town. But after a recent extreme makeover—that I had encouraged—she'd been transformed into a more glamorous version of Betty Boop. However, she didn't look like Betty Boop to me right now. She looked more like one of those cheesy blow-up dolls that they propped up in the windows in adult sex product stores. No, that description of her was too mild. She looked like the devil. She had eased her wretched ass into my life, my husband's bed, and now my home.

Like with a terminal illness, when dealing with the devil, a person didn't know what all to expect. I sure didn't. If my husband and his she-devil had told me that Pee Wee's barbershop, which provided the lion's share of our impressive income, had burned to the ground or that they had been robbed, it would have been less painful than what they had just told me.

"You're in love, Lizzie? In love with who?" I asked, my eyes burning, my ears ringing. "I know you are not standing here telling me

. . . you and my husband . . ." I couldn't even finish my sentence because I could not believe my ears. Even though I knew in my heart that what I'd just heard was true, I still managed to laugh.

I was the only one laughing.

I stopped laughing because my throat suddenly felt like I had a rock stuck in it. I had to cough hard, so hard I almost choked on some air, to clear my throat before I could speak again. "Come on, you two. What is this really about?" I asked. I almost didn't recognize my own voice. It was so hoarse and husky I sounded like a man. I shook my head, rubbed my ear, and blinked. "What is really going on here?" I demanded. The words felt like rocks in my mouth, but I laughed again anyway. "Who are you in love with, Lizzie? Did Pee Wee finally hook you up with one of his friends?"

My mind felt as raggedy as a bowl of sauerkraut. I was talking out of my head. It made no sense for Lizzie to be telling me that she didn't want to hurt me if the person she was in love with was one of Pee Wee's friends. But what was becoming more and more obvious to me didn't make any sense either.

"Annette, maybe you should sit back down," Pee Wee suggested, nodding toward the chair I had risen from. "You might take this better sitting down."

"Sit down my ass!" I screamed, my lips trembling. I kicked the chair over and slammed my fist on the top of the table so hard that the newspaper and everything else on it fell to the floor, even that Krispy Kreme donut box. "Talk to me, dammit!"

Pee Wee's hand was in the air again and it was still shaking. "Hold on now! You ain't got to tear the house down!" he advised. For the first time, this man looked ugly to me. He had on the crisp white smock that he worked in, and the way I was feeling it could just as well be his shroud. I wanted to kill him, but first I needed to know exactly *why* I wanted to kill him.

"If you don't talk to me and tell me everything, this house won't be the only thing I tear down!" I threatened, kicking another one of the four chairs to the floor. My feet must have been heavier or stronger than I thought. Because when I kicked that second chair over, it landed with such a thud the radio on the counter came back on by itself. I was glad to see that I had put some fear into Lizzie. Her eyes got big and I could see the terror in her face. Now

I knew why she had worn running shoes to my house. There was a strong possibility that she might have to leave in a hurry.

"Annette, please try to understand," Pee Wee's voice trembled as he spoke. As frightened as they both appeared to be, I couldn't figure out why they'd been brave enough to face me in my own house in the first place. "I don't know how to tell you . . ."

"All I want is for you to finish what you came here to tell me!" I roared. My head was throbbing so hard now, my ears went numb. "Keep going and give me the whole story!"

Pee Wee put his arm around Lizzie's shoulder and pulled her closer to him. My eyes burned as I watched this scene unfold in front of me like a cheap beach towel.

"Uh, I didn't mean for this to happen, but it . . . but . . . it . . . did," he stammered. "And I feel the same way Lizzie feels. You are the last woman in the world that I ever wanted to hurt. I mean, look what you done for me," he said, making a sweeping gesture around the kitchen with his hand. He swallowed so hard he had to lift his chin. "You made a good home for me, and you gave me a beautiful daughter. I will always appreciate that. But"—he stopped and shook his head. He even smiled, but that smile was so empty and false that it stayed on his face for just a split second.

Then he gave me the most pitiful look that another human being had ever aimed in my direction. "I think I'd be happier with Lizzie for now. I am sure enough sorry, Annette! Honest to God I am!" he wailed.

My heart felt like it had been pierced by a poisoned dart. I couldn't think straight for a moment, and it took me a few more moments to get a grip on myself.

In the meantime, Pee Wee's words rang in my ears like a death sentence. And as far as I was concerned, that was exactly what it was.

# CHAPTER 5

There was a taste in my mouth that was so sour and nasty you would have thought that those donuts I'd eaten had been glazed with shit. I slid my tongue up, down, and around the walls inside of my mouth, hoping it would dissolve the coat of slime that was threatening to make me sick. It didn't help. All it did was move that slime from one spot to another, and that made my stomach roll with nausea. If somebody had dropped a piano on the top of my head, I could not have been more stunned. I slapped the side of my head with the palm of my hand and rubbed my ear. I blinked hard, because not only was I not sure of what I was hearing, I was not sure of what I was seeing. But there was nothing wrong with my vision. My husband and a woman whom I had considered a friend, were standing in front of me telling me that they were in love. It made zero sense.

I closed my eyes and shook my head. When I opened my eyes, Pee Wee was looking at me like I was the most pitiful and disgusting woman on the planet. And that was exactly how I felt. I was getting sick of the way he and Lizzie kept looking at each other before they turned to look at me at the same time. I had to wonder how long they had been rehearsing their performance in this real-life soap opera. "Wait a minute. Are you telling me that you and Little

Leg Lizzie are already having an affair?" I wanted to know, hands on my hips.

Their silence, and the fact that they couldn't look me in the face, was the only confirmation I needed.

"Like I just said, I'm sorry, baby," he mumbled, looking at me and pulling his lover even closer to him.

I appreciated a joke as much as the next person, if it was good. This was one of the lamest, most ridiculous jokes I'd ever heard. "This *has* to be a joke, and it's a bad one at that," I mouthed, glaring from Pee Wee to Lizzie. "Pee Wee, you ought to be ashamed of yourself," I scolded, giving him a dismissive wave and a slightly contemptuous look. At the same time, my mind was reeling, trying to find some reason for my husband to be standing in front of me telling me such a stupid joke. . . .

"Look, lady—this is no joke!" Lizzie had the nerve to say. And I knew she was not joking. I think I had known from the moment I'd heard this unimaginable news that it was not a joke. I just couldn't bring myself to believe it right away. I didn't know why then, and to this day I don't, but for some reason I'd thought that if I prolonged the conversation, it would ease the pain. It didn't. By then my stomach was churning like a volcano about to erupt.

I had to rub my stomach before I could speak again. As soon as I opened my mouth, tiny drops of puke shot out with the words. "Bitch, you'd better talk to me with some respect. You and your funky ass are in *my* house now. And you do not come up into my house talking to me like I am just another aging ghetto skank— like you! Not unless you want to leave here in a body bag," I warned, wiping vomit off my lips and chin with the back of my fist.

"You don't have to get so nasty, Annette! I'm trying to talk to you in a civilized manner! You are the one acting ghetto!" Lizzie shrieked like a shrew. In spite of her bravura, she seemed to shrink before my eyes. Even though she was about the same height as I was, she suddenly looked about four inches tall. I didn't know if that was because I had reduced her to almost nothing in my mind or because I was hallucinating. If I was hallucinating, then what I was seeing and hearing was not what I thought.

I couldn't have been more wrong.

"I'm taking Pee Wee," she told me with a snort and a smug look.

My hand was already in a fist and I was one step from sucker punching that smug look off of her face. "Taking him where, BITCH?"

Instead of answering my question, she turned to him and said, "I told you we should have told her in a letter! We both know how unstable this woman is. There's no telling what she might do. . . ."

Those words hit me like a cannonball. A sharp spasm attacked my leg, almost making me drop to the floor. "You got that right!" I told her, raising my fist.

Lizzie gasped and reared back on her legs, like she was about to run or duck. But instead of running or ducking, she clung to my husband even harder and looked at me with her eyes narrowed into slits. The expression on her face was so intense I could feel it. It felt like she was shining a flashlight in my face, a big one with a lot of heat and a painful glare like the kind cops used. Even though that hateful look she was giving me made my eyes burn, I refused to blink or rub them as long as hers were still on me. I didn't want to give her the satisfaction of seeing any more discomfort on my part than she was already seeing. It was a small gesture, but each time I managed to "hold my ground," so to speak, it made me feel better.

"Baby, let's get your things and get the hell up out of here!" Lizzie bellowed into my husband's ear. His eyes got big as he looked from her to me. This was one man who didn't know how lucky he was that he was still alive. In all of the days of my life, I had never seriously thought about committing homicide until now. It didn't take me long to dismiss that thought. If I was going to spend the rest of my days in jail, it was not going to be because I'd killed a man for dumping me for another woman. I was glad that I was still lucid enough to realize that *no* man was worth that.

However, I was not about to let them down gently. No matter what happened now, my name would remain on their lips and minds for a long time.

"Is my suitcase still in the bathroom closet?" Pee Wee asked me in a meek voice.

I ignored him as I turned to Lizzie. "Woman, I hired you to work for my husband. Are you standing here telling me that you are fucking him, too?" It was no secret around Richland that Lizzie

had led such a sheltered life she was still unattached at the age of
forty-seven. "You've never had a boyfriend or a husband before in
your life, but you are willing to settle for . . . for my leftovers? You
think so little of yourself that you will settle for licking the jar, scraping the bone?"

Pee Wee gasped so hard he stumbled, like he was the one who
had just been pushed into an abyss by two of the people he trusted
most in the world. "Annette, is that the way you saw me? The bottom of a jar? A bone?"

"Yes! And not a very tasty bone at that!" I roared. "I stayed with
your black ass because I thought you were a good man!"

"I was—*I am a good man!*" he defended, whimpering like a wounded
puppy.

"Well, if you don't get the fuck out of my house, you're going to
be a dead man, too!" I warned. "Go get that suitcase, pack up all
your shit, and get the fuck out of my face!" I dismissed them both
with a vigorous wave, but they didn't move.

"Annette, be reasonable. This man deserves to be happy," Lizzie
said, words oozing out of her mouth like syrup. "He needs *me*,"
she whimpered. I could not believe that she was talking to me like
we were discussing a recipe or a yard sale.

"Look, bitch, a good ass-whupping is what you need! And that is
exactly what you are going to get if you don't get the hell out of my
house," I warned. With my arms folded, I clip-clopped across the
floor like a stallion. I stopped with my face so close to Pee Wee's, I
could feel and smell his sour breath. "You better tell me what the
hell is going on here, and you better tell me now!"

Pee Wee's mouth dropped open and he stood still for several
seconds, looking at me in slack-jawed amazement. It seemed like
he was stalling for more time, more time to make me even more
miserable. I kept my eyes on his, and for the first time I noticed
how dead his eyes had become. The pupils were no longer a
sparkling shade of brown. They were now a shadowy shade of black,
with deep, dark circles above and below. *When did that happen?* I
wondered. *And why?* Well, whatever the reason was, it was too late
for me to fix.

"What the—how many more times do I have to tell you? Are you deaf! Do you want me to spell it out on a piece of paper or what? *I'm leavin' you*," he boomed.

I shrugged and muttered some gibberish under my breath like a lunatic. "Then go," I advised in a voice that was so calm it scared me. I didn't remain calm for long. My voice took on a life of its own, flying out of my mouth like a missile. "Get out before I throw you out!" I yelled, shaking my head and both fists.

He just stood there staring at me. The longer he stayed in my presence, the more danger he was in.

# CHAPTER 6

"I . . . I tried to let you down easy," Pee Wee told me.

"I don't believe what I'm hearing." I shook my head again; then I rubbed my ears with both hands as if that would change what I'd just heard. "I thought you were leaving," I quipped, waving toward the door.

"I am. But I just want to make sure you're all right before I leave," he said gently.

"What makes you think I won't be all right?"

He gave me a pitiful look; then he spoke in a slow, clear manner, as if he was addressing an idiot. And maybe he was. Something had to be wrong with me, because even after what he'd already told me, I still couldn't believe what was happening. "You don't seem to understand what's goin' on. You look a little . . . delirious. And just now you were talkin' some kind of gibberish. If you want me to call you a doctor, or Reverend Upshaw, I will."

"If you do call somebody, it won't be for me, because there is nothing wrong with me. I can take care of myself. And you of all people know me well enough by now to know that if you see me wrestling with a bear, you'd better help the bear."

He flinched when I shook a warning fist in his face. I had mauled his head with my fist before, so he knew what I was capable of doing if I got mad enough. Lizzie whimpered and moved closer to the door.

"I just . . . I just want to make sure you realize what I'm doin'," he told me.

The fact that he was taking his time leaving confused me. And the way Lizzie was shifting her weight from one foot to the other and glancing at her watch, I could see how impatient she had become.

Since this particular act of betrayal was a first for me, and the most devastating, I honestly didn't know what I was supposed to say or do. That was one reason I kept asking the obvious. "I got the message. You're leaving me." I sniffed. "But can you tell me WHY?" Now that was one of the dumbest things I'd said so far. I was handling this nightmare in such an awkward manner that it made me almost as angry with myself as I was with Pee Wee and Lizzie. "Well, I won't stop you!" I hollered, rotating my neck and grinding my teeth. I was surprised that he was still standing, because I was giving him looks that could have brought down a giant. "But before you leave me for this—this enema bag, let me tell you something! I won't have any trouble replacing your sorry-ass dick with a good vibrator!"

A horrified look swept across Pee Wee's face like a sandstorm; but that lasted only a few seconds. Before his face could relax, another miserable expression presented itself, making him look even more horrified. This one was so severe it scared me. In all of the years that I'd known him, I had never seen him display so much misery. Not even when he had to be medicated for some mysterious ailment called *grippe*, and a month later for gout. Or the time he fell off the roof and landed on his back on a rake. I had not met a man yet who didn't get wild-eyed when a woman gave his bedroom performance a low rating. Especially when it was not true. His eyes looked like they belonged on a creature from a black lagoon. My comment had startled him that much. Pee Wee was the best lover I'd ever had and he knew it. "Now look, we don't need to go there. I was a good husband," he said, tears flooding his lying eyes.

"A *good* husband doesn't fuck his wife's friend!" I boomed.

"You can dog me all you want, but it won't change a damn thing. I'm in love with Lizzie and I'm leavin' you for her."

It felt like somebody had batted my head with a sledgehammer. The pain was so intense that I got dizzy and started to sway from side to side.

When Pee Wee grabbed me by my shoulders to keep me from falling, I slapped his hands away. Then I pinched them. It was only then that I realized how much I hated the hair on the back of his hands. This was the first time that they reminded me of a monkey's paws.

I almost laughed when I thought about the fact that I was standing in my own kitchen making a fuss over a man who had turned into a creature right before my eyes. Within seconds, my mind was as sharp as a tack, but my vision was off the chart. For the next couple of seconds the only thing I could see in that kitchen was Pee Wee's face. But it wasn't the face of a creature. It was the face of the only man I had ever really loved. And I wanted to slap that face through the wall. If this situation didn't justify a violent crime of passion, nothing did.

I knew that if I got ugly, somebody was going to end up hurt.

I took a deep breath. One so deep that my tongue felt like it was about to slide down my throat. As angry as I was, I was surprised that I was so composed. "You know what? You two deserve each other!" I yelled, shaking a finger in Pee Wee's face, looking from him to her, then back to him.

He nodded, "You're right." That was not what I expected to hear. He had already broken my heart. Now it felt like he was dancing a jig on it. "Me and Lizzie do deserve each other."

"So this is not just a little fling, huh?" I croaked, determined not to cry until I was alone. "Do you honestly think that you will be happier with her?"

He nodded again.

It took a few moments for me to get my next sentence out. "But—but *why*? We were doing so well trying to get back to where we were—"

Pee Wee held his hand up and gave me a stern look. "We don't need to go into all that now. The bottom line is, me and Lizzie have been in love for a while now, and we don't want to keep on sneakin' around."

"A while? Just how . . . how long has this mess been going on?" I asked, looking at Lizzie.

"Mess? I don't appreciate you usin' such a tacky word," he informed me. "We are all grown, reasonable adults up in here. You could show a little more respect. I am bein' very civil about this, ain't I? And so is Lizzie."

"Like I said, I want to know how long this . . . this *mess* has been going on?" I demanded through clenched teeth.

"What difference does it make?" Pee Wee answered. I stumbled forward and I guess he must have thought I was lunging for Lizzie because he shielded her body with his. "I . . . uh . . . we already put a deposit on an apartment. Life is too short—"

"And yours is going to be shorter than you think if you don't come to your senses!" I threatened.

Pee Wee gave me another wild-eyed look. "Me come to my senses? Woman, you got a lot of nerve sayin' some shit like that to me! Especially after what *you* did with that punk-ass *gigolo* last year!"

There was a large plastic bowl on the counter by the sink. It contained cold water up to the rim. I had used the water the night before to wash some Chinese mustard greens that I planned to cook for dinner this evening. My fussy daughter, Charlotte, a spoiled child who regarded good old down-home soul food like it was a cancer, had screamed and bolted from the kitchen in terror when she saw the greens. A few minutes later, she returned and played in that same water, pushing a tiny sailboat with a little man in it that resembled a young John Travolta. What fascinated her about the water was that it was so clear she could see her face in it. I could see my face in it now, but it wasn't a face I wanted to see, or one I recognized. There was so much anger in my eyes that it had sharpened my vision. I could see the red veins that had popped up in the whites of my eyes around my dilated pupils. My lips were twisted and my cheeks were trembling. I looked like some kind of wild-eyed creature from a black lagoon myself, just like Pee Wee. I felt like one, too. I knew that if Pee Wee and his bitch didn't vacate the premises soon, they'd have to deal with my full-blown wrath. Unfortunately for them, they didn't leave in time.

I could no longer contain myself. My fist connected with the side of Pee Wee's face so hard one of his teeth flew out of his mouth, sounding like a coin when it hit my freshly waxed linoleum floor. He howled and stumbled into Lizzie's arms, moaning and rubbing his cheek with both hands.

"Do you realize what you've just done?" she screeched, giving me a frantic look.

"I realize you're next!" I responded. She ducked when I swung my fist toward her face, but ducking didn't help her. I grabbed a rolling pin off the counter and batted her head a few times before she crumbled to the floor, taking Pee Wee down with her. They looked like two mangled rag dolls lying there on my floor. When Lizzie spat out some blood onto my clean floor, I kicked her in the side for doing that.

"Pee Wee, I knew you were going to bring that up! I knew you were going to bring up Louis Baines to make yourself look better!" I roared, standing over them with one hand on my hip and the rolling pin still in my other hand. "That's over and done with, and you know why I got involved with another man! You had stopped treating me like a woman. You didn't touch me in the bedroom for a whole year! What else could I do? But what's your excuse? What reason did you have to go outside of your marriage?"

"Annette, I told you I'm in love with Lizzie," Pee Wee said with a heavy sigh.

They wobbled up from the floor at the same time, holding hands like a couple of teenaged lovebirds. That pissed me off even more, and I raised my hand to let them have it again. But I didn't. I was afraid that if I didn't stop, I'd kill them both. Prison was not where I wanted to spend even a minute of my golden years.

Pee Wee continued, "I didn't know it was going to come to this, but it did. And the sooner you get that through your head, the better for all of us. You and I have a daughter together, so I hope we can still be friendly enough so it won't be hard on her."

Lizzie peeked at me from around Pee Wee's shoulder. What I could not understand was how any woman in her right mind could enter the house of the woman whose man she was taking!

"And I want you to know right now that when Pee Wee brings your daughter around, I will treat her like she's my own," Lizzie declared.

I must have hit Lizzie harder than I thought. A bruise that looked like a bull's-eye had already formed in the center of her forehead.

Shaking my fist in her direction, I said, "Look, bitch. Do me a favor and go wait in the car. There is nothing you have to say now that I want to hear." I swallowed hard and gave Lizzie the most menacing look I could manage. But she still didn't move. I gave Pee Wee a sharp look. "I can't believe that all this time—all of these last few weeks you were romancing me and talking all that trash about how important your marriage was to you, you were already planning this shit!"

"It just happened, baby!" Pee Wee claimed in a small voice. For a moment I *still* thought that he was going to break into a grin and tell me that this was all a bad joke. If only that were the case—*if only*! But he didn't. He gave me an indifferent look; then he wrapped his arm around Lizzie's waist and squeezed her. "That's life," he added with a shrug.

"That's bullshit!" I screamed.

Things were happening too fast for me. I had just made passionate love to this man a few hours earlier, and now here he was standing in my kitchen telling me he was leaving me for another woman? Oh, HELL no!

My marriage was the biggest investment I'd ever made in my life, and I was not about to let it end easily.

# CHAPTER 7

"Look, Pee Wee, I know I've made some bad mistakes lately, and I know it might take a while for you to get over some of the things I've done, but I can't believe that you are walking out on me and our daughter like this!" I didn't realize I was crying until I tasted the tears on my lips. "Whatever was wrong, you could have at least talked to me about it!"

Now I was the one stalling, or buying more time was a better way of looking at it. On one hand, I wanted Pee Wee and Lizzie to get out of my sight because I knew that I was no longer responsible for my actions. But on the other hand, I had to keep them in place as I tried to make some sense out of what was happening. "I am your wife and this is your home! You can't just up and walk out like this," I insisted, making a sweeping gesture with my hand.

I knew that if we didn't settle this mess within the next minute or two, I was going to be either on the floor in a heap or chasing Pee Wee and his bitch out of town on a rail.

"Why can't he?" Little Leg Lizzie asked, looking at me with her eyes narrowed into slits. For a woman in her position, she had a lot of nerve. From the look on her face now and the tone of her voice, you would have thought that I was the one breaking up her marriage. "He should have left you right after he found out you were cheating on him last summer—with a common flimflam man at that! And you were even *stupid* enough to give him money! I want you to know that I told Pee Wee that if he had had any sense, he would have left you then!"

I gasped. Pee Wee and I had just mentioned the affair that I had last summer, and I didn't care about Lizzie knowing that now. But I did have a problem with her *already* knowing about the affair. "Pee Wee, you told her all about me and Louis Baines?" I asked, more hot tears forming in my eyes. "You put our business out in the street?" He just blinked. "Can't you even answer my question?" He bowed his head and looked at the floor.

"Can't you put two and two together? Does everything have to be spelled out for you? Yes, Pee Wee told me about you and your little boy toy. And I swear to God, when I heard how you had given that . . . your . . . *gigolo* some money, I lost all respect for you, Annette. I never thought you'd be that stupid." Lizzie snorted. "And I always thought you had a little more class than the rest of the hoochie mamas in Richland. Tsk, tsk, tsk!"

Lizzie sucking on her teeth grated on my nerves like fingernails on a blackboard. As if I didn't already feel bad enough, my body felt like it was about to shed my skin like a snake.

"Look, I just want to get some of my things this morning. I'll come for the rest later, after you cool off," Pee Wee said in a low voice. There was raw fear in his demeanor. He was frightened and he had every reason to be. As a matter of fact, he looked like he was in pain. Well, since I was in serious pain myself, I was glad to see that he was, too. "My cousin Steve said I could use his truck. . . ."

I didn't know how many more times I was going to gasp, but I gasped again, this time so hard my eyes crossed. I had to shut my eyes for a moment and shake my head before I could focus again. I looked at Pee Wee like I was seeing him for the first time. He looked like a stranger. I could not interpret the look on his face. If I had to guess, I would have to say that it was a look of contempt. But it was only half as potent as the one on my face.

I glared at him so hard he grimaced. "Steve knows? Your cousin Steve, a man with a mouth as big as the Grand Canyon knows and I'm just now hearing about that? I . . . I . . . can't believe my ears," I whispered, stumbling back to the table. "A couple of meddlesome people dropped a few hints around me from time to time that you and Lizzie were fooling around." I had to stop talking so I could catch my breath. I rubbed my chest, blinked hard a few times, and shook my head. "I let them know that I didn't believe them. I made it clear to them that you would never cheat on me. At least not with Lizzie . . ."

"Well, you were wrong again," my husband taunted. "Now, if you don't mind, I'll grab a few things and be on my way." Pee Wee and Lizzie rushed out of the kitchen, scurrying across the floor like roaches. Then they sounded like two horses stampeding up the stairs to the second floor of a house that now felt like a chamber of horrors to me.

I must have blacked out for a few moments, because I was barely aware of what happened next. I was sitting at the kitchen table staring at the wall when my husband and his lover came galloping down the stairs and back into the kitchen with two suitcases that contained some of his things.

"I might be back later today. And I'll sit Charlotte down and explain things to her," Pee Wee offered. "I don't want my daughter to hear about this from anybody but me."

I looked at him. I was so stunned I couldn't even focus. For a split second he looked like a demon from hell. His eyes were red; his thin, graying hair was askew.

And the cheek that I had hit looked like a raw piece of meat, and that scared me. His tooth, the root covered in blood, was still on the floor looking like a discarded pebble. I didn't know it was that easy to knock somebody's tooth out!

"I want you to tell me how in the world you let something like this happen? Have you lost your fucking mind?" I barked. "Please tell me that, Pee Wee!"

"Uh, when I get settled, I'll come by and we can talk about it," he grunted. "I'll tell you all the things that were wrong with our marriage then."

All the things that were *wrong* with our marriage? How was it that Pee Wee could see what was wrong with our marriage and I couldn't?

"It's not important enough for you to tell me now?" I whimpered. "Is it so bad that it can't be repaired?" One thing about myself that I was proud of was the fact that I'd never tried to cling to a man who didn't want to be clung to. Now here I was acting like Pee Wee was the last conscious man in the world. My mother had practically crawled on her belly like a serpent the day my daddy left us. I hated seeing her like that. Even though I was a toddler back then, I was precocious enough to know that a woman crawling after a man looked like a desperate fool. I was so glad that my own daughter was not around to see me looking and acting like a desperate fool.

Had I seen this coming, I would have been better prepared. I could have handled it in a much more dignified manner. Hell, had I known in time that Pee Wee no longer loved me and wanted to be with another woman, I probably would have helped him pack! I had enough going for me that my life didn't revolve around my husband.

If Pee Wee had dumped me when he found out about me and Louis, it would have made sense, and I would not have protested the way I was doing now. I would have been hurt, but I would have moved on with my life. Shit! He was the one who had adamantly refused to consider a divorce! It seemed so cruel of him to lift my spirits so high these past few months and then to drop me like a bad habit.

"This is not a good time, Annette," he said hotly.

"And why is this not a good time? If it's a good time for you to bring your whore into my house, it's a good time for you to talk to me about it!" It seemed like I was getting angrier by the second. I knew that if this episode didn't conclude soon, somebody was going to be *real* sorry.

"Look, woman! I'm tryin' to make this as painless as possible." Pee Wee eased the door open with his foot and beckoned with his head for Lizzie to leave. She scrambled out like the rat she was.

I grabbed his arm and he stopped, shaking his head. "Turn me loose," he ordered. He set down one of his suitcases and rubbed the cheek I'd coldcocked. "And I advise you not to hit me no more!"

Right after he said that I throttled and boxed the back of his head with both of my fists. All he did was yelp, grab the suitcase he had set on the floor, and move faster out the door.

I followed him onto the porch. "Just like that? You are leaving me, just like that? Don't you know I can make you suffer?"

"Annette, you've already done that," he smirked. "Why do you think I' leavin'?" he said, trotting to his car.

"Hurry up! That bitch is crazy!" Lizzie yelled. She had already opened the trunk to Pee Wee's car and was sitting in the front passenger seat. To add insult to injury, she quickly rolled up the window, locked the door, and was now looking at me like I was a carjacker.

Pee Wee dropped the suitcases into the trunk. I stomped out to the driveway and stood in front of his car with my hands on my hips.

"There's one more thing before you go!" I sneered.

"Annette, get out of the way," he ordered. "I am tryin' to be nice about this!"

I walked up to him and boxed his head some more. All he did was close his eyes and moan. He didn't even try to defend himself. Then I kicked him in the shins. He yelled and stumbled, but he didn't fall. Lizzie jumped out of the car and ran around to help him. That was when I slammed her in the side with my elbow. She yelled and fell to the ground, but she was up again within seconds.

This time I cold punched her in the face with both of my fists at the same time. Pee Wee seemed too dazed to move or stop me from assaulting Lizzie. Right about then, Moshay, my nosy mailman, strolled over.

"Annette, you want me to call the cops?" he asked, looking amused.

"No, you don't need to call the cops!" I told him. "If you call anybody, it better be Jesus."

Some of my neighbors came out onto their porches and into their yards, some still in housecoats, some in work clothes, looking and shaking their heads. But that didn't stop me. I was in so much pain at this point, I didn't even care if I got arrested now.

I slapped Lizzie's face so hard I almost dislocated my wrist. She yelled as tears streamed down her face. She managed to get back into the car and lock the door before I could get my hands on her throat.

Since Pee Wee was still outside of his car, I turned my attention and wrath back to him. He stood as stock-still as a lamppost when I marched back up to him. I stomped on his right foot with both of my feet, like I was trying to put out a fire. I knew that that had to hurt him because it hurt me to do it!

The bottoms of my feet felt like I'd stepped on some nine-inch nails. But he didn't utter a sound. That only made me angrier. I stomped on his feet some more. He still didn't make a sound. "You son-of-a-bitch," I snarled. He stumbled to the driver's side of his car, wheezing and puffing as he got in, falling clumsily into the seat like a sack of flour. It looked like he had aged ten years in the last five minutes. And I felt like I'd aged twenty years since he'd dropped his bombshell on me.

"Like I said, I'll be back later to get the rest of my stuff. If you don't mind, can I go now?" he whimpered. I couldn't believe how calm he was!

"You do that! You'd better get your black ass out of my sight while you still can!" I hollered, standing by the side of his car with my arms folded.

My neighbors and my mailman were snickering like they were watching a bad movie.

"Damn right! I am sure enough leavin' this place!" Pee Wee assured me.

And that was exactly what he did.

# CHAPTER 8

Within days after Pee Wee's departure, I felt like an overcooked rump roast. My meat felt like it wanted to fall off my bones. I didn't even look like myself. My eyes had a hollow look to them. My hair wouldn't curl, even when I used a hot curling iron. I had to wear a scarf when I went out in public.

He wasted no time pouring more salt into my wounds. The affair got so serious so fast that Pee Wee started parading Lizzie all over town. He even took her to some of the places that I went to. And the apartment that they'd moved into—that he paid for with money that belonged partly to me—was in a new high-rise just three blocks from my office. If all of that wasn't unspeakable and painful enough, I had to face all of our friends—the same ones who had once envied my "perfect" marriage.

It seemed to get worse with each passing day. One Sunday night, after he'd been gone for almost three weeks, my mother steamrolled into my house with her wig on sideways, the way men at baseball games wore their caps. There was enough rouge on her cheeks to paint a cruise ship. I could tell that she'd been upset for a while. She was still in her church usher's uniform and clutching one of the hymn books that she passed out in church. "Did you know that Pee Wee brought that woman to church today?" she screamed.

"Brother Mitchell had to hold me up to keep me from falling to the floor! How could you let this happen?"

"Let what happen?" I asked in a calm voice. Muh'Dear was hysterical enough for both of us. I saw no reason to let her know just how upset I really was.

"You let that *white* woman take your husband? How could you let that happen?"

I shrugged. "I guess the same way you let a white woman take your husband," I responded with a smirk. That was not what my mother wanted to hear.

"But Frank was a fool! We all know that now. He was, and still is, limited—and still a straight-up fool if you ask me! He didn't know no better. He ain't responsible for his actions, and he'll at least get slightly singed by the fires of hell some day. But you—I raised you to be a strong woman. You ain't worldly. I know you used to be in the world, but you are a righteous, pious, virtuous woman now. Women in your position don't let their men run amok! I just want to know how you could let your husband drag his whore up into the same church where I worship? Where you worship when you ain't too lazy to come to church?"

As difficult as it was, I managed to remain calm. "It is a free country, Muh'Dear."

"Well, Pee Wee ain't a free man! He can't be actin' like one and get away with it! You need to take a brick and bounce it off his head! I am ashamed to see you bein' this weak!"

"Like I said, this is a free country. Pee Wee can take his lady friend anywhere he wants to take her." I was in the kitchen folding the laundry I'd just removed from the dryer. I was glad Charlotte was in her room.

"And you ain't gwine to do nothin' about him takin' his lady friend around all of your friends? *My* friends? Bah! What will Reverend Upshaw's mama say when she hears this? What are you gwine to do about this apocalypse?"

"Like what?" I asked with a weak shrug. "What do you expect me to do about it? And I'm not into bouncing bricks off of anybody's head."

Muh'Dear didn't have an answer, and I guess she got tired of asking me questions to which I responded with dumb answers. She threw up her hands and left, running out my front door like a woman on fire, mumbling Biblical phrases under her breath. I waited a couple of minutes to make sure she had driven off before I sat down and had myself a brief cry.

One of the things that angered me the most was that my husband didn't just betray me, he betrayed our daughter as well. However, my daughter's reaction was a whole lot different from mine. She was reasonably confused and hurt, but not for long. Like any other eleven-year-old, she focused on the benefits of having another female adult in her life whose goal was to make her happy.

No matter what I did for my daughter, my husband's mistress tried to upstage me.

The first weekend that my daughter spent with her daddy and her new "stepmother," she came home with new clothes, new toys, and the kind of smile that I saw on her face only on a Christmas morning. And she inevitably made comparisons between me and my new nemesis. "Mama, Lizzie doesn't make me eat greens and beans like you do. She lets me stay up late. She lets me do this, that . . ."

I got highly upset each time my daughter made a reference to that woman. After a while, everything she said about Lizzie sounded like gibberish. "Lizzie, yadda, yadda, yip yip, blah, blah, blah . . ." The words rang in my ears like bells.

"I don't give a *damn* what that *damn* woman does or doesn't do. I am still your *damn* mother and don't you ever forget that," I usually replied, shaking my head and sometimes rubbing my ears.

"And another thing . . . Lizzie don't use cuss words in front of me," my daughter revealed, giving me the kind of look I usually gave to her when she stepped out of line.

Like any other woman in my situation, I was hurt and mad as hell. Not just about my husband's betrayal, but now I had to worry about losing my daughter's allegiance, too. Somehow I managed to promise myself that I was going to rise above my pain and be even stronger. I was not about to let my anger cripple my spirit like it did some women. One of those women was my mother.

My father's desertion had almost destroyed her. She ended up resenting men and life in general for years. And even though my mother eventually found love again—with my daddy after a thirty-year separation—she still held on to some of her bitterness.

I had to face the most difficult challenge in my life: I had to find a way to get over losing my husband, and I had to deal with that slut who had stolen him right from under my nose. I knew that I was going to be angry for a while, but I was not about to let my husband's affair make me so bitter that I wouldn't be able to get on with my life. What I had to do now was decide *how* I was going to get this mess out of my system. Somehow I would maintain my dignity, but I wasn't going to sit back and let Pee Wee and Lizzie quietly ease into a new life and live happily ever after at my expense.

In spite of all my anger, I tried to remain realistic. I knew I couldn't force my husband to come back to me, and even if I could, I didn't want him back *that* badly. However, I planned to make sure he didn't forget me anytime soon. My name alone was going to be a major thorn in his side and her ass for a very long time.

I knew that from what I'd seen so far, Lizzie was not about to let him go too soon, or that easily. She worshipped the ground he walked on.

The more I thought about my husband's affair, the more I was convinced that it had been a long time coming. Pee Wee, whose real name was Jerry Lee Davis, was the kind of brother who women of all ages and colors usually chased like dogs in heat. It didn't matter that he was forty-seven and had already begun to lose his looks, hair, memory, and teeth. None of that mattered when you looked at the whole package. He owned and operated a successful business, he was generous, he was well respected in our church and community, he loved kids, and he was as considerate as a man could be. He was also a strong, caring man who went out of his way to keep the people he loved happy. All of that was more than enough for other women to be attracted to him. And some continued to cast their roving eyes in his direction even after he married me.

Before the breakup of my marriage, a lot of people had accused me of being smug. Yes, I had been smug for years because I had convinced myself that my marriage was rock solid. The last time I asked my husband if he would ever get in another woman's bed while he was married to me, he said, "Only if a storm blew me into it." I kept my guard up and my eyes open because I was not about to let another woman take my husband away from me. Well, clearly I hadn't kept my eyes open wide enough, because another woman took him from me anyway.

*How in the world did this happen to me?* I asked myself. I didn't know where to look for answers. I didn't really want to know all the details as to how it had happened anyway. Unfortunately, I already suspected that my past behavior had a major role in my life's latest drama.

# CHAPTER 9

Extramarital affairs were not new to me. The preacher before the current preacher at my Baptist church had been caught in bed with his wife's younger sister two years ago. The man I worked for was in the middle of a nasty divorce because his wife had left him for his business partner. The list of philanderers I knew about was very long.

Unfortunately, my first experience with an extramarital affair involved my own parents. In a way, it was the end of my innocence, because from that point on, I had to grow up real fast. For years, people teased me by telling me that I was the "oldest" little girl they knew. To this day, sharp pains shoot through my chest every time I think about my parents' breakup.

Out of nowhere, Daddy decided to run off with a white woman. They got married, and he had three more kids with her. Even as a child I could not understand why a pampered white woman from a prominent family, and during the turbulent fifties at that, would give up all that for a black man.

Well, that bold white woman's fascination with black men didn't last long. According to Daddy's version of the events, she eventually couldn't deal with the pressure of being married to a black man in the South. Segregation still ruled at the time, and black folks who didn't stay in their place often ended up dead. Daddy's new wife's rebellion toward her family fizzled out in a big way. When the going got too tough for her, she got going. Not long after giving birth to her third child with Daddy, she ran off with a white man. When she died in an automobile accident, her family didn't even mention Daddy or her three half-black kids in her obituary.

More than thirty years later, my parents got back together and now had one of the strongest marriages in Richland. It had not been easy for my mother to take Daddy back. Even though he put his hand on the Bible and swore to her that he'd never cheat on her again, she assured him that she would never trust him again anyway. She also threw his betrayal up in his face on a regular basis. Daddy was so afraid to look at another woman now, especially a white woman, that he behaved like a blind man when he had to be around one—no matter how young and pretty she was. He wouldn't even go to a female doctor; and if a woman got too friendly with him in public, in Muh'Dear's presence, he became hostile. It was no wonder that I avoided going anywhere with him as much as possible.

The bottom line was, cheating was nothing new to me. "We all have to deal with it sooner or later," Muh'Dear had warned me years ago. "Ninety percent of marriages is the *Titanic* with a slow leak . . . bound to hit the bottom sooner or later. If you are lucky, you can plug it up and keep it afloat, but just for a while. Because sooner or later, somebody is gwine to punch another hole in it." And so far, my mother had been right. I couldn't think of a single one of her female friends, or mine, who hadn't been cheated on. Even Rhoda O'Toole, my best friend, had not been spared this universal indignity.

Rhoda's husband, Otis, had cheated on her at one of the most vulnerable times in a woman's life. She had just given birth to her daughter. She had been experiencing post partum depression, and dealing with a huge weight gain. But Rhoda was not the kind of woman to take anything lying down. She would rise up during her autopsy to get revenge. She'd paid her husband back in spades. Otis's ill-fated affair had lasted only a few weeks. It probably would have gone on a lot longer if Rhoda had not paid the other woman a visit and roughed her up a bit. But that was only part of her revenge. She resumed a relationship with a previous lover, who also happened to be her husband's best friend. That man was still in the picture after more than twenty-five years! Rhoda told me on a regular basis that she was not about to end the affair, so that if her husband ever strayed again, she'd be ten steps ahead of him already.

I had never condoned Rhoda's affair, and until last summer I was the kind of woman who had always looked down on married people who had affairs. I felt that way until I had one myself. But since I'd done so many other stupid things in my life, which included prostitution, having an affair with a man young enough to be my son was not that much of a stretch.

Rhoda knew about my affair from the beginning, and she had encouraged it. At the time, she was the only other person who knew that my husband had stopped making love to me. "Girl, you live in the same house with Pee Wee and he treats you like a stranger with bad breath. If that's not a reason for you to sleep with another man, I don't know what is," she told me a few weeks before I took her advice.

"But Pee Wee is such a good man. I don't want to hurt him," I protested.

"Then don't. If you can spend the rest of your life without sex and not go crazy, then it doesn't matter." Rhoda always gave me sly looks when she said things like that. I always knew that when she really wanted me to do something, she didn't stop until I did it.

"You want me to cheat on my husband so you won't feel so guilty about you cheating on yours, don't you?"

"Honey, I don't know what makes you think I feel guilty about cheatin' on my husband." Rhoda chuckled. "My husband has nothin' to complain about. I'm a good wife."

"That's because he doesn't know you've been sleeping with his best friend all these years," I reminded. "I'm a good wife, too."

I was a good wife, but when my husband went a year without touching me, even being a "good wife" didn't stop me from crawling into bed with Louis Baines.

Louis seemed too good to be true. Unfortunately, that had been the case. He turned out to be a common con man. But he was one of the most dangerous kind—a smart one. He had me believing that he was in love with me and that he had no interest whatsoever in the fact that I had a high-paying job and access to large sums of money. He would ease sob stories into our conversations about one thing or another that were related to his "financial difficulties," but he never asked me for money. He was so cunning he didn't have to. All he had to do was display a puppy-dog face, break a few dates with me, and mention that his financial difficulties might impact our relationship, and I'd reach for my wallet. I had been a goose just waiting to get cooked, and he'd cooked my goose to a crisp. I'd given him thousands of dollars.

My ill-fated affair would probably still be going on if I had not overheard a telephone conversation between Louis and the fiancée he had back in North Carolina that I didn't know about. Laughing like a hyena, he told her how he was going to shake me down for one last lump sum and then be on his merry way back to her. I cringed when I recalled some of the nasty names that he had used to refer to me, like "greasy black bitch" and "that funky, old, fat woman."

After an ugly confrontation, where he attempted to blackmail me for more money, I had no choice but to run home and tell Pee Wee what I had been up to. It was one of the most difficult things I ever had to do in my life.

"Annette, I can forgive you for sleepin' with another man, but I won't ever forget it. If we want this marriage to work, both of us are goin' to have to do our part," Pee Wee said during one of our conversations after I'd confessed.

"Baby, I will work double time, triple time, night shift, day shift, three shifts in a row to repair this marriage," I vowed.

That was just what I had been doing since the day we had that conversation.

# CHAPTER 10

There were certain moments of bliss with my husband that I could not get out of my head, especially if a certain song came on the radio or the TV, or if somebody said something that reminded me of him. There was no way I was going to forget all of the pleasant experiences that we had shared together.

There were those loathsome weekend fishing trips that I used to pretend I enjoyed, but only to please him. There were the picnics and camping trips in the summertime where I'd invariably get poison ivy on almost every square inch of my legs. There were the trips to the Bahamas, the trips to the spas in Cleveland, and even the cheap dates he took me on to greasy, back-alley restaurants in parts of town you couldn't get a gangster to go to. Those were some fond memories for me. Despite the fact that I'd once been engaged to marry another man, Pee Wee had been my soul mate for years. I'd also wallowed around in bed with a slew of other men along the way, but Pee Wee was my only true love. I'd been with him longer, and in a more serious relationship—even before we got married—than I'd ever been with another man. We had a strong history, and because of our daughter, we would still have some kind of a future together.

And it was going to take more than a woman like Little Leg

Lizzie to make me forget those moments of bliss. They kept me afloat just when it felt like I was about to go under.

I was compelled to reflect on my recent past to see if I could get a better understanding of what had gone wrong. I had to think back to events and conversations between Pee Wee and me that might have indicated that something was amiss. Not that it would do me much good now. But even if it was too late, I still wanted to know.

Even though Pee Wee was gone, he was still in my daily thoughts; things he'd said, things he'd done. It was almost like I could still hear his voice. "Woman, you are goin' to spoil me! I must be the luckiest man in the world," he declared one January evening about a week into the new year—just a couple of months ago! I had met him at the door with a cold beer and his slippers. He took a sip of the beer and let out a loud burp. He paused long enough to give me a hungry little kiss on the cheek. I sucked in my breath, and hauled off and kissed him so hard on the lips he stumbled backward and hit the wall. "Girl, please. Let me get in the house and get out my work clothes first." He laughed. "Damn, you act like you just got out of prison."

"I'm just happy to see you," I told him, leading him to the couch in the living room. "I left work early today so I could get home in time to make your favorite dinner. As soon as the cornbread gets done, we can eat."

"I bet you plannin' on dumpin' me in that tub full of bubble bath again," Pee Wee whispered with an anxious look on his face.

"I sure am," I purred, trying to sound as seductive as I could.

"And another one of them hot-oil foot massages, too?"

"And another hot-oil foot massage, too," I said with a nod. "Later, if you feel up to it, I want to make love to you like I've never made love to you before."

"Hmmm. That's the same thing you said yesterday when I got home. You know, you don't have to be doin' all this. We ain't so young no more. Listen up, all them positions that you twistin' me in and out of these days, they are fun, but my back ain't what it used to be, baby." He laughed. I laughed, too.

"Do you want me to stop giving you so much special attention?" I asked with an exaggerated pout.

"Naw, you ain't got to stop showin' me so much attention. But it would make more sense if you showed me the kind of attention that wasn't so physical. At the rate we're goin', I'll be dead soon."

I continued to pamper my husband, but only half as much. He seemed pleased and appreciative. By the end of that month, things had become downright humdrum. I got tired just looking at his face as he slumped in his ancient La-Z-Boy snoring like a moose.

Despite all of my efforts, Pee Wee reminded me of the same old sad sack that he'd been when I had the affair! I made up excuses to get out of the house so I wouldn't have to look at his long face.

Thankfully, he continued to make love to me. And if he had stopped doing that again, too, I was still determined *not* to have another affair again.

There was no way I was going to let another affair disrupt or ruin my marriage.

"Baby, you've been down in the dumps a lot lately, and I don't like to see you like that," I told Pee Wee over dinner one evening. He had come home from the barbershop looking more depressed than ever. Our daughter, Charlotte, noticed it, too.

"Daddy, you look like a grumpy old man," she told him, rushing through dinner so she could flee and go do whatever it was kids her age liked to do. Unlike me, Charlotte had never had to worry about her weight. She had just gobbled up three spicy chicken legs and a mountain of mashed potatoes. I'd steamed a skinless chicken breast and stir-fried some vegetables for myself. I ate fried chicken and most of the other fatty foods that I had consumed over the years only once or twice a week now. And since I'd shared a slab of ribs with Pee Wee and Charlotte for dinner the day before, I planned to eat skinless chicken and steamed veggies for a while.

"I am a grumpy old man, and I'm goin' to be one until I'm a dead old man," Pee Wee said with a straight face.

Charlotte, who had her father's rich mocha skin, cute features, and long, thin arms, rolled her eyes and shook her head. "Can I be excused?" she asked, glancing at the Mickey Mouse watch on her narrow wrist. "I get bored sitting around old people."

"You go clean up your room," I ordered, using the sternest tone of voice that I could manage.

"Oh, I'd rather sit here and be bored than do that," my daughter decided, rubbing her small, button-like nose.

"I think she should go clean up that pigsty of a room," Pee Wee said, nodding in agreement.

"I want you to go over that room with a fine-toothed comb until you find that earring of mine that I told you to stop playing with," I told my daughter. "And don't you ever get into my jewelry box again. Do you hear me?"

"Yes, ma'am. Do I have to look for that old earring now?"

"Yes, you do, so get on it." Pee Wee cleared his throat. It was impossible for me not to notice how distracted and nervous he was acting. I knew him well enough to know that there was something on his mind, and it was probably something I didn't want to hear. My first thought was that it was something physical. That thought chilled me down to the bottom of my feet. I didn't think I could deal with that. Last year when he had that cancer scare, he had not even told me about it until he received a clean bill of health from his doctor. That news had almost destroyed me—even after I knew that he was going to be all right. A very qualified doctor had treated him and assured him that he had nothing else to worry about. But doctors didn't know everything. And even with all the knowledge they possessed today, they were often wrong. Before Pee Wee could utter his next sentence, I began to anticipate his funeral and my eventual nervous breakdown. "I need to talk to your mama about somethin' anyway," he added, making me even more apprehensive.

Charlotte and I looked at Pee Wee at the same time, then at each other. "Shoot. I hope we ain't getting no divorce," she said with a worried look. "Jimmy Proctor's mama and daddy just got a divorce and now he ain't no fun no more. Always sad . . ."

Divorce? I had not thought of that; but now that it had been mentioned, it was running a close second place to cancer! If it was either one, I was doomed! Now it was my funeral that I was anticipating.

Somehow I managed to force myself to remain calm. But the truth of the matter was, I was in mild agony. To me, divorce and cancer were two of the most feared words in the English language.

"Nobody is thinking about divorce," I said weakly, addressing Charlotte but looking at my husband. My daughter released a loud sigh of relief before she strutted backward out of the kitchen and ran upstairs to her room. I turned to Pee Wee and held my breath. "Are we?"

"Are we what?"

"Is anybody *in this room* thinking about a divorce?"

"If it is, it ain't me. How many times do I have to tell you that I don't want no divorce."

I felt relieved, but only for a split second. With divorce off the plate, that left the demon that I feared the most. "Are you sick?" I rasped.

"No, I'm not. This ain't got nothin' to do with my health, praise the Lord."

To say that I was even more relieved would have been putting it mildly. I was ecstatic. But that lasted only a few moments, because from the look on Pee Wee's face, something was still very wrong.

"Then what do you want to talk to me about?" I asked him, my voice, hands, and half of everything else on my body trembling. One of my knees was shaking so hard it was tapping against the leg of the table like a baton.

He took his time answering my question. And when he did, he didn't even look me in the eye. He tilted his head to the side, scratched his neck, and then spoke with his lips barely moving. "Baby, I need a change. I need a real change in my life, and I need it now."

# CHAPTER 11

"Mama, why are you looking so crazy?" My daughter had slunk back into the kitchen before I could respond to Pee Wee's comments. "You are looking so mean, people would think somebody stole something from you."

Charlotte was just inside the doorway, leaning against the counter. I didn't like the look on her face, or her tone of voice. One thing I could say about my relationship with my daughter was that I never let her forget which one of us was the parent and which one of us was the child. Whenever I got too liberal with her, to reestablish my role, I just thought about the incorrigible kids of some of the people I knew, and all of the problems that they were embroiled in. Like the kids acting out in school, talking back, running wild in the streets, doing drugs, fucking their brains out, and so on. That all reminded me of how good my relationship with my child was. But to save myself some time, I thought about children like Jade, Rhoda's only daughter.

Even though Rhoda was a stern parent who kept a tight rein on her little devil, Jade made my daughter seem like the poster child of innocence. That was one of the many things that I had to be thankful for. Nevertheless, I gave Charlotte one of my meanest looks. But before I could deal with her the way I wanted to, her daddy took over.

"I know you didn't clean up that room that quick," Pee Wee said, shaking a finger in Charlotte's direction. "Did you find your mama's earring?"

"I couldn't even find the fine-toothed comb that Mama told me to go over my room with!" she hollered with a hopeless look on her face.

My daughter said and did some cute things. And when she did, Pee Wee and I usually laughed at the same time. But not this time.

"What's a fine-toothed comb anyway? And how is it going to help me find an earring?" Charlotte gave me a wide-eyed look.

"Don't worry about the earring right now. Just go to your room," I ordered.

As soon as Charlotte disappeared, I turned to Pee Wee. "What's going on? What kind of change are you talking about?"

He shrugged his shoulders first; then he looked me in the eye. "I'm bored," was all he said. He shrugged again. But this time the way he did it made it seem like he was in pain. And from the frown on his face, he must have been. There were tears in his eyes, and his forehead had deep lines stretched across it. I had never noticed them before, but they must have been there for a while, and quite permanent, because when the frown left his face, the lines remained.

I gave him a puzzled look as I sat there waiting for him to give me more information. "And?"

"And what?" he replied with his mouth resembling a hole in the ground.

"So you're bored. What else?"

"That's it. I'm bored." He shrugged again. His whole face twitched for a few seconds, making him look like a confused rabbit.

"Is that all? Is that why you are sitting here looking like Methuselah's granddaddy? Is that the reason you got me all nervous and scared? I was sitting here thinking that you wanted a divorce or that you're sick with something. And all this time your only problem is that you're *bored*!" It took all of my strength for me to keep from laughing out loud. But I didn't laugh, and I wouldn't laugh until he told me what he was bored with. "You're bored with . . ."

He laughed before I could finish my sentence. "Don't worry. You ain't what I'm bored with. It's just everything else. Runnin' the shop so many years has become such a routine that I could cut hair in my sleep. The main reason I wanted my own business in the first place was so I wouldn't have to worry about slavin' away at a job I didn't like, or a job that ended up borin' me to death. Well, I got my own business and it's so borin' now that I can hardly stand to go in anymore."

"This is making no sense at all. You love being a barber. When we were kids that was all you talked about doing. And if you're tired of being a barber, what else in the world do you think you can do at your age?"

"I didn't say I was tired of bein' a barber," he mumbled, looking at me with an uncertain look in his eyes. He didn't sound very convinced, so I didn't know what to think. "Life is passin' me by, so maybe I should look into somethin' else before it's too late."

"Too late? As my mother often tells me, you've already got one foot and a big toe in the grave," I scoffed.

"You don't have to be so optimistic, Annette," he snapped. The sarcasm in his voice was so thick I could have cut it with a butcher knife. "The least you can be is a little more sympathetic. Shit, I ain't dead yet, so it ain't too late for me to do nothin'." He shot a piercing look in my direction but I didn't even feel it.

I sucked in some air and then finally gave him the sympathetic look he was whining about; but I also delivered some pretty harsh words. "Baby, you are no longer twenty-five. You are not even in the same dimension with youth anymore. No matter what else you try to do, you're a decade late and a thousand dollars short."

"A *day* late and a *dollar* short would have been enough. Do you have to bury me that deep?"

"I'm sorry," I said, and I really was. I had just made a pretty heavy-handed comment. Sadly, it was the way I really felt. . . .

"Like I just said, I'm not dead yet, Annette. As long as I'm alive and kickin', I can still do other things with my life," he said sharply, and with a fierce scowl.

One of the reasons I didn't like for people to confide in me about a serious matter was that no matter what I said, they copped an attitude. I didn't even want to think about what Pee Wee would say if I agreed with him that life was passing him by and that it was time for him to pursue a change. And the reason I didn't go in that direction was because no matter what he decided to do, it would have an impact on my life. After all I'd already been through, all I really wanted to do now was spend the rest of my years living a quiet, happy life. I didn't want to make any more changes. I finally had everything I needed to be happy; so as far as I was concerned, the only thing left for me to do was enjoy myself and keep Pee Wee happy.

"Maybe you need a hobby," I suggested. "Or some other kind of social outlet." I felt like I was grabbing at straws, or a life jacket or something. Whatever it was that I was trying to get a hold on, it was a lifeline because I felt like Pee Wee was sinking fast into some kind of abyss and he was dragging me down with him. "Brother Barnes and some of the other brothers from church get together every week and play Chinese checkers. Deacon Maize has a domino club."

Pee Wee looked at me like I'd slapped him. "Brother Barnes and Deacon Maize and all their checker and domino playin' buddies are in their seventies and eighties!"

"Well, so what? If it's not too late for them to put some spark in their lives, it's not too late for you. I think a hobby would do you a lot of good," I insisted. It still felt like we were both sinking.

"I already got all the hobbies I need!" he retorted. "I go fishin', I spend time playin' pool and drinkin' with my boys—what I need another hobby for?"

Not only was I getting tired of this conversation, I was also getting impatient and bored. "But exactly what do you really want to do?"

"That's what I'm tryin' to figure out, baby," he replied.

"All right, let's look at things from a different perspective."

"Such as?"

"Remember when your boy Victor Ford closed up his sports bar and went on that round-the-world trip when his wife ran off with that musician? He sold his house, his SUV, his furniture, everything. He didn't even make it halfway around the world before he came running back to Richland. He ended up opening another sports bar, but it was ten steps behind where he was before he sold the first one. You are a barber, that's what you were born to do. And what about all your loyal customers? If you even think about going out of business, what will become of them? There's only one other black barber in town now, but you get most of the business."

I rose from my seat, went around the table, and stood behind Pee Wee. He covered his face with his hands and released some of the deepest, loudest, most painful-sounding moans I'd ever heard.

It scared me to death because it sounded like he was dying.

# CHAPTER 12

Nothing was more painful to me than to see one of my loved ones in such a hopeless manner like Pee Wee was in now. I hadn't even seen him look or act this hopeless at any of the many funerals we had attended together.

I placed my hands on his shoulders and began to massage him, but I stopped almost immediately because that only made him moan even louder. "Why don't you take a few weeks or a month off, baby?" I said gently. My hands were massaging his shoulders again. "Go down to the Bahamas and kick back on the beach and watch the sunrise. Go to that little bar Rhoda and Otis took us to that time, and drink so much rum that you'll be able to fly back to Ohio without the plane. Just enjoy yourself until you feel better. I know Muh'Dear can arrange it with the Jacobs for you to stay at their beach house for free. Think of all the fishing and all of the kicking back doing nothing that you can do. Unfortunately, as much fun as that sounds, it'll only be a temporary solution to your frustration. You'd eventually get bored with that, too. I can assure you that you will be glad to get back to Richland and your boring life as a barber. I'll call Muh'Dear and tell her to call somebody in the Jacobs family right away and see if their beach house is available. It's a good thing I made you renew your passport last month."

"Will you come with me?" he asked, turning to face me. "It

wouldn't be no fun if I went to a paradise like the Bahamas by my-self."

I let out a loud breath and returned to my seat. "I wish I could. But things are so busy at work now, I don't think Mr. Mizelle would let me take off even a few days right now." I lifted Pee Wee's hand. It felt like a piece of dead meat. A cold piece of dead meat at that. It made my fingers tingle. I shivered and released his hand with my fingers still tingling. "Pee Wee, there is something you're not telling me. Now if we want to work as a team to resolve any issues that will affect us both, I need to know everything. I find it hard to believe that the only thing wrong with you right now is that you are just bored being a barber after all these years. If there is something else going on, I want to know and I want to know now. If we can discuss things like . . . uh . . . what happened last year, we can dis-cuss anything."

"What happened last year? You mean that cancer thing?" he asked.

"Uh, yeah . . ." I replied. For some reason the thing that hap-pened last year that danced around in my brain the most was that awful affair I'd slid into. But I was glad to know that that was not the case with him. "Cancer. If we got through that in one piece, we can get through a little bitty thing like you being bored, Pee Wee."

He let out a great sigh and cocked his head to the side. I looked at the one side of his head, noticing how much more gray hair he had since the last time I paid attention to his appearance. Normally, I would have mentioned it and offered to trot over to the Grab and Go to get him some of that Grecian Formula hair dye for men, but his gray hair was the least of my worries at the moment.

He shifted in his seat and released another moan, but this one sounded more like a rumbling growl. I didn't know if I was gaining or losing ground, because he didn't seem to be feeling, acting, or looking any better. If anything, he looked even more depressed than he did before we started this unpleasant conversation.

He shifted some more and cleared his throat, honking into a napkin. "There is more to it than me just bein' bored. I'm feelin' the sting of competition. I've never had to deal with it on this level before, Annette." He balled the nasty napkin and flipped it across the room, where it landed in the trash can by the sink.

I gasped. "What competition? You own the most successful black barbershop in town! That's always been the case."

Pee Wee blinked and gave me a pitiful look. "Annette, you women don't always know what's goin' on with us men. I am not just bored, I'm pissed off, too, see."

I gave him a curious look. He was in no hurry to offer me any more information. "Well, are you going to tell me about it, or am I going to sit here and try and pull it out of you?" I snapped. "We've been having this conversation long enough, and to tell you the truth, it's beginning to get on my nerves. And I'm just as bored and pissed off as you—because of this conversation!"

"You know Henry Boykin?"

I nodded. "Who doesn't?" I said with disgust. "He's one of the younger boys in that rough family who owns that big white house on Pike Street, right? A real asshole?"

"That's Henry."

I glanced toward the doorway to make sure Charlotte was not lurking about again before I spoke once more, whispering this time. "You used to buy weed from his uncle. The uncle that got killed by some drug dealers up in Cleveland a few years ago."

"Well, Henry took up where his uncle left off. But he's such an asshole, I'd rather buy my weed from the Klan before I put a nickel in his pocket."

"You don't need to be buying weed or any other stimulant from anybody. I've told you about that more than once, and I hope it doesn't keep coming up."

Pee Wee snapped his fingers and gave me a dismissive look. "Can we stay on the subject?"

"Exactly what is the subject now?"

"I'm tryin' to talk to you about Henry!" he yelled.

"Then talk to me about Henry!" I yelled back, stomping my foot.

"Anyway, that punk Henry Boykin got out of the drug business after he got busted and now he's runnin' Soul Cuts barbershop over by the skating rink."

"Oh yeah, that's right. I had almost forgotten about that because nobody ever mentions him to me."

"Well, they mention him to me. Every time I run into one of my former customers, they go on and on about how happy they are to be goin' to Henry! He is takin' away all of the young business that I used to have," Pee Wee complained. There was a worried look on his face, but there was also one on my face now, too.

"Oh? And how is he doing that?" I asked, feeling his pain and frustration. One thing about my relationship with my family was that when one of them was in pain, I felt it, too. And in some instances, it seemed like I felt their pain more than they did.

"Well, for one thing, he's young. Twentysomething. The kids can relate to him. And you seen his shop lately?"

I nodded. "I went by there with Daddy the other day when he got his bald spots oiled." I shrugged. "So what?"

Pee Wee's face froze and he just stared at me with his mouth hanging open like a gourd. Then it dawned on me why he was doing that.

"Oh! Um . . . see, Daddy only went there because he couldn't get an appointment with you!" I said quickly.

"Your daddy went to my competition? He had to get his bald spots oiled so fast he couldn't wait on me? And me havin' a full schedule never stopped him from comin' to me before. The last time I had him come by after hours."

"I didn't mean to tell you about that," I admitted, bowing my aching head. "Please don't tell Daddy I told you."

"You don't have to worry about that. If my own father-in-law don't want to do business with me, I can't do nothin' about it."

"You know how mad Muh'Dear gets when she hears about us going to dinner at Antonosanti's instead of eating at her restaurant," I reminded. "I guess that's no different than Daddy going to Henry's barbershop instead of yours, huh?"

"I guess not." Pee Wee waved his hands in the air in frustration. "Don't tell your daddy I even mentioned him goin' over to Henry's place. I don't want him to know how disappointed I am. . . ."

"I won't tell him I told you," I mumbled. "Anyway, what all is Henry doing to lure your customers away?"

"For one thing, he tryin' to be like all of them uppity barbershops on every corner, in every black neighborhood in Cleveland. He got that big-screen TV settin' up in a corner—right next to a condom machine and a calendar with a woman in a string bikini on it! I tell you, some people ain't got no shame! You would think he was runnin' a tittie bar instead of a barbershop. He doles out free peanuts, provides free bottled water and free sodas, and he has the nerve to run raffles for free haircuts every now and then. I got a good mind to have the law check him out and make sure he ain't breakin' no laws."

"So you think that all of that's the reason he's able to woo away some of your customers?"

"It must be! What else could it be? Shit. Your own daddy done jumped ship, and I had been cuttin' his hair for over ten years! But the other day when Otis didn't keep his appointment to get his dreads trimmed, that was the last straw."

Otis O'Toole was Rhoda's Jamaican husband, and one of my husband's best friends. We had all attended high school together. It was bad enough that my daddy was giving his business to my husband's competition, but I was more than a little disappointed to hear that Otis was doing it, too. I couldn't wait to talk to Rhoda about it, and I was surprised that she had not already mentioned it. She told me everything else.

"Henry spent a lot of money to make his shop so attractive to folks," Pee Wee lamented. "I wish I had proof that he got his money to take over that shop with drug money. I wish I could prove he's dealin' again. He'd be cuttin' some warden's hair for free for the state of Ohio."

# CHAPTER 13

My husband was a smart man, but there were times when he said something so stupid I couldn't believe my ears. This was one of those times.

"Do you know how ridiculous you sound? Would running Henry out of business and sending him back to prison make you feel better?" I asked. Pee Wee just gave me a blank look. "You're still doing well. Lack of business is not the problem. Well, it's not the main problem. You still have enough customers to stay in business. And look on the bright side, you can retire in a few years. Between the two of us, we'll be very comfortable in our golden years."

Pee Wee looked terrified for a few seconds. Then one of the most hopeless looks I'd ever seen appeared on his already tortured-looking face. You would have thought that I'd just told him he had a terminal illness. I was immediately sorry that I had made the "golden years" remark. It was too close to "last years." And because of that serious medical situation that he had faced last year, a male-related condition that could have ended his life, his mortality was one subject we both avoided. Even though he'd beaten the odds and was now as healthy as I was, he still didn't like to discuss it.

"Retire?" he said, making the word sound so obscene I almost expected him to spit it out and honk it across the room. "Re . . . tire?"

The second time he said the word it sounded so bad I wanted to spit it out and honk it across the room myself.

"Uh . . . yeah," I stammered, wishing I could take back what I'd just said.

"I don't want to retire. That's the beginnin' of the end! What in the hell would I do with myself if I retired? Sit around the house every day waitin' to die?"

"There are a lot of things a retired person can do!"

"Like what?"

"You can go fishing more, fool around with other retired men, and relax more, lots of things."

"All that shit is part of the reason I'm bored, woman! What's wrong with you? If you think I'm in bad shape now, I don't even want to think about how bad off I'd be if I retired early!"

"Yes, you're bored now, but if being bored is your biggest complaint, you need to do something to change that."

"Don't you think I've given that some thought? Do you think I'm discussin' this for my health? I've been thinkin' about makin' some changes for a long time."

"Thinking about doing something and doing it are two different things. Look, honey, Henry's shop is so popular because he's giving his customers what they want. Men like looking at a big-screen TV while they are waiting to get their hair cut. Especially when some stupid ball game is on! And all those damn free peanuts, free sodas, and raffles for free haircuts? So what! If that's all Henry's doing, why can't you do something like that?"

Pee Wee's facial expressions changed so rapidly from one moment to the next, it was like he was changing masks. There was a soft, thoughtful look on his face now. It was a huge improvement. The look that he had displayed a few seconds before, a long, melted jaw–looking grimace, had made him resemble a dachshund.

"You sayin' that if I can't beat 'em, I should join 'em?"

"That's not what I'm saying, but since you brought it up, why not? Yeah, Henry probably got his money from dealing drugs. But you've made a nice little fortune over the years. We've got a mighty big nest egg sitting in Richland First National Bank. Use some of it to spruce up your place. Get a big-screen TV and some peanuts."

"You make it sound so easy," Pee Wee said. I didn't like the fact that he was being resistant. "Having the same things in my shop that Henry got in his might not even work. If I can't do all of that and a little somethin' different, somethin' that will attract more business and liven things up, what would be the point?"

I gave my husband another thoughtful look. So far I'd given him so many "thoughtful" looks that my eyes had begun to burn. And if that wasn't enough to make me want to conclude this conversation, the sides of my face felt tight and constricted. I tried to clear my throat, but the lump that had lodged itself there refused to move. When I spoke again, I had to lift my chin and breathe hard to clear the passageway in my throat enough so that I could hold back the bile that was threatening to erupt. That was how frustrated this conversation had made me. "You know that white barbershop across the street from my office? The one owned by Maury Klein?" I didn't wait for Pee Wee to respond. "You would think he had strippers working for him the way his customers line up outside. Maury doesn't even have a big-screen TV."

Pee Wee stared at me with a disappointed look. "How would *you* know? Please don't tell me that you been goin' to the Jews to get your hair trimmed. I heard that a few black folks were goin' there. Lord have mercy on my soul! If I got to compete with the *Jews*—who own most of everything successful in this town already—I may as well retire and crawl into a hole right now. I guess the next thing you'll be tellin' me is that my black customers, and you, will start goin' to the synagogue, too, huh?" He looked at the telephone on the wall. "Where you put Reverend Upshaw's phone number? I'm sure he'd want to know that he got to compete with Jews now. . . ."

"Now don't you start bad-mouthing the Jews. Mel Lowenstein has been your accountant for over twenty years, and he's one of your closest friends," I reminded Pee Wee. "Last time I checked, he was still Jewish."

"We ain't talkin' about Mel. We're talkin' about Maury and you goin' up in his shop to do business with him." Pee Wee growled under his breath. "What else have you been doin' behind my back? If you can run to Maury to get your hair trimmed, what else will you do?"

"Be serious. You know me better than that. If I don't get my hair trimmed at your shop, you know I go to Claudette's beauty shop, not Maury Klein."

"Why are you bringin' up Maury Klein anyway?" Pee Wee sounded so tired and defeated I was surprised that he was still engaged in this conversation. "Maury ain't the one runnin' me out of business."

"Maury's got a manicurist in his barbershop. A lot of men like to keep their nails looking good."

"So?"

"So that's one thing you might want to consider doing," I pointed out. "If it works for Maury, it could work for you."

Pee Wee gave me an impatient look and then rolled his eyes. "What's wrong with you, woman? I don't need a bunch of sissies comin' up in my place. You know how black folks behave when it comes to things like that. Remember that sissy preacher they ran out the pulpit at New Hope Baptist church last year? My business would drop off sure enough if I started caterin' to a bunch of fags."

"I wish you wouldn't use words like *sissies* and *fags*," I said, looking away. "You know I don't like it when you do."

"I'm sorry, baby. I know you hate them words because when we was kids, everybody thought I was one."

"Uh, that's right." He was right. The fact that he'd been accused of being gay when we were kids was one of the reasons I hated words like *fag* and *sissy*.

There was another reason, and it was more recent and more painful. Pee Wee, and just about everybody else I knew, had implied that Louis Baines, the man I had cheated with, was gay. Pee Wee had been so adamant about it that he couldn't use Louis's name without including one of those derogatory terms in the same sentence.

I didn't like the way this conversation was going at all, so I knew I had to lighten it up or end it immediately. But from the look on Pee Wee's face, ending it didn't seem like the best option.

# CHAPTER 14

I forced myself to look and sound more cheerful and enthusiastic. "You can outdo both of them," I said.

I must have sounded and looked too cheerful and too enthusiastic, because Pee Wee gave me a bewildered look. "What?" he muttered, looking at me out of the corner of his eye.

"You can get a big-screen TV and everything else that Henry's got. But you can do even more—hire a manicurist. All the women who work with me go to Maury. They are always looking for ways to get on my good side. I can send them all to you."

I was happy to see that Pee Wee was giving my suggestion some serious thought. "I didn't know you had that many black women workin' for you. Last time I heard, it was just you and two others."

"You need to stop thinking about everything in black and white. But for your information, I have four white women, one Asian, and two Hispanic women working for me, too. And before you hear it from somebody else, half of them have already been to Henry's place to get their hair trimmed because they don't want to stand in that long line to get into Maury's."

"You think you can send 'em my way if I hire a manicurist?"

"I am sure I can do that."

"Hmmm. I guess I could run an ad in the newspaper for a manicurist. Shit. I don't want some fly-by-night that might run off when business gets good. You know how women are."

"Then don't hire a woman. Hire a man. They have male manicurists—and they are not all gay."

"That's somethin' to think about, but whether it's a man or a woman, it could be more trouble than it's worth. If I hire a young woman, she might run off and get married. An older woman might call in sick with a different female ailment every other week. A man, well, whether the man was a f—uh, gay man or not, people would think he was."

"Let me find somebody for you."

"You? You want to find somebody to work for me in my shop? Since when did you become a headhunter? I don't know about you gettin' involved in this."

"I can talk to Claudette and some of the women who come to her beauty shop. They know everything that's going on in this town. They'll even know a good manicurist's dog's business."

"I don't know about that Claudette. I hear she spreads more gossip than the *Enquirer*."

My jaw dropped. "Look, do you want me to help you or not? I have to talk to somebody to get the information we need. And Claudette is a good place to start. She knows everybody and everything. Being a gossipmonger is good for something."

"All right, all right. If that's what you want to do, go ahead and do it."

"Maybe I should stay out of it. If I do something you don't like, or if something doesn't go the way you want it to go, I'll never hear the end of it. And to be honest with you, I don't want to have another conversation like the one we had today anytime soon. Now, do you want me to talk to Claudette or not? Because if you want to deal with this problem on your own, that's fine with me. I'm getting tired." My outburst seemed to help.

Pee Wee attempted to smile, but he was taking his time replying.

"Well, do you or don't you want me to talk to Claudette, or somebody? At this point, I'd be willing to talk to Satan if it'll help," I said.

Pee Wee abruptly stopped trying to smile. He sniffed and moved his lips in silence for a few seconds. It seemed like he was having a hard time getting his words out now. When he did, it sounded like he had a frog in his throat.

Whether he was done with this discussion or not, I was. I looked at my watch and then at the door, and I was glad he saw me doing that. I wanted him to see that I was impatient. "Well, if you're goin' to do it, you better get on it right away," he said with a heavy sigh.

"Don't worry. I am going to find you somebody that you won't be able to live without. Trust me," I told him, squeezing his hand.

It felt good to know that I had a new mission to accomplish. One that would benefit me as much as it would Pee Wee, and everybody else concerned, for that matter.

Unfortunately, the problems I usually faced had a domino effect. I knew that if I didn't resolve this one, it would eventually muddy my relationships with everybody else. I didn't need any more of that right now.

I smiled to myself because I was feeling so much better now. I was confident enough to know that I *would* find just the right person to help bring my husband out of the doldrums.

And it definitely had to be somebody who could fulfill all of his needs. I had no idea at the time that I would end up regretting those thoughts in the worst way.

I already had enough problems in my life, but I seemed to be adding more and more all the time. And if it wasn't one thing that drove me up the wall, it was another. One of the "new" problems that I had in my life now was that I was often so preoccupied that when people addressed me, it took me a few moments to react. I didn't know if it was part of the "reward" I got for reaching middle age or what. But it was not something I spent a lot of time worrying about. My mother did enough of that for me. When I visited her the day after my conversation with Pee Wee, she jumped on me like a grasshopper.

"What is wrong with you, girl? You look like your mind is a thousand miles away this mornin'." My mother's loud voice cut into my thoughts like a sling blade.

"Huh? Oh! I'm sorry, Muh'Dear. I wasn't listening. I was thinking about something else," I explained. "What were you saying?"

"I asked if you been takin' them hormone pills I gave you? And from the way you sittin' here thinkin' about somethin' else, I guess you ain't." Muh'Dear grunted. "I done told you, you can't get through menopause in one piece without help."

"I am not exactly at that point," I reminded.

"You close enough to it! I don't care if you still see a few drops of blood every month. That don't mean nothin'. By the time I was your age, I had already been into the menopause for two years. And I wish you would stop tellin' me you ain't exactly at that point yet. I know better." My mother paused and stared at the side of my head with raw exasperation. "Me, I know when a woman is gwine through the change, whether she know it or not. Baby, there ain't no sugar left in your bowl, and you are about as bloated as one of them Macy's Thanksgiving Day parade floats. If that ain't enough to send a man on a walk of shame to another woman's bedroom, I don't know what is. Now, I asked you, are you takin' them hormone pills I gave you? At your age, you need all the help you can get if you want to hang on to your husband. . . ."

"Muh'Dear, I told you those pills made me retain water," I said, giving her an apologetic look. "And they made me nervous so I stopped taking them."

"Well, excuse me! If you can get through menopause with no help, you in better shape than I was when I went through it."

"Hell's bells! Do I have to sit here in this restaurant and listen to all this talk about female problems?" Daddy complained.

"Let me tell you one thing, mister. Just because you got that limp piece of raw meat between your thighs, don't think you in the clear. When you got women in your life, her female problems become your problem. And, brother, you got plenty. Just look at your daughter!" Muh'Dear waved at me like I was a wrecked car.

And I felt like one, too.

# CHAPTER 15

"What's wrong with this girl?" Daddy asked my mother, looking at me with his eyes squinted. "What's wrong with you now, girl?" he asked me.

"Nothing is wrong with me," I said with a chuckle, hoping that it would convince them that their unflattering assessment of me wasn't bothering me that much.

"See, ain't nothin' wrong with her, other than the obvious fact that she done lost too much weight. Gussie Mae, you the one brought up this female mess." Daddy paused and glared at my mother. "I have hard enough time gettin' a good appetite as it is. Pass me them biscuits. Them puppies is screamin' this mornin'. You really put your foot in this grub you cooked this mornin'." As soon as my father mentioned food, my mother's mood and expression changed.

"Why thank you, Frank." Even though my mother received a compliment on her cooking all the time, each time she did, she acted like she was hearing it for the first time. She beamed like she had just been crowned queen for a day. "Wait until you taste them turkey necks I'm cookin' for dinner."

My mother loved it when people complimented her cooking. Cooking was more than a profession to her. Not only had it become a way of life for her over the years, but it had also been the one lifeline that she had always been able to count on. And as long as people had to eat, Muh'Dear would never go hungry, or broke. She even had business cards that read: EAT HERE OR WE'LL BOTH STARVE.

My mother owned the Buttercup, the most successful black-owned restaurant in Richland. It was not a particularly fancy or ornate place, but it was full of down-home charm with its maroon table cloths and matching carpet. My late stepfather had left the business to my mother in his will. Next to me and my daughter, it was her most precious pride and joy. She had made a few improvements. She had replaced the old carpets and reupholstered the booths. And she had replaced all of the old autographed pictures of dead celebrities with some of celebrities who were still alive.

One thing Muh'Dear had promptly made sure of was that when she passed on, the restaurant and everything else she left behind would belong to me. Even though she had remarried my father, she was still bitter about him leaving us for that white woman. And she made damn sure he would not benefit from her hard work. She adored Pee Wee, but she had strongly advised me to draw up a last will and testament that would make sure *he* didn't get his paws on the deed to the restaurant or the house that he and I lived in, which was in my name only.

Not only was the restaurant in a nice, quiet, safe neighborhood, it catered to Richland's most upscale residents. It was not unusual to see the mayor or a corporate CEO sitting at a table or in a booth, humped over a large plate and some of the lemonade that my mother made, which included a dash of lime in each glass. "Serve up somethin' unique and it'll keep 'em comin' back" was her motto. And she was right. She had a large group of loyal customers whom she treated like family. They appreciated her hard work and dedication to her business, and they never failed to let her know. The few times that they didn't remind her of how inspirational she was, she did. Muh'Dear never stopped talking about how she had once cleaned toilets and lived in shacks. Now she lived like a queen, and most of the time, she acted like one, too. She wore expensive outfits, got her hair and nails done every week, took trips to exotic locations, but she still treated me like I was two years old.

If I didn't stop by the Buttercup or the house that Muh'Dear owned a few blocks from it at least one day a week to have a meal with her and my cantankerous father, they'd hound me until I did. It did me no good to remind my mother that I had changed my eating habits. I no longer gobbled up the large, unhealthy feasts that she'd introduced me to in the first place. Throughout my childhood, she had pacified me with every fattening, greasy, unhealthy thing that she could get her hands on. What was so ironic about all of that was, she was the main person warning me back then about how I was going to end up as big as a moose. Even after I'd ballooned up to the size of a small moose, she continued to unintentionally sabotage every diet I tried. She had ambushed me with so many fried potato sandwiches that throughout my teens my skin resembled a potato hull.

"Why do you keep lookin' toward the door? You expectin' somebody?" Muh'Dear asked me.

"Uh, I was hoping Rhoda would come," I muttered. I sloshed the coffee around in the large cup that Muh'Dear had set in front of me. I tried to ignore the platter a few inches from my face that contained a mountain of grits swimming in a pool of butter, scrambled eggs, and a stack of wheat toast on a saucer—each slice slathered with butter, jelly, and enough greasy bacon to bring down a horse. "You know how Rhoda loves your cooking."

"Well, she ought to show it more! That woman is as thin as a rail. She eats less than a gnat when she comes up in here. And me with my crazy self, in that kitchen sweatin' over that hot stove and whatnot—just wastin' my time on a skinny minnie like her! Poor Rhoda. I been tryin' to put some meat on them hip bones of hers for years. Men like healthy women. Rhoda don't watch her step and thicken them thighs of hers, she gwine to lose her husband," Muh'Dear predicted. "Eat your food before it gets cold."

I bit off a tiny piece of bacon and looked toward the door again.

Rhoda usually accompanied me to the restaurant, and I used her as an excuse to make a quick getaway. But when she couldn't leave her house, where she ran a licensed childcare center for preschoolers, she called the restaurant at a time that we had agreed upon to tell me she had an emergency situation and needed my help. She was five minutes late today. I slid back the sleeve of the red silk blouse that I had on and checked my watch.

"Why do you keep lookin' at your watch?" Daddy asked, biscuit crumbs decorating his bushy gray beard like confetti. For a man pushing eighty, my father had a lot of energy. He got up every morning at the crack of dawn and walked the four blocks from the house he shared with my mother to the restaurant. My mother got up even earlier, and by the time Daddy made it to the restaurant, she had his breakfast ready. She also had a laundry list of chores for him to do that day and a list of complaints that she wanted him to address. Today, I was on that list of complaints. "Your mama tells me that you been runnin' all over town tryin' to find some makeup artist to work for Pee Wee. What's wrong with you, girl? What Pee Wee need a makeup artist for? He already look like a clown." Daddy had a serious look on his face, but my mother snickered.

"Manicurist," I corrected, stabbing one of the seven slices of crispy bacon on my plate with my fork. Despite the fact that I had shed over a hundred pounds, my mother still tried to feed me like I was Hulk Hogan. I had barely touched the feast in front of me. She had also set a coffeepot with enough coffee for eight people next to the platter. Even though I'd been taking my coffee black for months, next to it was a container full of Half n' Half and sugar.

The Buttercup was already busy, and it was only ten thirty. Construction workers, a few cops, people who were coming off the night shift, men and women in office attire, and a few young people from a nearby business college occupied almost every table and booth. I had left my office at nine thirty. The only way I was going to make it back in time to interview the first candidate who had applied for the manicurist position was if Rhoda rescued me within the next ten minutes. Bless her heart. She would if she could, and that was what I was counting on.

Before I could form my next thought, Hazel Strong, Muh'Dear's day shift bartender, motioned to me from the bar counter across the room that I had a phone call. "Annette, Rhoda's on the phone. She say she got an emergency, but she won't tell me what it is," Hazel reported in her loud, nasally voice.

"I'll be right there," I told her.

Hazel looked disappointed, and I knew that it was because she was dying to know why Rhoda was calling me. Like with my mother and so many other people I knew, collecting and spreading gossip was a form of creative nourishment. It kept their brains and their tongues sharp.

"Where are you gwine, gal? I know you don't think you gettin' your sorry tail up out of here leavin' all that good food on your plate!" Muh'Dear hollered.

"Box it up for me. I have to take this call," I hollered back, already trotting across the floor to the telephone on the counter next to the cash register. "It's about time," I said to Rhoda as soon as I picked up the receiver. "Where the hell are you?" I glanced around and lowered my voice to a whisper. Rhoda knew Hazel well enough not to tell her what the "emergency" was that she was calling me about, so Hazel was trying to eavesdrop. She stood a few inches from me, wiping the same spots on the counter over and over. That was why I was whispering. "You're supposed to rescue me. I'm sinking like a block of cement in a bowl of quicksand over here."

"Listen, I've got an emergency situation," Rhoda replied in a tired voice.

"Did you hear what I just said? Rhoda, it's *me*. You can cancel that emergency ruse," I said, still speaking in a low voice because Hazel was still trying to eavesdrop and still wiping the same spots. "Girl, you called in the nick of time. Uh, my mother was well on her way to roasting me like a fatted calf."

"No, I'm serious. I do have an emergency, so I can't accommodate you this time."

I held my breath as I waited for Rhoda to elaborate. She remained ominously silent, and that made me more than a little nervous. "Is something wrong?"

"Big time," Rhoda sputtered. "And it's not somethin' that you are goin' to want to hear. . . ."

"Well, if it's something you don't think I want to hear, do I need to hear it at all? And if it is, is it something that you can tell me in five words or less?" I was no longer whispering, but I kept my voice low.

"I can tell you in three: Jade Marie O'Toole."

"Oh, dear God no!" I gasped and stumbled. Hazel moved closer to me with her arms outstretched, as if expecting me to fall to the floor. My legs got so weak I almost did fall. Somehow I managed to contain myself by holding on to the counter. I motioned for Hazel to move back. "Rhoda, I'm having a bad enough day already. Please tell me you're joking, and if you are, this is not funny."

"What makes you think I'm jokin'?"

The seriousness of Rhoda's tone scared me. I knew that this was one subject neither she nor I would ever make a joke out of.

Other than cancer and divorce, *Jade Marie O'Toole* were the other three words in the English language that sent the most shivers up and down my spine. But I had three more words of my own that described Rhoda's daughter even better: Bride of Satan.

# CHAPTER 16

Rhoda's daughter, Jade, who was going to turn twenty-one this year, had caused almost as much pain and destruction to the people in her orbit as a hurricane.

I was no exception. I had experienced the full force of her wrath.

The year before last, she had tried to take my husband from me by harassing me with threatening phone calls and obscene letters. When that scheme blew up in her face, she moved to Louisiana to live with Rhoda's parents and to attend college. But Jade cared as much about education as a mule did. She fought with her professors, other girls, her boyfriends, and everybody in between. She promptly flunked out of college and ran off to Cancún, Mexico, with some of her friends on spring break. Down there, that girl had gone hog-happy wild.

Rhoda had never told me the whole story about Jade's visit to Mexico, but it had to be one for the books. What she shared with me had come out in bits and pieces, and it had given me chicken skin shivers. Jade's south of the border jaunt had generated a chilling, middle of the night telephone call from the Mexican authorities to Rhoda's father. He had immediately hopped on a chartered plane and flown down there to rescue Jade, and to straighten out whatever mess she had gotten herself into. Whatever kind of mess he had to bail her out of, it had cost him thousands of dollars and several meetings with an official from the consulate. Jade was never allowed to set foot on Mexican ground again for the rest of her life. Those were all of the details that Rhoda had shared with me, and that was only because I told her I didn't want to know any more than that. I was still recovering from my own emotional wounds from my showdown with Jade. She returned to Richland straight from Mexico with twelve pieces of designer luggage and her Mexican fiancé, Marcelo.

Jade was without a doubt the "ugliest" beautiful female I knew. Despite her good looks, she was an offshoot of Godzilla—mean, violent, and mainly concerned about her needs way before anybody else's. And it didn't take her fiancé long to figure that out. He'd left her at the altar last year, and to save face, she'd promptly fled to Alabama. According to Rhoda's regular updates, the girl had driven almost everybody in Alabama crazy with her antics, which included smoking weed, cussing out people in public, a smackdown that involved the wife of one of her new lovers, and even a night in jail for slapping a cab driver because he wouldn't carry her lazy, doped-up ass from his cab to her doorway after a wild party. Oh, there were some lovely stories about this child.

"What did Jade do now?" I asked, my hand clutching the telephone.

"She's come back home," Rhoda said with a heavy sigh.

"When?" I had just talked to Rhoda a couple of hours ago and she had not even mentioned Jade.

There was a short pause before Rhoda responded. "She just stumbled in the front door a few minutes ago." Rhoda paused again. "With twelve pieces of luggage again. She had to hire two cabs to bring her and all of her shit from the airport."

"Lord. Well, I guess I won't be seeing you today, huh?" I was more than a little disappointed. My heart skipped a few beats. Then it started thumping around inside my chest so hard I had to hold my breath and massage the throbbing space below my breasts to ease the discomfort.

"Maybe later. I hope you understand." Rhoda lowered her voice to a whisper. "It sounds like Jade is back there tearin' down the house."

"I do understand." I let out such a deep and heavy sigh, I felt it all the way to my armpits. "Lord knows you've got a mess on your hands now. How long do you think she's going to stay this time?"

"Only God knows. She had a major falling out with my son the other night, which is what prompted her to hop on a plane and come back here. She claims one of his boyfriends insulted her. He claims she started the mess, and that anything the boyfriend said to her, it was because she had it coming." I didn't have to see Rhoda's face to know that she was thoroughly disgusted. I could hear it in her voice. "Jade resents the fact that her big brother is gay, you know? She always has. You and I know how some black people are when it comes to homosexuality."

"Tell me about it. Pee Wee told me in no uncertain terms not to interview any men for that manicurist position he wants to fill."

"I know at least two male manicurists, and neither one of them is gay. You know Beanie Ross, that white boy who works at the mall where we get our nails done sometimes?" Rhoda's tone took a sharp detour. "He's one of the biggest womanizers in town." She seemed relieved to be discussing something other than Jade, and so was I.

"I've already talked to Beanie. He didn't say it in so many words, but what he did say told me enough. He's afraid to work for a black man in a black neighborhood. He got mugged coming out of Antonosanti's last month."

"Antonosanti's is in the most exclusive white neighborhood in Richland!" Rhoda declared.

"Yeah, I know. But it was a black man who mugged Beanie."

"Oh well."

"I've got two prospects lined up for today and a maybe for tomorrow."

"I hope you took my advice."

"I did. They are both straight-up homely." I managed a quick laugh and under the circumstances, it felt good. "Marlene, the older one, who also happens to be a retired schoolteacher, she must be God's homeliest creation since the rhinoceros."

"Hmmm. That sounds a bit extreme. We don't want Pee Wee's customers to take one look at her and run, now do we?"

Rhoda laughed this time and I laughed again some more, too. The more I laughed, the better I felt. But I knew that my euphoria was not going to last long. With Pee Wee's mess on my hands and now Jade, well, I knew that I wouldn't be laughing much after I got off of the telephone. As far as Jade was concerned, she was the kind of problem with no easy solution. She was more like an ongoing disease; a person just had to learn to tolerate her. I didn't like the fact that my mind kept wandering back to Jade while Rhoda and I were discussing a manicurist for Pee Wee.

I redirected my thoughts back to the manicurist position. "Marlene's not that bad," I admitted with a chuckle. "And I think she'd make a good employee for Pee Wee. Anyway, you are the one who said it would be too dangerous to hire a pretty woman."

"And I meant that, too. But I didn't mean for you to go overboard. However, even if you hired a woman who looks like Moms Mabley, it would be better than you hirin' a Janet Jackson lookalike. If you hire one of these cute little wenches runnin' around Richland, you will have trouble from day one. Men and boys will be in and out of that barbershop tryin' to set up dates so they could get some pussy. Their women will get jealous and might make their men change barbers."

I was still reeling from the news about Jade, so I could offer Rhoda only a weak sigh before I resumed my end of the conversation. "Well, if I am going to hire anybody, I'd better get a move on now if I want to make it back to my office in time for the interview that I have set up. Where's Jade now?"

Rhoda moaned first. Then she took a deep, loud breath. "She's about to take one of her two-hour-long bubble baths," Rhoda replied, surprising me with a chuckle. "Poor thing. That Alabama sun wreaked havoc on her beautiful complexion. The first thing I noticed when she walked in the door was those dark splotches on her chin. I guess I'll have to run over to the Grab and Go and get her some Noxzema."

The fact that Rhoda was rambling off the top of her head concerned me. I knew that I could avoid Jade, but she couldn't. If it made her feel better to ramble on and on about that soulless daughter of hers like she was some helpless Little Miss Muffet, the least I could do was listen.

"I know my daughter is a real piece of work, but she's done some good things, wouldn't you say?" Rhoda inquired. "Even for you."

I had to clear my throat and smile first, because as odd as it sounded, what Rhoda had just said was true. I could not ignore the fact that had Jade not tormented me on such a brutal level that it had drastically altered my eating habits, *I would not be looking so good right now!* I'd still be wearing a size 24 and digging my grave with a fork and spoon. I patted my firm waist and said, "That's true . . ."

# CHAPTER 17

Rhoda was trying to paint such a rosy picture of Jade that I had to interrupt because I was getting sick to my stomach. "I'm sure Jade is still as pretty as ever, though," I offered. It gave me a bad taste in my mouth to say something complimentary about Jade.

"Oh, and with those lips, those eyes, that nose—she is still such a livin' doll! Now she looks more like Naomi Campbell than ever before. Just like me." Rhoda paused and sucked on her teeth. There was a dreamy tone to her voice, and I could almost see the wheels in her head spinning out of control, trying to convince herself that Jade was not the monster she really was. "It's a damn shame she's not tall enough to model. If she had a few more inches, I'd take her to New York myself and march her into Eileen Ford's office, where I know they'd beg her to sign a contract. Don't you agree?"

"I agree," I muttered. "Jade is too gorgeous to ignore. She should take advantage of her beauty while she still has time." Now I was the one rambling.

"I don't know how many more times I have to tell her that if she wants to look like me when she's our age, she's goin' to have to take better care of herself. The first thing she did when she arrived home was to grab a Snickers bar out of the candy dish. The only difference between stickin' a loaded gun in the mouth and a candy bar is, the candy bar will do more damage to her waistline!"

Other than the miserable conversation that I'd had with Pee Wee about his "boredom," this conversation was one of the worst I'd had in years. I couldn't wait for it to end. But the last thing I would ever do to Rhoda was brush her off. She was always there for me when I needed her, and as long as I could, I would do the same for her.

"Well, at least she didn't drag home another fiancé with her like she did when she came back from Mexico. You can be thankful for that," I stated, almost biting the tip of my tongue because this conversation had become so awkward for me. Rhoda was taking a long time to answer and that made me curious. "Or did she?"

"No, she didn't bring home a fiancé this time. She brought home a husband." Rhoda chuckled for a few seconds; then she mumbled a slew of profanities under her breath.

I was speechless. The last time I had asked Rhoda about Jade's love life, which was just last month, she told me that the girl was between boyfriends. Now here she was telling me that she'd found a new boyfriend and married him in less than a month!

For the first time, Pee Wee's idea about us packing up and moving to another state sounded somewhat attractive. There was no way I was going to be able to avoid regular confrontations with Rhoda's daughter. Ever since our falling out, Jade went out of her way to antagonize me—even when she was not even in town. Last Christmas, she'd sent me a dime-store greeting card from New Orleans with my name misspelled in the address and postage due.

"Who you talkin' to, gal?" Daddy asked, walking toward me with his hands on his hips.

"Uh, I'll talk to you later," I told Rhoda, abruptly hanging up the telephone.

"Your mama done already told you your food is gettin' cold," Daddy said, nodding toward the booth near the kitchen where Muh'Dear was still seated, looking at me with a cross look on her face.

"Put it in a box and I will pick it up later. I have to get back to my office now," I said. Hazel had not left her spot behind the counter, but she had stopped wiping it. Now she was wiping and rearranging glasses. I assumed she still thought that she was going to hear me say something that she could get some gossip mileage out of.

"Your mama told me to tell you that she might have a good person for that nail whatnot thing job Pee Wee got open," Daddy announced, his arm around my shoulder as we walked back to the booth.

Before I could ask who, Muh'Dear answered that question.

"You remember Lizzie, that gal who does my nails? She works in that salon down the street from here."

"Lizzie who?"

"Elizabeth Stovall."

I shrugged. "Do I know her?"

"I thought you did. Y'all the same age and she asks about you every time she does my nails." Muh'Dear paused and leaned back in her seat like she was about to attack somebody. In a way, she did. "Her mama is a *white* woman!"

My mother had a lot of white friends and a lot of white folks ate at her restaurant. Her lead cook was a white woman, and next to Scary Mary, she was Muh'Dear's closest female friend, so I knew my mother was not prejudiced. I could not understand why she still held some animosity toward white women. Daddy was not the first black man to desert his family for a white woman, and he wouldn't be the last. Another thing I couldn't understand was, if Muh'Dear could forgive him enough to take him back, why did she still resent those women? I was glad that Daddy had not left us for a black woman. . . .

"Oh, yes. That Lizzie. I went to school with her," I said, suddenly interested. "She was the girl with that leg."

"That leg? You make her sound like a car part."

"Well, I didn't mean to. You know I never make fun of people's handicaps. Lizzie had polio, or something, when she was real young. One of her legs is a little thinner than the other one. But she was a really nice girl," I said with eager anticipation. For once, Muh'Dear had aroused my interest.

Muh'Dear nodded. "Little Leg Lizzie. Last week she told me how she was ready for a change. She'd been passin', you know. Like that half sister of yours that Frank had with *his* white woman."

At this point, Daddy bowed his head and shifted his weight from one foot to the other. Even though my mother had "forgiven" him for leaving her to marry a white woman, she would never let him forget it. Muh'Dear's voice slid down to a sinister tone. "Once them white folks found out she had a black daddy, they stopped lettin' her do their nails. I guess they thought they'd catch some kind of blackitis disease or somethin'. Some white folks is so strange. We done raised their kids, cooked their food, and some of us done had their babies, and they still think we some kind of subhuman race. If we ever wanted to strike them down with some kind of affliction, don't they think we would have done it by now? Where I come from, some of them sisters in my generation know enough voodoo to bring the whole white race to its knees."

One thing about my mother was, if you didn't want her to hold you hostage for hours on end, you didn't encourage her to elaborate on any of her off-the-wall comments. "Do you have Lizzie's phone number?" I asked, looking at my watch. "I really have to be on my way," I said firmly.

By the way she pursed and stuck her bottom lip out, Muh'Dear was clearly disappointed that I was about to depart. She reached in her bra and fumbled around in it for at least two minutes before she fished out a folded piece of paper. "Here. Here's Lizzie's number. Now she is a little on the homely side, so it might take some of them customers a while to take a shine to her. And with that shrunk-up polio leg, she won't be posin' for no pictures in *Jet* magazine or *Playboy* no time soon, so she'll be stable. She ain't never had no man, so you ain't got to worry about her runnin' off gettin' married and leavin' Pee Wee in a lurch neither." Muh'Dear gave me a look that I couldn't interpret. All I knew was that it made me nervous. "But a woman that ain't never, uh, had her fruit plucked ain't normal, so you might be gettin' some kind of pig-in-poke. . . ."

I knew that if I didn't leave soon, Muh'Dear's comments and remarks would wear me down to a frazzle. At the rate she was going, she had almost convinced me *not* to interview Elizabeth or anybody else to work for my husband. I felt like I was on a treadmill. I had Rhoda telling me to hire a plain woman, but not too plain. Muh'Dear was telling me to hire Lizzie, but since Lizzie wasn't "normal" she might not work out.

"I really do need to get out of here," I insisted. *"Now."*

Daddy plopped back down in his seat and took up the conversation where Muh'Dear had left off. "What Gussie is tryin' to say is,

Little Leg Lizzie ain't perfect, but she might be perfect for Pee Wee. As slow as she is mental wise, she still know how to do some nails. Hold up your hands, Gussie Mae." Daddy grabbed Muh'Dear's right hand and held it up to my face, the front of her French-tipped nails facing me. Muh'Dear proudly displayed her left hand, waving it in my face like she was trying to hypnotize me. Lizzie's handiwork was good, but it was no better or different from any of the other manicurists' work I'd seen.

"Nice work," I agreed with a nod. "I'll call Lizzie and see if she's interested. Pee Wee is getting impatient."

"He ain't got to be impatient for long. Not if you get to Lizzie before some other nail person snatches her up. Like I said, she can change Pee Wee's life." Daddy released Muh'Dear's hand and turned to me again. "He'll be a changed man in no time," he told me with a nod.

"I sure hope so," I said.

# CHAPTER 18

I had interviewed a lot of people in my office for positions at my company, but I didn't feel comfortable interviewing people for my husband's business on Mizelle's property and time. I had each applicant meet me at a cute little coffee shop, where I often took my coffee breaks, two doors down the block from my office building. Whatever time I used to conduct the interview, I made up for it by not taking lunch or my two daily coffee breaks.

I didn't like interviews. It didn't matter whether I was the one being interviewed or I was the one interviewing somebody. For one thing, it was awkward for me to talk to a stranger. And in some cases, it was possibly dangerous. At least it was for a collection agent. Three years ago, I'd sent a process server to a man who had ignored an unpaid bill with the phone company for months. I hauled him into court and he still refused to pay. I had no choice but to have his wages attached. What was so bizarre about that case was, the man had once worked for the telephone company! A couple of weeks later when I had to interview applicants for a vacant position, he applied for it under a different name. This was a ruse that he'd concocted so he could get me alone somewhere to cuss me out and threaten me. And it had happened in my office during lunch. I was on the premises alone with just our meek, 100-pound receptionist. As soon as I'd closed my office door, that man started cussing at me. He blocked the door so I couldn't escape; then he grabbed me and held me in place so I couldn't make it to the phone on my desk. The receptionist heard the commotion and called the cops.

Now when I interviewed for positions at my company, I made sure to keep my office door open and that at least two of my male employees and our security guard are on the premises. I didn't think I had to worry about any of that in the case of Pee Wee's manicurist position. My main concern was whether he or she could do the job. But I also had to consider their appearance, their work history, their qualifications, and so on.

Another thing was that no matter how good the applicant looked on their résumé and application, that was rarely the person you met in the interview. Not only did people lie and exaggerate during interviews, they usually told you whatever they thought you wanted to hear.

It didn't take long for me to realize that people who really didn't want to work came to interviews with that attitude. None of the ragtag group of people I interviewed seemed that interested in working for my husband. And from the indifference and slovenly appearances of each one, they probably didn't want to work for anybody else either.

The first applicant I interviewed was still employed, and for an asshole who monitored every move she made. Her lunch hour and breaks combined didn't add up to enough time for her to do an interview with me that could possibly be an hour long. She was afraid to take off any time and practically begged me to interview her after business hours. In her case, I was glad to schedule an after-business-hours appointment. Despite the fact that she had arrived on time and seemed like a good candidate, she was a huge disappointment. She chomped and cracked a wad of chewing gum during the whole interview, and even told me, "I'm just looking for something now until I can get hired at the water company."

Another applicant admitted that she'd come to check out the job only because she thought that by working in a barbershop, she'd meet more men. The one that I'd really been interested in didn't bother to show up for her interview, or call to cancel or reschedule.

When Lizzie called to confirm her appointment, I told her to just meet me at the coffee shop. It was February and there was still a lot of snow on the ground, so it was cold enough for overcoats and boots. There was some ice and sleet on the streets, so a lot of people didn't like to drive or even walk around outside if they didn't have to. Muh'Dear had told me that Lizzie had a car, but public parking was so bad on the street where I worked I wasn't sure she'd be on time, so I arrived fifteen minutes later than the time I told her to meet me. I was surprised and embarrassed when I got to the coffee shop and she was already there.

As soon as I entered Mike's Place and saw her, I felt hopeful. I didn't know just how handicapped she was because of her leg. I wasn't even sure that that word applied to her. She had been in my PE classes all through high school and she'd done everything that the rest of us had done, including jumping jacks and cartwheels. Even when our classmates had laughed at her when we did square dances, she had done as many do-si-dos as the rest of us, and with a smile.

I had not seen Lizzie since high-school graduation night, but I would have recognized her anywhere. The poor thing. She was as plain as ever. She occupied one of the six red plastic tables with matching chairs next to the ladies' room. There was a huge smile on her face when she saw me walking toward her.

"Lizzie, it's so good to see you again," I squealed, pulling out a chair across from her. She surprised me by rising and extending her hand. She had a firm grip for a petite woman. "I'm sorry I'm a little late," I told her as I plopped down in my chair. "We had a small emergency back at the office that I had to take care of." I beckoned for the waitress to bring me a cup of coffee. "Would you like a bear claw or something? This place doesn't look like much, but they are giving Starbucks a run for their money. The pastries here are fantastic."

"Oh, no thanks. I'm trying to watch my weight," she told me with a shy smile as she eased back down in her seat, scooting it closer to the table.

"I heard that," I mouthed. I sucked in my stomach, not that I had to do that anymore, but out of habit. We both ordered just a cup of black coffee, decaf for her.

I sniffed and discreetly looked her over with a critical eye. I smiled and grinned a lot so I wouldn't be too obvious. Lizzie didn't look like she had to worry about her weight. I didn't see any bulges or lumps on her body. Like me, she was of average height. From what I could see, none of her body parts were bigger or smaller than they were supposed to be. Unfortunately, I couldn't say the same thing about the rest of her. Her shoulder-length hair was thick and had once been jet black. Well, some of it was still jet black, but most of it had already turned gray. Her lopsided ponytail, held in place by a red rubber band, was flat and stiff. Each time she shook or bobbed her head, that drab ponytail flip-flopped from side to side like a beaver's tail.

There was no makeup on her round, almost porcelain white face, but for the first time, I realized she had nice features. In spite of the saucer-size, Coke bottle–like glasses she wore, I could see that she had nice, big brown eyes and long, thick lashes. She had a cute little nose that wiggled slightly each time she smiled. I could tell from the laugh lines around her mouth and eyes that she smiled a lot. She worried a lot, too. I could tell that from the lines on her forehead and the noticeable dark shadows beneath her eyes.

She had draped a plaid coat across the back of her chair. It was a style that I had not seen since the seventies. It had what looked like a Nehru collar and black buttons as big around as silver dollars. Her drab, pea-colored woolen dress reminded me of a long night-gown that my mother used to sleep in. I couldn't see her feet, so there was no telling what kind of shoes she wore. What I couldn't understand was how a woman her age could let herself go to the point of ground zero. By anybody's standards, Lizzie was a rag doll. She was one woman who was screaming for a makeover.

"So I hear you're looking for a change?" I began.

"I am not going to lie to you. Yes, I could sure use a change," she responded with another eager smile on her face. "And if anybody can help me, it's you, Annette. Please don't think that I am kissing up to you, because I am not. People think that because I'm real quiet and shy that I don't know how to speak up for myself. But when I want something bad enough, I go for it." At this point, Lizzie paused and sucked in some air.

"Have you been in Richland all this time?"

"What do you mean?"

"Well, we've been out of school for decades and I lost track of a lot of people."

"I lost track of people, too. Me, I spent a couple of years with some of my mama's folks on their farm in West Virginia. I had a few problems down there because of my daddy's blood. I worked in a country deli, and a lot of those rednecks didn't want my 'black' hands making their fried frog leg sandwiches. I didn't put up with that mess long. I came back to Ohio and went to cosmetology school, and I took a few other courses in the beauty field." Lizzie stopped talking and let out a dry laugh as she patted her hair. "It surprises most people when I tell them that. They expect me to look more glamorous, I guess."

"I'm sure you remember what a frump I was in school," I said quickly with a grimace on my face.

"But you are no frump now."

"You should have seen me about a year ago. I was almost twice as big as I am now. Back in school, I was miserable like a lot of kids. Most of them left this hick town running. I was one of them."

"Oh yeah. I think somebody told me that not long after graduation, you took off to Pennsylvania with a man. . . ."

I rolled my eyes. "I took off to Pennsylvania, but it was not with a man. I was on my own. I didn't even have a boyfriend then. You can't believe everything you hear in this town. Anyway, things didn't work out for me in Pennsylvania, so I came back here. I worked hard to improve my life, and I did."

"I am not surprised that you got that high-level job at the collection agency, and that you married a big shot like Pee Wee. I remember how smart you were in Mr. Brown's debate class. All of the kids wanted to be on your team because you always made your team win. Annette, I know I said I wasn't trying to kiss up to you, but I know that what I am going to say next might sound like I am.

The truth is, I want to be where you are some day. I want the same things you've got."

"Thank you," I said, beaming proudly.

"I hope you can help me make that happen."

"Oh, I hope I can, too." I gave Lizzie a hopeful look. "And my husband will treat you better than your last boss," I assured her.

# CHAPTER 19

I could tell a lot about a person by the way they sat in a chair. And from the stiff-backed way Lizzie was sitting with both hands wrapped around her coffee cup, she was not comfortable with a lot of things. Another way that I could tell she was uncomfortable was the way she looked. She kept blinking her eyes, fiddling with her hair, and licking her lips. From the movies I'd seen and some of the things I'd read and heard, I had decided a long time ago that being biracial was not a picnic for some mixed-blood people. My half sister Lillimae was biracial, but she was the exception to the rule. She was one of the most confident and well-adjusted women I knew. Lizzie looked and behaved like a frightened deer. Her mother was a rather plain-looking white woman, and her biological father was a pure-blooded Jamaican with skin that was so black it looked purple in certain light. However, Lizzie had inherited her mother's European features, which she could have used to her advantage if she lived in a big city where people didn't know her ethnic background. Living in a small town like Richland, where everybody knew everybody else's business, she could not have passed for white successfully for long; no matter how hard she tried. I just found it hard to believe that in this day and age she'd lost her job because of her mixed blood, like Muh'Dear had told me.

"Do you mind telling me why you quit your last job?"

"I didn't exactly quit. . . ."

"Oh. Lizzie, I don't know if what I heard is true, but it doesn't matter to me."

"What did you hear?" she asked, looking me in the eye without blinking. She suddenly seemed defensive.

I shrugged. "I heard a rumor that some of the white customers had a problem with you doing their nails?" I put it in the form of a question.

"I don't know if that had anything to do with them asking me to leave. Everybody was always so nice to me, especially the customers. But the real reason is because my boss's baby brother—a beady-eyed so and so with no teeth—came on to me." Lizzie paused and gave me a wan look. I couldn't tell what she was thinking, but I couldn't control my thoughts about what she'd just said.

"You're kidding," I wailed, looking at her in disbelief.

"No, I am not kidding."

Sexual harassment was one phrase that I couldn't fathom being used in regard to Lizzie. She was the last person I'd expect to have to worry about somebody trying to get into her panties. One of our former classmates, an ugly, pimply-faced boy at that, had once told her in front of me and several other classmates that she was as appealing as an enema, and that he would not fuck her with a dog's dick. I didn't like what I was thinking. If anybody should have known better, it was me. Sex was not always about how somebody looked. One of my mother's former men friends had taught me that. During the ten years that Mr. Boatwright raped me, he had me convinced that because I was so black and ugly, nobody else would want to fuck me. Therefore, he *had* to do it because he felt sorry for me.

Apparently, that old pervert's convoluted opinions had rubbed off on me.

"I'm sorry to hear that, Lizzie," I said, apologizing more for my thoughts than I was about what she'd just told me.

"When I rejected him, he made a lot of noise about me having black blood and thinking I was better than 'real' white folks. It caused such a disruption my boss thought it'd be better for me to work someplace else. He also said something about a 'conflict of interest.' "

"Was it the baby brother's word against yours?"

"Yeah. He came after me one evening when I was the last one in the shop. I was waiting on a cab when he practically forced me to get in his truck so he could give me a ride home. He started talking nasty before he even turned on the motor. That's when he told me about a bet he'd made with his friends to see which one of them could get me into bed first. The winner was to get twenty dollars."

"Oh?"

"Twenty dollars. That was all I was worth to him. Can you imagine what that did to my self-esteem?"

"I can imagine. . . ."

"He even tried to . . . pay me to . . . you know. For *ten* dollars." Her face tightened, and she seemed to be anxious and even more uncomfortable now. "He had the nerve to tell me that I should be flattered that a man like him would want to, excuse my language, 'fuck a douche bag' like me," she said with a smirk. "I'm not that desperate," she insisted. "I care a lot about myself, Annette. I want a man that I can be proud of. I know I don't look it, but I am not the type to let people walk all over me. I am not a pushover, and if you hire me, you will see that right off the bat."

I nodded. "So you're telling me that you got fired because you made your boss's toothless brother mad?"

"That's about the size of it."

"Lizzie, I know it was not easy for you to tell me your story, but I appreciate you being honest. I won't bother to call your former boss to verify what you just told me. I already know he will have a totally different version of the events." I winked at Lizzie. This gesture put her more at ease. The tight look disappeared from her face and she smiled again.

We spent only a few minutes discussing her qualifications and expectations. Then we spent the next half hour reminiscing about our junior high and high school days. For each horror story she shared about a bully-related incident that she had survived, I had one of my own.

"I was so beaten down by the time I graduated from Richland High, all I wanted to do was crawl into a hole and stay here," she told me with tears in her eyes. She went on to tell me that other than her mother, her stepfather, and a few friends and relatives, she didn't associate with a lot of people. She drove a Ford station wagon that she referred to as her "baby." Now that was pathetic. I had heard of people referring to their pets like that, but this was the first time I heard somebody use that word in reference to a car. Lizzie seemed to like talking about herself, so I encouraged her by listening with wide eyes and nodding at the appropriate times.

She told me that when she was at home, she watched TV with her parents and spent the rest of her spare time in the bedroom she shared with her dreams, doing crossword puzzles and reading romance novels.

It was hard, but I forced myself not to give Lizzie too many pitiful looks. "How come you never got married?" I asked dumbly.

A panic-stricken look promptly appeared on her face. "Married? Who me? I have never even had a boyfriend or a date. Except the times I go line dancing with my cross-eyed cousin, Lawrence."

"Oh, that's too bad."

"Well, I am not dead yet. And I'm not that old, so there's still a chance that I will find a man and get married. I've had fun along the way, though." Then she gave me a mysterious look. "Did you know I went to Woodstock?"

Now that was a shocking piece of information. "You? No, I didn't know."

She nodded. "And during the summer of '69, I spent a couple of months in Berkeley, too. I have some distant cousins out there." She paused and a faraway look appeared on her face. Her voice sounded disembodied as she continued speaking. "We happened to be in L.A. for a folk music concert that August when the Manson murders occurred. I couldn't get back to Berkeley fast enough. I stayed high on acid for the next five days." She must have noticed how my face stiffened, because right after that admission, she said, "I haven't touched drugs since! Not even weed."

It was hard for me to put drugs and Lizzie in the same thought. But I didn't like to judge people. I didn't even want to think what my straight-laced boss, and some of the people from church, would think or say if they knew I'd occasionally smoked weed with

Pee Wee. Or worse yet, the fact that I'd once worked as a prostitute. I was proof that it was possible for people to change for the better.

"You've come a long way," I said.

"I had to. Woodstock and Berkeley were too much for me. The drugs, the wall-to-wall sex . . ."

"Oh. Uh, did you meet anybody interesting during that time, or any other time?" I didn't want to get too personal. I wondered if she was still a virgin like my mother had implied. Not that it mattered, but after some of the things that Muh'Dear had said about Lizzie, I had become quite curious about her.

"I haven't met anybody interesting recently, but back in the sixties when I was in Berkeley I got caught up in that hippie thing." Lizzie suddenly shut down. Her mood changed and she didn't seem as animated as she'd been a few minutes before. "If I hadn't come back home when I did, I might not be here today."

"Well, I am glad you are here today."

A sad look appeared on her face and she locked eyes with me. "Mama is so worried that after she dies I'll grow old alone," she bleated. It sounded almost like a cry for help. "I've been ready to settle down for a long time."

"Tell me about it. I didn't get married until about ten years ago," I told her.

"You know, I hate it when people bring up that subject." She gave me a misty-eyed look and I wanted to crawl under the table.

"Oh, I'm sorry. I just thought . . ."

"I understand, Annette. I brought it up this time, and only because it might influence your decision," she said, holding up her hand, drawing my attention to her nails. She had small, slender hands like the kind you see on models on TV and in magazine ads. But her nails looked like a dog had been gnawing on them. That was not so unusual. Most of the women who did my nails at the various shops I went to neglected their own. I had decided a long time ago that raggedy nails had to be a job requirement in some nail shops, so that was one flaw in her that I could overlook. "I know what you mean, and I know you are not trying to hurt my feelings. That's more than I can say about some of the people I know. Most of the people I come in contact with think that a woman my age has done something with her life, and I have. I usually get jobs I like, I live in a nice house, and I have plenty of food to eat, and I've got my health." She tilted her chin up and stuck out her chest, which was almost as flat as her ponytail. "I enjoy spending time with my mama, and that's more than a lot of people can say. And as far as the romantic side of my life goes, well . . ." Lizzie paused and shrugged. "I truly believe that there is somebody out there for me."

"Lizzie, let me assure you that there is somebody out there for you. It took me a long time to find my soul mate." I laughed. "And the funny thing about it was, he was right up under my nose all that time. We'd been friends all along!" It had been a long time since I'd had such a "girly" conversation with a woman other than Rhoda. And even though Lizzie could never compete with Rhoda, she was a refreshing diversion.

"That's right! You and Pee Wee were friends all through our school years." Lizzie and I both laughed. "Well, like I said, I believe there is somebody out there for me. And my soul mate might already be right up under my nose, too, huh?"

"He sure could be, girl," I said. I had no idea how prophetic my statement was.

# CHAPTER 20

Lizzie seemed like such a sweet person. She seemed like the kind of woman who would go out of her way to please a man—if she had one. She reminded me of myself in that respect; always willing to accommodate somebody else. However, I was hoping that she was more interested in employment than romance right now. Despite what I'd just said to her about her finding her soul mate, I didn't think she'd be writhing in ecstasy in any man's arms anytime soon.

"Are you interested in anyone right now, Lizzie?" I asked. "I hope I am not being too personal, and I don't want you to think I'm asking you this because I'm nosy," I said with my hand in the air. "The only reason I'm asking is because my husband doesn't want to hire someone, then have her up and run off to get married and leave him in a lurch."

Lizzie shook her head vigorously and sighed. "I'm still looking for Mr. Right." Then she gave me a sad, brief smile. "I am very picky. I have high standards. I refuse to settle for just any man who comes along. I don't care how long I live and how lonely I get, I would never up and marry somebody just for the sake of it. And it doesn't bother me that people laugh at me behind my back because they *think* I'm *still* a virgin. That's one of the things I am most proud of—the fact that I don't sleep around. There are some women who stay virgins all their lives. Besides, people have been laughing at me behind my back since I was a baby because of my leg. But I'm happier than most people, so I don't let any of that bother me."

"Whether you're still a virgin or not is your business." Despite what I'd just said, I was dying of curiosity.

The more Lizzie revealed about herself, the more I wanted to get to know her better. She was a dark horse, but she had a very bright outlook on life. With her positive attitude she was going to make it through life with a smile on her face, whether she landed a husband, and a good job, or not. She knew it, too, because there was a confident twinkle in her eyes. I hoped that if things did work out between her and Pee Wee, she would not be just another employee. It would be nice to have her as our friend as well.

"And guess what, Annette? My car is paid for, and it drives as good now as it did when I bought it off that used car lot in Akron four years ago." Right after she finished her last sentence, she leaned back in her seat and gave me a broad smile, revealing some of the healthiest looking and whitest teeth I'd ever seen. You would have thought that she'd just shared a naughty little secret with me about a tryst with Mr. Right, not a used Ford station wagon.

"Would you have a problem working with only male coworkers? My husband's barbershop caters mainly to men. However, he gets a few women in there to get their hair trimmed from time to time."

Lizzie shook her head again. "Not at all! When I worked at a barbershop in Cleveland a few years ago, all of my coworkers were men. That didn't bother me. Besides, the shop I just got fired from catered to women, but it was because of a situation with a man that I got let go. I am real flexible. I can adapt to just about anything. Being surrounded by males is not a problem for me. And another thing, I was the only girl in Mr. Hand's shop class back in eleventh grade."

Her last statement led us back to discussing the "good old days" at Richland High. That was all we talked about for the next few minutes. I didn't realize how much time had passed until our waitress asked us if we'd be ordering lunch.

"Oh!" I looked at my watch. "Uh, Lizzie, I didn't mean to take up this much of your time," I said, giving her and our waitress an apologetic look. "If you don't have any other appointments, or any other place to go this morning, I would love to treat you to a nice lunch."

"I'd like a Caesar salad and a diet Coke," Lizzie told the waitress.

"Make that two," I added.

We started poking at our salads as soon as they arrived and ordered more coffee. "Annette, I don't know how many folks you've already interviewed, or how many more you plan to talk to, but I want you to know right now that I want this job. I'm good at what I do, I am dependable, and I never complain."

I nodded. "I think you'd be good for the job, but I'd like to give it a little more thought before I make a decision."

"Oh." Her face dropped.

"I just need a little more time to make a final decision," I said quickly.

"Uh, will that be soon? They didn't give me any notice at my other job, so I'm going to be in a financial pickle this month if I don't find another job in time. Our water heater just broke, we need to have the wiring redone before the house catches afire and burns to the ground, my stepfather needs a new walker, and my mother needs me to help pay for her train ticket to go to Cleveland next week to visit my uncle Dennis in that veteran's hospital."

Before I could respond to Lizzie's overblown tale of financial woe, a deep male voice interrupted my thoughts. "Annette, is that *you?*"

I looked up into the face of Henry Boykin, the ex-drug dealer from the south side of town, and my husband's rival.

"Hello, Henry. Good to see you," I responded with a grunt.

"Sister, what happened to you?" he yelled, looking me over like he was doing an appraisal. "Damn, woman! I almost didn't recognize you!" Henry was talking so loud everybody in the café looked in my direction. I suddenly felt like a used car with a for sale sign on my face.

"I lost some weight," I muttered with a forced smile.

"You sure did! I ain't seen you since Jack Brown's funeral! Praise God, you finally lost most of that blubber! You look almost as good as a government check now! The last time I seen you, I said to myself, 'Please tell me that ain't Annette's butt followin' behind her.'"

Henry paused and turned sharply to look down at my ass, which was twitching in my seat like I was sitting on a tack. "Yes, ma'am. You finally got it goin' on! Umph! You oldsters are really givin' them young girls a run for the money these days! If you get any hotter, I'm gonna have to call a fire truck!"

"When did you get out?" I chided. I knew Henry had been out of prison for at least a year.

He laughed. "Girl, I been out long enough to get myself on the right track. I guess you know I took over that barbershop across from the skatin' rink?" he said, grinning from ear to ear. "And I'm hittin' it real good! I'm makin' as much money as I did when I was involved in . . . uh, the pharmaceutical business. And I plan to stay on the straight and narrow! Jail ain't no place for a man with my talents." He looked at Lizzie, smiling like a snake-oil salesman. "Ain't you the lady that works in one of them white folks' nail shop?"

"I used to be," Lizzie replied. I didn't like the way she was smiling back at him, but it was good to know that she could be friendly in the company of a low-life like Henry.

"Hmmm. Well, this is a dog-eat-dog world. You gotta do what you gotta do to make it. Me, I always find me a good hustle." With his long, greasy cornrows, his whiplash of a mustache, a tattoo of a dragon on his neck, and his loud-colored windbreaker, he still looked like the kind of person you'd expect to see involved in something shady. "How come you ain't workin' for the man no more?" he asked Lizzie as he blinked his shifty eyes.

"Uh, it was because of a conflict-of-interest issue," she answered.

"Is that all? That ain't a good reason to let a employee go—if they good!"

"I was very good at my job, Henry. I was at that shop for years. And if anybody tells you I wasn't good, they are a damn liar, and you can tell them I said so. Like I said, there was a conflict-of-interest issue, so they had to let me go." Lizzie kept surprising me. I was stunned and impressed by the way she stood up to Henry. "And I'll tell you the reason behind the 'conflict-of-interest' issue before you hear it from somebody else: My boss's brother tried to hit on me."

Henry tilted his head back and looked so surprised I thought he was going to laugh. "I'm a man," he announced, looking from me to Lizzie like we didn't already know what he was. "We do some stupid shit when it comes to poontang and our manly urges. Some of us don't care who we stick our dicks in."

Lizzie didn't flinch, but what Henry had just said bothered me. It took a lot of willpower for me not to say what was on my mind. But I wasn't about to let an ignoramus like Henry spoil the good mood I was in.

"Well, look here, Lizzie. I'm all for givin' back to the community. I make it a point of helpin' whoever I can. My mama used to go to the bingo hall with your mama. And for years, your mama loaned my mama money when she needed it, so I feel a little kinship toward you. If you don't find another job soon, come by my place. I just might have somethin' for you to do. My aunt Marie could use some part-time help keepin' the place clean. Sweepin' up hair, dustin' off the equipment, keepin' everything neat and organized. And once she go in for her hip surgery next month, I will need somebody full time."

Lizzie perked up, obviously interested in another job opportunity.

"Uh, Henry, you got here just a few minutes too late. Lizzie is, uh, going to work for my husband," I sputtered. Lizzie looked as surprised as I was by what I'd just said. I reached across the table and patted her hand. "Pee Wee's going to be offering manicures in his barbershop now and Lizzie is going to be doing them." I meant to sniff, but it ended up coming out sounding more like a snort. I shifted in my seat; then I sat up straighter, hoping that that made me look more poised and confident. "Lizzie, I was just about to tell you that the salary is negotiable, but I can assure you that you'll be pleased with whatever we decide to settle on." I winked at Lizzie. You would have thought that she'd just won a lottery jackpot. She looked just that happy. I assumed it didn't take much to make a woman happy whose main interests included bingo and taking Sunday drives in her used station wagon.

"Hmmm. Is that right?" Henry mouthed, caressing his lopsided chin. "Well, you tell Pee Wee I said hello, Annette. And tell him a few people have been askin' about him on the basketball court at the Y. But I understand, see. I know he's gettin' on in years, so I can understand him slowin' down a bit."

"I'll tell him what you said, Henry," I responded. "Now you have a blessed day," I added, giving him a dismissive wave.

As soon as he left, strolling across the floor like he was some proper British gentleman, Lizzie gasped and leaned across the table.

"You're going to give me that job?" she asked, with her eyes stretched open so wide it looked like her eyelids had disappeared into her forehead.

I looked toward the exit. Henry was still in the doorway, hugging on a cute Hispanic woman in her mid-twenties, which was around his age.

"If you still want it," I said, turning to Lizzie. "I think you'll make my husband very happy."

# CHAPTER 21

After Lizzie and I finished eating our lunch, we spent a few more minutes reminiscing about high school. She brought up things that had happened to me that had been so painful I had forgotten them.

"Remember that time JoAnn Springer and Judy Sharpe jumped on you in the girls' bathroom and tried to make you eat dog food?" she asked with a pinched look on her face.

It took me a few moments to recall that incident. And when I did, it made my stomach turn. "Uh-huh. JoAnn's on death row in Texas for killing her husband. And Judy got killed while trying to rob a bank in Cincinnati to get money to buy heroin," I reported, feeling a sense of triumph. Almost every other person who had bullied or abused me at some point was now either dead or in prison.

Lizzie shook her head, but she didn't look like she felt sorry about what had happened to our former classmates. "That just goes to show that God don't like ugly. You always get what you have coming to you."

I was pleased to see that there was a philosophical side to her. I knew that if I really made an effort to get to know her better, it would benefit us both. I'd have somebody to fall back on when Rhoda wasn't available, and Lizzie would have somebody to talk to and do things with other than her parents, her cross-eyed cousin, and that bingo-playing crowd.

We reluctantly ended our meeting, but on a high note. Lizzie admired the black leather boots I had on and squealed with delight when I told her that they were still available at half price at a boutique just two blocks from where she lived. Once she stood up, I got a chance to see what she had on her feet. It was not a pretty sight. She had on a pair of round-toed, black vinyl shoes with snaps in the place of shoestrings. I didn't know enough about her leg to know if she had some special requirements when it came to footwear. But if that was the case, why did she want to know where to buy a pair of boots? I didn't have to wonder about that long.

"I wear these shoes because of the ice on the ground. But I also like to wear heels and boots. People don't realize that my affliction, if you want to call it that, is with my leg, not my foot. I could even wear stiletto heels if I wanted to."

"I'm glad to hear that because I always know where the good shoe sales are," I said. Lizzie squealed with delight again. "Well, I'll be in touch," I added as we exited the café. She limped down the sidewalk in the opposite direction. I watched until she was out of sight. Suddenly, a great sadness came over me. And I wasn't sure why. Lizzie was obviously a well-adjusted person. She didn't need my pity.

But she did need a job.

I didn't like calling Pee Wee at work right after the lunch hour because that was when the men who worked night shifts came by to get haircuts and shaves. It was a busy time in the shop and very hard for Pee Wee to carry on telephone conversations, especially personal calls. But this time was an exception. I called him as soon as I got back to my office. I was anxious to tell him about my interview with Lizzie and how she had impressed me.

I wanted to promptly wrap up the situation with her, in case she ran into Henry again. He was the type of person who would do things just to piss off his competition. When he was dealing drugs from the front yard of the house that he lived in with his mama, he used to barbeque ribs at the same time. If somebody didn't come by looking to purchase drugs, they almost always ended up buying a rib sandwich. And from what I'd heard, everybody who purchased barbeque from Henry eventually ended up buying some drugs, too.

Henry had customers streaming in and out of his front yard like ants. And it wasn't just the ghetto folks from the armpits of Richland. His customers included rich yuppies and buppies from the suburbs. That drove the other local drug dealers crazy, especially the veterans and the OGs, who had opened the doors to the drug trade in the first place for the newcomers. Henry had been physically attacked a few times, and one night somebody riddled the front of his mother's house with bullets from an assault rifle.

If somebody had not ratted Henry out to the cops, he probably would not have lived much longer. I didn't wish for anything bad to happen to anybody, but I didn't want Henry in my life in any way. I didn't like the idea that a man like him was now one of my husband's biggest worries. Now that he knew Pee Wee was interested in hiring Lizzie, he might pull a fast one and hire her first, just to get back at Pee Wee. I didn't know if she was desperate enough to accept a job as a cleaning woman in Henry's shop, but I didn't want to take that chance.

"Annette, are you crazy?" Pee Wee screamed as soon as I told him why I was calling. "Hold on, baby!" He left me hanging on the telephone for several minutes. I could hear him fussing at somebody in the background about a steamed towel being too hot. "I can't be settin' myself up for no lawsuit!" Then he dropped the phone on something hard before he spoke again. "I'm sorry for leavin' you on hold so long, baby. This place is a madhouse today! Everybody wants to look good for that charity banquet comin' up at the country club in a few days. I swear to God, people just don't take pride in their work no more. Bobby just slapped a towel around Deacon Carter's face that was hot enough to steam a lobster."

"Why don't I call you back later today when things are not as hectic," I suggested.

"Things will be hectic the rest of this day. We had a power outage a couple of hours ago, so we are a little behind. I swear to God, with all the money the utility company charges us, you would think that they'd have their act together so we wouldn't be havin' no power outages at all in this day and age." I waited for him to take a few deep breaths. I was going to conclude the call and talk to him about Lizzie later that evening at home, but before I could do that he spoke again. "Now back to what you just told me—are you crazy?"

"No, I'm not crazy, Pee Wee."

"Well, you must be! You want me to hire a retarded woman?" He laughed. A moment later, I heard him mumbling something to somebody in the background; then they laughed with him.

"I wish you'd be more serious. I am trying to help you. We've discussed this and I thought this was what you wanted," I complained.

"Look, baby. If this is your idea of a joke, it ain't nowhere near funny. I got politicians and pimps—that'll get real ugly if I don't please them—comin' here to get shaves and haircuts, and they might want a manicure. I can't have no retarded woman choppin' up their nails. What's wrong with you, Annette? Can you see Mayor Banks sittin' in my shop with *that woman* buffin' his nails and droolin' all over his Italian-made shoes? Now go do somethin' constructive today. Go shoppin', go get a facial, or go get that mammogram you been puttin' off, and let me get back to work. Shit." He snickered. "You got some nerve callin' me up to tell me you offered *that woman* a job in my shop."

"Look, *that woman* is named Lizzie. And she is not retarded," I said, speaking through clenched teeth.

He muttered something under his breath; then he laughed some more.

"And I don't appreciate you making fun of my efforts. I am only trying to help you." I paused and let out a disgusted sigh for his benefit. "Well, if you're not interested, she can go work for Henry. . . ."

I heard him release a muffled growl. "I doubt that. That nasty young punk wouldn't have nobody like Lizzie workin' in his shop. You know what a snob he is."

"Suit yourself. I think you're making a mistake by not hiring Lizzie, so I'll set up a few more interviews. Maybe I'll have them meet me in your shop so you can sit in on the interviews."

"I already told you that I ain't got time to be interviewin' nobody. You volunteered to do it for me, and I hope you find somebody soon. I heard this mornin' that two more of my regulars been seen comin' out of Henry's place."

"Don't worry, honey. I'll keep looking for you, and I will find somebody soon. The way I'm doing it is not working out, though. I ran that ad in the paper, but I think it would have been better for me to call one of those employment agencies. That's what I'll do next."

"Good! Get on it," Pee Wee advised.

"I'd better call Lizzie and tell her to go ahead and accept that job with Henry that he offered her today. . . ."

Pee Wee's silence told me I had pushed the right button. "Oh? Henry Boykin offered Lizzie Stovall a job doin' manicures in his shop?"

"Yep, he offered her a job in his barbershop." I was telling half of the truth. If Pee Wee ever found out that the job Henry offered to Lizzie was a cleaning position, he wouldn't hear it from me if I could help it.

"You know, now that I think about it, wasn't she in one of them special ed classes back in school? She wasn't really retarded, was she?"

"Pee Wee, you and I attended a regular school. There were some special classes for the kids who were a little slow, but there were no retarded kids in our school."

"So she's more like a Forrest Gump type? Like the slow dude that my man Tom Hanks played in the movie. Like him, she's slow, but she's too smart to be called retarded?"

"You're the only one who is calling her retarded," I snapped. "And I don't know why you are doing that, because it's not true."

"If I am goin' to hire somebody to work for me, I need to know if I got to be worried about them burnin' my place down, or havin' some kind of fit or somethin'. Now, didn't this Lizzie woman ride in that short orange school bus with that flat-headed boy who used to spit on kids?"

As Pee Wee talked on about Lizzie, my heart sank because the more I thought about her, the more I wanted to help her.

"I don't know anything about all that," I said sharply. "All I know is Lizzie Stovall does good work and she's available. And when I talked to her this morning, she didn't seem retarded or even slightly slow to me. As a matter of fact, she seemed real smart. She came to the interview with a copy of the *Wall Street Journal* sticking out of her purse. Does that sound like a retarded person to you?"

"She could have been usin' that newpaper as a fan. That's all I use it for. Or she might have been usin' it to make a paper hat for all you know. You didn't see her readin' it, did you?"

"Look, Muh'Dear swears by her. The way she and Daddy went on and on about Lizzie, you would have thought that she'd worked in the White House. I've interviewed a few people. So far Lizzie is the best candidate. And she's the only one who said she's willing to work for minimum wage and tips only. The others wanted that, plus two weeks' vacation every year, starting with the first year. They wanted bonuses, employee discounts for their relatives, and one even had the nerve to say that she wanted you to provide all of her equipment and supplies."

"Well, I can't say I don't blame them. They want the best they can get, and so do I."

"Then take my advice. Listen to me," I insisted.

"I am listenin'," Pee Wee said, his impatience coming through loud and clear.

"Let Lizzie Stovall come work for you. Now that Henry knows you are upgrading your shop, he'll find another way to try and upstage you. I know you'll be glad you hired Lizzie."

# CHAPTER 22

"Baby, if I want to keep up with Henry, I have to maintain a certain image," Pee Wee told me. I could not believe that after all I'd just said, he was still being resistant.

"That's what I am trying to help you do," I insisted.

"If I take your advice and hire Lizzie, people might get the wrong impression about me."

"And what the hell do you mean by that? You're running a barbershop, not the Playboy Mansion."

"Look, I have to be honest with you. Now, I didn't want to bring this up, but since you won't let up on me, I need to put this out there. I want to say this in a nice way . . ." Apparently, Pee Wee didn't know how to say what was on his mind, because it was taking him a long time to get the words out of his mouth.

"Pee Wee, I don't know about you, but I have to get back to work soon. Can you move your lips a little faster?" I said.

Once I said that, he couldn't speak fast enough. The words seemed to roll out of his mouth like rocks rolling down the side of a mountain during an avalanche. "There's another thing I'm concerned about with this Lizzie woman. Ain't she kind of . . . *ugly?*"

I had to organize my thoughts before I could address what he'd just said. The last thing I wanted to do was come off sounding just as off-the-wall as he did. "I wouldn't call Lizzie ugly," I mumbled.

I was glad that nobody could hear my end of this conversation. For one thing, it brought back some painful memories. I knew first-hand how some people discriminated against plain people. I'd been in Lizzie's shoes too many times myself. I knew for a fact that I'd missed out on some jobs because at the time I was too fat and too ugly. And to some people, I was also too black. Now here I was trying to do the opposite. I was trying to hire somebody mainly be-cause she *was* plain, and it was not working! I didn't know what the world was coming to.

"Well, if she ain't straight-up ugly, I don't know who is."

Had I known that it was going to be this hard for me to help Pee Wee hire somebody, I never would have volunteered to help. But I was not about to let all my hard work go to waste. Somebody was going to benefit from it, and I had no trouble with that somebody being me. With Lizzie's determination and drive, and the fact that she needed a job, if he didn't want her, maybe I could find some-thing for her on my team. I was going to bring that up next if I had to.

"I will admit that I think she is a little on the plain side," I said, beginning to sound and feel tired. This conversation and this sub-ject had begun to wear me out. "So what? You're no Denzel . . ."

"You ain't funny. People want to leave my place lookin' good. They see a homely woman up in here, floppin' around with one leg lookin' like a mop handle, they might get nervous. You know how black folks are when it comes to handicapped folks. Even though they got enough sense to know that thinkin' like that don't make no sense."

"I know what you mean. With all of the gay black people in the world, you'd think black folks would lighten up on them some."

"I know where you goin' with this conversation and I'm tellin' you now, I ain't goin' into no argument about gay people again. I was just tryin' to make a point."

"If you don't like the way some black folks look down on handi-capped people, you need to check yourself."

"Now you stop right there! I never said nothin' about not likin' handicapped folks. I got a cousin in Erie who's been in a wheel-chair all his life, and he's one of my best friends. A lot of my other friends is handicapped, too. Since I was a kid I always treated those people with respect. Other than you, what kid in our neighborhood was as nice to old one-legged Mr. Boatwright who used to live with you and your mama?"

"Oh, I am really ready to end this call," I said hotly, bile coating the inside of my mouth. "I am not in the mood to glorify the man who raped me throughout my entire childhood." I choked back a sob.

"Oh, shit. Baby, you know I'm sorry to bring up old Boatwright and them bad memories about what he did to you." Pee Wee sounded so contrite I thought he was going to sob, too.

"Let's get back on the subject. The one I called you about. Now, do you want the woman to work for you or not? She's got another interview lined up with a shop in Canton. I am sure that if she doesn't take that job, she'll take the one with Henry."

Pee Wee wasted no time responding. "All right! But if she makes a fool out of me and my customers, or steals somethin' or breaks any of my equipment, I am goin' to hold you responsible!" he told me in a threatening manner.

As soon as I got off the telephone with him, I called up Lizzie. Despite all I had said to her in the café, she was surprised to hear from me. "Annette, what's this about? That was my stepdaddy who answered the phone. He said you needed to talk to me right away."

I was immediately taken aback. Maybe she was not as sharp as I thought she was after all.

"Uh, are you still interested in the job at my husband's barbershop?" I asked in a reserved tone of voice. I had to remind myself that since I didn't know Lizzie that well, she could turn out to be just as big a nut as some of the other people I had interviewed.

"Oh, my God! Are you serious? I thought about what you'd said in front of Henry and the more I thought about it, the more it seemed like you were saying it for his benefit. I didn't know you were really that serious about hiring me!"

"When can you start?" I asked.

"I got the job?" she squealed.

"If you still want it, you can start right away. Now, take a couple of hours and think about it, and call me back at my office."

"Can I start tomorrow?"

"Sure, be at my husband's shop at nine."

\* \* \*

I didn't like to call Rhoda's house now that Jade was back in the picture. I usually waited until she called me. But I couldn't wait this time. I called her as soon as I got off the phone with Lizzie. To my horror, Jade answered the telephone.

"Hello, Annette. Are you still with that fine-ass husband of yours?"

"Hello, Jade. Yes, I am still with that fine-ass husband of mine," I said stiffly.

"Hmmph! I guess anything is possible. To tell you the truth, I thought he'd have moved on by now. And you, too."

"What's that supposed to mean, Jade?"

"Well, I have a hard time believing that a man like Pee Wee is still married to a woman like you."

"If my husband ever leaves me for another woman, you will be the first person I tell. Now, if your mother is available, please put her on the phone."

"She's in the den having a drink with my husband," Jade reported.

"Oh yeah! She told me you got married. Congratulations!"

"You don't have to worry about getting me a gift this time."

"I won't." I covered my mouth so she wouldn't hear the snicker that I couldn't hold back. "Hmmm. Well, Jade, they say you can't keep a good woman down. You're living proof that that's true. You've had *two* nervous breakdowns, flunked out of college, and had your first fiancé desert you on your wedding day, and you're still going strong. I admire you."

"Look, lady! If you or anybody else thinks that I am going to curl up into a ball and slide into a hole because Marcelo jilted me, you're wrong—with your piggly wiggly self! Do you hear me? I could marry any man I want, and I did! LaVerne loves me to death! And he does everything, and I do mean everything, that I tell him to do! See, he *knows* what he's supposed to do to keep a woman like me happy!" Jade's outburst did not surprise me, and her hostility didn't faze me the way it used to.

"Have a blessed day, Jade."

"Ugh," she grunted.

I was very anxious to meet her husband now, so I could see with my own eyes what a real fool looked like.

The next voice I heard belonged to Rhoda. "I hope my daughter didn't say anything nasty to you."

"To be honest with you, I couldn't tell if she was being nasty to me or if she was being her usual self. Anyway, I called to tell you that I hired somebody to work for Pee Wee, and she's going to start tomorrow. She was just that anxious. Remember Lizzie Stovall?"

"Lizzie . . . Lizzie—oh yeah! Your mama and I were just talkin' about her the other day. Of course I remember her. Poor thing. She was that lame-legged girl who used to sit behind me in Miss Kline's homeroom. Lizzie was so sweet! She used to bring the whole class homemade chocolate-chip cookies twice a week. You couldn't have found a better person to work for Pee Wee. I am so happy to hear this news!"

I laughed. "Rhoda, calm down. It's just a manicurist job, not a walk on the moon."

"Well, it's an important job, and I know that Lizzie will look at it as such. Not only is she dependable and loyal, she's as appealing as a sow's ear. You won't have to worry about her runnin' off to get married or comin' in to work late because she was out partyin' the night before at the Red Rose."

"Based on what she told me, if her social life was any slower, she'd be dead. She doesn't even date much either."

"Much? Honey, she doesn't date at all. Can you believe that in this day and age? She's even a couple of months older than I am. And accordin' to the gossips at Claudette's beauty shop, that poor woman is still a virgin, or at least close to it."

"That's her business," I remarked.

"Well, she does good work. If you like her, you'd better make sure Pee Wee treats her well so she'll stay."

"I'm sure he will," I told Rhoda.

# CHAPTER 23

The northern part of Ohio was enduring one of the worst winters in years. There was so much snow on the ground the last Friday in February, the schools and some businesses had to close until the weather got better. I was not lucky enough to get any time off. We had too many cases pending. Some were fairly recent, like people who had overspent on Christmas a couple of months ago. They were the people who had acquired new credit cards just before the holiday season. Then they'd maxed them out and failed to make the first payment. The merchants wasted no time turning them over to us. But the majority of the delinquent accounts were from the previous year, and the years before. Mizelle's Collection Agency kept the local process servers in business.

I still looked forward to going to work. It was a tough job, but that was one of the things I liked about it. It kept me on my toes and well grounded. It also made me appreciate all of the things that I had to be thankful for, like my husband and my daughter. Speaking of Charlotte, she was as happy as a clam that she didn't have to go to school that Friday or Monday, and her plan was to lounge around the house and watch music videos. Her daddy had other ideas. He decided to take that Monday off, too, but he didn't plan on sitting back and letting Charlotte goof off.

The weather got even worse. By Tuesday evening, it was so bad they had to close some of the streets, so I couldn't drive home from work or get home any other way. The closest motel to my office was one that I swore I'd never set foot in again because it was where I'd spent a lot of my time sexing my young lover last summer. But it was spend the night at the Do Drop Inn, my office, or my car. It was too cold and dangerous for me to sleep in my car. The few die-hard employees who reported to me who had come to work that day had all managed to get rooms at the Do Drop Inn because they'd called early enough. By the time I called for a room, there were no vacancies left. Just as I was about to get comfortable on the vinyl couch in my office, using my tweed coat for a blanket, the motel manager called me back and told me they had a cancellation. I didn't think to call Pee Wee up to tell him where I'd be. But the next morning when he called my office, he didn't sound too happy.

"Where the hell did you spend the night, woman?" I didn't like his gruff voice, and I had told him more than once that I didn't like it when he referred to me as "woman."

"I told you that I couldn't get home because the roads over in this part of town had been closed down by the city."

"That ain't what I asked you!" he bellowed.

I didn't respond right away, and that seemed to upset him even more. "Annette, did you sleep in your car or what?"

"No," I mumbled.

"Well, you didn't sleep in your office like you said you was goin' to do. I called your office four times, and you didn't answer your phone. Now, was there someplace at your work where you slept that was so far away you didn't hear the phone ringin' in your office?"

"I slept at a motel. Most of the people who work with me had rooms there, too. Happy?"

"You slept at that fuck-nest where you fucked that punk last year, didn't you?"

"Yes, I slept at the Do Drop Inn. I had no choice. Like I said, the roads were closed. They kept coming on the radio telling people not to try and drive. I couldn't fly, so I couldn't come home. What else could I do?"

"Did you sleep alone?"

"Of course I slept alone, dammit. What the hell makes you think I didn't? I wouldn't lie to you about something like that."

"You did before."

"Well, I am not lying now!" I must have been talking pretty loud because the receptionist knocked on my door. "Yes!" I shrieked.

"Annette, is everything all right?" Donna asked in a shaky voice.

"Everything is fine!" I hollered back. "Pee Wee, you got some kind of nerve coming at me with this foolishness. I spent the night at that motel last night, and if I can't get home tonight, I will spend tonight there, too. If you don't like it—you can kiss my ass!"

"I just . . . see I . . . for one thing, you could have called me from the Do Drop Inn to let me know you were there!"

"So you could talk all that trash about it being that fuck-nest where I screwed Louis Baines? Look, I am not in the mood to deal with you right now. I'm sitting here in the same funky underwear and clothes that I wore yesterday, and even though I took a shower before I left that fuck-nest, I feel nasty as hell. I am warning your black ass that if you continue this foolishness when I get home this evening—if I can get home—you will be sorry." I slammed down the telephone.

An hour later, he called again. "Look, baby, I'm sorry. You know I didn't mean no harm."

"You told me that you wouldn't throw my affair in my face," I whined. "And it was the first thing you could think of . . ."

"I said I was sorry. Now, I just called to apologize, so when you get home this evenin', we won't mention it. All right?"

"Well, I can assure you that I won't mention it. Now, if you don't mind, I have a meeting to go to."

He didn't mention our heated discussion when I got home that evening. He didn't mention much of anything, and neither did I. We talked only when we had to. It was a tense week. He slept in the same bed with me, but he slept so close to the edge that the only way I knew he was even in the bedroom was by his loud-ass snoring.

Since he was so grouchy, I waited until the end of the week to ask him how Lizzie was working out. He had softened a lot by then. A sour look immediately formed on his face, so I braced myself.

"You and your bright ideas," he said with a dry laugh. He stood by the sink in the kitchen working on his second cup of coffee that morning. He was already dressed for work. He looked so good standing there in his crisp white smock and black pants. Right after I'd sent Charlotte off to school, Pee Wee and I rushed to our bedroom and made love for the first time since our argument. We had just returned to the kitchen.

"Oops," I said, cringing. "Things aren't going that well, huh?"

He shrugged. "I won't say things ain't goin' well. It's just that things ain't goin' the way I expected them to be goin' by now." He set his empty cup in the sink and joined me at the table. "Henry might run me out of business after all."

# CHAPTER 24

"**P**lease stop singing that tired old song!"

"Baby, I am just bein' up front with you. Hirin' Lizzie might not be the answer to my problem with Henry after all."

"Exactly what is the problem with her?" I wanted to know, crossing my legs.

"She's kind of quiet when she's workin' on a customer's nails. You know how much socializin' we do over there."

"Tell me about it. I know all about the whooping and hollering that goes on in that shop. I've walked by there more than once when you and your boys were on such a rowdy roll, I didn't bother to enter."

"It's just barbershop stuff, baby. We ain't no louder up in there than you and your women friends are at Claudette's beauty shop. I've walked by there a few times myself and I was scared to enter."

"The thing is, you just might be a little too rowdy for a woman as shy and conservative as Lizzie. If you want her to feel more comfortable, and more like a part of your team, encourage her to participate in the conversations. They say that still waters run deep. Maybe all she needs is for something to stir her up a little."

"I can do that, I guess," Pee Wee offered. He paused and gave me a sad look. That told me that there was more to this than just Lizzie being too quiet. There were times when it was hard to get information out of Pee Wee. I wondered if I didn't drag certain things out of his mouth, if he'd ever tell me on his own. This was one of those times. He had me all worked up about his problem with Lizzie and, as usual, it looked like he was going to leave it up to me to sort it out. And by making me drag the information out of him that I needed to work with, it made my role in this mess that much harder. And I didn't like it one bit. As a matter of fact, I promised myself that in the future when he had a problem that was related to his business, I'd let him handle it on his own. That is, unless it involved me directly.

"Pee Wee, something tells me that there is something else you want to complain about regarding Lizzie. If that is the case, would you please do so? Or do I have to sit here and play twenty questions, or some other kind of guessing game?"

He covered his mouth and released a quiet cough. Then he started talking real slow and in a low voice. "We need to discuss her appearance."

"Her appearance? What's wrong with her appearance?" I laughed. "Now look. Even in school Little Leg Lizzie was no femme fatale. She didn't have any fashion sense then, and she doesn't have any now. So what? You don't need some hoochie coochie woman up in that barbershop with her titties and her booty hanging out of a see-through mini-dress, now do you?" I laughed again.

"That ain't exactly what I'm talkin' about." Pee Wee paused and gave me an "I'm not sure what to say next" look. He waited, looking at me like I was supposed to know what was coming next.

"Baby, my mind-reading skills are kind of rusty, so could you help me out here?"

"See, she ain't exactly ugly after all, or nothin' like that, but a little eye makeup and some rouge wouldn't hurt. Women customers might get the wrong idea when they see her. They might get offended. . . ."

"What do you mean by that? You make the woman sound as gruesome as a one-eyed Cyclops." I pushed my half-empty coffee cup to the side.

"If you went into a beauty shop and saw the woman who was goin' to work on you to make you beautiful, wouldn't you feel better if she was already lookin' mighty spiffy herself?"

I blinked.

"I'm just sayin' that we have to look the part. We can't expect our customers to have much confidence in us makin' them look good if we ain't lookin' good. Is that makin' any sense to you?" Pee Wee rubbed my shoulder. "I mean, I like Lizzie and I know she needs a job. But if I am goin' to hold my own against Henry Boykin, I need all the help I can get. I heard a real reliable rumor that he's got some of his boys out on the street passin' out flyers advertisin' all kinds of deals and puttin' coupons on folks' windshield wipers at the mall parkin' lot."

"So? You can be just as enterprising as Henry."

Pee Wee kept talking, as if he had not heard a word I'd just said. "He's got so many new customers; if I didn't know any better, I'd swear he was dealin' drugs again. If that's the case, I don't have a chance to move up to the next level. I will need all of the help I can get just to stay in business. And I don't think Lizzie can help that cause. There's a lot of young people out there. The hip-hop crowd. They don't want to come into my place with a grandmammy-lookin' woman like Lizzie workin' for me. It's bad enough that Henry is part of that generation, so he's already got that edge on me."

I gave Pee Wee's words some thought. "You're right. The only way to fight fire is with fire. And you have to really get on the ball in this case."

"Meanin' what?"

"We could give Henry a run for his money if we do things right. We need to do something extreme."

"Like hirin' one of them cute little Asian gals to work for me?"

"Not *that* extreme," I chided. I was only half joking. "I'm telling you now that if you do hire an Asian woman, she'd better look like Charlie Chan," I snapped, surprised and annoyed that a man as sensible as Pee Wee would make such a frivolous remark. "You know I'm just kidding. You can hire anybody you want to hire as long as she's competent. But I hope you give Lizzie a good reason when you fire her."

"I don't want to fire Lizzie. I just want to spruce her up some," Pee Wee said quickly. "She's a really nice woman."

"And you know what else? I got a real close-up look at her that day in the café when I interviewed her. She's not nearly as homely as people make her out to be. As a matter of fact, she's got some really nice features to work with. With the right hairdo and the right make-up, she could shine like a new dime. I know you can remember how people used to treat me like a frump—and I was."

Pee Wee gave me one of the most loving looks I had ever received from him. I could have looked like Mighty Joe Young, but from the way he was looking at me, you would have thought that I looked like Sade, Janet Jackson, and Mariah Carey all rolled into one. "Let me tell you one thing right now, you ain't *never* been no frump to me. Since the day I met you, I have always thought you looked like a film star."

"That's not saying much. Godzilla was a film star." I chuckled. From the stiff look on his face, it was obvious that Pee Wee didn't see any humor in my comment, so I cleared my throat and got serious again. "Anyway, because I worked on my appearance, and lost all of that weight, the same people who used to make fun of me are now stopping me on the street to tell me how good I look. I don't care what people say about looks not being everything, that's a damn lie. People respond to the way you look. Why don't you tell Lizzie in a nice way to fix herself up a little." I didn't think that there was anything wrong with my suggestion, but the way Pee Wee reacted you would have thought that I'd just told him to cut off Lizzie's head.

"Shit! I don't want to hurt her feelin's. She might up and quit, and I don't want her to do that. Not after all I've told so many of my regulars about her."

"Do you want me to talk to her? She might take it better if another woman told her to fix herself up."

Pee Wee caressed his chin and thought about what I'd just said. "Let me drop a few subtle hints in her direction first. If that don't work, then maybe I'll have you or Rhoda put a June bug in her ear. Maybe y'all can take her to the Red Rose and get her drunk. Then take her over to Claudette's beauty shop and have them give her a makeover or somethin'. When she sobers up and sees how cute she looks, maybe she'll get the hint. Claudette knows what to do. She's been turnin' hound dogs into poodles for years. She can do the same thing for Lizzie! You know what I mean; brush some rouge and shit on her face. Maybe even slap a wig on her head."

Pee Wee's interpretation of a makeover was downright scary. I didn't even bother to tell him that it involved more than having a woman "brush some rouge and shit on her face" and "slap a wig on her head" to make herself look good. I couldn't imagine what he was going to say to Lizzie for her to get some beauty treatments. And I would have been glad to talk to her myself if he'd asked me. But he didn't.

Exactly one week to the day after my conversation with Pee Wee about Lizzie's appearance, Muh'Dear called me up at my office right after I returned from lunch. Just from the low, sweet tone of her voice, I knew she was calling me up with some disturbing news. It didn't take her long. She got under my skin quicker than a tick. "If I was you, I'd be worried about my husband workin' with such a pretty woman. . . ."

"Huh?" I responded. My first thought was that Pee Wee had fired Lizzie and hired one of those cute little Asian girls anyway. "What pretty woman are you talking about?" I held the telephone close to my ear so I could make sure I heard everything. "Did he fire Lizzie? I knew this was going to happen!" I slapped the side of my forehead with the palm of my hand. "Muh'Dear, I tried. I did everything I could to help Lizzie. Look, if you see her before I do, let her know how sorry I am about her getting fired. No, that's all right. I'll give her a call myself. I hope she didn't take it too hard."

"He didn't fire that woman. She's the pretty woman I'm talkin' about." Muh'Dear sucked on her teeth.

"Lizzie? What did she do to herself? Pee Wee had told me that he was going to drop a few hints to her that might make her get herself fixed up some. You know, some rouge and shit. And maybe a wig . . ."

"Well, he must have dropped some mighty big hints because that Little Leg Lizzie sure is lookin' good these days." I didn't like the smug tone in my mother's voice, but I had gotten used to it over the years. She couldn't help herself. She was one of those old sisters who usually did more harm than good when she tried to "help" somebody.

"Excuse me?" I said. I had visited my OB/GYN earlier that morning and had my annual Pap test and a mammogram. I was still slightly sore from all the poking and prodding I'd endured, so I was in a testy mood. It was hard for me to sound cheerful. But for once, my mother didn't even comment on how harsh I sounded. "What in the world are you talking about? And if you don't mind, could you tell me in ten minutes or less? I have a lot of work to do and I got in late, so I can't spend a lot of time on the phone."

"You want me to call you when you get home, then?"

"No! I want you to tell me what you called to tell me now," I hollered.

"You know I'm just tryin' to help you. I didn't know you was gwine to get this sassy by me callin' you—"

"Muh'Dear, please get to the point," I begged.

"I seen Lizzie comin' out of Claudette's beauty shop as I was goin' in to get my scalp massaged this mornin'. She looks like a film star."

"Oh? Hmmm. Lizzie got a makeover? That was quick. I'm glad he didn't waste any time."

"What was quick?"

"Well, now that she's working for Pee Wee, we wanted her to be a little more glamorous."

"We? We who?"

"Pee Wee and I."

There was a long moment of uncomfortable silence.

"Muh'Dear, are you still there?"

"Yeah, I'm still here. I was just thinkin' about what you just said." More silence. "Why would you want that woman to look more glamorous?"

"It's good for business, Muh'Dear."

"A glamorous woman is good for a lot of other things, too."

# CHAPTER 25

I felt like I was fighting a battle that nobody could win. I felt like I was still on the same treadmill that I'd been on longer than I cared to admit, and I couldn't get off.

Before Lizzie's makeover, Muh'Dear had recommended her for the job. Then she was concerned that Lizzie might not be the right choice for the job, all because she had not had her "fruit plucked" by a man yet. And that she didn't have the right look. But now that Lizzie was looking "glamorous," Muh'Dear didn't want Lizzie working for my husband because of *that*! This was one subject that was really getting on my nerves. It had become a no-win situation as far as I was concerned. The bottom line was, Lizzie had been hired and it appeared that things were working out for her, and for my husband's business. That was all I cared about.

"Muh'Dear, Pee Wee and I talked about it last week. He told me that he was going to tell Lizzie, or have some female tell her, in a nice way to fix herself up. But I didn't know he was going to do it so soon!"

"Hmph!"

"What was that grunt for?"

"Nothin', I guess." Muh'Dear snorted and cleared her throat. "It ain't really none of my business."

"Muh'Dear, if you are trying to say something, just go on and say it," I ordered with a disgusted sigh.

"I ain't tryin' to say nothin'."

"Then why are we talking about Lizzie? Is that what you called me up for?"

"I called your house last night."

"And?"

"You was by yourself."

"I'm by myself a lot. Where is this conversation going?"

"It was four o'clock in the mornin' and Pee Wee hadn't come home yet. You told me that yourself."

"Pee Wee is a grown man. He can do whatever he wants to do." As soon as I finished my last sentence I realized how stupid it sounded. I knew that my meddlesome mother was going to take those statements and run with them. And she sure did.

"He sure enough will!" she hollered. "Girl, you better watch your step if you want to keep that man. Your tooth is mighty long these days; you ain't no teenager and you don't look like Diana Ross. You got a lot of limitations."

"Uh, Muh'Dear, my other line is ringing. Can I call you back later?"

"You comin' to have breakfast with me and your daddy this week? We got some of that beef bacon in that you like. Or maybe lunch would be better. Them catfish is jumpin' out the skillet they so anxious for somebody to see how good they taste with that new curry recipe I just started usin' today." Muh'Dear sounded so sweet now, you would have thought that she was a different woman than the woman who'd been berating me in such a harsh voice a few moments ago.

"Not today," I said quickly. "I'm supposed to meet Pee Wee for lunch," I lied. "Bye!" I hung up and dialed Pee Wee's shop immediately. I was stunned when one of the two young apprentices who worked for him told me that he had taken Lizzie to lunch.

"Well, when he returns, will you tell him to call his wife, Cedric?"

"Yes, ma'am. He got your number?"

"Yes, he's got my number!" I snapped. I didn't mean to take out my frustration on poor Cedric. The boy was slow, and usually said something stupid when I called or dropped by the shop. But my mother had really gotten to me. Bless Rhoda's heart. Before I could make up my mind about calling her, she called me.

"It's Jade. That girl is drivin' me up the wall and back down the other side already," she complained.

"What has Jade done?" I asked, glad that I wouldn't have to unload my complaint first. If I spent a few minutes listening to Rhoda rant, it would give me time to cool off.

"She's hopeless. She's useless." Rhoda laughed. "Otis gave Vernie a high-level position down at the plant. A desk position at that, so he can go to work lookin' real dapper in a suit and tie like she wants. But that's still not good enough for Jade. She thinks the boy should be supervisin'. Can you believe that she'd think that?"

"Yes, I can . . ."

"Other than a few fast-food joints, he's never worked a day in his life! She's been cryin' like a baby all mornin'." Rhoda cleared her throat, then growled under her breath. "And I'm not in the mood for it."

"You're getting hysterical and that's not going to help."

"I am not hysterical!" Rhoda boomed.

I waited for the dust to settle before I spoke again. "Then stop acting like it," I suggested.

"I'm sorry. You know me. Some days I sound like a fishwife." She added a dry laugh.

I remained as calm as I possibly could. It would have done no good for us both to be hysterical. Besides, I needed to save all of my hysterical energy for my own problems.

"Have you tried to talk to your daughter?"

"Yes, I have tried to talk to my daughter. It was like tryin' to talk to a brick wall. Her daddy's tried to talk to her, too. Her husband has tried to talk to her. Her brain is as nimble as a block of cement."

"One good thing about it, the girl is consistent."

"My ass! If she doesn't watch her step, I am goin' to consistently whup her ass."

"I sure hope it doesn't come to that. Jade's a grown woman. . . ."

"As if I'd let that stop me from beatin' some sense into her!"

It seemed like the more we talked, the more hysterical Rhoda sounded. It was hard for me to remain composed. "You want to have lunch, or meet for a drink or something so we can talk about this?" I asked.

"Only if you agree to be the designated driver for the next few days."

I laughed. "You mean it's going to take more than one liquid lunch?"

"At least. Oh, if only Bully were here." Rhoda's lover was in London taking care of some business. He owned some hotels, so he could afford to live a lavish lifestyle, which meant he spent a great deal of his time in the States kicking back in Rhoda's house and making love to her on a regular basis. How he managed to still be sleeping with her right up under Otis's nose was a mystery to me. Since my affair had backfired last summer, I didn't encourage Rhoda to bring hers up. But somehow we always managed to discuss cheating spouses.

"You're not going to believe what Muh'Dear tried to imply a few minutes ago." I guffawed.

"Try me."

"Lizzie got a makeover this morning. I haven't seen her, but Muh'Dear ran into her coming out of Claudette's beauty shop. And you know my mother; she's going crazy. Claudette must have performed a miracle on Lizzie if Muh'Dear's worried about her stealing my husband." I guffawed again.

"Your mother said that?"

"Well, not in those exact words. But that's what she meant. Can you imagine Pee Wee with Lizzie?"

Rhoda sighed so hard it almost choked her. I was glad to know that she thought the whole idea was just as ludicrous as I did.

# CHAPTER 26

I was in no hurry to see Jade face-to-face. Her return impacted me like a boil on my butt! But I had heard so many nice things about her new husband, LaVerne "Vernie" Staples, from Rhoda and a few other people that I was really looking forward to meeting him.

"He's no Adonis like Marcelo, and he is kind of meek, but he's good for Jade," Rhoda told me, giving me a guarded look over drinks.

We occupied a table near the ladies' room at the Red Rose, our version of the wildly popular bar on the old TV show *Cheers*. Rhoda beckoned for our waiter, a knock-kneed woman named O'Linda who didn't hesitate to cuss out patrons who didn't tip her after each drink she delivered.

"He'll be a good father, and Jade wants to get pregnant right away. I know you don't want to hear this, but she said she doesn't want to be old enough to be a grandmother when she gives birth to her first child, like you. She wants to be a young mother. She wants to grow up with her kids, like I did." Rhoda paused, finished her glass of Chianti, and fished a couple of dollars from her wallet, which she handed to O'Linda as soon as she set down two more glasses of wine. "Isn't that cute? Jade's not even twenty-one yet and she's concerned about old age already."

I didn't think it was necessary for Rhoda to tell me what Jade had said about me being old enough to be a grandmother when I had my daughter. Even though it was true. I wanted to respond to that comment by implying that Jade would probably be a *great* grandmother by the time she was my age at the rate she was going. I didn't. I knew Rhoda well enough to know that when she told me something mean and nasty that somebody had said about me, it wasn't to make me feel bad. And she knew me well enough to know that I always wanted to know where I stood with somebody. As if Jade would not let me know what she thought about me herself. That heifer had such a long reach that during the few months she spent in Alabama, just hearing somebody mention her name made my stomach turn.

With Jade back on the scene, I had to plan my visits to Rhoda's house more carefully. I wanted to avoid Jade as much as possible, so I didn't visit when I knew she was on the premises. However, I didn't let Jade's presence stop me from visiting my best friend. She usually rolled out of bed around noon, so it was fairly safe for me to drop by during the early morning hours. She went to the clubs several times a week, so it was safe for me to visit between the club hours, too.

My next visit to Rhoda's house was the morning after we'd had drinks at the Red Rose. I'd arrived around eleven thirty. Rhoda had seated me in her kitchen, my favorite room in her house. She loved to cook Betty Crocker treats for her sweet-toothed husband, so her kitchen always smelled like cakes and cookies. Anyway, there I was sitting in Rhoda's kitchen sipping from a can of Coors Light and admiring her new granite countertops. We were in the middle of discussing her son-in-law again when she had to attend to a minor problem in her basement with the man from the gas company. There was no one else in the house, so it was very quiet. But it didn't stay that way long. I was startled by a loud, nasty voice.

"I thought *you* were here," Jade huffed. I looked toward the kitchen doorway and there she stood, still in her sexy nightgown, looking as friendly as the grim reaper. "I guess you won't stop until you wear out your welcome."

"Hello, Jade," I said, forcing myself to smile.

"Did Mama burn something?" she asked, looking around and sniffing with a sour look on her face.

"No, not that I know of."

Jade glared at me for a few moments before she disappeared. Rhoda had returned to the kitchen by the time Jade came back with a can of room deodorizer. Without looking at me, or saying anything to her mother, she started spraying the kitchen, saturating the air with a pine-scented fragrance.

"Good mornin', honey. I didn't know you were up," Rhoda said in a sweet voice. She removed another can of Coors from her refrigerator and started drinking from it right away.

"How can a person sleep in this house with such a foul smell coming from this kitchen? I thought a mouse or some funky creature had died up in here." Jade looked directly at me and sprayed some more. During my last visit, she had sprayed the telephone with Lysol after I'd used it, so this didn't bother me much.

"I don't smell anything foul," Rhoda said, looking from Jade to me. "Do you, Annette?"

"It is kind of stale in here if you don't mind me saying so," I replied, looking directly at Jade. She shot me a smirk before she left the room. I turned to face Rhoda and resumed our conversation. "How does Vernie feel about Jade wanting to have children so soon?" I asked, looking toward the door.

"I really don't know," she responded, easing onto a high stool by the counter, sliding her hand over that new granite top. "The boy is so mysterious it's hard to figure him out. He's so quiet, he usually doesn't even speak unless he's spoken to. I don't know if he likes livin' here in Ohio—he'd never even been out of the state of Alabama until now. I don't even know if he likes workin' for my husband and livin' with us. Jade does all the talkin' for him." Rhoda stared toward the wall for a few seconds with a blank expression on her face. "I'm concerned about that," she told me in a worried tone of voice.

"There's nothing wrong with being quiet," I said.

Rhoda shook her head. "I meant him bein' so mysterious."

"Well, I haven't met him yet so I can't offer an opinion; but from what I've heard from people who have met him, he makes a really nice first impression, Rhoda."

"So did Ted Bundy and Jeffrey Dahmer. And I am sure that Charles Manson must have made a good first impression, too, on somebody," she quipped, drinking some more beer with a belch.

"I think you're going way overboard. It sounds like the boy is the type who likes to keep to himself, that's all. And there is nothing wrong with that."

I took a long drink from my can and shook my head. Jade pranced past the doorway, coughing and rubbing her nose like she'd stumbled upon a skunk. I ignored her, but Rhoda gave me the usual hopeless look that invariably accompanied a Jade appearance.

"Anyway, as I was sayin'—keep to himself? Vernie? Uh-uh. That's one of the things you give up when you get married. If that's the case with him, there is just no tellin' what's on that boy's mind."

"Cut the boy some slack. Be glad he's the quiet type. As long as he remains that way, you won't have to worry about him embarrassing you or Jade in public."

"You're right and I know you are. It's just that . . . well, never mind. He's a sweet young man, and I think he's a good addition to my family. Even though . . ." Rhoda stopped and pursed her lips.

"Even though what?"

"He seems more like a stowaway than a newlywed husband."

I chuckled. "That's cute, Rhoda. Even if he is a stowaway, you should make him feel welcome." I sipped some beer. "Maybe Jade will pick up some of his habits."

"Such as?"

"Since he's so quiet, maybe she'll tone her image down a bit."

"Ha! That'll be the day. I can only hope. Listen, I know how busy you are these days dealin' with Pee Wee and his concerns about his business, but I appreciate you listenin' to me rant and rave about that daughter of mine."

"You are always there for me, Rhoda. And I know Jade and I have our issues, but I only wish the best for her. She's still young enough to make some drastic changes in herself."

I pressed my lips together and anxiously awaited Rhoda's response. All she did was stare off into space. As tough as she was, being the mother of a pistol like Jade had to be a daunting task.

"Has Vernie made any new friends yet?" I asked.

I had to snap my fingers to get Rhoda's attention back. It took her a few seconds to respond. But first she had to shake her head and blink a few times, like she was coming out of a daze. And I guess she was. I didn't even have to see or talk to Jade every day like she did, and I was in a mild daze myself.

"What did you just say?" she asked.

"Has Jade's husband made any new friends yet?" I asked gently.

"Not exactly. The Puerto Ricans across the street invited him over for a drink yesterday after he helped the husband jump-start that old jalopy of his. But just as he was about to go out the door, Jade put her foot down and told him she couldn't have him socializin' with people like that."

"People like what? I thought you told me those people were very nice."

"They are nice people. But ever since Marcelo jilted Jade, she's had it in for the whole Hispanic population. Jennifer Lopez flashed on the TV screen last night, and Jade called her everything but a child of God."

"That Jade. Do you think she's ever going to come to her senses?"

Rhoda whimpered and looked at me like I was speaking Greek. "What's that supposed to mean? My daughter is not crazy," she protested.

"You know what I mean. She's got some . . . uh . . . issues."

Rhoda nodded and released a mild sigh. "I know that. And I'm the first person to say that she's not exactly Little Bo Peep. She takes after the women on my daddy's side. Aunt Lola and Aunt Moline are real feisty. You know that; you met them when they came up here for my grandma's funeral. And by the way, my granny was as hot as a six-shooter herself. She is the one who Jade is the most like. Talk about a snake! That woman was a cross between a cobra and a python! Whew!"

I gave Rhoda a pensive look.

"What's that look for?" she asked with both eyebrows raised.

"I was thinking about what you just said. You think Jade's a snake?"

Rhoda rolled her eyes and let out another mild sigh. "In a way, I guess I do."

I patted her hand and gave her one of my most sympathetic looks. "Honey, for every snake there is a mongoose."

"I know," Rhoda agreed, dropping her head. She kept her eyes on the countertop for a few moments; but when she looked up again, all I could see was sadness. "And that scares the hell out of me. My daughter won't be lucky like I was when I was raisin' hell. You know what kind of shit I did along the way. . . ." Rhoda paused and tilted her head to the side. "Remember all of that stuff I shared with you?" she whispered.

"How could I forget any of it?" I whispered back. It seemed hard to believe that the woman sharing the kitchen with me, my best friend, had killed five people—and gotten away with it. "I just hope that Jade never . . . you know . . . does the same things you've done."

"I doubt she'll go that far. Me, I'm old school. Jade belongs to what I call the dot.com generation. There are too many things at her disposal for her to get too caught up on any one thing in particular. Look how quick she bounced back after Marcelo left her. And remember how fast she bounced back after that little misunderstandin' she had with you?"

I was still bouncing back from that "little misunderstanding" between Jade and myself that had occurred a little over a year ago. It still hurt when I thought about how she'd harassed me with anonymous nasty phone calls, vicious notes, and vile packages, hoping to send me to the nut house so she could move in with my husband.

"And Jade's still bouncing," I muttered under my breath.

"What was that? I didn't hear you," Rhoda said, tapping her fingers on the table.

"It was nothing," I said with a dry laugh. "I was just saying how lucky we all are to have so many blessings. . . ."

# CHAPTER 27

I counted my blessings each and every day. I had so much to be thankful for. Not just material things, my health, and my family, but emotional and spiritual things, too.

I was not perfect, so I knew that I could still lose my way again if I wasn't careful. My affair had cost me dearly—most of my self-respect and my husband's trust—so I was determined to put it so far on the backburner that I would forget how good I thought it was during the time that it was going on. I realized now just how much I had to lose, and that it could all happen in the blink of an eye—not just for myself but my family as well.

It had taken me a lot of years to get to where I was, and I prayed that I had a lot of years left to enjoy it. Thankfully, there was no reason for me to believe that I didn't have a lot of years left. I had been fortunate enough to reach middle age and longevity seemed to run in my family. Both of my parents were now close to their eighties. And even though they were both as fussy as toddlers some days, they were still enjoying healthy and productive lives. One of the things that I was most grateful for was that they were still sharp enough to live on their own. I dreaded the day that I'd have to either put them in a home or move them in with me. The way my mother rode my back by badgering and preaching to me, it wouldn't take long for my sanity to fly out the window if she lived with me.

"Annette, God been good to you, but God ain't through yet," Muh'Dear reminded me on a regular basis. She was right. God had been good to me; not by randomly dropping things into my lap, but because I had worked hard for everything I had. Therefore, I tried not to take anything for granted.

Besides, if God wasn't through with me yet, I was anxious to see what other good things He had in store for me.

One of my best blessings was my job. I loved being employed as a manager at Mizelle's Collection Agency. The pay was good, my boss loved me to death, and I was finally at a point where I got along with all of the people I supervised. Counting myself, we were a staff of seventeen. It would have been eighteen, had I not scared off one of my husband's most loyal client's twenty-five-year-old nephew, Michael Dench, last December.

It was hard to find good workers, especially for jobs as unpopular as credit collection agents. You had to be strong to put up with some of the crap we got from the deadbeats we went after.

Well, Michael had submitted a résumé that looked too good to be true. I could not ignore the fact that he was so eager to work for me that he had walked all the way to my office from across town for his interview because he didn't have bus fare.

It was the week before Christmas. He had arrived on time, which meant he had to leave the house he shared with his mama at least two hours earlier. One of the reasons Michael was so anxious and determined to get a job was because he wanted to earn some money so he could send his terminally ill grandmother to Disneyland for her eighty-fifth birthday, which was coming up in a few weeks. I really liked this young man and his enthusiasm.

"I just hope my granny lasts that long," he told me during the interview, looking away too late for me not to see the tears in his eyes.

"I hope so, too, Michael. Uh, if things work out for you, you can do all of the overtime you can stand. And you can even take work home from time to time—if you don't mind calling up deadbeats during the hours when most people your age are out dancing and having a good time," I said, sounding as giddy as a teenager. That sweetened a pie that was already sweet to him, but I didn't stop there. "We also have bonus incentives."

The more I talked, the more he smiled. Because we were short handed that day and two of my employees were out sick, I adjusted the rules and decided to hire Michael on the spot, but on a temporary basis. He got so excited he started grinning from ear to ear.

"Let me check out your references and do the background check. If everything goes well, we can talk about a permanent arrangement," I told Michael as I concluded the interview. Even though he was twenty-five, he still looked like a teenager, and I had some concerns about the fact that he was so cute.

"Um, thank you," Michael said, suddenly looking nervous.

My staff included a couple of predatory women who ate cute young things like Michael for breakfast. Michael would have been just a quick snack, like a bag of Fritos, for those heifers. He wore a loose-fitting white shirt that day with a maroon tie. But his black pants were tight enough for me to see how firm his thighs were. With his small, pearly white teeth, juicy lips, cinnamon brown skin, cleft chin, and light brown eyes, he was a recipe for disaster. Had he come around last year, he might have been the one that I lost my mind over instead of that fool Louis Baines. They looked just that much alike. But I was a changed woman. There was not another man on earth who was going to come between me and my husband again. Michael could have been sitting in front of me naked and it would not have aroused me.

"Uh, in the meantime, you can come in tomorrow morning at nine, fill out the necessary paperwork, and I can put you to work right away." I smiled.

"I'll be here tomorrow morning at nine o'clock sharp." The palm of his hand was covered in sweat when I shook it before his departure.

That boy was so anxious to start working for me, he arrived at the office before I did that first morning. I was pleasantly surprised when I stumbled across the parking lot and discovered him squatting on the ground in front of the bus stop a few yards from my office building. By the end of the first day, he had roped in two of our most difficult and elusive debtors, and locked them into firm commitments to bring their delinquent accounts up to date. "Thank you for taking a chance on me, Mrs. Davis," he said on his way out at closing time.

I knew for a fact that a lot of employers didn't always check all references, because I fell into that category myself. One reason was that if I had a good feeling about a job candidate, I usually went with that. Another reason was that sometimes tracking down references took up too much time. As much as I didn't want to admit it to myself, Michael's good looks had a lot to do with me wanting to check his background. After my disastrous affair with that pretty boy Louis Baines, I was now convinced that a good-looking man was a pig-in-a-poke. That and the fact that the uncle who had referred him to Pee Wee was a pimp *and* a drug dealer with a record as long as one of Magic Johnson's legs.

On the third day of his temporary assignment I got around to checking out his background. Just as I had suspected, it was a disaster. One of his "references" was a man named Logan Hotchkins, his parole officer. His other reference was fictitious.

According to Michael's résumé, he had spent two years studying business and finance at Kent State. As it turned out, he had dropped out of school in the tenth grade. He also had a felony record that included assault and battery, indecent exposure, and grand theft. I had some concerns about hiring him because he would be a security risk, and he would be a risk in other areas as well. But then so was I.

Not only had I worked as a prostitute, I'd embezzled money from my employer to give to that fool I was screwing around with last year. But I was lucky and had never been arrested. Unlike Michael, my record was as clean as a whistle, and now that I was on the right track, it was going to stay clean. I felt sorry for Michael and wanted to help him as much as I could. I decided to overlook his background report and hire him anyway. I firmly believed that everybody deserved a second chance.

Michael must have sensed something that day. I had left a note on his desk that I needed to talk to him as soon as he returned from lunch regarding his references, his background check, and his future with my company. I was on the phone with Rhoda when he came back, and by the time I ended the call and made my way out onto the floor he was gone.

Later that afternoon, a woman with a loud, menacing voice called me up and told me that Michael was not coming back. After mumbling a few profanities and calling me some choice names, she also told me in no uncertain ghetto terms where I could spend eternity and where to send the check that Michael had earned for the few days he'd worked.

I had thought about Michael almost every day since that day. I even prayed that he'd turn his life around and that somebody else would eventually give him a job. But things didn't work out that way for him. The same day that I interviewed Lizzie, I heard on the local news that Michael had committed suicide. An unidentified relative had told a newspaper reporter: "The boy made a lot of mistakes, but he had paid his debt to society. He tried to find a job, but nobody wanted to give him a chance. He was trying so hard he was on the verge of a nervous breakdown. That last job thing was his last hope. By then he was super duper depressed. But he was still confident that he'd do well as a collection agent—if he had the chance! But that woman who interviewed him turned out to be a coldhearted witch. . . ."

I hoped that nobody else thought of me as a coldhearted witch. Life had knocked me down a few dozen times over the years, but it had not destroyed me. I was now in a position to give back, and that's what I always tried to do.

Had Michael come to see me like I'd instructed in the note I left on his desk that day, he would have found out that, in spite of his references and bleak background, I was going to convert his temporary assignment to a permanent position.

Lizzie's situation had not been nearly as bad as Michael's, but knowing that I had helped her made me feel good about myself. Now all I hoped for was that things between her and my husband would go as well as I wanted them to.

Things must have been going well. It had been a week since Pee Wee mentioned Lizzie, and when he came home from work each day, he was more cheerful than he'd been in months. When I brought up the subject myself, he usually said something like, "Oh, Lizzie's doin' fine! Everything is turnin' out real good! What's for supper?"

And I left it at that.

# CHAPTER 28

Two weeks had gone by and I had not had a chance to go by my husband's barbershop like I had planned. Several people had told me about all of the changes he'd made to the place. I knew he'd installed a big-screen TV that included cable, but other than that—and Lizzie doing manicures—that was all I knew about.

"I noticed a huge mob walkin' into Pee Wee's barbershop the other day when I drove by there," my mother told me. "And I notice he's been stayin' open later than usual. Is he givin' out free haircuts or what?"

"Not that I know of." I laughed. "He's doing a lot of things to increase business."

"Lizzie workin' out all right?"

"She is as far as I know." It was hard for me not to mention my part in all these recent developments. "I am so glad I got him to hire Lizzie. She was just what he needed."

"Umph! I just bet she is," my mother said, her voice dripping with sarcasm and innuendo. I knew she was trying to initiate something unpleasant and juicy so she could contribute some new gossip to the mill, but I promptly ended the call by claiming somebody was at my door.

Every time I attempted to go by Pee Wee's work, something came up. One day when I was supposed to meet him at the shop for lunch, my daddy drove himself to a mall in Canton to look for some new fishing equipment in a sporting goods establishment. After he left the store, he couldn't locate his truck in the parking lot so he wanted me to come pick him up. By the time I got there, the police had arrived and Daddy was sitting in the backseat of a squad car. His thin gray hair was askew and his clothes were disheveled. As a matter of fact, he had his plaid flannel shirt on inside out. From what I could piece together, Daddy had mistaken his truck for somebody else's and had attacked the real owner with a stick. Witnesses had thought that it was a carjacking taking place and called the cops.

As it turned out, my daddy had parked on the other side of the mall. The police located his truck, and I called Rhoda to take a cab to the mall so she could drive Daddy's truck back to his house. I drove him home myself, and by the time we got to his house, he had forgotten why he was in my car in the first place.

Another time when I was scheduled to meet my husband for lunch, Rhoda had a crisis that I had to help her get through.

This time the cops had been called in reference to an incident involving Jade's husband. Vernie had been attacked and beaten to the ground in broad daylight, in front of witnesses. My first thought was that he'd been the victim of an attempted robbery. I had no idea how wrong I was about that.

By the time I got to the hospital where Rhoda sat by her son-in-law's bedside stroking the side of his face, I had forgotten all about my lunch date with Pee Wee.

"This is a hell of a way for us to meet for the first time, Miss Annette," Vernie managed. I could tell that he was in a lot of pain from the grimace on his face. Whoever had attacked him had meant business. There were long scratches all over his swollen face, and he had two black eyes. "I've heard a lot about you," he said, coughing.

"I wish we could have met sooner," I said, forcing myself to smile. I nodded at Rhoda, who sat there with a grim expression on her face. "I got here as soon as I could," I told her, looking at my watch.

Just then, Rhoda's husband, Otis, entered the room. "Annette, good to see you," he said, giving his chin a quick lift to enhance his greeting. He still had on the khaki uniform he wore to work every day, and there was a thin coat of brick dust on his hands. I knew that Otis loved his job as a lead supervisor at the Richland Steel Mill, and so did Rhoda because he made a damn good salary doing it. Like my husband, Otis was no longer as trim and handsome as he'd once been. But with his strong chiseled features and neat, shoulder-length dreadlocks, he was also the kind of man whom most of the women we knew dreamed about. And according to Rhoda, Vernie was, too. Which made it even worse that somebody had attacked him.

"Did the police catch who did this?" I asked, looking from Otis to Vernie. Rhoda was looking at her hands when I turned to her. There was something else wrong with this picture. "Where's Jade?" I wanted to know, still looking from face to face. I noticed how Vernie flinched at the mention of Jade's name.

"She's at the house," Rhoda mumbled as she twiddled her thumbs.

"Oh. Well, it's a good thing she wasn't with Vernie. Whoever attacked him might have hurt her, too," I said, sighing with relief.

"You're right!" Otis said quickly. "Me baby girl is a lucky bird. . . ."

Rhoda let out a loud breath and a muffled sob. She quickly looked away when I looked at her.

"Is there anything I can get for you, Vernie? Some bottled water maybe. Or would you like a snack from the vending machines?" I asked, not knowing what else to say.

"I'm fine, but thank you very much, ma'am," Vernie said, speaking with a very slight southern accent. He seemed like such a nice, polite young man. He was a cute one, too, but not as cute as the Mexican whom Jade had scared off, though. Since he was stretched out on his back, I could not tell how tall he was. But just by looking at his finely chiseled face and long arms, I could tell that he was concealing a fairly nice body under those hospital bedcovers. And Rhoda had said something about him working out at the gym several times a week. He had thick, curly black hair and small brown eyes. His nose was a bit sharp for a black man, but he had a nice, neatly trimmed mustache and a pair of the most kissable lips I'd ever seen on a man. I could see why Jade had been attracted to him. She was the kind of girl who wouldn't be found dead in the arms of a homely man.

But why was she at home and not with him now? That was one question that I was afraid to ask.

Otis disappeared from the room and returned a few minutes later with coffee in paper cups for me and Rhoda. We made small talk for a few more minutes; then I left. Before I could make it into the elevator, Rhoda caught up with me.

"Are you going back to your office?" she asked in a gruff voice.

I looked at my watch. "I guess so. I was supposed to meet Pee Wee for lunch, but it's too late for that now. I'll just grab a sandwich and eat it at my desk." I looked down the hall toward Vernie's room. Two rosy-cheeked doctors swished by us with the tails of their long white smocks flapping like parachutes.

"I need to talk to you about somethin'," Rhoda told me in a nervous voice.

"You want to call me when I get back to my office? Or do you want to go somewhere now and talk about it over a drink?"

I had not pushed the button for the elevator, but the door opened anyway. A plump nurse exited, scribbling on a chart. Rhoda surprised me by guiding me into the elevator and pressing the button for the lobby. As soon as the door closed behind us, she turned to me with a wild-eyed look. "She did it!" Her words exploded through gnashing teeth.

"What? She who? And . . . what . . . did she do?" I stammered.

"Vernie didn't get mugged!" Rhoda claimed. "At least not by a stranger."

"What—did Jade do that to him?" I asked.

"Yes, she did. Jade did that to Vernie."

"Oh, God no," I muttered, not the least bit surprised to hear this nasty piece of information.

One of the many things that Rhoda and I rarely discussed was Jade's hostile nature and what she might eventually do to somebody some day. Her level of aggression was extreme. The girl had a temper and could fly off the handle over the most trivial of things. To my knowledge, she had never physically assaulted another person; her attacks had always been verbal. That was no longer true.

I could not ignore the grim thoughts running through my mind. Rhoda had committed several murders. Was it possible that Jade was going in a homicidal direction, too? I shuddered. The thought of it made my flesh crawl. Even though Rhoda and Jade looked alike and had a lot of the same personality traits, Rhoda was a somewhat sensible person when it came to chastising her enemies. If there was such a thing as a "considerate" killer, that was Rhoda. She had killed some pretty nasty, evil people. The kind of devils that normal people like me had often fantasized about killing. But the fact that Jade was so irrational made this prospect even more chilling. "Rhoda, please tell me you're joking."

"I wish I could." She released a rapid chorus of choking sobs. I waited for her to compose herself.

"You're upset. Do you want to talk about this later?" I asked, clapping her on the back.

"No, I'm fine. I want to talk about this now, if you don't mind. Just give me a few seconds." I waited some more as Rhoda coughed a few times and cleared her throat. It sounded like she was in pain, and I knew she was. Her voice sounded so sad and desperate when she started talking again. "Yes, she attacked him, and it's not the first time."

I didn't want to make things any worse than they already were by asking unnecessary questions. The situation was grim enough, and I could see how hard it was for Rhoda to discuss it. But I couldn't keep my thoughts to myself, or my mouth from revealing them. "And I have a feeling it won't be the last time," I said.

# CHAPTER 29

After Rhoda and I exited the elevator, we stood in the hospital lobby on the first floor near the registration desk. Had the weather been nicer, I would have led her to the atrium outside. I didn't like to look at all of the injured folks coming in to get medical attention. One was a little boy with so much blood on his face that I couldn't tell what race he was.

"Rhoda, if there is anything I can do, just let me know," I told her, squeezing her shoulder. "If you want to talk about it some more, just call me."

I checked to make sure the buttons on my coat were done as I prepared to walk toward the exit. But from the look on Rhoda's face, I decided she wanted me to stay.

"Are you going to be all right?" I asked.

She shook her head and gave me a dry look. "Yeah, I will—I don't know, Annette. Instead of gettin' better, Jade seems to be gettin' worse." Rhoda looked toward the elevator and then around the lobby before she returned her attention to me. "My son called me up and told me that just before she came back up here, she bounced her cell phone off Vernie's head just because he spoke to an old girlfriend—in church! He said that right after Vernie fell to the floor with his head bleedin', she got so aggressive that the pew they were sittin' in turned over! Can you imagine that? It took three ushers and my son to restrain her. Poor Vernie. He's a smart boy, so he should have known better. He shouldn't have messed with her."

*He shouldn't have messed with her?* I was so taken aback by Rhoda's last statement that I almost choked on some air. Something told me that Jade would eventually meet her match. I wondered if Rhoda was going to say that person shouldn't have messed with Jade, too.

The more I heard, the more I feared for Vernie's safety. But I was in no position to intervene. For the time being, all I could do was listen. "I know now that I should have never sent her to Alabama. I should have kept her up here so I could keep her under control."

"Under control? Rhoda, if you can't even keep yourself under control, you can't keep Jade under control!"

"The hell I can't!"

We were talking loud enough for some of the nurses and incoming patients to hear. I moved back a few steps, closer to the exit, with Rhoda following. I resumed my end of the conversation in a voice that was just above a whisper. "If what you call yourself doing now is keeping Jade under control, I'd hate to see the kind of damage she could do if you weren't keeping her under control. Honey, your daughter needs some professional help."

Rhoda looked at me like I had just revealed the secrets of the universe. It was good to see the way she'd suddenly perked up.

"Maybe you're right! I've been thinkin' about somethin' like that for years, but I guess it's time for me to stop just thinkin' about it."

"It's a start," I added.

She agreed with me by offering me a nod and a weak smile. Then her mood seemed to darken again. "What did you mean a few moments ago when you said this wasn't goin' to be the 'last time' Jade does somethin' like this to Vernie? I gave her a good talkin' to. Do you think she will do somethin' like this again?"

"Why wouldn't she? And by the way, why did she attack him this time? Did he provoke her?"

"I guess you could say that. As far as Jade was concerned he did." An embarrassed look crossed Rhoda's face.

"It must have been pretty bad," I mouthed.

"To her it was. You know how sensitive she is. Well, he sassed her in public. She attacked him with one of those metal chairs at Big Bobby's Burger joint where they were havin' lunch today. All because he smiled at the waitress and back talked to Jade when she complained about it."

"I'm surprised somebody didn't call the cops," I said, shaking my head.

"They did. Remember that goofy-ass Lonnie Shoemaker from school? The brother with that peanut-shaped head who was a year ahead of us? He's a cop now. And still just as big a butthole as he was in school."

"I know. He gave me a speeding ticket last week, and one the week before."

"Anyway, I get there, and right away I try to talk him out of arrestin' my child. Otis had already arrived and was in the ambulance with Vernie. Jade was a wreck, hollerin' and screamin' like a banshee. A blind man could have seen that the girl was delirious. By the way, she'd been smokin' some weed with a couple of her she-devil, clonelike girlfriends before she met up with Vernie. She was a little light-headed and, you know, confused. I've told Vernie over and over to run when she's smokin' that shit. And I've told her over and over to stop smokin' that shit. But that's a moot point because it's in her blood. She's half Jamaican. Every damn time she goes down to the island to visit her daddy's folks, or sit around in the same room with her daddy and her uncle Bully, they pass around thick blunts like candy. That's the real reason she wasn't really *that* responsible for her actions this time. . . ."

"As far as I'm concerned, her smoking marijuana doesn't justify what she did to Vernie," I said firmly. "I know a lot of people who smoke it, and they've never done anything stupid because of it. Myself included—back when I was a kid myself, of course."

"I agree with you. Weed is more harmless than a glass of wine. If anything, she should be more mellow when she smokes it. And she usually is—but not this time. Vernie must have really looked at that waitress with a hungry eye for Jade to react so violently."

"Rhoda, if Vernie had fucked that waitress in front of Jade, she still had no right to attack him with a chair," I insisted.

"Look who's talking!" Rhoda blasted, giving me an amused look. "What about you beatin' the crap out of Louis when you found out he was playin' you?"

I rolled my eyes and chuckled. "That . . . that was different," I stammered, my face burning with shame. "I shouldn't have done that."

"But you did," Rhoda said, nodding.

"Well, it won't happen again, I hope," I bleated. "You know that that wasn't the real me."

"Anyway, Shoemaker had a crush on me one time, so he's got a soft spot where I'm concerned. Jade claimed self-defense, so he didn't arrest her. Poor thing." Rhoda paused and took several deep breaths. "She wouldn't last an hour in a jail cell. I couldn't have that." Rhoda pressed her lips together and shook her head. "And damn that Shoemaker! He had the nerve to talk trash to *me*! All because I told him I wasn't goin' to leave the premises until he promised me that he wouldn't even put my daughter's name on his report. I told him that he had to refer to her as 'an unidentified perpetrator who got away before he could detain her.' With his four-generations-livin'-in-the-same-house ghetto self! He agreed to write up his report that way, but he still told me that if I didn't get out of his face, he was goin' to plant some weed on *me*! I don't know what this world is comin' to!"

I could tell that Rhoda was disgusted beyond belief. But I couldn't tell if she was more disgusted about what Jade had done to Vernie or the fact that a cop had "talked trash" to her.

I felt so sorry for Rhoda. She was one of the smartest women I knew, but one of the most pathetic, too. She still thought that the world revolved around her. And apparently, so did Jade.

"Hmmm. Well, your daughter was lucky this time." I gave Rhoda a stern look.

She gave me a stern look back. "What do you mean 'this time'? This will never happen again," Rhoda vowed. "I will see to it; you'll see. Oh, and by the way, you've got a daughter, too. Raisin' daughters is not easy. This could happen to you."

"True. But little kids, little problems. Big kids, big problems. Right now we need to focus on your daughter," I said.

I didn't go back to my office. I left for the day. Since I had flaked out on another lunch date with my husband, I decided that he deserved some special attention, and a special dinner.

# CHAPTER 30

Despite my weight loss, and the fact that I no longer ate like a hog, I still liked to cook. My husband enjoyed the usual down-home plates that almost every other black person I knew who had southern roots enjoyed. I usually planned our meals so that I didn't have to come home from work and then scramble around the kitchen trying to decide what to cook. I was not the kind of home-maker who would fiddle around with microwave plates unless I had to. When greens were on the menu, I took the time to pick and wash them the night before. I always made sure I had thawed out a chicken in time for me to cook it for dinner, and if I was going to make some cornbread, I made sure I had all of the ingre-dients at my disposal. My daughter, Charlotte, didn't appreciate my hard work in the kitchen, but that didn't bother me. She was no different from most of the other kids her age. She hated almost everything I cooked, so at least once a week, if she'd been good, I ordered a pizza or took her out for a fast-food treat.

After I'd left Rhoda at the hospital, I stopped at the grocery store and picked up all of the things that I needed to prepare one of Pee Wee's favorite meals. We usually ate dinner between six and six thirty, but there were always exceptions to that rule. Some days we ate as early as six or as late as eight. It was a toss-up on weekends and holidays. Then there were days when one, or all three of us, walked around the house nibbling on something off and on all day. On days like that, I didn't even set the table. When Pee Wee had not come home by seven that evening, I set the table and summoned Charlotte.

"Yuck! Mama, how could you? Greens, squash, and pork butt, slimy okra and cornbread *again*," she complained, frowning at the plate I'd just prepared for her. "Eyow!"

"You can 'yuck' and 'eyow' all you want, Miss Thing, but you'd better eat everything on your plate. Do you hear me?"

"Yes, ma'am." Charlotte picked up her fork and stared at the contents on the plate in front of her like she was looking at a pile of horse manure. "And where's Daddy?"

"Uh, he's working late again," I told her. "Eat your dinner. And hurry so you can do your homework, then go wash your rusty little body."

I fixed myself a plate, just a small portion of greens. No meat and no bread.

"Is that all you're going to eat? You making me eat all this slop, and all you're going to eat is some of those nasty greens. Mama, you know that ain't fair!"

One of the things that I didn't like, or tolerate, was a child mouthing off to an adult. Especially when that child was mine and I was the adult. I didn't say a word. I simply lunged at Charlotte with my fist poised and gently mauled the side of her head—the same way my mother used to do to me when I got out of line.

She howled and then sniffled for a few seconds, but she dug into her meal the way she was supposed to. We ate our dinner in cold-blooded silence.

Charlotte winced with each bite she took. From the looks on her face, you would have thought she was being forced to eat a skunk. I felt so sorry for kids like her who didn't know how to appreciate real food. When I was her age, a plate of greens and cornbread used to make my eyes and mouth water. And that was still true to this day. I just didn't eat as much.

Every time I heard a car outside, I ran to the window, thinking it was Pee Wee.

Charlotte swallowed hard and took a sip of her water. She still had a lot of food on her plate to eat, but she was taking her time, prolonging her agony. A few minutes ago, she'd stopped eating to run to the bathroom. A minute after she returned, she stopped eating to run outside to make sure she had put her bicycle on the back porch like she'd been taught. When she returned from doing that, she had a piece of paper in her hand.

"Mama, look at this application I filled out today," she said, pushing the paper across the table toward me. "It's a mock credit card application. Miss Fagan said it'll familiarize us more with bank procedures."

I gave my daughter a puzzled look. When I was her age, I didn't even know what a credit card application was. Back in my elementary school days, kids did finger painting and drew stick people on the blackboard. It saddened me to know how far I had come. And it saddened me even more not to know where I was going.

"It's going to be years before you have to worry about credit card app . . . applications," I said, my voice falling apart because I was so angry about Pee Wee not being home yet. I looked at the document in front of me. I was proud to see that my daughter's penmanship was so neat and professional looking, even though the words were a blur because I had a few tears in my eyes. For the most part, I scanned the application with indifference. And then I saw something that made me laugh. In the spot where it asked for NAME OF YOUR CURRENT BANK, Charlotte had written: PIGGY.

"What are you laughing at?" she asked, snatching her application out of my hand. "This ain't supposed to be funny, Mama!"

"I know, baby. I was laughing because it's so cute. I can't wait to show it to your daddy," I said, looking toward the window again.

Her daddy hadn't called, and he had not come home by eleven, when I went to bed.

That sucker had some serious explaining to do. And if it didn't appease me, he would have even more explaining to do!

I couldn't get to sleep because by now I was worried. First, I called up both of the young men who worked for him. "Nome, I don't know where he at," one told me. "He left work at six like we all did," the other one told me. I called a few of his boys, but none claimed to know where he was. And knowing men as well as I thought I did, I had a feeling that even if they did know where he was, they wouldn't tell me. I even called up Rhoda. She had not seen him either. And since she and Otis had just come from the only hospital in Richland, it was reasonable to assume that Pee Wee had not been admitted with a broken leg or a bullet in his head.

Somehow I managed to get to sleep until the phone on my nightstand rang. I glanced at the clock on the radio next to it first. It was three thirty in the morning. Even though I was somewhat disoriented, the first thing that came to my mind was that something had happened to one or both of my parents. My heart started racing, and I felt like I was going to hyperventilate. It took me a few seconds to compose myself.

The other side of the bed was still empty, but that didn't mean Pee Wee had not come home. He often slept downstairs in the living room in that old La-Z-Boy chair that he was so fond of. I assumed that's where he was until I answered the telephone.

"Hi, Annette." It was the voice of a woman who spent a great deal of her time meddling in other people's business. Scary Mary was my mother's oldest friend and my unofficial godmother. She was also a notorious madam with a history of violence and corruption. "This is Scary Mary and I was just thinkin' about you, so I decided to call you up just to see how you're doin'. I ain't seen or talked to you in a few days. You asleep?"

"Yes, I was asleep," I hissed, sitting up. The most recent issue of *Black Enterprise* magazine, which I had been reading before I fell asleep, slid to the floor. "What's the matter?"

"Is Pee Wee there?" the old madam cooed, her voice so sweet it made my head spin. I knew her well enough to know that this was her "up to something" voice.

"Um, he's asleep," I said with a sniff. "What's wrong?" I wanted to know. "Are you all right?"

"I asked where your husband was."

"I just told you that he's asleep."

"Where at?" Scary Mary didn't have the voice of a woman her age, which was incredibly around ninety. She sounded more like a woman my age.

I softened my tone because I had always been taught to "respect" my elders, even ones as meddlesome and pushy as Scary Mary.

"What do you want with my husband?" I was wide awake by now, and getting angrier by the second. "It's three thirty in the morning," I said.

"I was wonderin' if he'd come by my place after work one day soon and take a look at the brakes on my van. I'm havin' a problem with them squeakin' like Mickey Mouse."

"I will ask him, and I will have him give you a call."

"When?"

"I'll have him call you back when it's convenient for him." I scratched the side of my neck, fuming with exasperation and impatience. I knew damn well that a problem with the brakes on her van was not the real reason that Scary Mary was calling me at this hour. "He's not home," I said finally, knowing that she'd take that piece of information and run with it.

"I was right," she cooed.

"You were right about what?"

"Well, I don't like to spread gossip or rumors unless it is necessary, but when I see somethin' takin' place with my own eyes, I have to address it."

"I presume you know something that involves me?"

"Indirectly. I would say it involves your husband more."

"Pee Wee is not here, so you can't discuss whatever it is with him. So tell me what it is that involves my husband so I can get off this telephone and get back to what I was doing." I didn't even try to hide the fact that I was annoyed. I hissed and snarled like a serpent. "And please hurry up with it." I also didn't care that I was speaking to an elderly woman.

"Hmmm. I thought that was your husband I seen drivin' down the street a few minutes ago. And I know he wasn't on his way to the store. . . ."

"Maybe he was on his way to the store. How do you know he wasn't?" I said, clearing my throat.

"I hope that's where he was going. Because the only places still open in this hick town this time of night is the Grab and Go convenience store and . . . a whore's thighs."

I was still trying to come up with a response, when she added, "And he was drivin' that car, leanin' like a pimp. Shame on him!"

"Well, he is a grown man, so he can drive his car any way he wants to drive it, and he can stay out as long as he wants to. I trust my husband." I couldn't believe how weak my voice had become in the last few moments.

"But don't you think this is a strange time for him to be out in the streets? He's a married man."

"What's so strange about it?"

"Well, this is a small city. It's hard to do dirt here and not get caught. Remember when you was bootyin' around with that young piece last year? I caught y'all together more than once, and I wasn't even tryin' to. You better get on the ball, girl."

# CHAPTER 31

"Listen, I just told you that if you've got something to say about my husband, just go on and say it, so we can end this conversation and I can go back to sleep."

Scary Mary gasped. "You sassin' me, girl?"

"No, I am not sassing you!" I toned down my voice. "I would never sass you."

"Then you better get a grip."

"Get a grip on what? What are you trying to imply?"

I awaited the old madam's response in agonizing silence. My heart was beating against the inside of my chest like a bongo drum.

"I love you as much as I love my own daughter, and I don't want to see you get hurt." She followed that statement with a rumbling cough. "Especially by a man. I been operatin' a . . . uh . . . hospitality house for more years than you been on the planet. And believe me when I tell you that if runnin' a whorehouse don't make you a good judge of people, nothin' will. Shit. I know more about human nature than Sigmund Fraud."

"Freud," I corrected.

She ignored me and continued her convoluted rant. "I didn't make it far in school, but I know a whole lot more than most people."

"I am sure you do," I agreed.

"You take time. The misuse of time is the worst thing a person can do. A lot of people say that the love of money is the root of all evil, but that's a dumb man's interpretation. People like me, we know better. You can have a zillion dollars and lose it, but you can always get another zillion dollars. But if you waste time, you can't never get it back. Tomorrow ain't promised to nobody. Even Jesus had to go when He had to go."

Scary Mary's philosophical comments made a lot of sense. But I still didn't know where she was going with this clumsy conversation.

"I agree. Time should not be wasted," was all I could think to say.

"I don't want you to waste your time with your head in the sand. Don't close your eyes and mind to what's happenin' around you. You followin' me, girl?"

"Yes, ma'am." She had lost me, but it didn't take long for me to follow her drift.

"Is Pee Wee havin' an affair?"

"Of course not! Why in the world would you think something like that? You know what kind of man he is. . . ."

"Let me tell you somethin', sugar pie, honey bunch. Don't you never think you know more about men than me. They ought to give me a master's degree in Penisology. If Pee Wee got a *good* reason to be out runnin' wild in the streets at this hour like a pimp, that's your business. But if he out here mishavin', it's my business. I ain't gwine to let nobody make a fool out of you if I can help it."

"Tell me, why do *you* think some men cheat?" I asked in a detached voice, knowing I had no choice but to listen to Scary Mary until she decided to release me.

"Honey, they cheat because they are men. It's as simple as that. That and the fact that they don't know what else to do with them dicks they got danglin' below their vile loins like bananas." She chuckled. "I bet they wouldn't be so randy if they were the ones that had to squeeze a newborn baby out of their holes. Buttholes in their case."

I was so exasperated that I couldn't even think or see straight anymore. All I wanted to do was end this conversation and go back to sleep. "I want to thank you for being so concerned about me, but I don't need your help," I said, trying to sound as cordial as possible. That was not easy. I was fuming. More because of what Scary Mary had said than I was about Pee Wee "out runnin' wild in the streets like a pimp at this hour." I sniffed and attempted to sound nonchalant. "I'll tell Pee Wee to call you about the brakes on your van."

"Huh? Brakes? My brakes? What about the brakes on my van, honey?"

"You said you wanted him to come take a look at them because they're squeaking," I reminded.

"Oh, that's right. All right. Bye, baby."

I didn't go back to sleep right away, but I did eventually. And when I woke up again, Pee Wee was on the other side of the bed, snoring like a moose.

He was gone by the time I got up to get ready for work.

"Where's Daddy now?" Charlotte asked, walking into the kitchen just as I was about to dial the number to his shop. I was pleased to see that she was already dressed for school. "He knows I like the way he prepares grits better than you. You and that ole nasty low-fat butter! Mama, please go back to being a great big fat lady. You were so much more fun then! And it was so much fun to sit on your squishy lap!"

I rolled my eyes and shook my head. Charlotte's reference to my former weight was endearing but painful. "He had to leave early today," I explained, wondering why that was so. "How about some cereal?"

I didn't know what I was going to say to Pee Wee when, and if, he answered the telephone at the shop. Whatever it was, I didn't want Charlotte to hear it. I fixed her a bowl of Fruit Loops; then I rushed upstairs and dialed the number to the shop from the telephone in my bedroom. He answered right away.

"Hello, baby. I didn't want to wake you up when I got in last night," he started. "It was real late."

"What time was that?" I asked. I didn't bother to remind him about all of the other times he'd come home late and woke me. He knew me well enough to know that something like that would not have bothered me. And he certainly knew me well enough to know that I worried about things a lot less serious than him staying out all night.

"To tell you the truth, I didn't look at the time," he said, speaking with hesitation. "But everything but the Grab and Go convenience store was closed when I drove through town. That's about the only thing still open that time of night. . . ."

*That and a whore's thighs,* I thought to myself. It was on the tip of my tongue but I managed to keep it there.

Then he started speaking so fast I had a hard time keeping up with his words. "I ran into Jesse Smart and a couple of our old army buddies. They said there's a rumor of another war brewin' somewhere. Another war is just what we need. Thank God I've passed the age to be of any good for this one! Anyway, we ended up at my homeboy Jesse's place guzzlin' beer and playin' poker, and reminiscin' about all the shit we experienced in 'Nam. Would you believe that Jesse got two different women—in the same family—pregnant before we left Saigon? Them Vietnamese chicks couldn't get enough of us brothers."

The last thing I was interested in discussing was what went on between American men and Vietnamese women during the war. It was beginning to feel like I had a "rumor of a war" on my hands, and I needed to be ready for it.

"Why didn't you call me to let me know what was going on?"

"Because I was so pissed off with myself that I couldn't even think straight! I lost everything but my citizenship in that card game. I know you didn't want to hear about that."

"It would have been nice to hear that you were not in a ditch somewhere with your head bashed in, like Jade's husband."

"Oh, now I heard all about that! It's already all over the grapevine how Jade beat that poor boy to a pulp."

"Let's stay on the subject," I suggested. "I wish you would let me know when you're going to stay out late."

"Baby, I'm sorry. My bad. It won't happen no more. Things happen, and if anybody knows that, it's you. Look how many times you've had to cancel havin' lunch with me," he pouted.

"I know and I am sorry about that. But I will get over there, hopefully within the next few days."

As usual, if it wasn't one thing, it was another that kept me from visiting Pee Wee's work. Last Monday, just before lunchtime, a disgruntled debtor showed up at my office with a baseball bat. He was upset because we had sent a process server to his house with a notice that he was being sued for not paying an outstanding credit card bill that had been past due for eighteen months. Not only did we have to involve the police, but two people had to go to the hospital because of injuries they suffered during a scuffle with the individual.

The next day, Charlotte fell off the monkey bars at school, and I had to run over there to make sure she was all right. She was so upset that all she wanted to do was go home. So I had to take off the rest of the day and tend to her. Other more minor events kept derailing my plans, but Pee Wee took it all in stride. "Baby, don't worry about not makin' it over here to have lunch with me. I know how busy you get," he said.

I felt a bit slighted because he didn't seem to be as disappointed about it as I was. But I didn't complain. Now that he was in such a good mood, I didn't want to rock the boat. Not only was he paying me a lot of attention in the bedroom lately, he was even bringing me flowers and other gifts almost every day. On the third day in a row that I received flowers at work, one of the women who reported to me made an ominous comment. "When a woman receives flowers from her husband every day, three days in a row, it can only mean one of two things: either he ran into a hell of a sale on flowers or he's up to no good. . . ."

I had laughed off her comment, but I didn't forget about it.

Another week went by before I made it over to Pee Wee's barbershop and when I did, I was stunned speechless by what I saw and heard.

# CHAPTER 32

I had told Pee Wee that following Thursday morning that if I could get away, I'd meet him at his office for lunch. "If something comes up *again* and I can't make it, I will call you," I told him.

"Baby, if you can make it, that's fine. If you can't make it, don't worry about it," he told me.

It seemed like he was now trying to discourage me from coming to the shop to meet him for lunch. That didn't make any sense—unless he really *didn't* want to have lunch with me now. And if that was the case, I knew it had to be for a good reason. However, until he told me not to come to the shop at all, I still planned to make it over there as soon as I could. It also occurred to me that him telling me not to worry about coming to the shop now was his way of "pouting" because he was disappointed about all of the other times that I had planned to meet him and something had come up.

Well, a few things did come up that morning, but I decided to delay dealing with them anyway. At the rate I was going, if I canceled my plans with my husband every time something "came up," I'd never find time to have lunch with him again.

I didn't call to let him know that I was on my way, and the only reason for that was because I had to rush out of my office before I got trapped in another situation. One of my workers had already begun to head in my direction with a frantic look on his face a few minutes before I scrambled out of my office. "Whatever it is, it's going to have to wait until I get back!" I yelled over my shoulder as I ran for the exit. I didn't stop running until I had made it to my car in the employee parking lot. I jumped into my car and zoomed out onto the street like an ambulance in service.

I parked on the street about a block and a half from Pee Wee's shop. Then I took my time walking the rest of the way. I had already decided that I was going to enjoy a nice long lunch with my man. I had even decided that if I had a drink or two, I wouldn't go back to work. My alternate plan was to lure my husband to that motel down the street from his shop—if he could get away.

Nobody heard me when I opened the door and entered, even though Pee Wee, his two male employees, Lizzie, and a customer were present. They all had their backs to me. Lizzie was scraping the dead skin off of Ronnie Dawson's big ashy feet. Everybody else was standing in front of Lizzie, watching her work.

I looked around and was pleased at what I saw. I knew that Pee Wee had installed a big-screen TV, but I was surprised to see two computers on a table by the wall with a sign indicating Internet service was free to paying customers. There were little bowls of peanuts and pretzels here and there, and the most current editions of the leading magazines were on display on the same table with the computers. The walls had been painted a bright yellow. This was the first time the place had been painted in ten years!

I smiled, but I remained silent. Lizzie was the only one talking, and from what I could determine, she was in the middle of regaling her audience with something that must have been quite amusing. They were guffawing like hyenas. And Pee Wee was the one who was laughing the loudest and the hardest. I decided to join in on the fun. I held my breath and listened as Lizzie continued.

". . . and my mama and my stepdaddy walked into my bedroom while I was getting it on with my new vibrator. 'Girl, what's that between your legs?' my stepdaddy asked. 'This is as close as I am going to get to a husband, so you all better get used to it,' I told him. A few days later, I come home from work and there was my stepdaddy sitting in the living room watching TV, and I could see and hear my vibrator buzzing up a storm on the couch pillow next to him! 'What in the world are you doing?' I asked my stepdaddy. He told me, 'I'm watching the game with my son-in-law.'"

The laughter that followed was thunderous. I had to laugh myself. It went on for a full minute before Pee Wee finally turned around and saw me standing in front of the door. He looked at me like I was a relative that he didn't like. That look hurt like hell. It hurt so bad that I could barely contain myself. My heart began to sink so fast that it felt like it was racing with the rest of my body parts to see which one could hit the floor first. He didn't waste any time trying to clean up his mess. The annoyed look disappeared from Pee Wee's face within seconds. But it was too late.

"Baby! When—how long—what you doin' up in here?" he hollered, almost jumping out of his skin. He whirled around to look at Lizzie, and it was only then that I really paid attention to her appearance. She was dazzling. Like me, she had a few wrinkles on her face, but I couldn't see hers now. That's how flawless her makeup was. She had replaced her thick Coke bottle glasses with a pair of blue contact lenses. She wore a floor-length, light blue, sleeveless dress. It looked more like something you'd wear to the beach, not something you'd wear to work in the middle of March! All of that drab gray hair and that flat ponytail that had made me feel so sorry for her were gone. Her hair had been dyed jet black and cut into a cute, tapered style with spit curls on both of her cheeks and across her forehead. I thought I was looking at a real live version of Betty Boop.

"I thought we were having lunch today," I said in a small voice. Pee Wee was obviously uneasy. I couldn't understand why, but everybody else in the room seemed to be uneasy, too. Even old big-footed Ronnie Dawson.

"Uh, Lizzie, how much longer before you buff my toenails? If I don't get back home soon, *my* wife will be comin' up in here next," Ronnie mouthed. Then he laughed at his own joke. He was the only one laughing this time.

"Just a few more minutes," Lizzie told Ronnie. Then she turned to me and gave me a look I didn't like, or will ever forget. She was looking at me like she resented my presence! I couldn't understand why, because I had every right to be in my husband's workplace.

"Hello, Annette," she said dryly. Even though she said it with a smile, I could still see that my presence annoyed her. "That's a nice pink blouse you got on. Is it new?"

"It is," I muttered. "That story you just told about the vibrator, it was funny." And it was. It was so funny, I laughed again. But this time nobody else did.

You would have thought that everybody else had suddenly become mute. That's how quiet they were. They all just stared at me.

"So, where are we having lunch, honey?" I asked Pee Wee.

He looked at me with his lips quivering; then he blinked like he was trying to blink something out of his eye. "Lunch? You want to do that today?" He stopped blinking and then started rubbing his eye, mumbling. Then he started to fidget with some hair-cutting instruments in his hands, placing them on the same table between his main chair and Lizzie's work table. It was obvious to me that he was trying to stall for time and divert my attention. He was too late. All I could think about was what I had walked in on and what I was seeing now: a cozy little setup that my intrusion had interrupted.

"Pee Wee, what about them pizzas that me and Lizzie ordered to be delivered?" Bobby, the younger of the two young men who worked for him, asked, looking from Pee Wee to Lizzie and then to me. "We didn't know you was comin', Annette. But we ordered large pizzas, so if you want to stay, you welcome."

"Uh, I just had pizza for lunch yesterday," I lied, cracking a smile that was so harsh it almost cracked the sides of my face. I looked at my watch. "I can't stay long anyway." I looked directly at Pee Wee and he looked like he wanted to crawl into the hole he'd dug for himself. "Can I see you outside for a minute?" I didn't wait for him to respond. I exited immediately and I was pleased to see that he was right behind me.

"Um, what's up, baby?" he asked, fidgeting.

"I see that Lizzie has come out of her shell," I commented with my arms folded, standing in front of the shop like a guard.

"She sure has!" he said quickly, nervously sliding his hands in and out of his pants pockets. "That makeover helped."

"And that story about the vibrator—whew!" We both laughed.

"Yeah, that was a mess! Ha ha ha. Yes . . . Yes, it was a funny story! I . . . I wonder if it's true," Pee Wee stammered. Now he was scratching his head and looking around.

"Is something wrong, Pee Wee? You seem nervous and agitated. Did I walk in on something I wasn't supposed to see or hear?" I glanced sharply over my shoulder toward the shop, then back at Pee Wee. "I know Ronnie is one of your boys, but is he up to something with Lizzie?" I shook my head. "Never mind. I should know better. I mean, when men in their forties, like you and Ronnie, cheat on their wives, it's usually with a much younger woman, right?"

"That's right!" Pee Wee quickly agreed.

"Then I guess Ronnie is not fooling around with Lizzie, huh?" I said, wondering why I was going in this direction. But I couldn't ignore what I'd just seen and felt. Something that involved Lizzie was going on.

"Not that I know of," Pee Wee mumbled, shrugging and swallowing so hard his Adam's apple looked like it was going to pop out of his neck. "He just come by to get them nasty-ass feet of his done, that's all. You wouldn't believe how long he'd let his toenails grow! I thought I was lookin' at a set of bear claws before Lizzie started doin' her thing. Him and Lizzie, they hit it off right away. She's really come out of her shell."

"Yes, she has. I said that already." I sniffed. "Listen, I'd better get back to the office."

"What about that lunch? Where do you wanna go?" Pee Wee looked like he was about as interested in having lunch with me as I was having lunch with the strange man who had just walked past us.

I gasped. "What about the pizzas you guys ordered?"

"Well, me and you can still go off somewhere else. Especially since you was countin' on it." The more he talked, the less interested he looked in us having lunch.

"Pfft! Don't worry about that," I said, dismissing the thought with a dramatic wave of my hand. He immediately looked relieved. "I should have called to let you know that I was going to be able to make it today." I exhaled; then I brushed off the sleeve on his smock. "I'm glad to see that Lizzie is taking such good care of you," I said in a sugar-coated voice. I didn't know if it was what I said or the way I'd said it, but his reaction stunned me.

His eyes bulged from the sockets like they were trying to escape.

# CHAPTER 33

As soon as Pee Wee's eyes returned back to the way they normally looked, he asked in a small voice, "What do you mean by that?"

"You had been walking around with a long face for a while before she started working for you. Now you're not. And the place looks so nice inside now!" I motioned toward the building with my head. "And I know a woman's touch when I see it."

"Yeah, Lizzie was the one who convinced me to get them walls painted. Yellow is her favorite color."

"I see. Hmmm. You know, she's such a godsend that the least we can do is have her over for dinner one Sunday. Maybe now that she's come so far out of her shell, you can introduce her to one of your boys—if you haven't done that already. You must have at least one middle-aged friend who would appreciate a middle-aged lady friend." I chuckled, he gasped.

"Uh, she ain't all the way out of her shell just yet. But she's, uh, gettin' there!" He was stumbling over his words like a man who had just learned to speak our language. "Um, I . . . a couple of my boys done already dropped a few hints about takin' her over to the Red Rose for a few drinks."

"That's nice." I leaned forward and kissed Pee Wee on the lips. He was surprised at first, but when he responded he overdid it. His lips covered mine and started sucking with so much vigor—like a toilet plunger—that I thought he was trying to swallow me whole. That was an unpleasant thought, but this was an unpleasant kiss.

"Baby, I'm so glad to see you," he said. "You look so nice today!"

"Now, if you are going to behave like Romeo, we'd better get a room," I teased, pulling away. "You've never sucked on my face like that," I quipped. "Is everything all right?"

"Like I said, I'm just glad to see you, baby," he insisted. He slid a finger along the side of my face. "We'll finish this when I get home this evenin'," he said with a wink.

I refused to listen to a little voice in my head that was telling me something was wrong. It was the same voice that had tried to get my attention when Jade was harassing me. My mama had told me that there'd be days like this, and she'd also offered me another one of her off-the-wall comments: "*De-nial* ain't just a river in Africa; sometimes it's a woman's biggest excuse. . . ." Was I denying to myself that I was in denial?

After I got back to my car, I sat in it for a few minutes, looking toward the barbershop. Lizzie was peeping from the front window like a nosy neighbor.

I didn't even wait to get back to my office to call Rhoda. I was so stupefied I couldn't. I stopped at the first payphone I saw, which was directly across the street from Pee Wee's barbershop. My eyes were still on his front window as I dialed Rhoda's number. What I saw next made the hair on the back of my neck rise. Lizzie put her arm around Pee Wee's shoulder and they walked toward the back of the shop. My mind was boiling like water for chocolate. "Rhoda, can you meet me at the little salad bar down the street from your house for a late lunch?" I asked as soon as she answered.

"Now?"

"Now," I insisted.

Rhoda was one of the most flawed people I knew, but she was also the only person I knew whom I could always count on when I had a potential crisis on my hands. In this case, I wasn't sure what I was facing: a crisis or an innocent misunderstanding. She was at the salad bar munching on some lettuce, when I got there. The lunch crowd had already left, so other than an elderly man in a booth by the counter, she and I were the only other customers. This was one of our favorite neighborhood lunch spots, and since we almost always ordered the same thing, she had ordered a plain green salad and a large glass of iced tea for me and for herself.

"What's up? You sounded stressed," she chirped, giving me a curious look as I eased down into the seat across from her.

"Have you seen Lizzie lately? She looks real nice," I said, watching Rhoda's face carefully. I could tell from the wan look she gave me that she had seen Lizzie.

She nodded. "I saw her day before yesterday at the Grab and Go. She looked nice and chic. We can't refer to her as a sow's ear anymore, can we?"

"I guess not. She is stunning now." I cleared my throat and shifted my butt around in my seat. I wasn't sure how to say what I wanted to say next, so I just let the words roll out of my mouth like they had a life of their own. "Does a vibrator count?" I asked, spearing some lettuce with the plastic fork that had come with my salad.

Rhoda gave me a stunned look before she choked on some lettuce. She had to drink some tea and cough a few times to clear her throat. Her big eyes were full of water and threatening to turn red. "Excuse me?"

"Is it considered sex when a woman uses a vibrator? Would that constitute her having a sex life?"

"Gee, I don't know," she told me, her head cocked to the side. I could imagine the wheels turning and the question marks dancing around in her head.

"If you ask me, when a woman pleasures herself with a vibrator, she's not a virgin," I stated.

"Hmmm. You've got a point there. I mean, nobody ever said a woman had to get laid in the traditional sense to be considered, uh, laid." Rhoda paused and furrowed both brows. She shook her head and spread her arms, hands up, both palms facing me. "Where is this conversation comin' from? And where is it goin'?" There was now an amused look on her face and I could understand why. What I'd just said sounded not only strange, but funny.

"If a woman doesn't date, but she uses a vibrator, does that still count?" I asked again, cringing this time.

"Count as what?"

"Does it mean that she's no longer a virgin; that she's got a sex life. That's all I want to know."

"Hell, I don't know. I sit around thinkin' about a lot of things from time to time, but that's not one of them. Why do you ask?" I could tell by the way Rhoda's lips were quivering, that she was trying not to laugh. But I was dead serious.

She stared at me with her mouth hanging open as I told her about the "party" that I'd walked in on at Pee Wee's barbershop. As soon as I stopped talking, she did laugh. "Let me tell you something, girl, Lizzie is not as innocent as you think. Trust me. I've been hearin' things."

My denial had already bitten me on the ass and I was still doing more "looking the other way" than all of the long-suffering Kennedy wives put together. "Rhoda, I don't want to hear a lot of gossip," I said quickly. "I still want to give Lizzie the benefit of the doubt. If she says she doesn't fool around with men, that's her business. And why should we care?"

"Honey, you brought it up!" Rhoda reminded me with a snicker.

"When I interviewed Lizzie, she gave me the impression that she has not had much experience in the romance department," I said dryly. "And even though she talked about finding a soul mate, I don't think she's that interested in men."

"That is so hard to believe," Rhoda snapped, putting so much emphasis on her words it scared me. "Even Mott, Scary Mary's severely retarded daughter, has been with a man. And I do mean fucked inside out. It happened at the same asylum where Mott is, and the dude is just as retarded as Mott is, so they didn't really know what they were doin'. They were just imitatin' some of the things that Mott had seen goin' on during Scary Mary's business hours. And Mott's not half as attractive as Lizzie. How do you know for sure that Lizzie's never been with a man? That's so hard to believe. After all, the woman is pushing fifty, not fifteen."

I shrugged. "I don't know for sure if Lizzie's *never* been with a man. And like I just said, her sex life is her business. But since we're on the subject, maybe she'll meet some new friends now and have more of a social life. Poor thing." I sighed.

"Now that she's gussied herself up, she's goin' to be gettin' a lot of attention. She can only fight the men off for so long." The mysterious look on Rhoda's face told me there was something behind her last statement.

"Is there something going on that I should know about?" I didn't like the way that Rhoda was staring off into space, not even blinking.

She looked me straight in the eye and gave me a pitiful look. "So what do you want me to tell you?"

"I can tell you what I don't want you to tell me, and that's some gossip. I am glad that Lizzie is coming out of her shell. If people are going to start gossiping about her just because she's looking good now, I can imagine some of the shit they said about me when I got myself made over."

"Well, what they were sayin' about you was true."

"What the hell are you talking about? Did somebody say something about me and Louis?"

"Not exactly. I mean, they didn't know about Louis, but there was some talk about you sneakin' around a lot."

My jaw dropped and my eyes got wide. "How come you didn't tell me people were talking about me behind my back?" I whined.

"You know how the people in this town are. They have *always* talked about you behind your back. And me and every other soul, too, for that matter. Get real. But as far as I know, none of the gossips knew about you and Louis."

"Scary Mary knew," I revealed.

"Phtt! That old battle-ax knows everything. I am sure she knows about me and Bully, too; but she knows when to keep her mouth shut."

I sighed and clucked. Rhoda sighed and clucked even louder. We sounded like a couple of old hens. "Are you goin' to keep your eye on Lizzie, or ask her what she's up to?"

I gasped and gave Rhoda a stunned look. I couldn't remember the last time she'd asked me such a ridiculous question. "Of course I'm *not* going to ask her that. Why would I?"

"You don't drag me to lunch at the spur of the moment unless you have a real concern."

"Well, I don't have a real concern yet. I just . . . I don't know what to think. After what I heard her say today, I don't know what to think about her, or anything else that's going on at my husband's barbershop."

"You want some advice?" Rhoda said, sounding more serious than she'd sounded in a long time. She didn't even wait for me to answer. "Keep your eyes open and on *everybody*," she advised.

The next morning, Pee Wee and Lizzie entered my kitchen while I was gobbling up Krispy Kreme donuts, and told me that they were in love and would be moving into an apartment together.

# CHAPTER 34

It seemed like on the days that something really bad happened to me, that day immediately shot into the category of doom in my mind. There were now too many doomsdays for me to remember, or forget. And every time a new one entered my zone, it reminded me of some of the ones from my past.

Mr. Boatwright, an oversexed, elderly old friend of the family, had been such a big bad wolf in sheep's clothing that he held a position of virtue as high as that of a saint until the day he died. He had started raping me when I was just seven years old.

As horrific as that whole episode had been, I couldn't remember the exact month or day that it started. I couldn't remember the exact day and month that Daddy left me and my mother either. As a matter of fact, the only day that a milestone event occurred in my life that I remembered down to the last detail was the day that Rhoda smothered old Mr. Boatwright to death—four days after the assassination of Dr. Martin Luther King Jr.

Dr. King's murder was the only way I was able to remember Rhoda's crime so well. Now I had another black day to add to the calendar in my mind: today. Because until the day I die, it would be known as the day that my husband left me for another woman. The fact that the other woman was a friend made it even more excruciating. I knew that no matter what happened next, this was going to be one of the most difficult and unbearable days on the calendar for me to get through in the years to come. And it would remain that way even if Pee Wee and I got back together.

But from what that hound from hell had told me, and the way he had thrown his affair and his whore up in my face in my own house, a reconciliation didn't even sound like a remote possibility. And I was so angry and disgusted with him, I wasn't sure that I wanted him back anyway!

The sun had come out and it looked like it was going to be a nice day after all. But nothing was going to make it a nice day for me. I felt like I had been knocked down and then run over by a tractor.

In addition to me thinking about all of the bleak days that I'd endured, I also thought about some of the other truly bad situations I'd faced that didn't just fall on any one day in particular. Like some of the people who had taken advantage of me and Muh'Dear after Daddy had run off. One woman, who had let us sleep in her barn because we had run out of money, made Muh'Dear clean her house and the houses of all her friends for free. Me, well, she'd made me be her personal slave. I had to haul water to and from her spring, feed her chickens, and do a variety of chores around her house that nobody in their right mind would make a child do. I thought about all of the nasty kids in school who had called me names and punched me for no reason at all. I even thought about the racism I'd encountered in Erie, Pennsylvania, when I tried to rent a motel room there almost thirty years ago. I had survived all of that shit, so I knew that I could probably survive anything. But that didn't stop me from being mad now. I didn't know how this drama was going to play out. However, there was one thing I knew for sure. And that was, no matter what happened or how this ended, I would never forgive Elizabeth Stovall.

That bitch!

I could still smell her perfume, Trésor, one of my favorites. I knew right then and there that I would never wear that fragrance again. Now it smelled like brimstone. Rubbing my nose didn't help; it only made it worse.

*   *   *

It had been just a few minutes since Pee Wee and Lizzie left my house together with his luggage. I stood in my driveway watching his car until it turned the corner. I didn't know why some of my neighbors were still watching me. All of the excitement was over— unless Pee Wee and Lizzie came back.

I turned to go back to my kitchen, dragging my feet like a dying mule. As soon as I made it back inside, I immediately dialed Rhoda's number. I knew she would stick by me, and console me, until this mess was resolved. She answered on the second ring.

"I need to talk to you," I blurted. I stood looking out of the window above my sink.

"Is somethin' wrong?" she asked, sounding more like a teenager than a woman in her mid-forties.

"Oh, hell yeah! Something is definitely wrong," I choked.

"Hmmm. Well, I hope it's not too bad. I've only got half a bottle of scotch in the house."

"Pee Wee is having an affair with Little Leg Lizzie."

"Excuse me?"

"My husband is having an affair *with that bitch I hired to work for him*! He just left the house with her, and some of his things. They . . . they are moving into an apartment together." I had to pause to catch my breath; it felt like it was trying to desert me, too. "Rhoda, it was awful. They had the nerve, the unmitigated gall to come into my house to tell me that they are in love and want to live together! Can you fucking believe that shit? What kind of woman would do that to her friend?" I exhaled and rubbed my chest. "I *knew* something was up when I went into that barbershop yesterday. But I refused to believe it was something this bad!"

Rhoda was taking too long to respond. I knew that she was going to take this hard. She was as much Pee Wee's friend as she was mine.

"Rhoda, I know you are upset. But I need for you to be strong for me," I sobbed. I released a few tears, wiping them away with the back of my hand. "Can you believe that man? He's been having an affair for I don't know how long with that two-faced, backstabbing woman—and now he only wants to be with her!" I couldn't even hear Rhoda breathing on the other end.

"I already knew," she finally said.

"Did you think—*you already knew?* What the hell do you mean by that?"

"I already knew that Pee Wee was havin' an affair with Lizzie and that he was goin' to leave you for her. But . . . I . . . see you and—honey, I saw it comin' a long time ago!"

It had been hard for me to share this painful information with Rhoda. But it was even harder for me to remain conscious after she told me she already knew! My best friend already knew that my husband was having an affair with another woman and didn't tell me! The world had gone to hell in an Easter basket and was taking me along with it.

I couldn't think straight. It felt like the parts of my brain were meandering around in my head, trying to figure out what thought to process next. Then it seemed like every thought in my head had merged into one. And that was unbearable. My head was aching all over. I had to be in the middle of a nightmare. But since I was wide awake, leaning against the sink to keep from falling, I knew this was not a nightmare.

"Rhoda, what the hell do you mean? Please tell me you are joking. Please tell me that you didn't know about Pee Wee and Lizzie." Her silence told me all I needed to know. "Then it's true? You knew about this already? You're not kidding?"

"Yes, I knew," she answered. She blew out some air that seemed to chase the words out of her mouth like she couldn't get rid of them fast enough.

# CHAPTER 35

"Rhoda, what kind of friend are you not to tell me?"

"Calm down, Annette—"

"Calm down my pussy! My husband just left me for another woman! And not just any woman! This is a woman that I hand-picked and then practically served my husband to her on a silver platter! This is a woman who I thought was a friend! How in the hell am I supposed to be calm after some shit like that?" I was seething. There were no words that could describe the pain I was in. It seemed like every cell in my body was on fire.

"Annette, we can't address this as long as you're behavin' like a fishwife. Let's discuss this calmly and rationally."

"When did you find out?" I didn't want to admit to Rhoda that I'd seen a few red flags myself. It was bad enough that I'd ignored the few red flags along the way during that fiasco with Jade. This was much worse. Despite the red flags each time that I even *thought* that Pee Wee was up to no good, I dismissed it. And that was because I had already accused him of fooling around several times before and I had been wrong.

"Annette, *everybody* knows," Rhoda said gently. "It sounds like you are the only one who didn't know."

I couldn't believe my ears. I thought I'd heard wrong. "What did you say?" I rasped. "I know that you didn't say what it sounded like you just said. *Everybody knows about my husband having an affair with Lizzie?*"

"Uh-huh. Scary Mary held me hostage at the Grab and Go a couple of nights ago and asked me how long it was going to be before you saw what everybody else sees. Yes, everybody knows about it. That's all they've been yip yappin' about at Claudette's beauty parlor these days . . . and at the bowlin' alley . . . and at the nail shop that I go to on State Street . . . and at church . . ."

"Apparently not *everybody*. I sure as hell didn't know!" I screamed, pounding the wall with my fist.

"I had been a little suspicious for a while, but I had no proof. I'd even been hearin' things from those heifers who work the cash registers at the Grab and Go checkout. And . . ." Rhoda paused and groaned. "And Otis even put a few bugs in my ear. It devastated him. You know how emotional my husband can get when it comes to relationships. He's Jamaican to the bone. You know how men tell each other everything. I guess Pee Wee took him aside one day and, you know, got off into that home-boy talkin' shit."

If a semitruck had rolled over me, I couldn't have felt any worse. Everything on me, from my eyes on down, felt like it was being poked with daggers. "Were you ever going to tell me? If I hadn't brought it up today, how long were you going to let me be the fool in the dark?" I asked, rubbing my forehead, then my cheek. My tongue was fighting with my bridgework to see which one could make it down my throat first. I swallowed some air, but it went down the wrong windpipe so I started choking and coughing.

"Are you all right?" Rhoda asked. "I am really beginnin' to worry about you, girl."

"I'm fine," I managed. "Keep talking. Answer what I just asked you." I pounded my chest with my fist.

"Now, you know me. I got your back now and I've always had your back. But you know Pee Wee was my best friend way before I met you. I didn't want to get in the middle of this mess by tellin' you before he made his move."

"What the hell does that mean?" I wailed.

"I didn't know he was goin' to up and leave you for Lizzie. I just thought he was gettin' him some pussy on the side. By the way, she was not really a virgin. She told him about a thing with some Russian guy that picked her up after bingo one night about ten years ago."

"I don't give a damn if Lizzie fucked the Pied Piper! She's fucking my husband now—and has been for God knows how long—and you knew about it and didn't tell me. That's what I care about!"

"Annette, you and my husband are very close. You are probably the closest female friend he has. At least in America. You know about me and Bully. You've known for years. Have you felt like it was your obligation to tell Otis?"

"You are getting way off the subject—"

"Just answer the question please. You know about me and Bully, but you don't feel it's your business to tell my husband, right?"

"So this is about your loyalty to your boy? Is that your excuse for not telling me?"

"Not exactly. Well, yes and no. But there is more to it than that." Rhoda got suspiciously quiet. "A couple of weeks ago, I spent an afternoon at the Do Drop Inn with Bully. He was goin' back to London the next day. With Jade and Vernie in the house, we can't, you know, do as much as we normally do. Not in the house, I mean. See, we, uh, get kind of loud when we get carried away. Anyway, while we were still in the motel office checkin' in, Pee Wee and Lizzie strolled in the door, arm in arm."

"Well do say!" I boomed.

If the Do Drop Inn burned to the ground, or if somebody's disgruntled mate tossed a bomb in the window and blew it to kingdom come tomorrow, it wouldn't be soon enough for me. That was one place that had become such a den of iniquity—of Biblical proportions—to me, that I would *never* set foot in it again.

"That evenin' Pee Wee called me up and told me to meet him at the Red Rose for a drink. As soon as I got there, he started askin' me about me and Bully. Under the circumstances, I had to come clean. I love my husband and I don't care how good Bully makes me feel, I am not leavin' my husband for him, or any other man. My husband is a happy man, and I want him to stay that way."

"Let me get this straight. You couldn't tell on Pee Wee because you didn't want him to tell on you and Bully. Is that the case?"

"I guess it is." Rhoda got silent again. "Listen, I want you to know that I already told Pee Wee not to ever bring that woman to my house, or even attempt to make her think that I will accept her. So you don't have to worry about her poppin' up at any of our private parties or our backyard cookouts. And in knowing that, I doubt if Pee Wee will be partyin' much with us anymore either."

"I won't miss his company," I spat.

"And if it'll make you feel any better, I was goin' to tell you everything anyway whether he did or not . . . eventually."

"Oh, really? And when were you eventually going to tell me?" I wailed.

"Pee Wee called me last night and told me about you comin' to the shop to meet him for lunch. He said he talked it over with Lizzie, and they both agreed that you were too good of a woman for him to be holdin' you back. You need to be with a man who appreciates a good woman like you."

# CHAPTER 36

The last thing I wanted to hear was somebody telling me again what a good woman I was. Good women didn't lose their husbands, because they were too smart and intuitive! They were savvy enough *not* to be so trusting that they would befriend a woman who probably had a plan from the very beginning. And that plan included using me and my naïvete to get what she wanted. Being a good woman was what got me into that mess with Jade! If this was what it meant to be a good woman, I was through with this "good" shit, and that was one thing that I was going to make known, loud and clear.

"Shut the hell up, Rhoda! I don't want to hear all of that shit anymore!"

One thing that was digging a hole in my brain was the fact that I didn't know which one had made the first move and all within a month. I knew Pee Wee, so I didn't believe that he was the one who had initiated this nasty business! Even if Lizzie had been the initiator, Pee Wee had fallen feetfirst into her trap, like a fly caught in a spider's web. The bottom line was, Pee Wee was no longer the man I used to know. But I had to wonder if I ever really knew him in the first place. I couldn't read his mind, so I never really knew what he was thinking until he told me. I had based all of my beliefs on his actions and what he'd said. Just like I had done with that

Louis Baines and he'd screwed me royally, in more ways than one. I had promised myself that I wasn't going to be the same fool twice. Well, the joke was on me because Pee Wee and Lizzie had conspired to play me in the worst possible way.

"Rhoda, do you think that hearing this riffraff about him letting me go so I could be with a man who appreciates me is making me feel any better?" I growled. "I do not want to hear any more shit like that from you!"

"No, but I—"

"Let me ask you again! When were you going to tell me?"

"That's what I'm tryin' to tell you! If you'd just let me finish." Rhoda snorted so loud it sounded like she was in my kitchen with me. "I told him last night that if he didn't tell you by today, I would. And I meant it. I didn't care if he blabbed to Otis about me and Bully. One thing I know for sure is that no matter what I do, my husband will never leave me. He'd be pissed off, but he tells me all the time he wouldn't leave me to go to heaven."

"Well, aren't you the lucky one. It's a damn shame all women are not as lucky as you!" I sneered. "Then what you just said about not telling on Pee Wee because he'd tell on you doesn't make any sense."

"Pee Wee begged me not to tell. He said it was his place to tell you, not mine. But like I said, I told him that if he didn't tell you today, I was goin' to. He was all right with that. So now you know."

"You said everybody else knows."

"Scary Mary knew from the get-go. She told me that she'd called you one night and tried to tell you, but that you didn't want to listen. She said she'd even let them use one of her rooms the first time they . . . got together. And before you go off on me, she just told me that last night."

"This is going to kill my mama and daddy when they find out," I managed.

"They already know," Rhoda reported. "I'm surprised you haven't heard from them yet."

"What?"

"Scary Mary told me that she told them last night. The man that Pee Wee and Lizzie are rentin' the apartment from is one of Scary

Mary's tricks. He owns that building over on Webb Street next to the brickyard."

"I—don't you tell me that my daughter already knows about this, too!"

"Not that I know of. Listen, I don't think you should go to work today. I can tell that you are a mess. Let me pick you up and we'll drive up to Cleveland, rent a room, go out to dinner, and get drunk." Rhoda sucked on her teeth. "I need to get out of this house anyway. I had to straighten out another mess between Jade and Vernie last night."

Jade and Vernie were the last two people in the universe that I wanted to discuss. I didn't even comment on what Rhoda had just said about them.

"After Pee Wee forgave me for sleeping with Louis, I thought that I didn't have to ever worry about losing him. So I never thought he would end up leaving me anyway!" I shouted, squeezing the telephone so hard my hand tingled. "And I know this is his way of getting back at me for sleeping with Louis last year. I just know it!"

"Do you think he really is in love with Little Leg Lizzie? Or do you think she's just the convenient excuse he needed to get back at you for Louis?"

"I . . . I don't know what to think right now!"

I blew out some stale air and glanced around the kitchen. Everything seemed surreal. It was like I was watching this tragedy unfold on a screen, because it didn't seem like it was happening. At least not to me! Especially since I'd been so good since I ended my affair with Louis. I had not even glanced at another man sideways since! I had bent over backward to keep Pee Wee happy. What else could I have done?

"I can tell you one thing, I will drag him through so much courtroom mud he will be farting mud pies by the time I'm done!" I declared.

"And what good would that do? Don't you think it's goin' to be ugly enough? Makin' it uglier will affect Charlotte more than it will you."

"You let me worry about my child!"

"Just don't do anything stupid!"

"Like what? It sounds like I've already done enough stupid shit! Damn that Louis Baines!"

"Girl, don't put all of the blame on Louis Baines. You don't know if that's the reason Pee Wee lost his mind."

"Pee Wee is having an affair because I had one. That's the only thing that makes any sense! I just can't believe that he'd choose Lizzie over me. She—she . . . you know. She's an old maid."

"Annette, you can sit there and mean-mouth the other woman all you want to, and it is not goin' to make a difference. My husband cheated on me with a bitch who looked like James Brown on a bad hair day. I wouldn't have felt any worse if he'd screwed Halle Berry. You know how men are. To them, tail is tail. Pee Wee is in love with another woman. If you think he is worth it, fight for him. Don't give up all you've invested."

"Rhoda, let's try to keep this in its proper perspective," I suggested.

"Fuck that shit!" Rhoda howled. "You want to know what the real proper perspective is?" She didn't bother to wait long enough for me to respond. "I'll tell you! Sister, you need to be a *sister* and go whup that bitch's ass!"

"I have never fought another woman over a man," I muttered, already wondering what I was going to say when Rhoda heard from one of my neighbors that I'd gotten violent before Pee Wee and Lizzie left my driveway. For the time being, I wanted her to think that I was still above violence. "And I'd feel kind of foolish starting that now at my age. Besides, I don't want to end up getting arrested and spending a few nights in jail."

"Well, it would be worth it, goddammit!"

"That won't change anything. It'd only make matters worse." I rubbed my neck like I was trying to reduce the lump in my throat. All the rubbing did was make my neck hurt even more. "If he comes back, he'll come back on his own. But I can tell you one thing, since he thinks I'd make some man such a good woman, I just might not be available if he decides to come back. Fuck him!"

"I still think I should take you out for a drink," Rhoda insisted.

"Rhoda, I have to be here when my child gets home from school. This is something she should hear from me. And I need to face my mama and daddy, and get that part of it over. Not to mention Scary

Mary—speak of the devil! She just parked in front of my house!" I moved a few feet away from the window.

"Call me after she leaves," Rhoda said sharply.

"And she's not alone! Muh'Dear and Daddy are with her. Lord, they're rushing across my yard like soldiers going to the Battle of Jericho!" I cringed.

"Oh shit! By the time they get through with you, you'll be in so many pieces, I'll have to scoop you up with a shovel."

I hung up the telephone, but I didn't move from my spot. My legs were so numb I couldn't move right away anyhow.

# CHAPTER 37

It was so quiet it was scary. You would have thought that I was the last person left alive on my block. But it didn't stay quiet for long. A few minutes later, my house became like a scene out of some horror movie. The last three individuals I wanted to see invaded my space like those sinister pods did in the old movie *Invasion of the Body Snatchers*. I was the body that was about to be violated.

They didn't even bother to knock. And I didn't even hear my front door open, but my parents and Scary Mary made their presence known immediately. Even with the thick carpets in my living room, I could hear them galloping across the floor like a herd of buffalo.

I was surprised and amazed that people their ages could move so fast through my house without running into a wall or two, or knocking over a piece of furniture.

As soon as my mother entered the kitchen, she screamed: "Annette, what did you do to that man to make him run off with a white woman! Addie Powell called me up a little while ago and told me that they moved into her buildin' this mornin'!"

I just stood there in the middle of the floor, blinking.

"And an ugly white woman at that!" Scary Mary added, shaking her gnarled fist at me.

"I told y'all that Pee Wee was cookin' up somethin' with that woman when I seen 'em all cozy and happy comin' out of the Red Rose the other night," Daddy tossed his words into the rant like a rock, looking nervous and uncertain at the same time.

"I see that news still travels fast around here," I began. "Would anybody like something to drink? I can make some iced tea." I was not surprised that they all ignored my offer.

I knew that there was no way I was going to get out of discussing my situation with this self-appointed committee. I let out a loud breath and twisted my face up the way that I thought they expected a woman in my position to do. I didn't start speaking until I was reasonably sure that I looked mean and scorned enough to suit them.

"You look like hell, baby," Muh'Dear said, rubbing my back. "Why don't you pack a bag and come stay with me and Frank for a few weeks."

I whirled around to face her. "I am not about to leave my house," I shouted.

"You damn right you ain't leavin' *your* house! If you did, that low-down funky black dog would move that woman up in here before you could say Jack Robinson," Scary Mary insisted.

"I don't think so. He's not *that* crazy," I protested. I was not trying to defend Pee Wee, that was for sure! But I didn't want my parents or anybody else to think that he would do something as bold as moving that woman into my house.

"Honey child, don't let this kill you. You can let it all out while we here to pick you up off the floor. Come on now . . . let it all out," Scary Mary told me, giving me a pitiful look. She hobbled over and stood next to Muh'Dear; then she started rubbing my back, too.

It took all of my strength for me to remain calm. But the truth of the matter was, I was falling apart inside. My guts felt like they were coiled up like a bedspring. And I knew that once I was alone, I probably would hit the floor.

"Speak, baby," Daddy urged.

I sniffed and they misinterpreted that. Muh'Dear whipped a starched handkerchief out of her bamboo purse and started blotting my nose.

"I'm all right," I told her, pushing her hand away. I looked from one concerned face to another. From the looks on those faces, you would have thought that they were looking at my corpse. "What I want to know is, why nobody told me until now?" I asked calmly. "I heard you let them use a room in your house," I said, looking directly at Scary Mary.

"Girl, you know I'm a businesswoman first. I need to get paid. I'd rent a room to the devil," the old madam said, giving me a stern look. Then she softened and wrapped her arm around my shoulder. "But, baby, I did try to tell you there was a fox in the hen house. You didn't want to listen to me when I called you up that night."

"Sit down before you fall down," Muh'Dear suggested, attempting to guide me to a chair at the table. Daddy had already fished a bottle of beer out of my refrigerator and dropped into a chair at the kitchen table.

"I don't want to sit down," I insisted, pushing her hand away. "I need to figure out what I'm going to do."

"Well, the first thing you need to do is whup that strumpet's ass," Muh'Dear roared. "Had I got my hands on that bitch that Frank run off with, I'd probably just be comin' up for parole."

"Me, too! Seven of my eight husbands cheated on me!" Scary Mary reported. "And the eighth one cheated on his wife with *me!*"

"Now, Gussie Mae, you be nice. Don't you be bringin' up the past," Daddy said in a low voice, looking at my mother. From the strained look on his face, I could tell that he was not where he wanted to be. I couldn't imagine how uncomfortable it was for him to be in the presence of three scorned women. "Uh, you want me to go and talk some sense into Pee Wee's head? He might listen to another man."

"And what good would that do?" Scary Mary boomed, glaring at my daddy like he had just slapped her face. "You just as triflin' as he is! With your white woman–lovin' self!"

"Lizzie ain't all white," he reminded. "I seen that tar baby daddy of hers."

"You all can stay here if you want, but I'm going to work," I said evenly. I snatched the coffee cup that I'd been drinking from off the table and set it in the sink. Then I grabbed the damp dishrag and wiped the counter.

"One of my best clients is that divorce lawyer over on Mahoning Street. Max Rosenberg. Pee Wee will be as naked as a jaybird by the time that smart-ass Jew gets through with his black ass." Scary Mary struck the front of my stove with her cane. "Let me get on that phone so I can call him up right now." Scary Mary headed toward the phone on the wall, but I blocked her way.

"I can take care of my own business, thank you," I insisted. "I know what I need to do."

"Is that right? Well, whatever it is, you better do it and you better do it quick!" Muh'Dear warned. "You too good of a woman for Pee Wee to be runnin' off like he done! If he smart, he'll bring his happy ass on back home before another man snatches you up."

The only reason my visitors left was because they thought I was about to leave for work. But I didn't go to work that day. I called in sick.

And I was.

I crawled into my bed, buried my face in my pillow, and cried and babbled like a baby. I remained that way off and on all day. Rhoda called every hour to check on me. She volunteered to pick my daughter up from school. I agreed to that, but I told her to take her to my parents' house. I needed some time alone, and I didn't want my daughter to see my swollen face and red eyes.

"Just make sure Daddy and Muh'Dear don't tell her about her daddy. I need to be the one to do that," I told Rhoda.

But I was too late. As soon as Rhoda dropped Charlotte off at my parents' house, Charlotte called me up herself. "Mama, why did Daddy leave you for Little Leg Lizzie? What did you do to him?" she asked.

"I didn't do anything to him."

"Then why did he leave?"

I sighed. "I don't know, Charlotte. I honestly don't know." And I didn't. I didn't know if he had left because he was still in pain over my affair and was trying to pay me back, or if he'd found Lizzie too hard to resist.

"Mama, it's going to be all right," my daughter told me, sounding more mature than she had ever sounded before in her life.

"I know," I managed. I was glad to see that Charlotte was not taking this nightmare as hard as I was.

As soon as I got off the telephone with her, I crawled back into my bed and stayed there for the next two days.

# CHAPTER 38

"Annette, you get your ass up out of that bed. You are givin' black women a bad name! You know we *real* sisters don't let a little thing like a man drag us down. You need to eat, and you need to pull yourself together." Rhoda had let herself into my house the following Sunday evening. I had not seen or heard from Pee Wee since he'd left with Lizzie.

She opened the curtains in my bedroom, then marched over to my bed and snatched off the covers. "You're not the first woman to lose her husband, and you won't be the last."

The radio on my nightstand was on to a news program, reporting mostly bad news, such as rapper Biggie Smalls getting shot and killed in L.A. last night. I had enough bad news of my own to deal with right now so I turned off the radio.

"Poor Biggie," Rhoda sniffed, shaking her head. "I hope he didn't get killed over a woman. No woman, or man, is worth gettin' killed over, or goin' crazy over like you seem to be doin'."

"Rhoda, I'm fine. I'd never go crazy over a man. You don't have to treat me like a baby," I moaned, struggling to sit up in my bed. My head was spinning like a top, my insides were dancing around in my stomach, and other parts on my body felt like they had been run over by a train. My poor legs felt like a steamroller had flattened them. Even the soles of my feet were in pain. They felt like I'd stomped out a bonfire with my bare feet.

For a moment, I couldn't remember what I had done the night before. But a glimpse at my nightstand told me at least one thing: I'd drunk until I passed out. A wine bottle, a vodka bottle, and two beer bottles sat on that nightstand—all were empty. I didn't see any glasses, so I must have drunk straight out of the bottles.

"Well, stop actin' like a baby if you don't want me to treat you like one," she snapped. She leaned forward and sniffed a few times. "And from the way you smell, you need a long, hot bath. Eww! Get up!" Rhoda clapped her hands together, looking at me with the same stern expression that she used when she was chastising that unruly Jade or those preschool kids she took care of at her daycare center.

"I feel like shit," I managed.

"And you look like shit, too. I am not goin' to let you ruin yourself because of that man. He's gone, and the best thing that you can do is get over it."

I shot Rhoda a hot look; then I offered her some choice words. "That's easy for you to say! He wasn't the man you loved. He wasn't your husband! He left me for another woman, and it's not going to be that easy for me to 'get over it,' and you should know better, Rhoda."

"I'm sorry. I'm out of line. It's just that I don't want to sit back and watch you go down the tubes. You're a strong woman, Annette. You've survived all kinds of shit. You can survive this, too."

"I know I've survived all kinds of shit, Rhoda," I said in a gentle voice, rising off the bed. I didn't realize I was naked until I looked down at myself. I plopped back down on the bed and covered myself with two pillows. Rhoda didn't even react to the fact that I was naked. She still had the same pitiful look on her face that had been there when she first stormed my room. "But this just might be the one thing that I can't survive," I told her, my voice cracking. "I never thought he'd do something like this to me. I thought he loved me."

"I'm sure he still does love you. But there is more to it than that. Men do some of the craziest shit for the craziest reasons. Maybe he just needs some time away from you. This could be his midlife crisis. After all, we've been through ours. His was just a longer time coming." Rhoda gave me a hopeful look.

"What the hell are you talking about? When did you or I go through a midlife crisis?" I asked, sitting up so straight one of the pillows slid to the floor.

"That thing you did last year with Louis was probably because of your midlife crisis." Rhoda blinked and leaned forward like she was waiting for me to respond. But the only thing that I could do was blink myself. "And me, well, I've been in a midlife crisis since I had Jade. How else can I justify my ongoin' affair with my husband's best friend?"

"Maybe you really love Bully," I said, knowing that I didn't care one way or the other about Rhoda and her lover. But talking about them eased my pain a little. No matter what else I thought about or said, what Pee Wee had done to me was at the front of my mind.

"I should go over there and shoot the shit out of both of those motherfuckers!" I roared. I hated the fact that violence kept entering my mind. I still considered myself to be a nonviolent person. However, it made me feel somewhat better knowing that the few times I had gotten violent, I had been adequately provoked. I pounded the mattress with my fist and stomped my foot on the floor.

"But you're not goin' to shoot anybody. At least not today. Now, you get dressed and come on downstairs so we can talk about this."

Rhoda waited downstairs while I took the first bath I'd taken since Pee Wee's departure. I was glad that my mother had insisted on keeping my daughter with her for a few days. But I had declined her offer for me to move in with her for a while, too.

"I just made a fresh pot of coffee," Rhoda said as I joined her in my kitchen. I had not been in the kitchen since that morning Pee Wee and Lizzie had infected it with the news of their affair. But I had left dishes in the sink, and a Krispy Kreme box with a few donuts in it and a half-empty coffee cup on the table. The rolling pin that I had bounced off Lizzie's face was still on the counter. Rhoda had washed my dishes and put everything else back in its place.

"Thanks," I muttered, plopping down with a groan into a seat at the table directly across from Rhoda. Most of the swelling around my eyes had gone down. I had cried so much that they had been almost swollen shut. And my hand had stopped throbbing from that monster punch I'd delivered to the side of Pee Wee's face. I looked at the floor and was glad to see that Rhoda had removed the tooth that I'd knocked out of his mouth.

"What did you hit him with?" she asked with an amused look on her face.

I didn't even bother to lie or act like I didn't know what she was talking about. "Just my fist," I admitted. "And I let that bitch have it with my rolling pin," I said proudly through clenched teeth, looking around the room. "They were both lucky I didn't have a few bricks lying around." The tip of my nose was itching so I rubbed it before I drank a few sips of the strong coffee Rhoda had made.

"Atta girl!" Rhoda said, giving me a vigorous black power salute with her raised fist.

"You know I am not the kind of woman to be fighting," I said, clearing my throat. "It wasn't worth it anyway."

"But you are glad you did it, right?"

I nodded. "I guess. I feel a little bit better knowing that I let them know just how pissed off I was." I exhaled a deep breath. "I need to get out of this house soon. It feels like these walls are closing in on me. That dog lied to me. He was supposed to come get the rest of his things and talk to me about what we are going to do next. And he was supposed to discuss this with his daughter."

"What do you want to do next? Are you goin' to fight to get him back?"

I gave Rhoda an incredulous look. "Hell no! I don't know what I'm going to do next, but I do know what I am not going to do. I'm not going to chase after him or beg him to come home. If he doesn't want to be here, I don't want him here."

That Monday, I lumbered into my office a few minutes before noon. I was glad to see that all of my workers were busy. As soon as I got myself a cup of coffee from the break room, I locked myself in my office and did more work in the next two hours than I normally did in a day.

I didn't even stop to eat lunch. I had not had much of an appetite since Pee Wee left. As a matter of fact, I hadn't even eaten anything since that morning! I must have dropped a few more pounds, because the navy blue pants I had on felt a size too big. I was happy with my current weight and didn't really want to lose any more. But I knew that if I didn't start back to taking care of myself, my weight wasn't the only thing I'd have to worry about losing. I didn't want to lose my grip on reality. One of my mother's employees had suffered a severe nervous breakdown last year when her husband left her. Sister Hawkins had been in the state hospital ever since, talking to herself and rubbing her own shit in her hair. The last thing I wanted was for some man to take credit for me losing my mind.

It was after six by the time I opened my office door and strolled out onto the main floor. Except for the janitor, everybody had left for the day. I stopped when I got to the cubicle that Michael Dench had occupied during his short stay. Even though it had been a while since he'd committed suicide, I still thought about him from time to time. As sad as it was to stand in the same spot that he had occupied, it offered me a brief distraction. The more I focused on other things, the less I had to deal with my own situation.

I finally ate something when I got home; some strawberry yogurt straight out of its container, as I stood in front of the refrigerator with the door open. As soon as I entered my bedroom, I knew that something was different. The closet door was ajar, and it looked like somebody had been sitting on the bed. I checked the closet and saw that Pee Wee had removed all of the clothes that he had left behind. I shuffled into the bathroom and saw that he'd also taken all of his toiletries.

The only messages on my answering machine were from my mother, Rhoda, Scary Mary, and my daughter. Just as I was about to fix myself a very stiff drink, the front door flew open and my daughter flew in like a bat out of hell.

"Hi, Mama! Grandma just dropped me off," she sang, dropping her backpack onto the living room sofa as she dashed toward the steps leading upstairs. "I gotta do my hair!"

I had not talked to her much about her daddy's departure. When she came back downstairs about twenty minutes later, I brought it up.

"Charlotte, I don't want you to think bad things about your

daddy. He's still a good man," I started, joining her at the kitchen table where she sat rolling up the end of her ponytail with some pink sponge rollers. "Uh, he's going to let me know when we can sit down with you and explain what is happening."

"Why?" Charlotte asked, giving me a puzzled look. "I already know what's happening between you and him. I got eyes. I got ears. I know how crazy you old people are." Her eyes seemed to see clean through me, like she knew more than I did. "What I don't understand is why any of y'all old people are still having sex in the first place."

# CHAPTER 39

"Look, girl. Sex is not just for young people. Some elderly people do it right up to the day they die," I said, stunned and saddened to hear that my daughter had even thought that much about sex at her age.

"Maybe that's why they die," she suggested.

It did me no good to sigh with exasperation. That went right over Charlotte's head. "Mama, stop looking so sad about Daddy leaving. At least you had him for a while. Some women don't keep their husbands half as long as you kept my daddy."

"Well, I am glad to see that his leaving doesn't bother you that much!"

"It does bother me, Mama. I am just not going to let it spoil my life like you. Dang." Charlotte's eyes suddenly lit up. "Me and all of my girlfriends said we're going to be like Liz Taylor and Zsa Zsa Gabor when we grow up. Each time a husband leaves us, we'll just get another one."

I shook my head. "There are a lot of things you don't understand. You're not mature enough yet. And in a way, that's a good thing. Stay a child as long as you can. . . ."

"Huh?"

"Baby, being an adult is hard," I admitted, my voice cracking.

"Mama, I don't have no idea what you're talking about," Charlotte complained, giving me a look of confusion that I'd never seen on a child's face.

"That's just it, baby. There are things going on that you don't understand, things that you can't understand. Things that only adults can deal with, and we need to explain them to you."

Charlotte rolled her eyes. "Like what? Dang, Mama, I'm eleven. I am not a baby no more," she said in a strong voice, sounding so mature it scared me. "I'm almost grown," she informed me. Right after she said that, she lifted a yellow water pistol off the table, and squirted water onto her bangs and on the roller she had just used to roll up the end of her ponytail.

It was heart wrenching to see just how innocent and young my daughter really was. If it had been up to me, she would have remained that way until the day she died. But I was realistic enough to know that I could protect her for only so long from the black boots of misery that were waiting to stomp her into the ground the way they'd done me. Even though all of the hard knocks I had survived had made me the woman I was today, I didn't want my daughter to walk in my shoes.

"You're not as grown as you think you are," I said.

She rolled her eyes again; then she dipped her head and looked at me with a dry expression on her face. "Too bad you and Daddy ain't like Rhoda and Otis."

Both of my eyebrows shot up. My breath caught in my throat and it took me a while to form the words I wanted to release. "What do you mean by that?"

"Rhoda and Otis are the perfect married couple. They love each other, and neither one of them would never be running around with somebody they wasn't married to like my daddy. Jade won't do something that nasty to her husband either."

I had no desire to discuss Jade and her marriage. But I was curious as to what made Charlotte think that Otis and Rhoda had the perfect marriage. But I was not curious enough to ask. The last thing I wanted to deal with right now was her asking me questions I didn't want to, or couldn't, answer.

However, I couldn't stop myself from bringing up Jade's name in another context. "I don't want you going over to Rhoda's house to spend time with Jade. I've already told you that it's better if you spend your time with kids your own age. Jade is a grown woman now. And she's married. You should not even be thinking about her."

"And that's another thing, Mama. I know the real reason you don't want me to hang with Jade no more. I know how you got mad at her. I seen her at the movies one day and she told me the whole story about how you was jealous of her."

"That's not the whole story," I protested.

"Mama, I don't care. I'd rather be around kids my own age anyway. Can I order a pizza for dinner?" Charlotte had already jumped out of her seat and was walking toward the telephone on the wall before I could answer.

"Make sure it's a small one," I told her.

As soon as she'd placed her order and returned to her seat, I started up again. "Your daddy is in love with another woman and he wants to be with her. We've had a few problems recently, and I think he's still trying to get over that. That's part of the reason he doesn't want to live with us right now."

"You didn't tell me what you did to make him fall in love with another woman yet. What did you do to him?"

"That's not important. Anyway, he still loves you, and no matter what he does to me, you should not let that stop you from loving him. Men his age sometimes feel that the love of a wife is no longer enough."

"What about you?"

"What about me?"

"Do women your age feel like that, too?" Charlotte gave me a guarded look as if she was trying to read my thoughts. "Are you going to get a boyfriend?"

"I don't know what I'm going to do. The important thing right now is for us to adjust to your daddy being gone."

Shortly after I'd put Charlotte to bed, I received another unwanted visit from Scary Mary. "I was just in the neighborhood," she lied, looking around my living room as she practically pushed her way in. "Pee Wee still gone?" She wore a beige trench coat with a black belt. She had on a pair of white house shoes. "I'm glad to see you ain't crawlin' around on your belly with grief."

"Yes, he's still gone, and you won't ever see me crawling around on my belly with grief. You want a drink?"

"A beer if you got one you don't need," she said, following me into the kitchen.

"I went back to work today," I told her. "And he came to the house while I was gone to get some more of his shit." I gave her a beer and poured myself a glass of milk; then I sat across from her at my kitchen table.

"That nasty puppy!" Scary Mary drank her beer; then she slammed her fist down hard on the table. "Mens, mens, mens! We can't live with 'em, we can't live without 'em." She stopped and gave me a curious look. "If I was you, I'd get me another one as soon as possible. You know what they say about fallin' off a horse. As soon as you fall off one, get on top of another."

"I think it's too soon for me to even be thinkin' about another man," I decided. I didn't know what made everybody think it was that easy for me to run out and get another man. Had it been *that* easy, every woman on the planet would have somebody, and most of the women's magazines would go out of business.

"Well, you ain't got all the time in the world, you know. And you ain't got what Janet Jackson got." The old madam glared at me for a moment, making me uncomfortable. Had I known she was lurking around my neighborhood, I would have turned off all of my lights and refused to answer the door. "I remember when Pee Wee was an itty bitty boy. He was scared of white folks then. Now he done fell in love with one and moved in with her. Tsk tsk tsk."

"I wish everybody would stop referring to Lizzie as a white woman. Nobody started saying that until this . . . this mess with Pee Wee."

"Her skin is as white as Michael Jackson's!"

"So what? Lizzie has always identified herself with the black community." Lizzie Stovall was the last person in the world that I wanted to defend. But after what I'd just said, and the way Scary Mary was looking at me, that was what it sounded like. "Not that I care what race she is. She's still a no-good whore who just happens to be the daughter of a white woman." I tilted my head to the side. "I guess it would make everybody happy if I got me a white man."

Scary Mary yelped and looked at me like I'd sprouted horns. "What white man would want to stick his dick into that pothole between your legs?"

I ignored the brutal insult that she'd hurled at me by pretending like I didn't hear it. "You want another drink?" I rose and rushed over to the cabinet where I kept several bottles of leaded fuel. The first bottle my hand touched was a fifth of gin. "Or do you want something stronger?" I asked, pouring myself a large glass of gin.

"Pour me one, and then you set down and shet up. I got a bug to put in your ear. A big one."

"What?" I asked in a nervous voice, easing back down into my chair.

"He done already talked to a lawyer, baby," she told me in a low voice, glancing toward the doorway. "That's what I rushed over here to tell you. I didn't want you to be caught off guard."

My mouth dropped open. I had to take a drink before I could speak again. With some of the liquid still in my mouth, I said, "Pee Wee is already talking to a lawyer. How . . . Who told you that?"

"Look, girl. I got eyes and ears all over this town. Don't nothin' go on around here that I don't find out." Scary Mary gave me an impatient look as she sucked on her teeth. "If you really must know, the lawyer in question is one of my regular tricks. He is one of them Republicans at that, so you better hire you a real big gun if you want to have a chance."

"So . . ." I said with such a huge sigh on my lips that I had to pause. "He's *not* coming back. But he told me that he would never want a divorce!" I mouthed, speaking more like I was talking to myself.

"And that wasn't the only thing he lied about!"

"Do you have any other lawyers on your list? Give me the name of the best one!" I yelled. "I'll beat him to the punch, and by the time I get through with his black ass, that barbershop and everything else he owns will be mine."

# CHAPTER 40

As soon as Scary Mary had left my house, I boiled a couple of hot dogs and was able to eat them both. After I took a long, hot bubble bath, I poured myself a glass of white wine. That helped me relax.

I had begun to wonder what in the world was going to happen to me next. It seemed like every time I got to a comfortable place, things blew up in my face. And what scared me so much was the fact that I didn't know why. Was I being punished for the things I'd done? There had been so many, and some had been so extreme that I had to wonder if karma had finally caught up with me. Or maybe the devil, and God, were testing me some more. I dismissed all of those thoughts. I knew that I was responsible, at least on some level, for the way my life had turned out. Now I had to figure out what to do to fix it.

I must have wandered around the house for at least an hour with my wineglass in one hand and the wine bottle in the other. One minute I was in the kitchen wiping off the counter and rearranging the dishes in the cupboard. After that, I wobbled to the dining room where I rearranged the chairs around the table, watered my plants, and brushed off the place mats. I eventually ended up in the living room, where I opened and closed drapes, straightened the area rugs, and dusted off the coffee and end tables.

No matter what I did, I couldn't ignore the pain that Pee Wee had caused me. I wanted him to be in pain, too. I couldn't wait to get lawyer information from Scary Mary. Before I went to bed, I pulled out my phone book and wrote down the numbers of three lawyers.

As soon as I got to work the next morning, I called the first one on my list and made an appointment. Ten minutes after I'd concluded that call, Pee Wee called me up. Just the sound of his voice made my heart jump and my breath freeze in my throat. I had decided that if he called to apologize and told me that he had made a terrible mistake, and that he wanted to come home, I'd cuss him out first. But then I'd tell him to come on back home where he belonged.

"I just wanted to talk to you," he began, sounding sad.

I leaned back in my seat trying to decide how to respond, especially since he was sounding so down in the dumps. I quickly decided that I wasn't going to cuss him out after all. What I really wanted was for us to work things out.

"Pee Wee, there is nothing in the world we can't work out. If you could get over what I did to you by getting involved with Louis, I can let this thing between you and Lizzie slide."

His silence stunned and disappointed me. He didn't break down and beg me to forgive him. He didn't even tell me that he missed me. "Annette, I'm in love with Lizzie."

Even though he had already told me that, those words chilled me all the way through my flesh to my bones. He got silent and I didn't know what to say next. I just sat there holding my breath, silently scolding myself for letting him know that I was such a lovesick fool, and that I was ready, willing, and able to take him back if that was what he wanted.

But that was not what he wanted, and he wasted no time making that clear. "Uh, all I wanted to do was to touch base with you," he said, talking in a stiff and impersonal voice. "I want you to know right off that you ain't got to worry about money."

"Who said I was?" I hissed. "If anybody should be worried about money, it's your scaly black ass. God don't like ugly, and He's the one you'll have to answer to for what you did to me!" I was amazed at how quickly I went from wanting him back to wanting to put a major curse on him.

"Maybe God can strike us both down at the same time," he muttered.

"I wish you would stop reminding me about my affair with Louis Baines!" I screeched.

"Baby, you are the one who usually brings it up. I can't stop talkin' about it if you don't."

"What did you call here for?" I asked, sounding as impatient as nature would allow me to. "And hurry up! I've got things to do, places to go!"

Despite what I was saying and feeling, I didn't want him to hang up. It had never occurred to me that it was going to be so hard to cancel the feelings that I still had for him. I loved him from the bottom of my heart, but at the same time I hated the ground he walked on. If those mixed emotions were not enough to confuse me and have me talking and acting like a fool, nothing was. "And just to let you know, I hope you don't plan on coming back, because I might not be here!"

"Annette, you can go wherever you want to go as long as you let me know how I can get in touch with my daughter. If not, you can leave her with me and go on to wherever you want to go," he said calmly.

I almost blacked out. This man had no shame whatsoever. I had not expected him to say anything like that. It seemed like the more we talked, the more pain this conversation caused. I figured that if I didn't want to end up in hysterics, the sooner I got off the telephone the better. "What did you call me up for?" I asked.

Pee Wee let out a loud sigh. I couldn't tell if it was a sigh of relief or a sigh of disgust. "I will continue to pay all your utilities, your car insurance, and all of the other household bills. I'll give you more than enough to keep Charlotte happy, but for the time being, you should be able to foot your own personal bills. You know, them beauty shop expenses and nails and stuff. Just until I get sorted out. It won't be easy for me to pay for two households."

"That's not my problem. *You* chose to take on two households, *motherfucker*," I said calmly. I was just waiting for him to tell me that he had already spoken to a lawyer.

"I want to see Charlotte at least three or four times a week. My new place has two bedrooms, one already done up for her. Toys and her own TV and stuff. There is a large backyard so she can run around like she wants to. I'll even finally get her that puppy she's always wanted, but that you wouldn't let her get because you didn't want to be cleanin' up behind it."

"Oh, that's so damn cozy. That's so . . . so *Leave It to Beaver* cute of you! I guess the next thing you tell me is that the Brady Bunch lives next door to you and your use-to-be hippie *valley girl*."

"Annette, I am not in the mood to fuss and fight with you," he whined. "I am tryin' to make this . . . this adjustment work for everybody concerned. A change might do you some good anyway."

"A change? What the fuck makes you think I need a damn change? I was happy with the way things were between us!"

"Annette, do I have to keep remindin' you that when I was happy with the way things were between us . . . never mind."

"If you bring up Louis Baines and that affair I had with him again, I am going to scream!"

"I am not goin' to bring up Louis Baines. That's one thing you do enough on your own. Right now my focus is my daughter."

"Well, let me tell you one thing, my daughter will not be spending much time wherever you moved to. The less she sees of that cow, the better."

"Let's get one thing straight right now. You can't keep me from spendin' time with my child! You are not goin' to interfere with my relationship with her!"

"I didn't say that. But I can keep your whore from spending time with her."

"Annette, I am surprised at you. One of the things I always admired about you was the fact that you didn't use foul language that much, and you didn't call people nasty names as easy as some people do."

It felt like somebody had set me on fire because I was just that hot. "Yeah, I am using a lot of foul language these days, and I am calling your BITCH some foul names. What did you expect?"

"Well, I guess I'll come to your house when I want to see my daughter, huh?"

"*Our* daughter. And let me remind you that I was the one who carried her. I was the one who suffered through hour after hour of labor to bring her into the world. She's more my daughter than she is yours."

"You'd better watch your step, woman."

"Don't call me woman! I am not your woman!"

"True. But after what you just said, I need to know something."

"What do you need to ask me?" I screeched.

"Is Charlotte my daughter?"

I thought my ears were going to fall off because the words that had just hit them felt like acid. "How dare you ask me a question like that!"

"Well, is she?"

"Of course she's your daughter. And if you don't believe me, you can easily find out by getting a DNA test! I can't believe you would even fix your lips to ask me something like that. Oh my God!"

"I'm sorry. I didn't mean to go there. Listen, all I want is to be able to see my child on a regular basis. And I plan to."

"I am sure you will. But if you ever bring that bitch back to my house again, people are going to read about you and her both in the newspaper! The obituaries!" I warned.

"I knew you were goin' to be talkin' all kinds of shit before I even picked up the telephone!"

"Then why did you call here, asshole? Look, can you hurry up and finish saying what you called to say. I've . . . I've got a date!"

"Uh-huh. I see you didn't waste no time."

"No, I didn't waste any time finding me somebody else. And guess what, he's a real man. He's not a punk. . . ."

"All right. This conversation is over—"

I didn't even let him finish his sentence. I slammed the phone down as hard as I could.

I was sorry about all of the profanity I had used and all of the hurtful things I'd said. I had always thought that I was a level-headed woman who didn't fly off the handle the way I'd seen some of the other black women in Richland do. But I couldn't even imagine a sister as regal and stately as Oprah *not* getting down and dirty in a situation like mine. If Pee Wee's actions didn't justify my behavior, what did?

I scolded myself for telling that lie about me already having a new man. But the one thing that I didn't want Pee Wee and Lizzie— or anybody else—to think was that nobody else wanted me.

Now all I had to do was find somebody who did.

# CHAPTER 41

As angry as I was, I knew it was not going to be easy for me to find a new lover and initiate a romance while I was still in love with my husband. But that was just what I was going to do. And I was not going to waste any time doing it. Well, I didn't have any time to lose.

I didn't expect to be rescued and wooed by a Prince Charming on a white horse. I didn't expect too many men in my age group, who had a lot of younger and prettier women to choose from, to choose me. Things just didn't happen that way in real life. If there was another available man out there for me, he was going to have a lot to live up to because I didn't want just any old body off the street. Even before I got married, and went for months at a time without a date, I had high standards. I didn't care how lonely or horny I got, I wasn't going to settle for too little.

But I was not naïve enough to think that it was going to be easy, *or even possible*, for me to find love again.

After all, I was a forty-seven-year-old woman who had been out of the dating game for more than ten years. I wasn't sure my affair with Louis Baines counted. Even if it did, I still didn't have any time to waste if I wanted to save my own face. There were still some good men out there, but there were still a lot of desperate women out there competing with each other for those men.

I had to laugh when I thought about all of the women who had coveted my man! It seemed so ironic that none of those women had pursued him (as far as I knew), and that the woman who I least expected to be a threat turned out to be my downfall. I was thankful that I had other things in my life to fall back on. In most situations, that was Rhoda.

"Can you meet me at the Red Rose tonight around nine? That band from Cleveland is playing tonight," I said to Rhoda, practically yelling into the telephone.

"I'd love to, but I promised Bully I'd go out and have a drink with him tonight."

"Oh. I thought he was in London." After all these years, I still got disappointed when Rhoda's lover interfered with my plans. I liked Bully, whose real name was Ian Bullard, and he liked me. But I wasn't always in the mood to socialize with him.

"He got back from London last night. Didn't I tell you he would be back this week?"

"You probably did. Well, maybe some other time," I said, knowing I sounded like a petulant two-year-old.

"If you don't mind his company, I can meet you this evenin'. You sound like you need to talk."

"Rhoda, I do need to talk and I don't care if Bully, his dog, and his grandfather comes with you."

"Uh-oh, this sounds pretty serious."

"It is. I had a real tense conversation with that man."

"That man you married I presume?"

"That man. He's not coming back."

"Well, didn't you already know that? He took most of his stuff, and he rented a new place. That sounds pretty serious to me. Did you think he was coming back?"

"I don't know what I thought! I thought I knew him. I thought I knew what kind of man he was."

"Annette, give this some time. If you love your husband and want him back, there is always a chance that that will happen. You can make it happen, or you can move on. Now it's up to you. I just want you to know that no matter what you do, I am behind you all the way."

"Bully won't mind us sitting there talking about my problems?

His wife dumped him, so he will be able to relate, too." I didn't wait for Rhoda to respond. "We can send him to the bar for drinks a few times, long enough for us to chat. So can you meet me there?"

"I can and I will," Rhoda told me. "It's been a tense day for me, too, so I need to get out of the house myself. See you there."

My mother had called my office six times during the day, and each time I'd lied and told her that I was on my way to a meeting. When she offered to come to my office and catch me between meetings, I told her I was going home early. "I need to talk to you," she told me. "I need to make sure you doin' all right."

"I'm doing just fine, Muh'Dear. Please don't worry about me." My voice wobbled and I hung up before she could hear me sobbing, which is what I did in my office for the next ten minutes.

One thing that amazed and pleased me was the fact that as far as my employees were concerned, I didn't have a care in the world. But when I left my office to go into the break room for some ice, Brian, a short blond with beady blue eyes, put his hand on my shoulder. "Annette, is everything all right? You look like you've been crying," he said in a gentle voice. Brian was as gay as a picnic basket, and he was also the biggest gossip in the office. He was the last person in the building that I wanted to know my business.

"Oh, I'm fine!" I quickly replied. As hard as I tried to hold it back, a single hiccup slipped past my quivering lips. "I spilled some ink on my hand when I was changing the toner in my printer, and then I rubbed my eyes before washing my hands."

"Oh. Well, I'm glad to hear that that's all it is. Of all the people I know, you are the only one who is not shackled with problems and ailments."

I spent the next ten minutes listening to a detailed account of Brian's high blood pressure problems, his shabby nerves, his bad back, his insomnia, a mysterious gum condition his dentist couldn't identify, and a variety of other afflictions. I was surprised that he was still alive. By the time he got through with me, I did feel somewhat better. I was glad that at least I still had my health.

When I got home, I found Muh'Dear had left six messages on my answering machine. She was the last person I wanted to talk to, so I didn't even bother to call her back and ask if I could drop

Charlotte off so I could go out. I arranged to send Charlotte across the street for a sleepover with one of her neighborhood friends.

"Whew! I was scared you was going to send me to Grandma's house, and I'd have to eat cabbage greens and cornbread!" she informed me on her way out the door with her sleeping bag and backpack.

"Well, whatever the Turners are having for dinner, don't you overdo it," I warned. I watched until she made it across the street to the Turner house where her little friend was waiting for her on the front porch steps.

I wore to the Red Rose the same red blouse and black pants that I had worn to work. As soon as I walked in the front door, I almost fainted. There was Rhoda sitting at our usual booth near the back. But she had company, and it was not Bully.

Her husband, Otis, was with her, his long arm wrapped around her like a newlywed, but it wasn't his presence that made my flesh crawl. Jade and Vernie were also with her, and that made my stomach churn. I slunk quietly back out of the door like a shy burglar. As I was sprinting back to my car where I had parked it on the street a block away, I heard footsteps. I kept running, but I turned around to see who it was, expecting to see either Rhoda or Otis. It was neither one of them. It was somebody from my past. I stopped in my tracks under a street light, so relieved I wanted to dance a jig. And he could not have timed our "reunion" better.

"Jacob Brewster," I swooned, holding my arms out to him. "I haven't seen you in years!"

"Girl, when I saw you come through that door, I didn't know who you were until the bartender told me! You've lost a ton of weight!" Jacob yelled, looking me up and down. He was obviously pleased to see me, and pleased to see how good I looked.

"I don't think it was *that* much weight, Jacob," I said with a chuckle as we embraced.

"How come you didn't come on in?" he asked, spinning me around so he could see my new frame better. You would have thought that I was posing for the cover of *Vogue* magazine the way I was showing off.

"Uh, I was, but I changed my mind," I mumbled.

"I'm out alone, and your girl Rhoda is in there," he added, beckoning toward the bar with his head. "She told me that she was supposed to be meeting you there."

"Yeah, she was," I said, feeling more relaxed. "I haven't seen you since you took me to that party about twelve or thirteen years ago. I always wondered what happened to you."

"Well, I thought you had flown the coup, given up on the north, and was sitting on a front porch down south somewhere!"

My jaw dropped. "As you can see, I am still here and I plan on staying here," I said proudly. "I did hear that you had married one of the Fisher girls."

"I did. I married one of the Hampton girls, too. And one of the Mason girls." A sad look appeared on Jacob's face. "I guess sooner or later one of my marriages will take."

"I hope so. . . ."

"I heard about you and Pee Wee busting up. You got you a new shoe yet?"

"No, not yet. But I . . . I mean, I am dating again, but nothing serious yet."

"You know, of all the women I dated, you were the only one who treated me like a real man. I kicked myself in the butt for years over how stupid I behaved at that party I took you to. You ended up hooking up with that punk-ass Cunningham brother that night."

"I was going to marry him, but that didn't work out," I said quickly. As far as I knew, Jerome Cunningham had not told anybody that he had dumped me because his uncle blabbed to him that I'd worked as a prostitute and that he'd been one of my tricks. If the Richland gossipmongers ever did hear it, it wouldn't be from me. "I didn't make it to your mama's funeral last year because I didn't hear about it in time," I said, gently touching his shoulder.

"She was a good woman and I miss her," Jacob mumbled in a low, sad voice. He blinked and let out a prolonged moan. But then his voice perked up like a shotgun blast. "Listen, if you don't have to rush off somewhere, come on back in and have a drink with me. I don't know about you, but I'd sure like to get reacquainted."

# CHAPTER 42

My previous relationship with Jacob had not lasted long enough for me to really get to know him that well. That was why he reacted the way he did when I suddenly wrapped my arms around his neck and planted a juicy kiss on his lips. His lips were dry and his breath was as foul as it ever was. As a matter of fact, his bad breath was legendary. When I was dating him, my friends rarely referred to him by his name when he came up in a conversation. Instead, they usually referred to him as "that brother with the foul breath."

I didn't care about Jacob's bad breath, or anything else, right now. The way I had embraced him, my stomach pressed up against his like a suit of armor, it looked like I was giving him the Heimlich maneuver. When I released him, he gasped. Then he let out a sharp laugh.

"Have mercy," he panted. "It sure enough is good for a woman to pay me this kind of attention." We were directly under the street light. A moth came out of nowhere and circled Jacob's head. I fanned it away, thumping the side of his head like a melon. That made us both laugh. His eyes looked into mine with so much intensity it was like he was trying to see my soul. I could tell that he was ripe for the picking. "Something told me to drag my tail on over to this bar tonight!"

What Jacob didn't know was that a few seconds earlier, I had spotted my husband cruising down the street out of the corner of my eye. The kiss had been for his benefit. I wanted that sucker to know that I wasn't sitting at home pining my life away over him.

Just as Pee Wee drove near the street light and spotted me, he jerked his head around so hard and fast, he almost ran up on the sidewalk. There was a slack-jawed look on his face. Behind and above Pee Wee's car was a large silver moon. It looked like a yo-yo suspended on an invisible string. Lizzie was with him, sitting so close to him it looked like she was on his lap. And that was not easy to do in a car with bucket seats! There was a stupefied look on her face, like I was doing something that she didn't approve of. I was suddenly attacked by a siege of indigestion. I was afraid that the Chinese chicken salad I'd eaten for lunch was going to rise up out of my stomach and squirt out of my mouth. Suddenly, I had trouble breathing. I felt like I was being smothered by a large pillow that had been cruelly placed over my face. Jacob said something, but I couldn't make out what it was. I was too busy trying to breathe and get the image of Pee Wee and Lizzie out of my mind. Somehow, I managed to contain myself.

"Annette, are you all right?" I barely heard Jacob ask in a concerned voice.

"I'm . . . I'm fine," I croaked. "What were we talking about now?" I cleared my throat and glanced at the moon again. It still looked like a yo-yo. I blinked and returned my attention to Jacob. "I haven't been feeling well," I said, hoping that would explain my odd behavior to his satisfaction. "It is so good to see you again," I squealed.

I kept my arms around Jacob's neck until Pee Wee's car was out of sight. It was only then that I was able to breathe again.

"Um, I am so glad I ran into you tonight. We've got a whole lot of catching up to do, huh?" Jacob said, looking so eager and excited I thought he was going to bite me. He grabbed my hand and led me back into the bar.

Rhoda gave me a helpless look as we joined her and her family in their booth. I was glad that the only two seats available were on the side next to Otis and Rhoda. Jade was on the opposite side, scowling like a convict posing for a mug shot.

I didn't notice the small birthday cake on the table until Jacob and I sat down.

"My baby girl angel is de grand ole twenty-one today!" Otis exclaimed, pounding a fist on the table. "And she's never had an unhappy moment since de day she was born!"

I had no idea how Otis could sit there and tell such a bald-faced lie with a straight face. I figured he was one of those kinds of parents who saw only what he wanted to see. Maybe Jade was an angel in his eyes. But from the way she was scowling and rolling her eyes at me, I was still convinced that she was the exact opposite. I gave Otis such an incredulous look, Rhoda kicked my foot under the table.

"Happy birthday, Jade," I said in the most pleasant tone of voice I could manage.

"Ugh," she replied, speaking out of the side of her mouth as she eyed me with undisguised suspicion. "Mama, can I have another margarita?" she said, turning to Rhoda with a pleading look on her face.

"Aye yi yi," Otis yelled, slapping his forehead with the palm of his hand so hard his dreadlocks slapped the side of his head. He grinned, kissed Jade's cheek, and summoned the waiter.

"Jade, you've had *four* drinks already," Rhoda said sternly. "Drinkin' is one thing you have to handle with care, unless you want to get slaphappy and act like a fool."

"And that's not a pretty sight for a woman," Vernie muttered.

"*You* shet up!" Jade snarled, shaking a finger in Vernie's direction.

"Now, Jade, you be nice," Rhoda advised with a frustrated look on her face. "You promised you would be."

"All right, Mommy," Jade cooed. She leaned over and kissed Vernie on his cheek. That must have made him happy because he offered a broad smile. Jade turned her attention to me with a pug-ugly expression on her face, like she had been sucking on a lemon. "Uh, Annette, I heard your husband finally left you. Is that true?"

"It's true," I told her. I didn't even remove my jacket. I knew that as long as Jade was present, my departure could occur at any minute, and it would not be soon enough as far as I was concerned.

Jade let out a loud breath, which really sounded more like a grunt of disgust. "Oh well. That's a damn shame. *Everybody* needs somebody. Even worms deserve mates. . . ." The lighting was dim in the bar, but not so dim that Jade had to shade her eyes so she could see Jacob better, but she shaded her eyes anyway. "Jacob? Jacob Brewster? Why—I thought you were dead!"

I was the only one at the table who didn't laugh.

"Sometimes I feel like it," Jacob said, laughing some more. He turned on a smile that was so bright it made his face glow.

"And what's that knot on your forehead? Cancer?"

"Oh no, it's nothing like that," Jacob answered quickly, rubbing a peanut-size pimple on the side of his forehead that I had not noticed until Jade pointed it out. "Just some allergy I've been dealing with the past couple of weeks." Jacob covered his mouth and coughed. "It's nothing serious."

That information didn't appease Jade. She looked at Jacob like he had just announced that he had leprosy. "Well, it looks contagious to me, so if you don't mind, please don't cough in my direction." She turned to Vernie. "Groom, trade seats with me." Like a well-trained puppy, Vernie complied.

I was already anxious to leave. I wanted to go home, slide into my bathrobe, and curl up on my living room couch with a good book. As soon as the waiter took our orders, I asked Rhoda to accompany me to the ladies' room.

"What in the hell is going on?" I asked before we even shut the ladies' room door. "I thought you said it was just going to be Bully and us."

"It was, but Bully was so tired from that long flight from London, he fell asleep on the couch before I knew it. We had planned to celebrate Jade's birthday at home, but all of a sudden she decided she wanted to have her first alcoholic drink in public."

"Her first alcoholic drink?" I asked with both my eyebrows raised and a cackle lurking in my lump-infested throat.

Rhoda gave me an impatient look. "Yes, her *first* alcoholic drink," she snapped defensively with a hand on her hip.

Jade had had her first alcoholic drink in my house—before I could stop her—more than five years ago. As a matter of fact, she had probably started way before then. It was one thing for Otis to be so naïve where Jade was concerned. But it was hard to believe that Rhoda thought that Jade was drinking for the first time tonight. Rhoda didn't know her daughter as well as she thought she did. Back when Jade was in her teens, Rhoda was concerned about Jade's first sexual experience, convinced that she was still a virgin. I knew for a fact that not only had Jade been fucking for years already by then, she'd also had two abortions. I knew from experience that, in some cases, it was better for me to mind my own business— unless I wanted to open a can of worms that might crawl all over everything and everybody. Even though I didn't like it, I totally understood why Rhoda had not told me about Pee Wee and Lizzie as soon as she found out. Nobody liked the thought of worms crawling out of a can. I decided that I would never tell Rhoda that Jade had already had her first drink.

"Before I could even tell Jade that I was going to meet you, she suggested this family night out on the town."

"I'm surprised that she didn't change her mind when she found out I was going to be here," I said, turning to the mirror to check my makeup. I had smeared my lipstick when I kissed Jacob, but all it took to repair it was for me to blot a few spots with a wet paper towel. "I would have understood."

"It's no big deal. I think that we are all civilized enough to get through tonight without a scene. Now . . ." Rhoda paused and sniffed, and widened her eyes. "What's up with you and Jacob?" She put her hands on her hips and stood closer to me, checking out her own makeup in the same mirror.

"I don't know yet." I turned to face Rhoda, giving her a thoughtful look. "He just might be what I need right now. And right on time." I told her about the scene that I'd performed under the streetlight outside for Pee Wee's benefit.

I didn't like the pitiful look she gave me. My first thought was that she didn't approve of what I had just confessed. I suddenly wished that I had not told her.

"Go ahead and say it! I know Pee Wee's your boy, and you love him to death, but he's my husband and he's betrayed me in the worst way. What do you expect me to do, Rhoda?"

The look on her face softened. She cleared her throat and nodded. "Good for you, girl! I'm glad Pee Wee saw you kissin' Jacob out in the open." Her response made me relax a little more.

"You don't think it was a tacky thing for me to do? I mean, I am still technically married, but I was glad to see Jacob."

"What you did is no more tacky than what Pee Wee's doin' out in the open. As far as I'm concerned, you should be doin' a lot more."

"What do you mean by that? Is there something else going on that I don't know about?"

"Well, Pee Wee's not bein' discreet, you know?"

"Can you make a little more sense? If you are trying to tell me something, just tell me."

Rhoda took a deep breath and gave me a sorry look. When she clapped me on my back and started rubbing like she was trying to rid me of a demon, I knew then that she was about to reveal something else that I was not going to like. I was right. "Since Pee Wee takes Lizzie to dinner at Antonosanti's some nights after they close up the barbershop—struttin' like a peacock with his arm curled around her shoulder like a bodyguard—you can kiss whomever you want to kiss out in the open."

# CHAPTER 43

"He takes her to dinner at an expensive place like Antonosanti's? I used to have to beg him to take me there!" My battered heart must have skipped three beats. And it felt like it was hanging from an invisible string like a yo-yo, just like that moon outside. Even though I knew that I'd lost my husband to another woman, hearing that the affair had become so public and blatant made my blood boil. I wanted to go back home and get my rolling pin. I hated the woman that I had become. Even though I still didn't condone violence, it had become a frequent visitor to my fractured thoughts. I was glad I didn't have access to a gun or a competent voodoo woman.

"Lizel and Wyrita drive past there every evenin' on the way home." Lizel and Wyrita were the two busybody young women who worked for Rhoda, helping her run her childcare center. "Pee Wee's car is in Antonosanti's parking lot almost every day around the same time. Yesterday and today, Lizel and Wyrita stopped there to order somethin' to go—or just to be nosy, I should say. Lizel said that both times Pee Wee and Lizzie were sittin' in a booth kissin' and huggin' like they were auditionin' for *The Love Connection.*"

"Oh well," I said with a shrug. My insides were crumbling like a house of cards. "He's on his own, so he can do whatever the hell he wants to do." Those words tasted like venom on my tongue. "I plan to do the same thing." Those words tasted much better. As a matter of fact, they tasted so good I wanted to savor them. "I plan to do the same thing," I repeated, this time with even more conviction. "By the way, did you know he's been talkin' to a lawyer? Scary Mary told me."

Rhoda's jaw dropped and she covered her mouth with her hand for a few seconds. "I didn't know that!"

"Well, you know it now. And I want you to be the first to know that I have an appointment to see a lawyer. I plan to serve Pee Wee with divorce papers as soon as I can."

"I don't blame you, girl. I mean, he's still my boy and he always will be, but you have to do what you have to do. Let him stay with his middle-aged might-or-might-not-be virgin." Rhoda paused and cackled. "Well, if she was still a virgin, I'm sure she's not a virgin anymore now. Still middle-aged, though."

"Hmph! She probably hasn't been a virgin for a long time," I snapped.

"I thought she'd never been married, or even had a real date."

"So? Half of the prostitutes who work for Scary Mary have never been married or had dates, at least not dates in the traditional sense." I gave Rhoda a serious look. "Did you know she went to Woodstock?"

"So did Mick Jagger and Jimi Hendrix, I think. What's your point?"

"And a year after we got out of high school, she spent some time in Berkeley doing that hippie thing."

Rhoda's brow furrowed. "Wasn't that the Summer of Love where everybody was fuckin' everybody while they were on acid or whatever drugs they could get their hands on?"

"From what I know, every summer was the summer of love during the hippie movement. Now, with all of that in mind, just how innocent could Lizzie be if she was there? And Woodstock? What about all of that?"

Rhoda considered my words with a frown. "Of course, if Lizzie really got into what was goin' on, she was well-fucked when she left Berkeley. And another thing, as far as I know, she has never said that she's still a virgin anyway, right? I mean, before Pee Wee gave her a beef injection . . ."

"She never told me she was. I don't know how Muh'Dear came

to that conclusion." I swallowed hard. "Oh, what the hell. What difference does it make? She's living with my husband now and I know he's fucking the hell out of her."

"This is some truly crazy shit, girl. How do you think somebody like her got to somebody like him?"

"I don't know who got to who in this case. And to be honest with you, I don't think I really want to know. But I am still ticked off with you for not telling me," I chided, shaking a finger in Rhoda's face.

"Don't think that I didn't want to tell you as soon as I found out. You have no idea how hard it was for me to keep from callin' you up that time I ran into them at the motel. I had even thought about sendin' you an anonymous note."

My mouth dropped open. "Well, after what Jade put me through with her cute little anonymous notes, I'm glad you didn't! Something like that would have pushed me closer to the edge faster than a bulldozer. I can't believe you would say something like that, Rhoda!"

"I'm sorry for even thinkin' of doin' somethin' like that, and I'm sorry for tellin' you. I just . . . I just want us all to be happy. Now, I know that you and Jade still have some issues, but let's try and get through tonight in one piece."

By the time Rhoda and I returned to our table, our drinks had been delivered. Jacob was squatting down on his knees on the floor facing the booth with a camera. He was snapping pictures of Jade as she leaned over her birthday cake, posing with Otis and Vernie. The way that the three of them were positioned with Jade seated, Vernie leaning forward over her so that his chin rested on top of her head, and with Otis in a similar position above Vernie, they resembled a short totem pole. It was a Kodak moment if ever there was one. "Rhoda, do you and Annette want to get in this picture?" Jacob asked.

Now that I looked so much better, I wasn't as camera shy as I used to be. But before I could respond and announce that I wanted to pose with the birthday girl, Rhoda spoke, "No thanks. I'm too bloated tonight," she said with a frown as she rubbed her belly. "I would come out lookin' like Moby Dick's mama." She, as well as everybody else present, looked at me.

"I feel the same way," I muttered.

The minute everybody returned to their seats, Jade's scowl returned to her face. And it was aimed in my direction. I couldn't raise my wineglass to my lips fast enough. I was glad that I had ordered some of the strongest Chardonnay in the house. I got an immediate buzz. It hit me so hard I didn't have time to stop the loud, long burp that popped out of my mouth as soon as I set the glass back on the table.

"Excuse me," I yelled, leaning toward Jacob. I beckoned for our waiter to bring me another drink.

The band—one plump, bald-headed brother tickling a red piano, another man strumming a square-shaped guitar, and two others tooting horns—was well known for the soft jazz instrumentals they played. The club was fairly crowded, and the atmosphere was so soothing it was easy for me to relax a little bit more. Even though Jade was present, with Jacob by my side now, I was actually glad that I had come back in. This was the first festive mood I'd felt since Pee Wee left me.

"So, Annette, I'm glad to see you didn't waste any time hooking up with a new man," Jade said with a grimace on her face that looked like it belonged on a crocodile. "And such a handsome man." She winked at Jacob. "Jacob, don't be blushing! You know you look good for a man your age. That wig store on State Street sells hairpieces that would cover up your receding hairline real good!" that crude heifer said. "But you could still use a few props." She took a drink from her glass and looked me in the eye. "Annette, I always thought you'd end up with just another mummy like Pee Wee, or some other dried-up old fossil. Ow! You surprised me!"

Rhoda cleared her throat and tried to divert the attention in another direction, but she didn't have to bother. Jade was two steps ahead of her.

"Groom?" Jade cooed, looking at Vernie like he was something good to eat. As soon as he whirled around to face her, she kissed the tip of his nose. Then she tapped his lips with the tip of her finger.

Vernie looked at her like she was the Queen of Sheba. "Yes, baby?"

"Dance with me, baby," Jade ordered. Jade grabbed Vernie by the hand before I could offer an appropriate response to her comments. And the fact that he didn't protest surprised me. He seemed more like her well-trained puppy than her husband.

I was glad when Otis and Rhoda got up to dance, too. It gave me the chance to investigate Jacob a little. Father Time had been good to him. He was still reasonably good looking and fit. As a matter of fact, he had the same dark brown skin and features that were similar to Pee Wee's. I was anxious to determine where he was coming from, and where he was going, as far as resuming a relationship with me.

"So, how do you spend your time these days?" I asked. I knew that if I was going to hold on to my sanity, it was going to take a lot of hard work. Now that I knew Pee Wee was parading his woman all over town, I knew that I had to at least make it look like I was having just as good a time as he was. I wasn't looking for another man to fall in love with. What I needed right now was a crutch, and Jacob was a good candidate to fill that role for the time being.

"I still like to go to parties and movies, and whatnot. The same things I liked to do when you and I were together," he told me, patting one of my hands for a few seconds, then the other. "I'm looking for the right woman to do that with. I'll be her fool," he said in a low voice, still patting my hands.

I didn't exactly want a fool in my life. And as soon as Jacob said that, he gave me a look that I didn't know how to interpret. He was staring at me like I was the only woman in the room. On one hand, it made me feel special; but on the other hand, it made me uncomfortable.

"I have a real busy social life," I reported, hoping that that statement would make him ease back a little.

"I'm sure you do. A fine sister like you. I should be so lucky to get you to go out with me again. But if I do, it'd be a blessing. Especially after all of the grief I've had to deal with lately."

"You mean your mama's passing?"

He nodded. "That's part of it." He paused and blinked a few times. When he spoke again, his voice was so low I had to lean closer toward him to hear. "My son by my high-school sweetheart passed, too. Suicide."

"Oh? I didn't know you had a son."

He nodded again. "When I got back from 'Nam, me and his

mama had him. My son's mother is a sister named Lois Dench. She didn't want to get married, but she wanted that baby. His name was Michael. Me and Lois broke up right after he was born, and they moved to Cleveland. The boy stayed in trouble up there, so they moved back down here. He took a shine to one of his uncles, who happened to be a straight-up thug, so he kept backsliding. He got into one mess after another down here."

"I didn't know you were related to the Dench family," I mumbled. "I knew Michael, and I had no idea he was your son. He used to work for the same company I work for."

The room suddenly seemed dark and more like a long black tunnel or some kind of cave. It was nowhere I wanted to be. I really wanted to flee the scene now. How in the world was I going to tell Jacob that some people held *me* responsible for his son's death?

# CHAPTER 44

"Your son . . . he was a sweet boy and a hard worker," I stammered. "And Michael is my favorite name for a boy."

"He was my only child." I could tell that Jacob was in pain, but he managed a weak smile. "He was smart, too. I bet he could have ended up working in a high-level management position some day. Yep, he was the only child that the good Lord saw fit to bless me with."

"Hmmm," I said, rubbing my chin.

"Hmmm what?" Jacob gave me a confused look.

"I am surprised to hear that you have only one child. Now, I hope you don't mind me saying this, but you got around in the bedroom, brother. And you got around in a lot of different bedrooms."

"Well, that's true. But he was the only one I had that I know about. And he will be the only one I ever do have. My baby-making days are over."

"Oh. I can understand that. With all the diseases we have to be concerned about these days, a lot of folks, just as many men as women, are choosing to abstain."

Jacob threw his head back and laughed long and loud. Now I was the one with a confused look on my face. "That's not what I meant! I don't plan on giving up my fun for at least another twenty or thirty years. And even then, if my motor needs a tune-up, I will make a beeline to a doctor and get myself a big supply of Viagra. Maybe by then they will have something even more potent."

"I'm sorry. But when you said you were through making babies, I thought . . ."

"You thought I was through having sex? You're not the first woman to think that when I mention my situation. But the truth of the matter is, I'd love to have more kids! It's just that I can't. See, a few years ago, I got some strange virus, and that ruined my chance of ever having any more biological children. That was why I really wanted to have a relationship with Michael."

"I always knew that you wanted kids, and I knew you'd make a good father, Jacob. At least we have one unique thing in common."

Jacob's eyes searched mine. Apparently he had no idea what I was talking about. "You had just the one child, I have just one child, and we both would like to have more," I stated. "I had my daughter late in life, and for a long time I was happy with just one child. But my daughter was not happy about that, and she was the one who told me, 'An only child is a lonely child.' "

"Is your equipment still working? You don't have to answer my question if you don't want to. It's just that the last woman I was involved with, she'd had a hysterectomy. And the one I was with before her, she'd had her tubes tied. I know that when a woman reaches middle age, her baby batter is usually a little stale by then. Having babies that late in life, there's no telling what kind of crossed-eyed gnome you might give birth to."

"Jacob, if my daughter was a crossed-eyed gnome, I wouldn't love her any less. But I am thankful that she is healthy and attractive. Your son was, too."

"Yeah, he was. Thanks for saying that, Annette."

"The females in my office couldn't take their eyes off of him," I said with a giggle.

"I guess he got his good looks from me," Jacob said with a straight face. I didn't comment on his comment, but it wasn't true. Jacob was no baboon, but he was no Mr. America either. The exceptionally good looks that his son had possessed had come from his mother.

"You'll be happy to know that I thought your son was one of the sweetest young men in Richland. And I'm sure he loved you."

"I appreciate you saying that, too. Too bad his mama didn't feel that way. She made it hard for me to see him. Every time I tracked her down, she moved."

"Didn't you have to pay child support?"

"Oh, I did that. I didn't miss a payment. But since I couldn't keep up with her, I paid her for his upkeep through the system. And the situation stayed that way until he reached legal age and I didn't have to support him anymore. But since he was grown by then and could make his own decisions, he let me know where he was staying at all times. We had just started to get close a few months ago. He got a job, but that didn't work out. They say that's what pushed him over the edge. I don't know all of the details, and nobody wants to discuss it with me." Jacob choked back a sob and I had to hold my breath to keep from doing the same thing myself. "Anyway," he continued, "I was visiting some of my mama's folks in DC when he hanged himself. It just broke my heart. I would have done anything in this world to help save my boy, and that's what I was trying to do. But I was too late."

"I got to know your son fairly well. Actually, I was his supervisor when he died," I admitted.

Jacob's eyes got so wide so fast he looked like an owl for a few seconds. "You? You were the one who fired my boy? I was told that it was some mean-ass bitch that had ice water in her veins! That doesn't sound like you!"

For a moment, I thought that Jacob was going to strike me. But he just stared into my face, like he was searching for an explanation as to what my role was in his son's death.

"I didn't know people saw me that way. I was just doing my job," I whined, knowing that that was the last thing that a grieving father wanted to hear.

"I see," Jacob said with a sniff. He suddenly looked so sad I thought he was going to burst into tears and weep like an old woman. I was glad he didn't, because the look on his face made me want to crawl under the table.

"And I didn't fire your boy. I got attached to him right away. I want you to know that if I had a son, I would have wanted him to be as polite and as ambitious as Michael was." I paused and swallowed one of the lumps in my throat. I was glad to see that Jacob didn't look as sad now. "The last day that he worked for me, I was prepared to offer him the job on a full-time basis, but he didn't give me a chance to talk to him about it."

Another unbelievable look of sadness crossed Jacob's face. This time I was the one patting his hand.

"He was a fine young man, and I am so sorry about what happened to him. I would give anything in this world if I could go back to that day. I would have met him at the door that morning and told him he had a permanent job. I wanted to help him, but I guess I was too late, too."

"Don't beat yourself up over something you can't change, Annette."

I still felt some guilt over Michael Dench's suicide, and the sooner I got over that, the better. I knew that if I could do anything to make Michael's family get over their tragedy faster, I had to do it.

If spending time with me meant so much to Jacob, it was the least I could do. In a way, it was like we were doing one another a favor, so to speak.

"Jacob, I hope you still like good home-cooked meals. Because if you do, I'd really like it if you'd come by the house some time soon to have dinner with my daughter and me."

"I'd love that," Jacob said, almost drooling.

"Jacob, what are you grinning about?" Jade asked as she stumbled off the dance floor and back to her seat, with Vernie, Rhoda, and Otis close behind. They all sat down at the same time. "Annette must be putting some real funny bugs in your ear for you to be showing so much of your gums."

"I hate to leave, but Jacob and I are going to go home and finish off a mess of collard greens and some hush puppies that I had left over from yesterday's dinner," I lied. Jacob didn't bat an eye, and he didn't even seem surprised by what I'd just said.

"Aw, shuck it! That's a damn shame. I wish you didn't have to leave so soon. I'd love to hear more about . . . uh . . . whatever it is you're doing these days to keep your mind off the fact that your husband left you for another woman, Annette," Jade babbled. As soon as she stopped speaking, a loud, viper-like breath hissed from her pouting lips. A veil of indifference covered her face.

"I am really sorry that I can't stay longer, too, Jade." Now I was the one being nasty and sarcastic, and I knew she knew that. I could tell by the glare on her evil face. Jade was an extremely beautiful young woman. Like Rhoda, she seemed to look more and more like supermodel Naomi Campbell with each passing day. But Jade's personality and demeanor were so ugly—at least as far as I was concerned—that I could only acknowledge her beauty through a pig's eye. You would have thought that I was Miss Piggy by the way I was looking at her now.

"Annette, why in the world are you staring at me like that with that stupid look on your face?" she asked, fidgeting sideways in her seat. If Vernie had not secured her in place by wrapping his arm around her shoulder, she would have slid to the floor. She was slurring her words and the whites of her eyes had begun to turn red.

"I was just thinking about how sweet you were when you were a little girl," I replied in a heavy voice.

She released a loud hiccup before she stammered, "I'm . . . I'm still sweet!" She looked from me to her parents and then to her confused-looking husband for confirmation. "Aren't I, Mama? Daddy? Vernie, you told me to my face one time that if God made a sweeter woman than me, He kept her for Himself. Didn't you?"

"I sure did," Vernie answered, his words fumbling over his lips like clumsy feet. "And that's still true today."

"Seeeeee," Jade sang. Her eyes looked like they were about to pop out of their sockets as she shot dagger looks at me.

I gave her a pitiful look and shook my head. That made her look even more indignant. "Good night, everybody," I said gently, not taking my eyes off of Jade. "Jade, happy birthday again. If I had known that you were going to be here tonight, I'd have brought you a present."

"And I wonder what that might have been?" Otis yelled. He was beginning to look and act drunk, too.

"Oh, there is just no telling!" Jade shouted, almost leaping out of her seat. "After all, Annette is the dollar-store queen."

Rhoda was obviously annoyed, and I had a feeling that she was as uncomfortable as I was. Somehow, she managed to keep a smile on her face.

"Annette, you don't want a piece of cake?" Otis asked. "Or are you still counting dem calories. You can still take a tiny sliver with you!"

"Don't force her, Daddy. Can't you see she's gained back some of that weight—and in all of the wrong places." Jade snickered, shaking her head as she lifted a knife and positioned it above her birthday cake. "Vernie, scoot over to the bar and see if they've got some milk—and make sure it's low fat!"

Vernie rose at the same time that Jacob and I did. He went one way and we went the other.

# CHAPTER 45

"Annette, this is Pee Wee. You know I don't like to talk to no answerin' machine, and knowin' you, you probably standin' right next to it listenin' to me talk. So pick up!" Pee Wee paused for about ten seconds.

I was in the living room where the telephone with the answering machine sat on one of the end tables next to my couch. I rolled my eyes and just stared at it. You would have thought that I was looking at a rotten apple, because I didn't even want to touch it.

When I didn't turn off the answering machine and pick up the telephone, Pee Wee continued speaking. "I don't want to say what I'm goin' to say to a machine, but you don't give me no choice." He paused again, and this time I heard ice cubes clinking against a glass so I knew that he was drinking. That made me really not want to pick up that telephone. It was hard enough trying to have a sensible conversation with him when he was sober. And now that I had so much red-hot anger practically cremating my peace of mind, the less I talked to him the better. At least until I cooled down to a sizzle.

"You listen here, woman!" He was yelling so loud his voice echoed. "I don't know who you've been talkin' to and who's been puttin' shit in your head, but you better straighten up and you'd better do it quick. I don't appreciate you sendin' a process server to the restaurant where I was havin' dinner with some friends this evenin'. Do you know how embarrassed I was? And if you think I'm goin' to make it easy for you to get a divorce, you got another think comin'. Shit!"

I could not believe that this was the same mild-mannered man I'd known for over thirty years. If a midlife crisis was responsible for the metamorphosis that had turned him into such a dick, there was no hope for the rest of the world.

I reached over to turn off the answering machine and take his call, but I was too slow. He had already slammed down the phone, and so abruptly and hard that it made me shudder.

I called him back immediately. He didn't answer. I hated talking to answering machines, too, but I did.

"Pee Wee, if you're there, please pick up the phone." I gave him a full minute to do so, but he didn't.

I had other things to do, so I wasn't going to waste any more time on him. I had invited Jacob to dinner, and I wanted the evening to go well.

I had left work early so I could take my time shopping for all the things I needed for this special occasion. Jacob was a meat and potatoes man, so I wasn't going to insult him by serving pizza like he had suggested.

I had picked out one of the best-looking rump roasts that I'd seen since my size 24 days. That and a pot of collard greens, some baked potatoes, and a peach cobbler seemed like the perfect reunion feast for me and Jacob to get reacquainted over.

He had been to my house a few times since that night at the Red Rose, but he'd stayed for only a couple of hours each time. Other than a few lingering kisses, and his hands roaming over a few intimate locations on my body, we had not taken our relationship to the next level. And I had my work cut out for me. I started by telling him that he needed to do something about his bad breath. He was surprised to hear that he even had that problem. And he was even more surprised when I told him that he'd always had that problem. I couldn't believe that nobody had told him about it in all of these years—especially the women he kissed. He thanked me for telling him, and from that point on, he kept an ample supply of breath mints and other breath-freshening products in his pocket.

And just to be on the safe side, I stocked my candy dishes with the same things for when he visited me.

Charlotte liked Jacob, especially since two of the times that he'd been to the house he'd brought gifts for her. When I told her that he was going to join us for dinner tonight, she got so excited you would have thought that he was her date. But only because she knew he'd be bringing her another gift. However, she had chosen to eat dinner and spend the night with the Turner kids across the street. She'd made that decision as soon as she found out I was planning to serve greens again for dinner. One reason my daughter, as well as most of the other kids in the neighborhood, liked to hang out at the Turner residence was because the Turners rarely cooked most of the foods on the average black child's hate list, like the collard greens and the rump roast that I had on the menu.

We rarely ate meals in my spacious dining room anymore. So since this was such a special occasion for me, I thought it would be nice to set the table with a new white linen tablecloth, candles, and a vase of fresh red and white roses. I had even purchased some maroon-colored place mats.

Jacob was due at six, so when I heard a car in the driveway, I assumed it was him. I glanced at my watch. It was only five thirty. Before I could make it to the window to peep out and see who it was, my kitchen door flew open.

Pee Wee stormed in looking like a mad man. "What the hell is this?" he screamed, waving some papers in my face.

I calmly took the papers and looked at the top page. "Hmmm. It looks like a notice that I'm divorcing you," I said, tilting my head. I looked around the kitchen to make sure my rolling pin was handy. Since the day that I'd used it on Lizzie, I kept it on the counter close to the door. Pee Wee saw me looking at it, so he moved back a few steps. "What did you think the papers were?"

He snatched the papers out of my hand. "I can read! I know what it is!" he hollered, shaking the paper like he was trying to shake off the words on it.

"Well, if you know what it is, why are you asking me what it is?" I folded my arms defiantly. "What did you expect? Did you think I was going to wait around for you to serve me?"

"Who said I was goin' to serve you?" There was a wounded look on his face. You would have thought that I'd already slapped him upside the head.

"Why else would you be talking to a lawyer?"

"What are you talking about?" he shrieked, flapping his arms like he was about to take off flying. He gave me a wide-eyed look, and he stopped flapping his arms as his body froze. "Who told you I was talkin' to a lawyer?"

"If you really must know, it was good old Scary Mary. The lawyer that you talked with just happens to be one of her regular tricks!"

"Shit!" he barked, the word shooting out of his mouth like a bullet. "That old lady pimp needs to mind her own damn business. That damn woman has been a thorn in my side since the day I met her!"

"Well, she is like family to me, so she looks out for me. By the way, she told me about that night you tried to rent one of her rooms so you and your whore could lay up."

"That's a damn lie. Lizzie had lost her house key, and her mama and stepdaddy were in Toledo. The motels didn't have any vacancies, and Lizzie didn't want to impose on you and spend the night on our couch."

"So you took a woman to a *brothel* to try and get a room? What did you think Scary Mary would make of that?"

"That old battle-ax didn't give me a chance to tell her why I was tryin' to rent a room that night. I was goin' to get Lizzie situated, and then I was goin' to come on home like I was supposed to."

"Yeah, right. So what were you talking to that lawyer about? Vietnam? Or was it some sporting event?"

Pee Wee's shoulders sagged. He stumbled as he made his way to the table, where he collapsed into a chair. "Annette, I was talkin' to that lawyer about a minor tax situation. I don't know what he told Scary Mary, but I know that old blabbermouth didn't say nothin' about me talkin' to him about a divorce. Now did she?"

"Well, no, she didn't. But under the circumstances, what else could she or I think?" I sat down across from him.

"I don't want a divorce," he said. He was very emphatic about it. "I told you that back when you, uh, you know."

"Yes, you told me you didn't want a divorce when you found out about me and Louis. But what do you want now?"

He covered his face with his hands and shook his head. When he looked at me again, he looked so confused I almost felt sorry for him. "I'm just tryin' to sort things out, that's all." He rose and started walking toward the living room. I was close behind him. "Where's my daughter?" he asked, still walking.

"She's having dinner with the Turners," I reported.

"I guess them greens done finally got to her. I got a feelin' that is what I smell right now." He sniffed a few times and continued walking. He stopped when he got to the dining room doorway.

"That's right," I said.

He looked at the table; then he turned and looked at me. I had on a hostess gown with a very low-cut neckline. "I—why are you dressed like *that?*"

"I'm expecting company for dinner this evening," I explained, smoothing down the sides of my gown with both hands.

Then he whirled back around and looked at the lavish spread on the table. "Well, if the company you expectin' ain't Gandhi, it better be Nelson Mandela! I know goddamn well you didn't go to all this trouble for that cheesy-ass motherfucker I seen you slobberin' all over that night outside the Red Rose!"

# CHAPTER 46

"Yes, I am expecting that . . . that particular man you just mentioned," I answered, glaring at Pee Wee. Now that we were no longer in the kitchen, I couldn't grab that rolling pin if I needed to. But I wouldn't hesitate to grab one of the thick wooden chairs from the table to "defend" myself. "What's it to you?" I leaned over the table and straightened the two place mats.

"What's it to me? I'll tell you what it is to me. Jacob ain't the kind of person I want my daughter around."

"That's too bad. I guess we still have at least one thing in common. Lizzie is not the kind of person I want my daughter around," I retorted.

"Lizzie is a good woman," he had the nerve to say.

"So you keep telling me. In that case, you'd better get on back home to her before she gets suspicious."

"Lizzie ain't got no reason in the world to think I'm foolin' around with another woman."

"I didn't either—or so I thought," I said glumly. "Now, if you don't mind, I'd like for you to leave. My company is going to be here soon, and I am not in the mood to deal with a confrontation."

"You told me a long time ago that Jacob Brewster wasn't your type. Do you remember tellin' me that?"

"Yes, I remember telling you that. What's your point?"

"So why him? Why of all the men in this town did you run after him?"

"Why not him?" I quipped. "And for the record, I didn't run after him. There isn't a man on this planet that irresistible to me."

A disappointed look spread across his face. "Not even me?"

"Especially you!"

Pee Wee looked at the floor; then he looked at me again. His eyes looked like they'd seen the devil. Then they started twitching. For a second I thought that he was going to throw some kind of a fit. But all he did was give me a dismissive wave before he rushed out the door like his pants were on fire.

And not a minute too soon. As soon as he drove back out onto the street, Jacob pulled up in a shiny silver luxury car and parked it in front of my house. I didn't know much about cars. As a matter of fact, all I really knew was how to drive one. I didn't even know how to change my oil, and I could barely pump gas. I loved my little Mazda, but the way Jacob stood looking at his vehicle, and the way that he was brushing a spot on the hood with the sleeve of his shirt, I could tell that that car meant a lot to him. I didn't know what it was about men and their cars, and the way they worshipped them. It was one of the many things that irritated me, especially when it involved a middle-aged man. Rhoda's husband treated his Jeep like a mistress. He was in love with it. Pee Wee was the same kind of fool when it came to that damn red Firebird he drove. I will never forget the day that car entered our lives. When the dealer delivered it directly to our house, Pee Wee snatched the key out of the dealer's hand and kissed it.

Jacob stood back and stared at this car; then he got back in it. He didn't see me looking out the window, but I watched as he moved the car closer to the curb. When he got out this time, he wiped another spot on the other side of his hood.

"I didn't know you had two cars," I said as soon as he made it inside. The other times he'd come to the house he'd driven a beat-up old rust-colored jalopy that I couldn't even identify. It had surprised me when I found out that it was an old Thunderbird.

"I use the T-bird most of the time. I only use the Lexus for special occasions, like tonight. I thought that after dinner, I'd take you to a movie or to that new bar out on Sawyer Road for a few late-night drinks," he told me all in one breath. He handed me a bottle of Chianti as he removed his thin cotton jacket. Like Pee Wee, Jacob was no fashion icon. He wore a pair of jeans, a white shirt, and a red tie.

"They must be paying you some long money down at that brickyard for you to be able to afford a brand-new Lexus," I teased.

I hung his jacket on the rack by the door and led him to the living room. I had already placed a bottle of wine and two wineglasses on the coffee table in front of my couch.

As soon as his butt hit the couch, he slid out of his shoes. Then he promptly raised his arms, stretched his mouth open like a lion, and released a fierce yawn. Something told me that this man was about to make himself right at home. And that was the way I wanted it to be. If I was going to be spending time with him, the sooner we got better acquainted the better. I had no time to lose.

"Oh, I don't make much money over there. The brick business is not what it used to be. But I stay there because I got tired of changing jobs every two or three years." He leaned slightly to the side so that his elbow rested on the arm of the couch.

"I am glad to see that you are still doing so well. Did you ever buy your own house? You used to talk about becoming a homeowner a lot back in the day."

"Yes and no. When my mama passed, I got the house. She had already paid off the mortgage. That was enough of a blessing. But like the old folks say, 'God is good.' And sure enough, He proved it. Come to find out, my mama had a two-hundred-thousand-dollar life insurance policy. Girl, when that insurance man contacted me and told me that I was the sole beneficiary, I had such a serious panic attack I quit the job I was working at the time on the spot!"

Jacob popped open the bottle of wine that he'd brought and poured himself a glass. I waited for him to pour some into my glass, but he didn't. That puzzled me, but it was not important enough for me to mention. I just hoped that he was having as much fun learning more about me as I was learning more about him. Our previous relationship had been so brief, I had only met his mother and a couple of his other older relatives. I didn't even know that he was a smoker until he fished a pack of Newports out of his shirt pocket.

"You got an ashtray?"

I scurried into the kitchen and returned with one of several ashtrays that I kept in a cabinet. I only brought them out when a smoking guest visited, or when Pee Wee lit up a joint.

"Like I was saying, my mama left me all that nice money. And since I was so overwhelmed, I needed to relax. I did that on a two-week cruise, visiting spots in the Caribbean that I'd always wanted to visit. I ate spit-roasted prime rib for breakfast! Had two cuties on my arms at all times. I got some sun, not that I need more sun with my black ass." He paused and guffawed long and loud. "I was living like a king for those two weeks." He gave me a misty-eyed look. "My mama sure was a thoughtful woman. She surprised the hell out of me!"

"Why? If you were her only child, who else would she make her insurance out to?"

"She's got a couple of greedy kinfolks who got a little upset when they found out she left me the house. They stopped speaking to me altogether when they found out about the insurance money, too. See, me and my mama didn't really get along that well. I didn't get to visit her that much in the last days and . . . and I feel kind of bad about that. But I can't change anything now!" Jacob slapped his thigh. "Anyway, I just went on that cruise and enjoyed myself. I'm the kind of man who enjoys and appreciates the good life."

"A cruise," I swooned. "That must have been nice."

"Uh-huh." He nodded; then he sniffed and looked toward the dining room where the aroma of the lavish dinner that I'd prepared was coming from.

"Collard greens and rump roast. And I remembered how much you liked peach cobbler," I said with glee.

"Is that right? Damn! I wish I hadn't eaten that super burrito before I left work. But don't worry, if I don't eat before I leave tonight, you can fix me a couple of plates to take home."

Jacob and I had talked about my cooking dinner for him several times in the last couple of days. I couldn't understand why he had eaten a super burrito just before the dinner that I had spent so much time and money on. I let all of that slide. But something told me right then and there that if I continued to see Jacob, there would be a lot of other things for me to let slide, too. And I didn't like that.

When he whipped out a book of matches and scraped one across the top of my coffee table, I let that slide. But the more cigarettes he smoked, the more I frowned. I didn't have a problem with people smoking in my house. But I did have a problem when people ignored the ashtrays that I put in front of them and still shook a few ashes onto my carpet! That's what Jacob was doing now.

"If you don't mind, would you please make sure your ashes land in the ashtray, not on my carpet," I said. "And please use the matchbook cover to strike your matches, not my coffee table."

"Oh! I'm so sorry. I'm just so excited to be here with you, I can't keep my mind straight." He had smoked only half of his fourth or fifth cigarette, but he mashed it out in the ashtray, then turned to me. "I'm going to make you a very happy woman, Annette. This time for sure. I shouldn't have let you get away from me that other time. If I hadn't, you wouldn't be sitting around depressed about that fool Pee Wee running out on you."

"I'm not exactly depressed, Jacob."

"The hell you're not. I know a depressed woman when I see one. Now give me some sugar."

I hesitated, but I puckered up and kissed him. From that point on, all he was interested in was my body.

# CHAPTER 47

After he had removed my clothes and his, he folded everything and placed it on top of the coffee table next to the wine-glasses. The latest edition of the *Richland Review* newspaper was already on the coffee table, opened to the sports section. He glanced at an article about Tiger Woods winning the Masters Tournament by a record of twelve strokes; a first for a black person. "Hmmm. I didn't know black folks played golf," he said with a snicker. That was such a stupid remark, I chose not to comment on it. Then he covered my body with his, spreading my legs open with his knee. We made love on my living room floor.

I was not the kind of woman who liked to do a lot of talking when I was this close to a man, but Jacob couldn't stop yapping. "Baby, you are going to love this," he promised, yelling into my ear. Now that was a bit irritating. When I moaned and turned my head to the side and shuddered, he thought that it was because I was in ecstasy. "See there!" he panted. He moaned a few times as he slammed into me. As soon as he caught his breath, he started yip yapping again. "I knew you were going to have a meltdown as soon as I got my hands on you. You'll be begging me not to stop! And it won't be long before I have you so sprung, you'll have to be weaned off me. I'm going to put something on you that a doctor can't take off. Oh baby!"

"As long as it's not some incurable case of VD," I joked, huffing and puffing and writhing as I tried to keep up with his thrashing hip movements.

We both laughed. For one thing, he wore a condom, so him putting something on me that a doctor couldn't take off wasn't likely to happen. However, he made me feel so good that, when he attempted to rise and return to the couch, I pinned him to the floor. I didn't release him until I was thoroughly satisfied.

It was nice. It was nice to be in a man's arms again, even if that man was not my husband. Jacob was a fairly good lover, and he seemed to be more interested in satisfying me than he was himself.

We eventually ended up in the same bed upstairs that I had shared with Pee Wee. But by that time we were both too tired to continue. I fell asleep with my head on his shoulder.

When we woke up at the same time a little while later, he licked up and down my chest and face, and played with my titties for a few minutes. I tickled his butt and fondled his balls, but that was all. And I was glad that that was all we did. I knew it was going to be hard for me to enjoy making love in the same bed that I'd shared with my husband for so many years. That was something that I wanted to ease into.

When Jacob left a few minutes after midnight, the scrumptious dinner that I had prepared for him was still on my dining room table. I put everything away, drank a glass of warm milk, and then took a shower before I returned to my bedroom. I straightened the sheets and blankets, and crawled back into bed, but I couldn't fall asleep. For some reason, I couldn't get comfortable on the same sheets where I'd just wallowed around with another man. Especially since the sheets were still damp with his sweat. I jumped up and changed the bedding; then I slid into the bed and slept like a baby.

The next morning when I called Rhoda and told her about Pee Wee's visit, then Jacob's, she couldn't stop laughing. "Maybe the next time you prepare a meal like that, you really should invite Gandhi. Or at least Nelson Mandela."

"The next time I go to that much trouble to prepare dinner, it won't be for a man," I vowed. "At the end of the day, it's all about sex with them. By the way, how is Bully?"

"Now don't you start talkin' trash about my sweetie. He's fine if you must know. He's fifty if he's a day, but he's in better shape than men half his age. I'm blessed. And you are, too."

"I don't know about that. I've lost my husband to another woman, and I've got some serious concerns about the man I'm with now."

"Jacob? He's harmless. And didn't you just tell me how good he was in bed? What more do you want?"

"He's too pushy for me. Also, he's got some hygiene habits I don't like. He doesn't like to use deodorant." I stopped talking and we remained silent for a long uncomfortable moment.

"Don't leave me hangin' just when it was gettin' good!" Rhoda yelled. "Explain what you just said."

"I don't like it when he shows up without calling. That's one thing. He did that the very first time he came to the house. I was not expecting him, so I looked like a fishwife and the house was a mess. And it's bad enough when it's my house involved, but he has already dropped by my office a few times with flowers for me. I don't share my personal business with the people I work with, but they know I'm married. I don't even want to think about what some of them must be thinking about his visits."

"Or what they are sayin'. You know how the people in this city like to spread gossip."

"Tell me about it. And another thing that I don't like about him is that, when he takes baths in my house, he leaves his dirty underwear on the floor, and he doesn't even bother to let the water out of the tub when he finishes."

"What is so bad about that? I have that same problem with Jade."

"Jacob is usually covered with that oily dust from the brickyard when he comes by after work. You wouldn't believe the black ring it leaves in my bathtub. And he leaves the soap in the water, too. So it melts and floats on top of the water. By the time I go into the bathroom to clean up after him, it's a mess."

"Well, sister-girl, all you have to do is tell him to clean up after himself. And don't leave it open for discussion. Shit. That's your house, and he should respect your rules. What about his house? Does he do the same thing there?"

"He does, but a woman cleans for him a couple of times a week."

"Hmmm. Well, no man is perfect. That's the one thing we have to keep in mind. We can't live with them, and we can't live without them, right?"

"That's one question I can't answer. But I will admit that I'd rather spend my time with Jacob than alone. He's good company. At least until . . ."

"Until Pee Wee comes back?"

"That's not what I was going to say!" I said quickly.

"Then what were you goin' to say?"

"Just that I'm going to cancel my divorce for now. Now that I know Pee Wee's not ready for it."

"But shouldn't you be more concerned about what *you're* ready for? He left you and he just might not come back. You need to get things in writing before somethin' happens to him."

"What do you mean?"

"Bein' apart but not divorced is like havin' a sword hangin' over your head."

"Where are you going with this?"

"Find out where you stand in regards to the financial position. What if he drops dead tomorrow and you find out his life insurance goes to that bitch or one of his relatives? What about that car he paid cash for?"

"You of all people know that I am about as financially secure as I can be. I can get along just fine without his insurance if he drops dead tomorrow."

"That's not the point. I know it's easy for you to say that now, but it'd be a different story if it happened. And what about Charlotte? Do you want Lizzie to end up with somethin' that should go to your child? Look, even if you don't go through with a divorce, you need to get some legal advice anyway. Change your will. Because as much as I hate to bring it up, that sword hangin' over your head cuts both ways."

"Stop talking like one of Joan Crawford's movie characters and say what you mean the first time," I ordered with a heavy groan. "You're giving me a headache."

"Annette, if something happens to you, Lizzie might end up raisin' your daughter, in the house that your mama left to you and you alone. I know you've got a couple of bucks in the bank, too.

You need to make sure it all goes into some kind of trust fund for Charlotte until she's of legal age. Have you thought about that?"

"No . . ."

"Then you'd better. And the next time you see or talk to Jacob, tell him I said hello."

"I don't plan on seeing him for a while. I am beginning to feel smothered, and I need some space right now. I'm going to spend less time with him."

# CHAPTER 48

The very next day, Jacob parked in front of my house and ran up to my front door with a bouquet of roses in his hand. "Baby, I hope you're ready," he said when I opened the door.

"Ready for what?" I asked, taking the flowers he waved in my face.

"I thought we were going out to dinner. Didn't you get my message?" he said with an anxious look on his face.

I stood there with my head cocked to the side, giving him a guarded look. "What message?"

He strolled in, slamming the door shut behind him. "Didn't that dingbat secretary tell you that I called? I told her to ask you if you wanted to go to Lomax's Steak House this evening. I told her to tell you that if I didn't hear back from you, I would assume you were going, and that I would make a reservation for seven o'clock. We could have a few drinks at the bar, listen to that soulful country western band, then enjoy a nice steak dinner with all the trimmings. I didn't hear back from you, so here I am." Jacob gave me a gummy smile as he spread his arms out like he was expecting me to fall into them and swoon.

I sighed and placed the roses, which were already in a nice vase, on the coffee table. "I didn't get the message. And in the future, don't leave messages and assume I'll get them."

"You need to talk to your girl at your office. She told me point-blank that she would make sure you got my message."

"That's not the point, Jacob. If you want to see me, you need to talk to *me*, not my dingbat secretary. Don't leave messages and assume that's all you need to do before you show up. I would appreciate your confirming things with me. That's just common courtesy."

"I'm sorry, baby. I'll go on back home," he pouted, heading back toward the door. "Tell Charlotte I asked about her."

"Charlotte is spending the night with her grandparents. And wait—you don't have to leave. Since you're already here, we might as well keep that reservation you made."

Despite the fact that Jacob was beginning to look like a first-class oaf, I still enjoyed his company. And he had selected a nice place for dinner. Lomax's was one of my favorite restaurants. As a matter of fact, some of the waiters still remembered me from the days I used to come in and eat enough for three people.

Jacob had instructed me to order whatever I wanted on the menu, and since I had not eaten lobster in a while, that was what I ordered. It was not a cheap place, and when the waiter placed the $190 check on our table, my eyes watered.

"Baby, can you go warm up the car while I take care of the bill?" Jacob asked, rising.

Jacob was not the kind of man to do gallant things, like helping me put on my coat or opening my car door. I rose and wrestled myself into the black spring coat that I'd worn over my light blue pantsuit. "The waiter will take the check and payment to the cashier. I'll wait for you," I told him. "Make sure you give him a good tip," I said in a low voice. "I am a regular here."

"No, no, you go on and warm up the car," he insisted, handing me the keys to his Lexus.

I shrugged, took the keys, and headed toward the door. I noticed our waiter looking at me with a puzzled expression on his face, but I kept walking. I didn't stop until I reached Jacob's car.

Just as I seated myself in the driver's seat and started the motor, Jacob came sprinting out of the restaurant with three waiters on his tail. "Let's go!" he yelled as he flung open the door on the passenger side and hopped in. "Drive like hell!"

I didn't have time to ask questions or react. I just drove. I drove like a bat out of hell, turning the first corner on two wheels. Finally, I asked, "What the hell is going on?"

Jacob didn't answer my question, but I answered it for him. "You ran out on the bill, didn't you?"

"Yes, I did. And do you want to know why?"

"Yes, I would like to know why. I have never done anything like this before in my life! Don't you know we could get arrested for doing shit like this?"

"Well, they have to catch us first." Jacob giggled like the Joker.

"If you didn't have enough money, you should have told me. I would have been glad to pay the bill."

"Naw, naw. This wasn't about me not having enough money to pay the bill."

"Don't tell me you do shit like this just for the thrill of it?" I yelled.

"It's a lot more serious than that. See, just before my mama died, I brought her to this restaurant for Mother's Day. When she complained about the way they had cooked her steak, instead of them cooking another one for her, they politely told her that if she didn't like the way they cooked, she should eat her steaks someplace else. My mother was a dignified woman, see. Everybody liked her. She didn't deserve to be treated like that. I called up the restaurant the next day and demanded to speak to the manager. When I tried to speak my mind, he hung up on me! This was the only way I could get back at them."

"By not paying your check? And why did you have to drag me into it?" I had to stop for a red light. I looked in the rearview mirror, glad not to see a police cruiser behind us. "What if they got your license plate number?"

"I thought about that. Now, you know I am no angel, never have been. I'm the kind of brother who will do what I have to do when necessary. I switched my real plates for this car with the stolen plates that my thug cousin Georgie uses when he needs to take care of some street business. The plates belong on the car of a little old white retired schoolteacher from Sandusky."

I was angry, but there was nothing I could do about what had happened. "Just promise me that the next time you have a point to make, don't involve me."

Things were too tense, so Jacob didn't attempt to come in once we got back to my house. He didn't kiss me or even walk me to the front door. "I'll see you soon," he yelled as I ran up on my porch.

And I knew he would.

When I spoke to Rhoda the next morning, I told her I'd had dinner with Jacob the night before. However, I didn't tell her about the scam he'd pulled. She would have never let me live that down.

"It sounds like he's tryin' so hard to please you," she told me. "I know he's kind of crude, but he sounds like he's the best man for you right now."

"The best man? That's funny. Is there such a thing anymore? Has there ever been such a thing on this planet?"

"The best man? Probably not. But there are men a lot worse than Jacob."

"That's for sure," I muttered. "Jacob's all right. He'll do for now, I guess."

"He'll do for now? That doesn't sound very hopeful. And I hope no man ever says somethin' that generic and indifferent about me." Rhoda laughed. "By the way, have you talked to your lawyer lately?"

"No, but I will. And I'm telling you now that if Jacob is the best I can do, I might cancel my divorce for good."

"So that means you think there is a chance for you and Pee Wee to reconcile? Is that why you might cancel the divorce?"

"I don't think I really need a divorce. I don't need one so I could rush into another marriage."

"What's that supposed to mean?"

"For one thing, there are too many Jacobs out there waiting to jump into the lives of women like me. I am going to make sure that all of my assets are protected, so a divorce is not a priority right now. I don't know if divorce is always the answer when a marriage goes sour. I know marriage is a partnership, but in America, most of the burden of keeping it together is on the woman's shoulders."

"Yeah, you're right. Look at me."

# CHAPTER 49

That following Wednesday morning, I went to see my lawyer so I could put my divorce on hold and revise my will. Rhoda was the only person who knew about my plans.

My mother, my father, and Scary Mary advised me daily to "straighten" out my life because they didn't want me to "suffer" or "be stupid enough to grow old alone." Each one had a different interpretation of what I needed to do to get out of the mess I was in. My mother assured me that no matter what man I ended up with, he'd still be a dog or a devil. To her, the three were interchangeable. It didn't matter how good or bad that man was, when it came to men, it was a one-size-fits-all situation. It was up to a woman to make the best of a relationship; men didn't have enough sense to do so. Scary Mary offered to share some voodoo secrets with me that would "take care of Pee Wee and that wench" he'd left me for. Daddy told me that whatever I wanted to do, it was my business. But he also told me that if I wanted him to help me find a new man, and I didn't have a problem with age, he had a lot of widowed friends that he could introduce me to.

I was nervous sitting in the lobby of David Weinstein's office with four other women, all younger than me. And each one was barking like a dog about one thing or another. I overheard one woman complain to one of the other women that her husband had left her because she'd gained seventy pounds. Another one told somebody that she was conversing with on her cellular phone that she was sorry she'd let herself go. I could see why. Her bright red hair looked like a well-used mop, she was as big as I once was, and her nose looked like a meatball. Another one, a dwarf who couldn't have stood more than three and a half feet tall, said she was going to beat up the woman her husband had left her for. I found that hard to believe. With her squeaky voice and abbreviated height, this woman looked about as menacing as Winnie the Pooh. I decided to keep my business to myself.

And I was glad that I had not let my physical appearance go to the dogs. Not only was I the most well-groomed woman waiting to see Mr. Weinstein, I noticed that I was the only woman in the room with a neck. But I was still in the same boat with these other four no-neck women: I couldn't hold on to my husband.

My lawyer agreed with everything Rhoda had told me: I had to protect my assets in case Pee Wee got greedy. After we'd revised my will, my lawyer complimented me on how nice I looked. I had worn a stylish black pantsuit with a yellow silk blouse. I had just come from the beauty shop, so my hair, nails, and face were all looking good. By the time I left, I was feeling so much better.

My euphoria didn't last long, though.

A stout black man about my age, wearing a blue suit at least two sizes too small, got in the elevator with me on the fourteenth floor. He wasn't particularly handsome, but he had a pleasant-looking face. He nodded at me, I nodded at him. Then he looked at me and did a double take. "These white folks! I been tryin' to settle a claim with the unemployment folks for two years, and I ain't no farther along than I was two years ago. Ain't white folks a mess?"

"I know what you mean," I said with a weak nod.

"It's a good thing I got me a side thing goin'. I'm gettin' paid under the table so I don't really need that pooh butt pocket change the unemployment crooks dole out anyway. But I want it 'cause I earned it! Know what I mean?"

"I know what you mean."

"I look at it this way, anytime we can pull somethin' over on the man, it's just part of that money they owe us for all that free labor our folks done for them as slaves. Know what I mean?"

"I know exactly what you mean," I agreed.

The man suddenly gave me a critical look. "Excuse me, sister, but you look like somebody I used to work with when I worked for the phone company. And them dogs was about as racist as could be. They fired me for no reason! I was late a few times when my car wouldn't start and I didn't get along with my supervisor; but other than that, I was a damn good employee. I done what they paid me to do, so that should have been enough. Anyway, there was this sister there that they all liked. They bent over backward to keep her happy, like she was their pet monkey. And in a way she was! Of course, she was one of them butt-kissin' mammies that the white folks love to death. A woman named Annette."

Damn! I must have been looking better than I thought if people didn't recognize me. Even though I didn't like what the man had just said about me being a butt-kissing mammy, I gave him one of my broadest smiles, and he smiled back.

"You know a sister named Annette Davis?" he asked, a puzzled look on his face.

I nodded. "Uh-huh," I said shyly, the smile still on my face.

"People ever tell you that you look a lot like her?"

I nodded again.

"Don't it make you mad?"

"Excuse me?" The smile left my face so fast my teeth ached.

"I mean, if people tell you that you look like Diana Ross, that's one thing. If people tell you that you look like somebody like that Annette—not that you ugly or nothing, that's another thing. But she sure wouldn't have won no first-prize blue ribbons for her looks. You look enough like her, but you look WAY better than her! Take me and my older brother, Pookie. We look enough alike people can tell we are related. But he's ugly, whereas I inherited all the good looks."

"No, it doesn't make me mad when people tell me I look like Annette Davis."

"Hmmm. You must be a real strong woman. What you say your name was?"

"Annette." I sniffed. "Annette Davis."

If I had slapped this man with a dead skunk, he could not have looked more startled.

"You do look a whole lot better than you used to look," he amended. "At least you got that goin' for you. What did you do to yourself? Get liposuction, or what?"

Before I could answer, the elevator stopped on the third floor and he bolted, even though he had punched the ground floor.

I remained mildly depressed for a couple of hours. But when Jacob showed up at my house unannounced that night and told me that he'd been thinking about me all day, I felt so much better. "Annette, this time I am going to do everything in the world to hold on to you."

Charlotte was with Pee Wee for only a few hours, so Jacob and I couldn't get too cozy.

We had just started on our first pitcher of lemonade when Pee Wee showed up with Charlotte in tow, hugging the new black-and-white backpack that he'd bought for her the day before.

"Hi, Mom. Hi, Jacob," she greeted before dashing up to her room.

Normally, when Pee Wee dropped Charlotte off, he didn't stay. But as soon as he realized I had a man in the living room, he made himself comfortable on the love seat that faced Jacob. I sat on the arm of the couch close to Jacob.

"What's up, dude?" Pee Wee grumbled, looking at Jacob with his eyes narrowed into slits.

"Hey!" Jacob jumped up from his seat and attempted to shake Pee Wee's hand. Pee Wee looked at Jacob's hand with a severe frown and ignored it. Then he looked at Jacob's bare feet. I didn't know Jacob had removed his shoes.

"I'm glad to see you and my ex seem to be gettin' so close so soon," Pee Wee sneered.

"Well, brother, let me put it like this. One man's shit is another man's fertilizer," Jacob announced with a smug look and a wink.

Pee Wee jumped up so fast he almost fell. Both his fists were clenched. I rose, too.

"I think you should leave," I said to Pee Wee, both my arms outstretched.

"I think I should, too!" he snapped.

I didn't say anything to Jacob until I heard Pee Wee's car roar out onto the street.

"That was a tacky thing for you to say," I scolded, shaking my finger in his face.

"It's true!" he boomed. "And the sooner you put that fool out of your mind, the better off we'll be. You need a husband who deserves you."

"Jacob, let's get something straight right now. We don't know where our relationship is going. I told you in the beginning that I am not looking for another husband anytime soon. And I am not looking to get too seriously involved with another man yet either."

"Well, let me tell you something right now, too. We are already seriously involved, sister."

I cringed when he kissed me. And I asked myself, *What have I gotten myself into now?*

# CHAPTER 50

Two days later, Jacob was at my door again, knocking so hard I thought he was trying to knock down the door. "I don't believe this shit!" I hollered out loud. "Does this man not listen, or does he not understand plain English?" I felt a little foolish standing in my living room having a conversation with myself. But I was at the end of my rope with Jacob's bad habits.

Since I had not invited him over, and he had not called to let me know that he was coming, I didn't answer the door. By now I had decided that the only way I was going to tolerate him was to be as crude and rude as he was. Well, maybe not that bad. But I wasn't going to make it easy for him to run our relationship in a way that suited him but not me.

I parted my living room window curtains just enough so I could see him. I waited and watched until he walked off the porch and back to his car. Then I went back into the kitchen and continued mixing the cornbread to go with the cabbage greens that I had planned to serve for dinner.

A couple of minutes went by and the next thing I knew, Jacob came prancing into the kitchen, grinning like one of those door-to-door salesmen. My daughter was right behind him. "Mama, didn't you hear Jacob knocking?" she asked, giving Jacob a sympathetic glance.

"Oh, was that you, Jacob? I thought I heard something," I muttered, wiping my hands on the tail of my apron.

"I just about came through that door. And the knuckles on my hand are still aching from all that knocking I did. You must be deaf," he complained.

"I didn't hear you," I said, forcing myself not to sound angry. I didn't like to get involved in confrontations when Charlotte was present—not with Pee Wee, and especially not with Jacob. I had no trouble admitting to myself that my generation was setting some pretty bad examples for Charlotte's generation. More than half of her friends lived in broken homes. But since I had no control over my situation with Pee Wee and I was stuck with Jacob, I tried to make the best of it. And that meant I couldn't let my guard down and act a fool by telling Jacob off in front of Charlotte but still letting him come to the house. That was one mixed message I didn't want to convey.

Charlotte had an anxious look on her face. She stared at me for a few seconds; then she turned to Jacob. "What you bring me? What you bring me?" she asked, already reaching for a small white bag he held in his hand.

"Just some mangoes," he responded.

I could tell from the look on her face that Jacob's latest gift didn't impress her at all. "Oh." She shrugged, looking from him to me. "Mama, what's a mango?"

"It's a fruit," I told her, taking the bag out of her hand and placing it on the counter. Somehow I managed to look at Jacob without scowling. "Have a seat," I mumbled, waving him to the table. I gave Charlotte the most exasperated look I could come up with, but she had no idea why. One thing I didn't want to do was involve her in my plan to gently ease Jacob out of my life. For one thing, I wasn't sure that that was what I wanted to do. I liked Jacob, and I was more than willing to continue the relationship as long as we kept it on a level that was comfortable for me.

"Do I smell cabbage greens?" he asked, sniffing and looking toward the stove where a pot of greens sat simmering.

"OH NO! NOT AGAIN!" Charlotte roared, stomping her foot on the floor so hard some empty pans on the counter rattled. "This house is turning into a chamber of horrors! If it's not one kind of greens for dinner, it's another. Yesterday, it was turnip greens. The day before that it was collard greens. The day before that it was collard greens *and* turnip greens—cooked up together in the same pot! I don't know what's wrong with the African American family these days! With all of the greens black people eat, one day we are going to turn into plant people!" She paused long enough to give me a pleading look. "Mama, why do you keep doing this to me?"

"I've been cooking the same meals for you for eleven years, and as long as you live in this house, I will continue to choose the meals here. When you get a job and can afford to feed yourself, you can cook what you want to cook."

"See, I told you," Charlotte said to Jacob. Then she did something that I didn't like. She leaned over and whispered something in his ear.

"Don't do that," I ordered. Charlotte and Jacob whirled around and looked at me at the same time. One looked just as startled as the other. "Whispering is rude," I said.

Jacob laughed and pulled Charlotte into his arms. "Little sister, you better be glad you didn't grow up in my house. We had greens *and* beans together every day, seven days a week."

"And she'd better be glad that she's not a member of some family in China or Somalia, where they are lucky to get *anything* to eat every day," I said, sitting down in the chair facing Jacob.

"Get me a beer out of the ice box, sugar," he said to Charlotte, slapping her on the butt as he released her from his embrace.

"What time are you taking me to the movies this Saturday afternoon, Jacob?" she asked, prancing back to the table with a can of Coors Light in her hand.

"What movie?" I asked quickly, looking from Jacob to Charlotte. I didn't like that he had made plans to do something with my child without my permission or knowledge. And I didn't like the fact that my daughter had gotten friendly enough with Jacob to be contemplating spending a Saturday afternoon with him at the movies. But what I really didn't like was that the two of them had become so close so soon. "I don't recall anybody asking me about a movie?"

"What's the big deal? Jacob took me to the movies last Saturday," Charlotte reported.

"Oh? How come I didn't know about it?" I had to think back to the previous Saturday afternoon. All I could remember was Charlotte mumbling something to me about going to the mall with a friend and asking if it was all right. After I'd given her some spending money and told her to be home before dark, I'd waved her out the door. She came home before dark, told me she'd enjoyed the movie, we ate dinner, and that was it. She had said nothing to me about Jacob being the "friend" whom she'd gone to the movies with. And I had no reason to ask.

"I was at Jacob's house and we got bored," she told me. The more she revealed, the more concerned I became.

"Charlotte, can you go into the living room so I can talk with Jacob?" As soon as she left, I turned to Jacob. "Jacob, don't do anything else with my daughter unless I know about it."

He blinked like an owl. "I understand. But I didn't see any harm in letting her into my house when she went to the trouble of riding her bicycle all the way over to Willow Street. And I didn't see any harm in taking her to the movies that afternoon."

"I didn't even know she knew where you lived! And she knows I warned her about talking to . . . uh . . . I've just warned her to be careful. We're living in a world gone mad."

I had endured one of the most painful childhoods imaginable. Old Mr. Boatwright had tainted my precious little body with the scourge of sexual abuse, and that was not going to happen to my daughter if I could help it.

"Look, you listen," Jacob said, a hand in the air, a finger wagging in my face. "Your child couldn't be safer with nobody more than she would with me. I love kids. You know how much I miss my own child. So don't you worry about Charlotte."

"No, you listen, brother. Charlotte is not your child, she's mine. I will be the one to worry about her safety. I am responsible for her. I don't want you, or anybody else, to interfere with the way I'm raising my daughter. Now, if you want to remain friends with me, that's the one thing you will stay out of. Do I make myself clear?"

"I understand. But don't you think it's going to confuse her if she can't be friends with me and here I am over here spending time with you, taking you out, and eating dinner with you and her? And I hope you don't think for one minute that she doesn't know what's going on behind closed doors. I mean, the last time I spent the night and made love to you, you screamed so loud she came running to your room. I can assure you that she didn't think you were in your room screaming because I was scaring you with a spider or stepping on your toe. Kids know more than we do these days."

"Jacob, I don't want to sit here all night discussing this subject. I just want us to be on the same page. Charlotte is my daughter. You can be her friend; but when it comes to her activities, that's my job. If you want to take her to the movies, or anywhere else, you check with me first. That's all I ask."

"That's fine with me. This is your house and I'm just a guest. I will behave as such from now on. . . ."

I excused myself to go to the bathroom and when I returned, Jacob was kicked back on my living room sofa, barefooted, shirtless, and with a plate of my greens on his lap. But what was more disturbing was the fact that Charlotte was sitting next to him with her arm around his neck.

# CHAPTER 51

"Don't you think that you're jumping to conclusions too fast?" Rhoda said when I called her up and told her about how affectionate Charlotte was with Jacob. "He's not crazy enough to do anything inappropriate."

"How do you know that?"

"How do you know I'm not right?"

"I'd be willing to bet a month's salary that anybody who knew Mr. Boatwright would have said the same thing about him. Even you."

"Well, Buttwright was a different story."

"Every story on this subject is different. But the end results are always the same. After what I went through, if I let something happen to my daughter, I'd never forgive myself."

"Annette, has Jacob done anything for you to be concerned about?"

"He's a grown man and he should not be encouraging a young girl to get too close to him. That's inappropriate, if you ask me."

"If you're so concerned about it, dump him. And don't even think about gettin' involved with anybody else. You'll run into the same problem with the next man, and it might be even worse."

"Let's change the subject," I suggested, blowing out a loud groan.

"That's fine with me. But you're the one who brought it up."

I got off the phone with Rhoda and did a few chores around the house for the next half hour. I would have continued doing that, but somebody knocked on my front door. I moved quietly from the kitchen to the living room; the broom I had been using to sweep my kitchen floor was still in my hand. I looked toward the stairs and around the room to make sure Charlotte was not lurking about. The last thing I wanted her to do was answer the door without my knowledge like she'd done the day before.

I looked through the peephole. But since I had not turned on the porch light, it was too dark for me to see who it was. I didn't see Jacob's car on the street, but that didn't mean anything. He could have walked or had somebody drop him off. I held my breath and placed my ear against the door until I heard the visitor walking away. I ran to the window and cracked open the curtains. Whoever it was had on some kind of hooded windbreaker. He had the hood on his head, and it covered the top part of his face, so I still couldn't tell who it was. He spotted me in the window, gave me a little wave, and lowered the hood so I could see his face. I was stunned to see Vernie. I snatched open the door.

"Vernie! Vernie, come on in," I yelled. I propped the broom up in the corner by the door and beckoned for Jade's husband to enter.

"Hi, Miss Davis," he mumbled, dragging his feet as I led him into my living room.

"Please call me Annette," I told him. I waved him to the couch and I sat on the love seat facing him. "I didn't know you knew where I lived. It's nice to see you."

"Uh, I hope you don't mind me coming by like this. I got your address out of Rhoda's address book. She . . . Jade . . . nobody knows I'm over here. And I'd appreciate it if you don't tell them that I came by here. I needed to talk to somebody. I don't know anybody else up here that well yet, but since you're a friend of the family I thought it'd be all right if I talked with you."

"I see," I said carefully, wondering what I was about to get myself involved in this time. "Vernie, would you like something to drink first?"

"Yes, ma'am. I think I need one. And the stronger the better."

I padded to the cabinet where I kept my liquor, then poured him a shot of scotch and myself a glass of white wine.

"Now, what's the problem?" I asked, returning to my seat and crossing my legs.

He had to take a sip from his glass first. Then he looked at me with tears in his eyes. "I need to talk to you about my wife." His hands were shaking so hard he spilled a few drops of his drink on the top of my coffee table. When he realized that, he set the glass down on a coaster; then he started wringing his hands. "I'm sorry. I didn't mean to come over here and make a mess."

"Don't worry about that. Talk to me," I told him.

"Like I just said, I need to talk to you about my wife." His hands started shaking even harder. I couldn't tell if it was because he was nervous, angry, or frightened. I had a feeling it was probably all three. "That woman is driving me stone crazy!" he sputtered, balling one hand into a fist. "She is! She is driving me crazy!" He shook his fist in the air.

"I figured that," I told him in a calm voice, looking him straight in the eye.

"Now, I know all about the bad blood between you and her. She told me her side of the story. She told me how you got jealous of her as soon as she got into her teens because she was so pretty and so slim, and you were, um, real fat and real plain back then. She told me how you used to talk trash about her, and call her names behind her back with people from the 'hood and stuff. She told me how you upset her so bad that one time that she had a mild break-down and had to be hospitalized. She told me how she had to leave town to get you off her back. And when she came back, you started trash talking her again. That's why she doesn't want me to get to know you."

As soon as Vernie stopped talking, I started. "Vernie, Jade told you her side of the story. Let me tell you my side." I uncrossed my legs. "I treated Jade like she was my own child. She, like a lot of young girls, developed a crush on my husband. She started sending me anonymous hate mail, she harassed me by phone, thinking it was going to run me out of town so she could be with my husband. To make a long story short, her plan backfired. She didn't get rid of me, and she didn't get my husband. All she got for her troubles was a stint in the hospital after she suffered a mild 'breakdown' and 'amnesia.' Her parents sent her to New Orleans. She flunked out of college, drove her grandparents crazy; then she ran off to Cancún on spring break and got loose with a Mexican. She returned to Ohio with the Mexican. She drove him crazy, so he left here running, leaving her at the altar. That's when she had another one of her breakdowns. Then she fled to Alabama. Now she's back here and you . . . well, you married her. But by now, you must have an idea of what kind of girl she is."

"Annette, I met Jade in a club one night. All I did was ask her to dance. From that point on, she decided I was 'the one' for her. Next thing I know, I'm standing in front of a preacher getting married to her!"

"Why did you go through with it?"

"She started cooking my goose the day she met me! She kept me drunk and sexed up, so half of the time I didn't know my butt from a hole in the ground. I didn't realize she was cooking up a wedding! It happened so fast! And I didn't see it coming!" Vernie paused and finished his drink. He raised his glass, indicating that he wanted a refill. I returned from the cabinet with the bottle, filled his glass again, and set the bottle on the coffee table in case he needed more. He wasted no time drinking his second glass of scotch. "I love the girl, but I wasn't ready for all this! Here I am, twenty-two and stuck with a wife and she's trying to get pregnant! All I wanted to do when I met her was have some fun. Now look at me!"

"Vernie, what are you going to do now? Do you plan to stay here and put up with Jade's mess, or do you plan to go back to Alabama? What about your family?"

"It's just my mama and my three sisters. They stopped speaking to me after Jade cussed 'em out and told them not to call up here. I do call home from payphones to check on my mama when I can. I don't want to worry or upset her or my sisters, so I don't let them talk to Jade. I'm the man in the family, and when my daddy died when I was sixteen, I promised them that I'd take care of them. Well, Jade got me going in so many different directions, I don't know which way is up. Her daddy hired me and pays me well, but she controls my paycheck. I can't send my mama anything like I had planned on doing. Jade goes with me to the bank, takes the bulk of my pay, goes shopping, gets her nails, hair, and face done, and then she *gives me the change*! I can't live like this!"

"What do you plan to do? What can I do to help you?"

"I just needed to talk to somebody. I was going crazy sitting in that house. The only place I go without Jade is to work."

"Where does she think you're at now?" I asked, giving him a worried look.

"She went out drinking with some of her girlfriends. Otis is working late, and Rhoda went off somewhere with Bully. I was in the house by myself," he said, looking at his watch. "I'll be back home before any of them." He rose.

"Do you need a ride home? How did you get over here?"

"I took a cab. I got out at the corner and walked the rest of the way."

"Well, can I offer you a ride home?"

"Oh, Lord no! If one of Jade's nosy neighbors saw me getting out of *your* car, she'd teach me a lesson I'd never forget. I appreciate your listening to me, and I'd appreciate it if you'd keep my visit a secret. I'll flag down another cab at the corner."

"You don't have to worry about me telling anybody about you coming over here. And please feel free to come again." I hugged Vernie and walked him to the door. "And, Vernie, I'll be praying for you," I told him as I clicked on the porch light.

He gave me a weak nod, pulled the hood on his windbreaker back up so that it covered the top part of his face again, and then trotted off the porch. I watched him move toward the street, dragging his feet like he was on the way to his execution. It broke my heart. I knew that if Vernie didn't get tough with Jade soon, he'd end up just like me: bitter and prone to violence.

I went back into the living room to finish my drink. A couple of minutes later, somebody knocked on my door again. I looked out the peephole, but even though I had turned on the porch light, I still couldn't see who was at my door this time. That meant that the visitor was covering my peephole. I moved over to my front window and cracked open my curtains. It was Jacob.

I snatched open the door and gave him an angry look. "Please tell me why you are here?" I demanded, one hand on my hip.

"Never mind all that! I want to know who that young nigger was that just left your house, bitch!"

# CHAPTER 52

I had promised myself a long time ago that the one place I was not going to tolerate somebody disrespecting me was in my own house. I grabbed the broom that I had placed by the door. Then I stood in my doorway looking at Jacob like he had lost his mind.

"You can't be coming over here talking to me like that!" I hollered with my fingers curled around the broom handle. "Who the hell do you think you are?"

"I am Jacob Lee Brewster, BITCH!"

"So?"

"I am your man!"

"Not anymore!" I screamed before I slammed the door in his face and locked it.

I was surprised that he didn't knock again. I waited until I heard him leave the porch before I put down the broom. I peeped out the window and saw him driving away, and that was when I went back to my drink.

The following day at lunchtime, Rhoda dropped by my office. She looked as gorgeous as ever. She wore a beige dress with a matching shawl and a pair of low-heeled black pumps. Her makeup was flawless, and her long, thick black hair was in a ponytail. She looked fifteen years younger.

"I tried to call you last night, but you didn't answer and your machine didn't pick up. Is everything all right?" she asked as soon as she entered my office. In addition to the vinyl sofa in my work area, there were a couple of chairs that faced my big cherry oak desk. She dragged one up close to me and placed her elbows on the top of my desk. "You look worried."

I looked at her and shook my head. "Same shit, different day," I said with a shrug. I couldn't tell her about Jacob's visit last night without telling her about Vernie. I decided to improvise. "I don't think things are going to work out between Jacob and me."

"Here we go again," she said, rolling her eyes. "Does this have anything to do with what we talked about yesterday? His relationship with your daughter?"

"It's not just that. He's too pushy and possessive for me. I need a man who knows how to behave."

Rhoda laughed. "Like my son-in-law?"

"What's that supposed to mean?" I sat up straighter in my chair and straightened a stack of manila folders on my desk.

"The boy is *so* docile. He'll do anything you ask him to do without protest. That kind of behavior can cause a person more grief than anything. I've told him that if he stood up to Jade, she would back off."

"Have you tried to talk to Jade about her cutting that boy some slack?"

Rhoda didn't even bother to answer that question. She just rolled her eyes. "Next question."

"Well, he seems like such a sweet young man. I hope she doesn't run him off like she did that sweet little Mexican dude. You can kick a dog around for only so long and he'll get tired. And when he gets tired enough, he's either going to retaliate or haul ass." I dipped my head and turned it slightly to the side as I gauged Rhoda's reaction.

"You don't think my beautiful daughter can hold on to her husband? The women in my family don't believe in divorce, you know."

"I know that. This is not about your beautiful daughter being able to keep her husband. He's got a mind, too. And sooner or later, he's going to put it to use."

"Let's change the subject," Rhoda suggested with a heavy sigh. "I had a rough night. Jade came home from a night out with her girls and as soon as she saw Vernie, she got all over him because he'd gone to bed when he should have waited up for her. Hell, it was three in the mornin' and everybody else in the house was in bed. What did she expect him to do? Anyway, she made him get up and go to the Grab and Go to get stuff to make her some tacos. He was gone only twenty minutes. When he returned, she met him in the driveway convinced that he'd taken so long because he'd met up with another woman. She choked, kicked, and punched him, and made him drop the taco things. By the time me and Otis got dressed and outside to calm her down, the package of ground beef, taco shells, and everything else was all over my front yard, all in the street, even up under my SUV, girl."

A sad thought crossed my mind. I couldn't get the image of Vernie's long face out of my head. I even tried to shake it out, but it remained there as I resumed my part of the conversation. "Rhoda, I don't know what to say about your daughter or my new man. But I think they both need some serious help."

Rhoda looked at me with renewed interest. "Is Jacob so bad that you want to cut him loose?"

"I . . . I don't know what I want to do about him. He's fun . . . sometimes. He's good for some, uh, maintenance sex. And . . . and he keeps me from feeling lonely. When I'm with him, I don't think much about Pee Wee and what I'm going to do about him. Let's go get something to eat."

I went to a salad bar with Rhoda and when I returned to my office, there was a huge floral arrangement on my desk from Jacob. He had also left four voice mail messages. In each one, he declared his love for me, and he moaned and groaned about how sorry he was for the way he had acted at my house the night before. Even though he sounded genuinely sorry, I still didn't want to talk to him or see him.

Two days later, when Pee Wee brought Charlotte home from a night out with him at the pizza parlor and the mall, he came in. He usually didn't come in when he returned her home, but since she had several bags, he did.

"I just wanted to help Char get her stuff in the house," he said, giving me an apologetic look as he entered the kitchen. "But don't worry, I ain't goin' to stay but a minute."

Charlotte must not have wanted me to see all the junk and other unnecessary mess she'd talked her daddy into buying, because she'd already dashed through the kitchen like a reindeer and on up to her room.

"You can stay as long as you want to stay," I told him. I took the remaining two shopping bags from him and set them on the counter. "You want a beer or something?"

I was so preoccupied I was not even aware of what I was saying. When I realized I'd invited him to "socialize" with me, I changed my tune. "Uh, you can take one with you if you want," I amended.

I pretended not to see the dry look that he shot at me. "You got company comin' or somethin'?" he asked, removing a beer from the refrigerator.

"That's right!" I said quickly. "He'll be here real soon."

I decided that my last statement would prompt him to leave immediately. It didn't. He dragged a chair from the table to the middle of the floor, turned it backward, and straddled it. From the look of things, he was going to take his good old time leaving.

"Uh, excuse me a minute. Charlotte sounds like she's tearing down the house. I'd better run upstairs to see what she's into," I said.

I dashed upstairs, taking the steps two at a time. I cracked open Charlotte's bedroom door, gave her a quick dirty look, scolded her about all of the noise she was making, and then ran into my bedroom and called up Jacob.

"Annette, baby, I'm so glad to hear your voice," he said as soon as he realized it was me on the other end of the line. "Baby, please give me another chance. I am sorry about barging up on your porch. But it was my dead son's birthday and I was depressed. I didn't mean to behave the way I did. I'd been drinking . . ."

"I got the flowers you sent today and I wanted to thank you. I also wanted to know if you'd like to come over for a little while tonight?"

I could tell he was surprised. The gasp that he released sounded like the hiss of a cobra. "I can be there in ten minutes!" he yelled, sounding so giddy it was frightening.

He lied. It didn't take him ten minutes to get to my house. Eight minutes later when I returned to my kitchen, where Pee Wee was still kicking back at the table drinking his beer, Jacob stumbled up on my front porch.

Charlotte let him in, squealing his name. He entered the kitchen with her riding him piggyback.

The minute Pee Wee saw Jacob's face and Charlotte riding his back, he rose so fast he almost knocked over his chair, grumbling with disgust under his breath.

"I didn't know you had company," Jacob said, looking embarrassed. There was so much tension in the room you needed a meat cleaver to cut through it. I was glad that Jacob immediately untangled Charlotte from his back and set her down on the floor. "Dude," he greeted Pee Wee, attempting to slap his palm. Pee Wee just glared at Jacob, looking at him like he wanted to punch him in the nose.

"Annette, I'll talk to you later," Pee Wee said, looking at me like he wanted to strike my face, too. Then he seemed to soften. "By the way, I wanted to thank you for droppin' the divorce. . . ." There was a smug look on his face as he turned to Jacob. Then he looked at me with his chin tilted upward, and his legs reared back like he was about to moonwalk.

I tried to look nonchalant so it would seem like the divorce was not that important to me for the time being. "Well, I *delayed* it so I could give it some more thought," I clarified. "You'll be hearing more from me and my lawyer eventually."

Pee Wee rubbed the top of Charlotte's head, kissed her on the cheek, and then left. He didn't even bother to look at me again; but from the way he looked at Jacob on his way out the door, if looks could kill, Jacob would have dropped dead on the spot.

# CHAPTER 53

They say that the more things change, the more they stay the same. Less than a week after I'd allowed Jacob back into my life and bed, he started acting a fool again.

I had dropped Charlotte off to spend Thursday night with Pee Wee so I could go to a bachelorette party with Rhoda that night. The agreement was, he'd keep her with him until he heard from me on Friday.

That Friday morning around ten, a folder ended up on my desk at work. It was red, which meant it was an extremely difficult case. Those were some of the ones that I usually handled. I groaned as soon as I saw it. I knew from past experiences that whoever the debtor was, he or she was going to cuss me out, talk about me like a dog, call me all kinds of obscene names, tell me to do something sexual to myself that was anatomically impossible, and then tell me where to go. That's what I usually had to put up with. I groaned again when I opened the folder and saw who that deadbeat was. Jacob's name leaped out at me like a panther.

"I'll be damned," I said to myself as I looked over the documents. I could not believe my eyes. Jacob had defaulted on a huge bill to the funeral home that had handled his mother's funeral!

That devil had not paid one penny of the six thousand plus dollars that he had agreed to pay! I squinted my eyes to make sure I was seeing right. I leaned back in my chair and gave this situation some thought. I knew that most people had insurance on their loved ones so that they'd be prepared to cover final expenses when the time came. I had such insurance on my parents, my daughter, and myself. I still had burial insurance on Pee Wee. I was glad that he had not made me mad enough for him to require a burial. And Jacob had told me to my face that his mother had made him her beneficiary on her life insurance policy—two hundred thousand dollars! He had used the money to go on that lavish cruise he'd told me about, purchase his new car, upgrade his wardrobe, and do some home improvements. Had he no shame?! Apparently, he did not.

It saddened me to know that there were people on the planet who cared more about material things than they did their mother's final arrangements. And this was the man whom I was involved with! That saddened me, too. When old Mr. Boatwright died, well, when Rhoda smothered him to death, I had treated him with utmost respect to the very end—and he'd sexually abused me for ten years! Despite that, I'd helped my mother plan his funeral, I'd prayed for his wretched soul, and I was there when my mother wrote a check to the undertaker to cover his funeral. Not once did she, or I, even think about not paying off that expense.

To my surprise, Mr. Boatwright had left instructions in his will stating that all of the money left over after his funeral expenses had been settled was to go to me. Even then I had a hard time spending that ten thousand dollars on myself. And it never occurred to me to spend it on something as frivolous as a cruise and a new car!

I got so light-headed that I had to stand up. I couldn't understand how anybody could do what Jacob had done. And he must not have cared because he had let it go into collection. His poor mother was probably spinning in her grave.

I looked at the telephone; then I looked at the folder in my hand. I had no idea how I was going to approach this mess. But it was my job and I had no choice.

I reached for the phone, but then I stopped when I realized he was at work. I didn't want to leave him a voice mail message, so I decided to confront him face-to-face. I knew that this shit was going to have a negative impact on what was left of our relationship, so I had to resolve it with a long-handled shovel.

I kept myself busy the rest of that afternoon, calling some of the other deadbeats. By the end of the day, I'd been cussed out and called every name in the book. I was still tired from staying late at the bachelorette party the night before, so I couldn't wait to get home.

I picked up some Chinese takeout after I left work. Around six that evening, I called up Pee Wee and asked him what time he was going to drop Charlotte off.

"Charlotte's not with me!" he said quickly, panic in his voice.

"But—but the girl from her school called me up and told me that her daddy was there to pick her up!" I hollered, clutching the telephone in my hand like it was trying to get away. "What—oh shit!"

"What in the hell is goin' on, woman? My child is missin'?"

"Um, that must have been Jacob that picked her up. You know white folks think we all look alike. That girl probably thought it was you!"

"Look, I don't care what the hell you do with that punk! But I sure as hell care about what he does with my daughter. Now, if you don't want to end up in court in a custody battle, you'd better get the spirit, sister!"

"I wish you would calm down. Jacob loves children!"

"That's what's got me so worried! And you, of all people, after what you told me you went through with Mr. Boatwright—"

"Hold on. I hear a car." I laid the kitchen phone down on the counter, ran to the living room window, and snatched open the curtains. There was Charlotte crawling out of Jacob's car with three shopping bags. As soon as I opened the door, he blew his horn, waved at me, and sped off like he was driving a getaway car.

I grabbed Charlotte by the arm and pulled her into the house.

"What the hell is the matter with you, girl? You don't leave school with anybody but me, Rhoda, your daddy, or your grandparents."

"Dang, Mama! Why are you tripping? I was with Jacob. He says he's more like family." She was clutching the straps of her shopping bags so tight she must have thought that I was going to take them from her. "He took me to that sale at the Barbie store in the mall. Then when I told him you had picked the stems off some greens last night so you could cook them up for dinner tonight, he felt sorry for me and took me for pizza."

"Go put your things away and get back down here. We need to have a long talk."

As soon as Charlotte stomped up the stairs with her lips poked out so far it looked like they'd been starched, I returned to the telephone. "Everything's fine. It was just a big misunderstanding," I told Pee Wee in a calm voice. "Jacob had picked her up from school."

"Shit! Oh, hell no!" He was frantic. "If you can't straighten out that punk, I will! If I hear about him pickin' my daughter up from school or doin' anything else with her that I don't think is right, I am goin' to kick his ass! Will you pass that on to him for me?"

"Pee Wee, you are overreacting. And as far as I'm concerned, this conversation is over." I hung up.

When Charlotte finally joined me in the kitchen, her face was so long it almost touched the floor. "You don't want me to have no fun," she said with a pout.

"Honey, I want you to have fun. I know it's important for a girl your age to be happy. But it's more important for you to be safe. The world is not what it used to be, and you can't trust everybody."

"What are you talking about, Mama? I was with Jacob, not the boogeyman. He wouldn't let anything happen to me."

"You don't understand. *Anybody* can be the boogeyman. . . ."

I could see that I had only confused her more. "Charlotte, when I was a little girl, younger than you, somebody my mama trusted took advantage of me."

"You got . . . *raped?*" She gasped; then she gave me a pitiful look.

"Yes," I said with a nod. "And it went on for years."

"Is he in jail?"

I shook my head. "He was an old man and he eventually died. I didn't tell my mama what had happened until he'd been dead for a long time. But it still hurts when I think about it. I don't want that to happen to you."

"You think Jacob . . . uh, can I go to my room now. I don't like talking about stuff like this."

"You can go to your room, but you can expect me to talk about stuff like this whenever I feel it's necessary. Now, I like Jacob; I like him a lot. But he's supposed to be courting me, not you. I don't like it, your daddy doesn't like it. And I don't even want to think of how crazy your grandparents will get if they knew about it."

"Oh, so you don't want me to speak to Jacob no more?"

"I didn't say that. I don't want you to ever leave school with him again—unless I know about it. I don't want you to ever go to his house again, without me knowing. That's one thing I've already warned you about. You haven't been back over there, have you?"

Charlotte dropped her head. Then she nodded. "I rode my bike over there yesterday to see his new goldfish. . . ."

# CHAPTER 54

"Charlotte, don't you *ever* go to Jacob's house again unless I'm with you. If you do, you will be severely punished. Now, do I make myself clear?"

She nodded. "Can I go over to Patsy Boone's house after school tomorrow?"

"Yes, you can go over to Patsy's house. She lives just down the block, so I can pick you up on my way home from work."

Charlotte couldn't get to her room fast enough. The phone rang, but I didn't pick up. I let it go to the answering machine. It was Muh'Dear talking loud and fast. "Annette, pick up that phone. I know you standin' there."

"Hi, Muh'Dear. I was in the bathroom," I lied.

"You been hidin' from us? Scary Mary said she seen you at the mall the other day and you ducked around a corner so fast she couldn't catch you. She thought you saw her but was tryin' to dodge her."

"I didn't see her."

"Tell Charlotte to come by after school tomorrow. I got some of that hard candy she likes."

"She's going to visit her friend after school tomorrow. You know that little Patsy girl, a grade ahead of Charlotte."

Muh'Dear gasped. "You let your baby run around with a pregnant girl?"

"What are you talking about? Patsy's only twelve. . . ."

"My mama had me when she was twelve!"

"Are you telling me that Patsy Boone, my daughter's friend, is going to have a baby?"

"Girl, I'm speakin' plain English. You can't understand what I'm sayin'?"

"How in the world did that happen?"

"Patsy's hotter than a six-shooter. I'm surprised it didn't happen before now."

I looked toward the stairs. "I'll talk to you later."

I rushed up to Charlotte's room and flung open her door. "Girl, why didn't you tell me that little Patsy girl was pregnant?"

There was a startled look on Charlotte's face. She stood in front of the mirror on the front of her closet door admiring the new jeans Jacob had purchased for her. With a shrug, she said, "I thought you already knew. Everybody else in town knows."

"Everybody except me," I said sadly.

I went back downstairs right away, moving my feet so slowly, it seemed like it was taking forever for me to make it to the living room.

A few minutes later, Scary Mary entered my house without knocking. She made herself comfortable, stretching out on my living room couch like a cat, staring at me with a sympathetic look on her face as I complained about my daughter's recent behavior. This was one of the few times I was glad to see her. I needed to talk to somebody after I'd heard about little Patsy's pregnancy. I had called up Rhoda's house, but Jade wouldn't call her to the phone. Then I'd called up Pee Wee. When Lizzie answered the phone, in such a cold and impersonal way—"Annette who?" she'd asked—I got so pissed off I just hung up.

"I didn't know that raising a child was going to be this hard," I lamented.

"Girl, you ain't seen nothin' yet. If you this worried about your girl and she ain't even in her teens yet, just imagine what you're going to go through then," Scary Mary said, taking a loud drink from the glass of bourbon she'd requested. "Now, you take me. I was a pistol back in my day. I lost my cherry when I was nine."

I could feel the sides of my face tighten. "Was it somebody in your family? Somebody you knew?"

"What do you mean?"

"Who took advantage of you?"

"What's wrong with you? Ain't nobody took advantage of me. I was ready to be popped!" She smacked her lips and winked at me.

"Oh," I muttered.

"He was the cutest boy on the planet. Big brown eyes, smooth butterscotch-colored skin. His daddy was Korean, his mama was black. He was so exotic I couldn't help myself! Of course, neither one of us knew about orgasms then, so when we came at the same time, we both thought we was havin' a spasm, and that that was the punishment from God that all the old folks had been scarin' us with. Heh, heh, heh." Scary Mary paused and shook her head. There was a wishful look on her face. "Boy, if I could go back in time, I'd be a totally different person if I had had more sense and more guidance." She sniffed and looked away, but not before a tear rolled out of the corner of her eye. I pretended not to see her wipe it away with the tip of her finger.

"Can I ask you something?"

"You can ask me anything you want to ask me. I ain't shy."

"How did you . . . how did you end up becoming a madam?"

"What kind of stupid question is that?"

"Most kids dream about being doctors and nurses and what-not. . . ."

"The young girls back in my day didn't have a lot of choices. Black and white, they was sellin' pussy—one way or the other. Hell, just gettin' married is a form of prostitution! A woman hooks up with a man and she marries him for what he can give her."

I shook my head. "There are a lot of women who don't need a man to take care of them. There are a lot of men who are hooking up with women so they can be taken care of."

"And that's why we call them suckers gigolos!" she yelled.

I laughed. She didn't. Instead, she gave me a serious look as she wiped away another tear. "When I found out I could make just as much money sellin' somebody else's pussy as I could mine, I did.

Shoot. My mama didn't raise no fool." She stopped talking and gave me a dry look.

"You don't have a problem with taking advantage of people like that?"

"Takin' advantage of who? I ain't never took advantage of nobody in my life! If my girls are fool enough to sell pussy and give me the money, I'm fool enough to take it! This is a mad world, and it's gettin' madder by the minute. Now look at you sittin' there worried to death about your daughter endin' up a fool."

"That's not exactly what I'm worried about. It's just that being a single parent is a lot harder than I thought it'd be. Since Pee Wee's departure, I feel like I've aged ten years."

"Don't mention age. As you know, I'm ninety if I'm a day, and I didn't live this long by bein' a fool. I stay three steps ahead of everybody. You remind me of myself when I was your age—strong and smart. Women like me and you, we sure enough don't take no mess. Somehow we always land on our feet like a kitty cat. Speaking of kitty cats, when you get a chance, drop by my house and meet my new booty. Her name is Weng Lu, and she's from one of them way off Asian cities. She's real popular with my adventuresome clients. They all want to see if that rumor's true about Asian gals' pussies bein' slanted in a *sideways* position in the crotch area." I rolled my eyes. The old madam, who looked like she belonged in a mummy's tomb, let out a great belch. "But even with you bein' strong and smart, you might make it alone and you might not! A woman raisin' kids alone got it hard."

"It's not like Charlotte's daddy's not in the picture," I reminded. I was glad that we were back on our original subject.

"He ain't in the house! And that's just as bad. If I was in your shoes, I'd be doin' everything I could to get my husband back."

My jaw dropped. "Don't forget; you were the one who wanted me to chastise him and make him suffer by putting a voodoo spell on him," I reminded.

"Well, you know as well as I do that them voodoo spells swing more than one way. You can use it to get rid of him, cripple him, or you can use it to get him back home!"

"I hope I never want a man bad enough to use voodoo to get him," I said, putting a lot of emphasis on my words. "I'd rather die alone than go to all that much trouble for love," I admitted with a shudder.

"Well, it's your funeral, baby. Mind if I have me another highball for the road?"

I didn't go to bed until midnight, and I didn't sleep much that night. As soon as I got up the next morning, I called up Jacob.

"Hey, baby. I was just on my way out the door to work," he told me.

"Will you stop by the house tonight. I need to talk to you," I said in a weak and uncertain voice.

"Listen, if it's about me picking Charlotte up from school, you don't have to worry about that anymore. I won't do it again unless you tell me to."

"That's one of the things that I need to talk to you about," I mumbled.

"Let's discuss it over dinner at that Italian place you like so much. I'll pick you up around six thirty. Is that cool? I owe you another good time, I think."

"I'll see you at six thirty," I replied.

It was one of the longest days I'd ever endured. Pee Wee had picked Charlotte up from school so she could spend the night with him. Jacob picked me up at six thirty just like he said he would. And all the way to the restaurant, he talked about how happy he was going to make me.

I didn't beat around the bush when we got to Antonosanti's. "Jacob, before we discuss our personal relationship, I need to ask you something. And this is business related," I began. I was glad the waiter had already delivered our wine. I took a long drink.

Jacob gave me a puzzled look. "Is there somebody else?" he wanted to know, his jaw twitching. "You don't want me anymore?"

"We'll discuss that later—"

"We'll discuss that now!"

Before I knew what was happening, he lunged across the table and grabbed my wrist. "Who is he?"

"I don't know what the hell you are talking about! And that's not what I want to discuss," I yelled, prying his fingers from around my wrist.

"You are my woman and I love you, BITCH! If I ever catch you, or find out you—"

I was so furious that when I rose, my chair fell over. "I am not going to stay here and argue with you in a place like this."

"You want to get down and funky, I will gladly take you over to the projects on Noble Street. That way we can go at it ghetto style."

"I'm out of here." I looked around. People on all sides were staring at us. Carlo, the cute young waiter who usually waited on me when I visited Antonosanti's, rushed in my direction.

"Annette, is there a problem?" Carlo asked, looking from me to Jacob.

I held up my hand. "It's all right, Carlo. Put the wine on my account. And please call me a taxi."

Before I could leave the table, Jacob leaped up from his seat and slapped my face so hard I saw stars and stripes.

# CHAPTER 55

There weren't that many black cops in Richland, but it seemed like every time a disturbance involved black people, black cops showed up. This time was no different. Lonnie Shoemaker, the cop who had handled the situation with Jade and Vernie in that burger place, steamrolled into the restaurant looking like he wanted to shoot up the world. He rushed over to the booth where I stood with a damp napkin, dabbing my busted lip. Jacob was slumped on the seat, crying like a baby, making faces that would make Jim Carrey jealous.

"What's the problem?" Lonnie demanded, one hand on his gun. He looked from me to Jacob. A small crowd had formed around us. I couldn't remember the last time I'd been so embarrassed. "Annette, it ain't like you to be involved in some mess like this! Now, who did what?"

"I'm fine," I managed, waving my hand with a limp wrist.

"I didn't ask you that! I asked you what the problem was?" Lonnie boomed. Lonnie was loud, but he didn't scare me. I didn't know of anybody who was actually afraid of him. He was too much of a Chris Rock type—in looks and personality—to be taken seriously. "Did Jacob hit you? Do you want to press charges?"

I didn't answer his questions. "I just want to go home," I insisted, shaking my head so hard it felt and sounded like something inside was rattling.

"Well, you can go anywhere you want to go after I find out why these folks called for the police."

"I . . . I just snapped," Jacob sobbed. "I didn't mean to hit her."

"He hit you?" Lonnie asked, whipping out a pair of handcuffs and tossing them to his frightened-looking young white partner. "Dean, cuff him up!" he ordered, shaking a finger at Jacob.

"I can't go back to jail! I'll lose my job! Brother, please cut me some slack!" Jacob hollered, rising.

Jail? I had no idea that Jacob had been in jail!

"Annette, you want to press charges?" Lonnie asked me again.

"I'm fine. I just want to go home," I said again.

"Can't you just let us slide this time?" Jacob begged. "I don't want my name in the newspaper. I don't want to lose my job! Please, *brother*, please, give a *brother* another chance!"

"Look, I got more important things to do with my time. Now, I am going to go easy this time. Annette, you leave first. Dean here will put you in my squad car, and I will personally escort you home." Lonnie stopped talking and gently squeezed my shoulder. Then he turned back to Jacob and said just loud enough for his partner and me and Jacob to hear, "And you, Jacob—you get your black ass out of my sight before I plant some weed on you!"

I knew Lonnie was not serious, but Jacob must have thought he was. He scrambled away from that table so fast he fell twice before he made it to the exit.

It seemed like every neighbor on my block just happened to be on their front porch when the police car with me in it stopped in front of my house about fifteen minutes later.

"Now, if you have any more trouble, you just give us a call," Lonnie told me as he walked me to my door.

"This won't be in the newspaper, will it?" I asked, fumbling for my keys.

"Don't worry about it, sister," he assured me. Lonnie was a dedicated and competent cop, but he still had a lot of his ghetto habits. He had a wife, and a few girlfriends on the side, but he still paid a lot of attention to other women. He was the kind of brother who would pat a woman on the back with one hand and at the same time, pat her on the butt with his other hand. He didn't even look around before he patted me on the back with one hand and on the butt with the other. Then he gave me a brief hug and gently pushed me into my house.

I didn't know why my hand was trembling when I flipped on the light switch. As the bright light flooded the room, I wrung my hands and looked around. I knew that there was *no* way I was going to continue my relationship with Jacob now. I had been prepared to tell him that, even though I was no longer interested in being his lover, we could still be friends. Now I didn't even want to do that. And there was still that humongous outstanding bill that he owed to the funeral parlor that I needed to talk to him about.

I still had my jacket on, and I was too restless to go on about my routine like this was any other day. I turned off the light and went out to my car. I headed straight toward Rhoda's house. This was something that I wanted to discuss with her in person.

As soon as I turned the corner on her street, I got another shock. There were two police cars with flashing lights in her driveway, and an ambulance.

There was a mob of Rhoda's nosy neighbors milling around in her front yard. I parked at the nearest available spot on the street and sprinted down the sidewalk.

"What happened?" I asked the woman who lived in the white house across the street from Rhoda. "Did Jade hurt her husband again?"

"I don't think so. He's the one the police just led out in handcuffs. He's sitting in the back of one of the squad cars now," the neighbor woman told me.

I squeezed my way through the crowd, but when I got to Rhoda's front door, a grim-faced black policeman prevented me from entering. "Sorry, ma'am. This is a crime scene!" he barked.

"What happened? I'm a friend of the family!" I wailed as I tried to look past the officer. I couldn't see or hear anything.

"Ma'am, please get back," the officer insisted, gently pushing me away from the door.

One of the police cars roared off down the street with the siren screaming. I turned for just a moment, and when I looked back at the door, the EMTs were coming out of Rhoda's house with some-body on a stretcher who looked so twisted and broken I thought I was looking at a large rag doll. The head was completely covered with a blood-soaked white towel. I stretched my neck and blinked hard so I could see better.

It was Jade.

The police finally got so aggressive they made every spectator leave the premises. I had to back away with the rest of the crowd as a stout policewoman led Rhoda out of her house. Otis and Bully, both looking like they had been mauled themselves, followed close behind. Rhoda had to be helped into the back of the ambu-lance. As soon as it shot down the street with the siren blasting, Otis and Bully scrambled into Otis's Jeep and followed it.

I didn't think it would do much good for me to go to the hospi-tal. At least not yet. One reason was that things were too chaotic and I probably would have just been in the way. Another reason was I knew Jade hated my company. And as long as Otis and Bully were there to support Rhoda, I knew she'd be all right. I decided to go home and wait until I heard from her. If she wanted me to be with her at the hospital too, I'd join her, whether Jade wanted me there or not.

While I was pacing my living room floor awaiting a call from Rhoda, Scary Mary stumbled up on my front porch again.

"Do you have any idea what happened at Rhoda's house this evening?" I asked as soon as she made it in. She was walking slower than usual, and with the cane she sometimes had to rely on to get around. She was huffing and puffing so hard I had to hold her up as I led her to my couch. "Do you know what happened to Jade?"

"Of course I know. I was at the hospital when they brought her into emergency. You know how bad it gets when my grippe acts up. This time it was the grippe and a severe case of piles." Scary Mary gave me a dry look as she focused her gaze on the half-full bottle of wine on my coffee table.

"Would you like a drink?" I asked, already heading to the kit-chen to get some glasses.

"Don't mind if I do," she said, fanning her face with a hand that resembled a piece of dried liver.

I literally ran back into the living room. "So what happened?" I asked, pouring myself a glass of wine, too. I plopped down on the love seat that faced Scary Mary. She took her time responding. First, she had to take a long swallow of wine.

"Now," she said, releasing a burp. "A few drops of bourbon or scotch would get this wine up on its feet," she commented, again looking toward my kitchen, where she knew I kept more liquor.

"Uh, I didn't make it to the liquor store, so wine is all I have right now," I lied.

She shrugged and finished her drink, then burped again. I was so impatient by now, I was ready to scream. But Scary Mary was the kind of person who did everything in her time. She wobbled up and hobbled across the floor. "I hope your bathroom is clean," she mumbled.

Rhoda called while Scary Mary was using my bathroom. "What in the world is going on?" I hollered, twisting the telephone cord around my fingers like a vine. "Why were all those cops and an *ambulance* at your house?"

"Vernie finally snapped," Rhoda replied, speaking in a flat voice. She sounded so tired that I got tired listening to her. "The boy snapped like a rubber band." She stopped talking and sobbed softly for a few seconds, making squeaky, jerking noises like an injured mouse. Then she told me in a stone-cold voice, "He's goin' down for murder."

# CHAPTER 56

"Oh no!" Despite all of the unnecessary turmoil that Jade had put me through, I did not want to see any harm come to her. I certainly didn't want to see her dead. "Is she . . . is she? Exactly what happened?" I had so many questions to ask, but I didn't want to upset Rhoda any more than she already was. "Do you feel like discussing it now?"

"She's still alive, but it's touch and go right now. I'm still at the hospital. Otis was so upset he had to be sedated, and Bully is too upset to drive. I'll find somebody else to drive him and Otis back home. But do you think you could come pick me up? We can talk then."

"Of course I can pick you up. I'll be there as fast as I can."

As soon as I hung up, Scary Mary came stumbling back into the living room.

"Where you runnin' off to?" she asked. "I thought you wanted me to tell you about what happened at Rhoda's house." She sat down hard on the sofa with a groan and a grimace.

"That was Rhoda who just called. She wants me to give her a ride home from the hospital. I'll get all of the details from her. But could you do me a favor? Call up Pee Wee and tell him what's going on, and tell him that I might leave Charlotte with him for a couple of days. I may need to spend some serious time with Rhoda," I said. "Before I go, I need to freshen up a little," I added as I ran to my bathroom.

When I returned to the living room, Scary Mary was on the telephone. She seemed agitated, so I decided to wait until she finished her call.

"Don't you worry about who this is, you mongrel floozy!" she snarled. "I eat cunts like you for breakfast! Always did!" After what she had just said, I couldn't wait for her to finish the call.

"Who in the world are you talking to?" I yelled, running across the floor to face her.

"I thought you wanted me to call up Pee Wee—"

I grabbed the phone out of Scary Mary's hand. "Lizzie, this is Annette."

There was a long silence before she responded. "Annette who?"

"Look, bitch. I don't have time for any of your games tonight. You put my husband on this telephone right now, or I'm going to come over there and shove it down your throat!" The next voice I heard belonged to Pee Wee.

"Annette, what's goin' on now?" he asked in a weary voice.

"I don't have time to go into detail, but there's been some kind of violent incident at Rhoda's house. Jade's in the hospital, Vernie's in jail—that's all I know. I need to give Rhoda a ride home and spend some time with her. I need to leave Charlotte with you until I know what's going on."

"Sure, I'll keep her here. Is there anything else I can do?"

"Not right now."

"When you get Rhoda home, either you have her call me or you call me and tell me what's goin' on. Rhoda's more like family to me than most of my family," he reminded.

"We'll call you."

I hung up and ran out of the door with Scary Mary on my heels. There were times when I wondered if she really needed the cane she carried with her at times. This time she was running behind me like a track star, waving her cane in the air. She got in her van, and I got in my car.

We made it to the hospital parking lot in record time. Once we got inside the hospital, it was like we'd stumbled into a madhouse.

Doctors, nurses, and police officers were all over the place. Otis and Bully were inconsolable. I was surprised to see Pee Wee there, looking like a wild man. I was glad that he had brought Charlotte with him. I didn't like it when he left my daughter alone with Lizzie. Jade was out of surgery. After the doctor assured Rhoda and Otis that their daughter was going to be all right, we all decided to leave.

Pee Wee ended up driving Otis and Bully home from the hospital in Otis's car. I had left my car in front of Rhoda's house and accompanied Scary Mary to the hospital in her van. She transported Rhoda home. I drove Pee Wee's car to Rhoda's house, with my daughter riding shotgun. It was a mess, and this was one night that I couldn't wait to end.

Charlotte said some interesting things to me on the way to Rhoda's house. "Mama, they got roaches almost as big as me," she said, forcing herself not to laugh by covering her mouth with her hand. But she couldn't help herself. She giggled long and loud.

"Who's got roaches?" I asked, keeping my eyes on the road.

"Daddy and Lizzie. You should hear him fussing at her about how nasty she is. She leaves used tampons on the floor in the bathroom. She don't always wash her hands when she uses the bathroom. Every time I go over there, the kitchen sink is full of dirty dishes. Remember last week when I went? She had dropped an egg on the kitchen floor. When I got there today, that same egg was still on the floor." Charlotte stopped talking and giggled some more. "There's dust and crumbs and stuff everywhere you look, even in the refrigerator. There is moldy food and dirty dishes in the refrigerator, too. And boy does it stink when you open the door! Whew! She hardly ever sweeps or vacuums; I do it for her. She's too busy in the mirror fussing with her hair and stuff. She hates doing laundry, too. When she runs out of clean panties, she wears Daddy's shorts! Or she runs to the mall and buys some new ones. And that's another thing. Daddy said she's spending his money like he was printing it in the basement. She's a mess, Mama. I only go over there because I know it makes Daddy happy to see me." Charlotte sighed before she laughed some more.

"Well, Lizzie's bad habits must not bother your daddy that much if he puts up with them," I snapped. I wanted to laugh myself, but I didn't.

"Oh yes, it does bother him! He's always telling her what a mistake he made leaving you for her. He told her tonight that you was worth five of her."

I was glad that I had to stop for a red light. I turned to Charlotte and gave her a thoughtful look. "He said that in front of you?"

"He didn't know I was listening. He thought I was in my room watching TV."

"I see. What else did you hear?"

"She told him that if you was so great, how come he didn't go back with you."

I was so interested in what my daughter was telling me that I didn't realize the light had turned green until the driver behind me honked his horn. I sped off. "And what did he say to that?" I asked.

"He told her that if he knew you would take him back, he'd move back home in a heartbeat. She said you was stupid, but you ain't stupid enough to dump Jacob for him. Boy did *that* make him mad."

"I'll bet it did," I muttered. "Uh, that's something I wanted to talk to you about. Jacob."

Out of the corner of my eye, I saw Charlotte give me a surprised look. "Why come? I like Jacob. He never cooks greens and all that other nasty icky stuff you cook when I go to his house. He cooks frozen dinners and orders pizza. Just like Lizzie does most of the time. That's another thing Daddy complains about. He said he hasn't had a decent meal since he left you. . . ."

"Charlotte, you haven't been back to Jacob's house since I told you not to go, have you?" I asked in a loud, menacing voice.

"Um, just once," she admitted, hunching down in her seat. "This evening before you called Daddy. I didn't stay long, though. And the only reason I went was because he had some Batman decals for me to put on my bike."

"Jacob and I decided to stop seeing each other. He won't be coming to the house anymore," I stated.

"Oh." I could tell from the tone of Charlotte's voice that this news disappointed her tremendously. "First you ran my daddy off, now Jacob. Dang, Mama! What did you do to *him*?"

"What's that supposed to mean?"

"What do you do to make men run off?"

"That's something we'll discuss in a few years. This is not the time." I stopped at a stop sign and looked at Charlotte. "So you are no longer allowed to visit Jacob's house, or that pregnant girl Patsy. Is that clear?"

"Well, who can I visit?"

"You have a lot of other friends. You can visit with any of them."

"Okay."

"Now, let's change the subject and talk about something more pleasant."

"Is Jade going to die?"

"No," I said in an uncertain voice. "I said let's talk about something pleasant."

"I heard Lizzie fussing at Daddy about taking you back," Charlotte blurted.

"I'm going to have a long talk with your daddy about being more careful about what he discusses when you're with him," I said, releasing an exasperated breath. "And if I have to talk to that . . . to Lizzie about watching her mouth when you're in the house, I will." I grunted. "You are too young to be hearing all that mess!"

"Mama, I already know about all that mess. I watch cable TV."

"That's different. And we are going to have to monitor what you watch on TV, too, I guess."

I pulled in front of Rhoda's house a minute later.

"Let's get inside so we can find out what's going on with Jade," I said. I parked Pee Wee's car right behind mine where I had left it on the street.

# CHAPTER 57

Pee Wee greeted me at the door with a clumsy hug. The only reason I hugged him back was because of what Charlotte had told me in the car.

I ran into the bathroom and splashed some cold water on my face. Then I joined Rhoda in her bedroom where she lay splayed on the bed with an ice pack on her forehead. There was blood all over the front of her pretty yellow dress.

"Rhoda, what happened?" I asked gently, sitting at the foot of the bed in her fairy-tale–like bedroom—a brass bed, pastels and frills everywhere.

She sat up, her back against the headboard. "Jade and Vernie were in their room when the fight started this time. I don't know what they were arguing about, but whatever it was, it pissed Jade off so bad, she chased Vernie out of the room into the hallway with a lamp—that expensive antique gooseneck lamp I bought in Cleveland. He tried to get away. He tried to protect his head with his hands. She grabbed one of his hands and bit the hell out of it. Then she did the same thing to his other hand. She knocked him down and straddled him, beating him about the chest with that lamp."

"You didn't try to stop her?"

"It happened so fast. Otis, Bully, and I saw the whole thing. We were all yellin' at her to put the lamp down before somebody got hurt. Otis got the lamp away from her. Bully grabbed her off of Vernie, and for a minute it seemed like everything was under control. As soon as we turned to go back into the living room, she grabbed that lamp again and raised it to bash Vernie some more. But he was ready for her this time. He got it away from her and brought it down on her head. She didn't move anymore. . . ."

"So he was just defending himself, right?"

Rhoda gave me a hopeless look.

"Rhoda," I began slowly and cautiously, "if he was only defending himself, you and Otis and Bully have to do the right thing."

"What are you gettin' at? My child is the one in the hospital at death's door, not Vernie!" Rhoda snapped.

"But Jade's going to be all right," I reminded her.

Rhoda's mouth dropped open and she blinked until the anger disappeared from her eyes. In a soft, hesitant voice, she whispered, "Didn't you see all that blood on my floors? She was out cold when they hauled her out of my house on a stretcher!"

"Yes, I saw all of that blood, and she was unconscious because she'd fainted. But her doctor said that she'll be fine if she takes it easy."

"I just hope we didn't get her to the hospital too late. If she has brain damage, she will never be the same again."

I had a feeling that Jade was going to come out of this mess with an even worse attitude, but I couldn't say that to Rhoda. "She'll be fine. Dr. Hall is on duty, so she's in good hands." I paused and cleared my throat. "The police took Vernie to jail."

"Well, that's just where he should be! The boy did attack her!" Rhoda yelled, giving me an incredulous look.

"Rhoda, honey, she attacked him first. You just told me that yourself," I said in a gentle voice, patting her shoulder. "What are you and Otis and Bully going to tell the police? Or have you already given them a statement?"

"No," she mumbled. "Thanks for remindin' me. Even though that's one thing I don't want to even think about."

"Well, you can't not think about it, Rhoda." I had pushed the thought of what had happened to me in the restaurant with Jacob to the back of my head. But I could not ignore it. When I did think about it, I recalled the sting of the slap he had delivered to my face. "This has been a long day for me, too. I'll . . . tell you about it later. I can't think straight right now," I managed to say through dried, cracked lips. I rubbed the spot where Jacob had slapped me. It stung just as much now as it did when he'd hit me.

"I can't think straight either," Rhoda moaned, massaging her head. "Please help me get through this."

I never thought that I'd see the day that I would be on my knees praying for Jade. But that's just what I was doing now. Rhoda was on one side of me, Scary Mary was on the other. We were all kneeling and swaying from side to side on the floor in front of Rhoda's bed, hands cupped in prayer with Scary Mary leading. ". . . and another thing, Lord, don't be too harsh on Vernie. He's limited and weak. . . . He didn't mean to hurt Jade so bad . . . didn't know what he was doin' . . . Amen." Scary Mary stumbled to rise but fell back to the floor, moaning in pain. "Praise the Lord!" she whispered, shaking her head and waving her arms and cane in the air. "God is good!"

Between breaths and holy references, she reminded us that she'd recently had hip replacement surgery *and* her gallbladder removed. Rhoda grabbed her by one arm and I grabbed her by the other. We all rose at the same time.

"Rhoda, go out yonder to wherever you keep your liquor and pour me a real strong highball," Scary Mary ordered, wobbling on her cane as she followed Rhoda and me to the living room.

From the mood in the living room, you would have thought that Jade was already dead and that people had come to pay their respects. Lizel and Wyrita, the two attractive young women who practically ran Rhoda's childcare center, were humped over on Rhoda's plush couch, with tears streaming down their faces.

Several people from the neighborhood were huddled by the window, mumbling, speaking in hushed tones, and shaking their heads. Since Jade had verbally trashed so many of them, I knew they were present more because of curiosity than concern.

I had my share of problems, but Rhoda had enough for an army. And most of them were centered around Jade. Despite all she had done to Vernie—and me and countless others—some of the people present were now talking about her like she was a cherub. Even Pee Wee.

"I just hope that child is goin' to be good as new," he muttered, giving Rhoda a concerned look. Over the years, Pee Wee had replaced the two older brothers that Rhoda had lost. One had died at the hands of an out-of-control cop, and her other brother had come back from Vietnam with so many mental setbacks, he was as good as dead. He was a permanent resident at an asylum in Louisiana near Rhoda's parents. I totally understood Pee Wee and Rhoda's allegiance to one another. He sat in an easy chair near the door. Charlotte, who was asleep, lay in his lap with her head on his chest.

"Jade's gwine to be fine! Devils don't go down easy. Look at me!" Scary Mary blurted with an animated look on her face.

Bully and Otis managed to chuckle; everybody else remained stoic. I moved closer to Pee Wee, mainly so I could rearrange Charlotte on his lap. The way she was positioned, with her head turned too far to one side, she was bound to have a sore neck the next day.

"Now ain't that nice," Scary Mary commented, looking from me to Pee Wee with her head tilted so far to one side that her floppy red wig shifted. "I'm so happy to see y'all gettin' along so nice." She sniffed and gave me a mysterious look. "Annette, ain't this a whole lot better than you sittin' in your house prostrate with grief over Pee Wee takin' off with that woman?"

I heard several snickers. Every head in the room turned to look at me as I leaned in front of Pee Wee with my legs about to buckle. Scary Mary had caught me off guard with her comments.

I cleared my throat and stood up straight. "I wouldn't say that I was prostrate with grief," I quickly clarified. "I've moved on with my life." My last sentence made everybody uneasy. The noncommittal expression on Pee Wee's face disappeared. "By the way, when do you plan to come by the house and remove the rest of your stuff?" I asked him.

He looked shocked, and a split second later he looked disappointed. "Uh, I'll talk to you about that later," he told me.

# CHAPTER 58

Scary Mary was the kind of person who made herself right at home, no matter whose home she was in. As old and "sickly" as she claimed to be, she hobbled in and out of Rhoda's living room like a young squirrel with a tray of drinks each time. She fussed at people for spilling alcohol on Rhoda's nice fluffy carpets, and she even volunteered to cook up a few snacks. People were drinking like fish, but only a few were interested in eating anything. That didn't stop Scary Mary from throwing together some cheese and crackers, and some other finger foods, and passing the trays around with such a relish that you would have thought we were at a block party.

I tried my best not to look at Pee Wee across the room, because it seemed like every time I looked in his direction, he was looking in mine. At one point, he looked like a lost puppy. His face was long, his eyes drooping, and his lips looked so tight I was surprised he was able to open them wide enough to shove in the cheese and crackers he kept snatching off the tray every time Scary Mary got close enough.

When Pee Wee ended up standing next to me, he suddenly remembered "a previous engagement," so he decided to leave. I knew that his leaving had a lot to do with what I'd said about him coming to get the rest of his belongings.

"It sure was good to see you, Annette. You are lookin' well," he told me, his eyes darting from side to side like a condemned man.

I had no idea why he felt so uncomfortable in my presence, especially this late in the game. There was nothing else he could do or say to upset me that he hadn't already done or said. Even though I still felt some pain and anger, I was also well on the road to recovery. But he was clearly agitated as he stumbled toward the door, almost walking into the wall to keep from looking me in the eye.

"I'd better be on my way," I told Rhoda about ten minutes after his departure.

"Is everything all right?" she asked.

"Not really. And to tell you the truth, Rhoda, I don't think that things will ever be 'all right' for me again."

When I got home, Pee Wee's car was parked in my driveway. He was in the driver's seat, looking like he didn't have a friend in the world. I had not expected to see him, and I was not happy to see him on my turf. As far as I was concerned, he had no right to show up unannounced. He had given up that right when he moved in with a woman he thought he'd be happier with.

By the time I parked my car, he had jumped out of his and run over to mine to open my door. "I . . . I just wanted to make sure you got home all right," he said, following me to my front porch doorsteps.

"You didn't have to do that. You don't have to do anything for me. I can take care of myself," I told him in a firm tone of voice. I already had the key to my front door in my hand. The last thing I wanted this man to think was that I was weak in any way. "I did it before you married me, I can do it now." I couldn't stop myself from adding that little dig.

Charlotte, still snoozing, was in my arms. Her body was as limp as a wet dishrag. Pee Wee was so close behind me I could feel his breath on my neck. Of course that irritated me and I almost dropped Charlotte as I stumbled toward the door. He attempted to take her, but I silently pushed his hands away. As soon as I got inside, I placed her on the couch, covering her with a light green blanket that I'd left on the couch from the night before.

"You can leave now. You don't have to worry about us," I assured Pee Wee. "We're getting along fine without you."

"I'm sure you are, Annette. You know how to get that point across real good. But that still don't mean I don't worry," he said, plopping down in that old La-Z-Boy chair of his.

I stood with my arms folded. "I'm surprised you haven't come back for that damn chair yet," I commented under my breath. He ignored my comment.

He was clearly uncomfortable, so I did not understand why he had bothered to come to the house on this particular night. We stared at each other for a few moments. He looked confused, then tense. When the phone rang, he looked relieved, and I heard him release a sigh of relief that was so profound it sounded like a hiss.

I was apprehensive about picking up the phone. The machine was on, but I didn't want the call to go to it. The speaker was on, and if the caller, meaning Jacob, said something stupid, I didn't want Pee Wee to hear it. I grabbed the phone in time and I was glad to hear the voice of Mr. Combs, the widower who lived in the big brown house across the street.

"Annette, I was just checking to make sure you're all right," the old man began. "I've been real worried about you. Is everything all right now?"

Now?

"I'm fine . . . now," I told him, puzzled.

"That's good. Did you straighten out that mess with that jitter-bug peeping in your front window? I hope so. Because the other night when he did it, he also peeped into your car. I told my grandson Harvey that that spook was up to something. If you come out to your car and find it vandalized, or sugar in the tank one morning, you'll know who done it."

"Mr. Combs, what are you talking about?" I glanced at Pee Wee. Like me, he looked thoroughly confused.

"Honey, you don't have to try and hide nothing from me. I'm only concerned about your welfare. You remind me of my niece in Biloxi."

I had to deal with old folks every day of my life. With my parents and Scary Mary racing with one another to see which one could drive me crazy first, I was used to the ways of the elderly. I thought I was going to have to go across the street and sit on Mr. Combs for him to cut to the chase. "Brother Combs, I have company right now, so I don't have a lot of time to talk. Could you please get to the point?"

He sputtered through a few coughs first. "Didn't the po'lice bring you home earlier tonight?"

"That's correct. Why?"

"Well, since you ain't disabled, coming home in a squad car had to be because you got a mess on your hands. And it must involve that sport I've seen visiting you on occasion since Pee Wee took off. He's the one I seen peeping in your front window and your car."

I could feel my blood rising and my heart sinking. "Oh, thank you for telling me," I said, trying not to sound too concerned. "You have a blessed night."

"God willing. You just be careful now. This is a close-knit neighborhood, and we look out for each other. Me and your daddy go fishing all the time. I keep my hunting rifle and a baseball bat handy. You need me, all you got to do is holler and I'll come running. Do you hear me?"

"Yes, sir. Mr. Combs, would you do me a favor and not mention any of this to my parents? I don't want to worry them."

"I won't say nothing about it to them. Now you make sure all your windows and doors is locked."

I hung up and turned to Pee Wee. He spoke before I did. "Who was that? What is it you don't want your parents to worry about?" he asked, giving me a tentative look. "Is there somethin' goin' on around here that I should know about?"

"That was Mr. Combs across the street. Uh, he told me there's been reports about a burglar breaking into houses on our street."

Pee Wee rose, hands on his hips. "What?"

I motioned with my hands for him to sit back down, but he didn't. Instead, he moved closer to me with his hands still on his hips.

"Don't overreact," I advised. "We've had break-ins in this neighborhood before."

"I'm goin' to get a pit bull for you! No—three pit bulls. I want you to keep one in the front yard, one in the back, and one in the house at all times. I'm goin' to have a burglar alarm installed first thing tomorrow mornin'."

"I told you that I can take care of myself, Pee Wee," I said weakly. I paused and exhaled a sour breath. I had drunk a glass of wine at

Rhoda's house and I could still taste it. "Do you think Lizzie would mind if you stayed with me and Charlotte tonight?" I asked, wringing my hands and looking toward the window. I knew Jacob had some issues, but his recent actions and what Mr. Combs had just told me made me realize that Jacob's issues were more serious than I thought. "You can sleep in your La-Z-Boy," I said quickly.

"No problem," Pee Wee said without hesitation. "Just get me a pillow and a blanket."

"What about Lizzie?"

"What about Lizzie?" he asked with a look of mild disgust on his face.

"Shouldn't you call and let her know you're staying here tonight? I don't want to cause you any problems with her."

"Baby, I've had problems with that woman from the day I moved in with her. But this is not the time to talk about that. I am more concerned about you and my daughter." He paused and shifted his eyes, like he was trying to decide what to say next. "You and Charlotte are my family."

# CHAPTER 59

I smelled bacon as soon as I rose out of bed the next morning. I grabbed my robe and padded down to the kitchen immediately. Pee Wee was gone, but he had prepared a breakfast fit for a queen.

"Mama, that sure smells good," Charlotte exclaimed, running into the kitchen. "So what is going to happen next with Jade? Is she going to be okay?" Charlotte asked, already spooning grits from the pot on the stove onto a plate. She plopped down in a seat at the table.

"Jade had an accident, but she's going to be all right," I answered. I wasn't hungry, but I poured myself a cup of coffee, and I plucked a piece of bacon off the tray on the stove. I quietly sat down at the table and faced Charlotte. She was humped over her plate like a pig at a hog-trough.

"An accident? Yeah right!" Her mouth was full of food. She talked and chewed at the same time. "Puh-leeze! Getting hit by a car or falling out of a tree is an accident! Mama, I'm not stupid. I don't know why you and everybody else keeps treating me like a child."

"Because you are still a child," I reminded her firmly, giving her the kind of look that made her sink down into her seat.

She swallowed hard and gave me a critical look. "I know Vernie beat Jade's butt and sent her to the hospital, and he didn't do it by accident."

I didn't like the amused look that was now on my daughter's face, but I could see the humor in the situation. "Get that stupid look off of your face, girl. What happened to Jade is not funny." It was a struggle for me to keep a grin off my face.

"And I know that Vernie is in jail, Mama. I already told you that I hear things when nobody knows I'm listening."

I gave Charlotte a threatening look. I wanted her to know that she was on thin ice. "You'd better stop listening, because sooner or later you're going to hear something you don't want to hear."

"Yes, ma'am." She licked her empty spoon and remained silent for a few moments. "So . . . since Daddy stayed the night here—I heard you and him talking last night when you thought I was asleep—does that mean you're going to let him come back home?"

"He stayed here last night because . . . because this is still his home. Technically, at least." I sipped some coffee. "Now shut up and finish your breakfast."

I called Rhoda's number twice during the day, and each time Bully told me she was too upset to take my call. I was tempted to go to her house again, but under the circumstances, I had a few issues of my own that I needed to focus on. One was, I still had to contact Jacob about the money he owed the funeral home.

I waited until the following Monday evening to make that call. I knew he worked during the day, and leaving messages on his machine would be a waste if time. I decided to call him around eight thirty that night.

"Jacob, this is Annette," I began. I was leaning over the counter in my kitchen. I had brought home the red folder that contained the paperwork related to his account. It was open to the first page, but I turned to the second page because I had dog-eared it. I was amazed to see that three of my employees had left that man a total of twenty-eight messages on his answering machine. He had had twenty-eight opportunities to make some arrangements to resolve this issue. He had ignored them all.

"Uh-huh! I figured you'd come crawling back to me soon! I am not perfect, but I'm a good man, and I know you will eventually see that and stop clowning me! I don't know what you expect in a man at your age. You ain't no Queen of Sheba."

"Jacob, this is a business call," I said calmly.

"You can call it whatever you want to call it. The thing is, I still have feelings for you."

"The thing is, I'm calling about a bill you still owe. I need to collect on it." It felt good to knock him off of the high horse he had climbed onto. There was complete silence on his end for what seemed like a very long moment. "Jacob, are you still on the phone?"

"Yeah." He paused again and cleared his throat, gurgling like he was choking on a bone. When he spoke again, his voice was so loud it sounded like he was talking through a megaphone. "A bill? What bill?! What the hell are you talking about? I don't owe you a damn thing. You must have me mixed up with one of your other punks! Like the one I saw sneaking off your porch that time!"

I was so tempted to tell him that the "punk" he'd seen "sneaking" off my front porch was Vernie. But since that poor boy was in jail and until I had all of the facts, I didn't even want to bring up his name to a fool like Jacob. Vernie was going to get demonized enough when all of the Richland meddlers got wind of his predicament.

"Jacob, in case you've forgotten, I work for the Mizelle Collection Agency. My job is to collect unpaid—"

"Wait a minute! Is this about that steak house thing *we* didn't pay?"

"No, this is not about that steak house thing *you* didn't pay. It's a real unpaid bill."

I heard him gasp so hard he choked on some air. I leaned back on my legs and braced myself.

"Woman, I know damn well you didn't call me up about a damn unpaid bill! I don't owe nothing to nobody in this world! You need to learn how to do your damn job right, because like I said, you must have confused my name with somebody else's! Shit! You just ruined my evening! And to think that I was about to call you up and ask if I could treat you to a nice Italian meal! You . . . you— now you're acting just like a black woman!"

"That's because I am a black woman," I reminded him.

"And that's your problem! I bet if I had me a half-white woman like Pee Wee, I wouldn't be going through all these changes!"

"I'm just doing my job."

"Fuck you and your *job*, BITCH!"

The only reason I didn't complain about Jacob's unnecessary use of profanity was because I was used to it. It came with the territory and I expected it. I couldn't remember the last time I'd had a pleasant conversation with a debtor.

"Do you want to dispute the claim from the funeral home?" I asked in a gentle, very professional voice. I wanted him to know that his hostile reaction didn't faze me.

"Huh?"

"Do you have proof that you paid off your mother's final expenses in full? Because if you do, then I apologize on behalf of my company. But if you didn't and need to set up some payment arrangements, I can assure you that we can negotiate—"

"You negotiate my dick, BITCH!" Jacob hung up so fast and hard, my eardrum started throbbing.

Before I snapped his folder shut, I removed a marker from my notions drawer and printed a note to myself on the front page: *Initiate garnishment of wages. Mr. Brewster has made it abundantly clear that he has no intentions of settling this account.*

Before I could leave the kitchen, the phone rang. I groaned and prayed that it was not Jacob calling me back. It was Pee Wee.

"I'm going to go see a man about them pit bulls later tonight. I should have you set up by tomorrow evening," he told me.

"I don't want to be cleaning up after three dogs. But I'd appreciate a very good security alarm. I think I'm going to need one now."

"Oh? Did something else happen? Was there another burglary in the neighborhood last night?"

"Not that I know of. I just . . . I'd just feel safer with a security system in place. Just in case."

"Annette, I know you. Is there somethin' goin' on that you don't want me to know about?"

"I really don't want to talk about it yet," I said. "I don't want to make a mountain out of a molehill."

"It's Lizzie, ain't it? She called you up about me spendin' the night over there!"

"What makes you think that?"

"Because she told me she was goin' to do it! She told me this mornin' when I got home that she was goin' to put you in your place—"

"You can stop right there!" I hollered, holding my hand up in the air like he could see it. "I've got enough mess going on in my life without Lizzie adding to it. You tell that nasty-ass bitch if she ever tries to 'put me in my place,' I will beat the dog shit out of her—again!" I hung up before Pee Wee could say another word.

I was so stunned I started breathing through my mouth. In addition to all of the other problems I already had, I was not going to add Lizzie to the mix. I knew that the most effective way to make sure that didn't happen was for her to hear it from me!

# CHAPTER 60

As soon as I got to work that morning, I called up Pee Wee's barbershop. I was glad Lizzie answered.

"Lizzie, this is Annette. We need to talk," I stated. I was too agitated and angry to sit down. I had the speaker on, so I talked as I paced back and forth in front of my desk.

"About what?" she asked, sounding nonchalant.

"About my husband. It's time we had a woman-to-woman talk about this situation."

"That's fine with me," she hissed. "What's your problem?"

"Look, you are one of my minor problems, but don't think I won't come over there and bitch-slap you in a major way! If you've got a problem with *my* husband coming to see me and *his* daughter, that's your damn problem, bitch. If you want to 'put me in my place,' all you have to do is tell me where to meet you. We can settle this once and for all."

"I am not about to fight you or any other woman over a man. And anyway, you've already lost the battle. Your husband lives with me!" Lizzie slammed down the telephone.

I didn't like to cuss, even though I had done it a lot lately. And I certainly didn't like to fight and act like I had been raised in a jungle among wild animals and savages. But the way things were going in my life, I knew that it was just a matter of time before I snapped.

And when that happened, I was not going to be responsible for my actions.

Just as I was about to slam my fist against the wall, Rhoda called.

"Thank God it's you," I told her. "I'm having a bad day."

"Who isn't? I've gone through two beers already this morning."

"How are you doing? How is Jade doing?"

"She's goin' to be fine. Listen, I've been thinkin' about what you said about Vernie, and me doin' the right thing. Uh, he was only tryin' to defend himself."

"Does that mean Jade's not going to press charges?"

"Oh, she wants to. She's been jumpin' up and down in that hospital bed. She wants to see him suffer."

"With all due respect, the boy's been suffering since the day he met her, Rhoda. What more does she want?"

"Well, I can tell you what she doesn't want, and that's a divorce. She said it would be too much of an embarrassment for a girl like her to get a divorce."

*"A girl like her?"*

"Yes, a girl like her!"

I couldn't stop myself from laughing. I covered my mouth as soon as I could so Rhoda couldn't hear it. "Are you telling me that she thinks things are going to go back to normal? And in her case, that's pretty scary."

"I know, I know." Rhoda groaned under her breath. "Otis bailed Vernie out of jail this mornin'."

"Oh? Well, that's a move in a positive direction. And I know he's not happy about what he did to Jade. How is Vernie feeling?"

"Annette, he wants to leave and go back to Alabama! He—he wants to desert my daughter the same way that Mexican did. When she hears about it, it's goin' to crush her! Oh—I'm at the end of my rope!"

"Calm down. You don't need to work yourself up into a frenzy again. Do you want me to meet you for lunch today? It sounds like you need a shoulder to cry on."

"Yes, please let's do lunch. Come by around noon. The puffiness around my eyes should be gone by then." Rhoda sniffed. "You don't know what a lucky woman you are, Annette."

"Come again."

"Well, other than Pee Wee leavin' you, you don't have a whole lot of drama goin' on right now. By the way, how are things between you and Jacob? When you talk to him, tell him I'd like to invite you and him over for dinner as soon as things settle down with Jade. Do you think you all can make it?"

"I can, but I don't think he can."

"Excuse me?"

"I won't be seeing Jacob anymore."

"Do you want to tell me about it?"

"Not over the telephone. Let's save it for lunch."

"That's fine. Let me ask you one more thing before you hang up. How's Pee Wee takin' the news about Lizzie wantin' to go work for his rival?"

"What did you say?"

"You didn't know? You didn't know that Lizzie went on an interview with Henry, and that she's goin' to go work for him?"

"I didn't know. I guess she decided she'd rather clean up his barbershop than do manicures, huh?"

"No, she's goin' over to Henry's to do manicures and pedicures. Pee Wee's business is boomin' and it's kickin' the hell out of Henry's. Now he wants a cute woman on his payroll. Lizzie has a lot of regular customers who will follow her to Henry's place. I don't know how they worked it, but she had to do some sneaky shit to be this far along so fast. I got the whole story from Scary Mary this mornin'. I thought you'd know by now."

"Well, I didn't. Uh, listen, I'm about to have a staff meeting. I'll see you at noon." I was still reeling from the bitch-slap that I'd received from Jacob. I didn't think that I could stand to hear more on the subject of Pee Wee and Lizzie at the moment. But as soon as I got off the phone with Rhoda, I called Pee Wee's barbershop. To my everlasting horror, Lizzie answered again. "Put my husband on this phone!" I ordered. Pee Wee came on immediately.

"What's wrong now?" he wanted to know.

"Why didn't you tell me that Lizzie was leaving you to go work for Henry Boykin to be his manicurist?"

His silence spoke volumes. "What? That's because I didn't know!" he snarled. "I—this is news to me! When is this supposed to happen?"

"Ask her," I said. Then I hung up.

\* \* \*

Rhoda had to cancel her plans to have lunch with me. The hospital had called her up after I'd talked to her, and told her that Jade had just suffered a setback. Rhoda was too upset to go into detail, but it had something to do with the fact that Vernie was planning to do a disappearing act.

I was sitting at my desk, toying with some lettuce on the salad that I'd picked up for lunch, when Pee Wee called. As soon as I heard his voice, I started talking. "I am not in the mood to waste any more of my time talking about that woman."

I was so sick and tired of dealing with one issue after another, I knew that I had to do something. One thing was, I was going to stop letting Lizzie and Pee Wee's actions get on my nerves anymore. The biggest concern I had now was Jacob. I had already started the process of having his wages attached. There was just no telling how he was going to react.

"I didn't call you to talk about Lizzie. I called to talk to you about our daughter," Pee Wee told me in a sorry voice.

A large lump immediately formed in my throat. "What about her?"

"If you didn't want her hangin' out with that pregnant child, why would you let her hang out with those Turner kids? They are way worse than that Patsy girl."

"Look, I have no idea what you are talking about. Yes, I told Charlotte to stay away from Patsy. A pregnant preteen is not the kind of kid I want my daughter hangin' out with. I know all of her other friends, and none of them is pregnant."

"You know that Jasmine Turner?"

"Of course I know Jasmine. She sleeps over at least twice a month. She goes to church *every* Sunday, which is more than I can say for Charlotte."

"Well, goin' to church every Sunday ain't doin' her much good. She smokes more weed than a Rasta man, and she's been screwin' around with some of them boys from the high school. Did you know she was into all of that?"

I was almost speechless. It was a struggle for me to find my voice. "I didn't know. And how did you find out?"

"Jonah Ripley came up in here for the first time to get his hair cut this mornin'. He's sick of goin' to Henry's place. He's related to the Turners, and he's the one who told me about Jasmine."

"I'll talk to Charlotte as soon as I get home this evening. And the Turner family is such a nice, quiet, churchgoing family . . ."

"I ain't finish," Pee Wee said quickly. "You know that Jasmine's got three older brothers?"

"Why are you asking me a question that you already know the answer to? One of those boys delivers my newspaper every day. You know that."

"That ain't all he delivers. He's got three different girls pregnant, and they are all due to give birth the same month. Did you know that? And I was told that every day, as soon as them Turner kids get home from school, they party like Rick James."

"Like I said, I'll be talking to Charlotte when I get home. I'll call you later."

"I'm comin' over there tonight," Pee Wee informed me. "Maybe you can't control my child, but I can!" He hung up. I sat at my desk, glaring at the telephone like it was a dirty diaper. I couldn't even finish the salad in front of me or concentrate on my work.

Somehow, I made it through the rest of the day. Charlotte was in the bathroom when I got home. I decided to wait for her in her room, sitting on her bed. Just as I stood up to leave, I noticed something sticking out from under her mattress. I pulled out what I thought was a T-shirt or one of her undershirts. It was a pair of her white cotton panties.

The crotch was covered in blood.

Of all the things that had happened to me in the past and in the present, this was my worst nightmare. Somebody had violated my child. And whoever that hound from hell was, he was going to have to answer to me.

# CHAPTER 61

Tears were streaming down the sides of my face like a waterfall. I stood there holding those bloody panties, trembling so hard I wanted to scream. Some old memories that I thought I had buried for good danced around in my head. I recalled the first time blood had appeared in my panties. It had happened when I was just seven years old, the first time Mr. Boatwright raped me.

"Mama, what are you doing?" Charlotte asked, stumbling into her room with a towel draped around the bottom half of her naked body. It had been a while since I'd seen her naked. I had no idea that she had started developing breasts. There was no telling what else I didn't know about my own child. But I was going to find out.

"When did this happen?" I asked, holding the panties up in the air.

"Yesterday," she muttered. I could see that she was nervous and frightened, and she had every reason to be! "I was going to tell you. . . ."

"Oh? Well, were you going to tell me who did it?"

"Who did what?"

"Did Jacob . . . have you been to Jacob's house? Did he . . . touch you?"

"Mama, what in the world are you talking about?" Charlotte moved back a few steps toward the door, clutching the towel tighter around her.

"Or was it one of Jasmine's horny, baby-making brothers?"

"Mama, I stopped going over to Jacob's house just like you told me. And Jasmine's brothers don't even like me. They like girls with big butts."

"What about the drugs?"

"What drugs?"

"Are you going to tell me that those boys don't smoke weed?"

"No, they do smoke weed."

"And have you?"

Charlotte looked so frightened I thought she was going to melt into the wall that she was now backed up against. "I only smoked weed one time."

I swayed like a palm tree. To this day I don't know how I managed to keep from falling to the ground. "You are not to ever go back to that house!" I hollered, steadying myself by leaning against the wall. "Do you hear me! If I ever hear about you going around those boys again, smoking that shit, I am going to file a complaint against them!"

"I didn't smoke weed with them! I found that roach on our floor."

"What?"

"Uh, Uncle Otis and Uncle Bully used to smoke weed all the time when they came over here. Daddy did, too—before you ran him off. They would send me to the store to get that Glade room freshener to spray the air before you got home. I didn't like it, so I'll never smoke again. Not even cigarettes."

"Do you mean to tell me that your daddy knew about this and he didn't tell me?" I didn't need the wall to steady myself now. I was so mad that I was stiff enough to stand up in a bowl of quicksand. I must have looked pretty menacing standing in front of my daughter; I had a scowl on my face, with one hand on my hip and my other hand holding her bloody panties.

"No, he didn't know. I done it behind his back. Uncle Otis told me to never do it again. Uncle Bully told me the same thing, and I told them I wouldn't. I don't want to grow up to be a fool like Jade."

"Your daddy is on his way over here. We are all going to sit down and have a long talk."

"About what?"

"About your behavior. Now get dressed and get your butt down-stairs. He'll be here any minute, or so he said," I told her, glancing at my watch.

Pee Wee didn't come, but he called. "Uh, I've got a situation here at my place that I need to address immediately. I'll try and get over there tomorrow."

"I know you have more important things to be concerned about than your daughter. But like I've told you before, I can handle my end. You take care of yours."

"You were right. Lizzie's leavin'. She's leavin' the shop, and she's movin' in with Henry's uncle Peabo. I . . . I found out that Peabo has been dippin' his spoon in her sugar bowl for weeks! Anyway, she's also goin' to be Henry's new manicurist. I guess that makes you happy, huh?"

"I don't know what makes you think that. But I will say one thing; it sounds like she's planning to milk every cow on the farm."

I was not happy to hear about Lizzie's new venture. The damage she'd done to me was still too fresh and it remained intact. That was more than enough pain for me to deal with at the time.

Pee Wee grunted. "That's the way it looks to me. Did you talk to Charlotte yet?"

"I've got things under control for now," I said.

"Are you sure? I do not want to ever hear about her hangin' around with Jasmine's brothers. You know how these young punks are these days."

"And the old punks are not too much better," I pointed out.

"Look, I am not in the mood for one of your mouthy beat-downs. I know I've caused you some grief these past few weeks."

"Yes, you sure have, but you're not the only old punk I was re-ferring to this time."

"What?"

"I don't want Charlotte around you and your friends when you all are smoking weed."

Pee Wee remained quiet for a few seconds. "Uh, don't worry about it. It won't happen again."

"You're damn right it won't. Call me when you get a chance. I've had a splitting headache all day, and it just got worse."

My head felt like it was going to explode by the time I got through "straightening out" my daughter. No matter how many times I asked her who was responsible for the blood in her panties, she wouldn't tell me. She continued to say, "I don't know!" By the time we went to bed, we were both in tears.

I took off work the next day and called to see if I could make an emergency appointment with my regular OB/GYN so I could have Charlotte examined. But there were no appointments available for another three weeks. I ended up dragging her to the free clinic on Morgan Street where the homeless people went. It took a young doctor just a few minutes to tell me what I should have known already: Charlotte had had her first menstrual period. That's why the blood was in her panties.

"She's only eleven," I yelled. Then it hit me: I had started my first period when I was her age. "Uh, thank you, doctor," I muttered, on my way out the door.

"Happy?" Charlotte said with a smirk on her face as soon as we got out into the hallway. "What you got to say now?"

I gave her a tired look. I drove in silence for the first few minutes. "Honey, you could have saved us both some grief if you'd just told me what it really was."

"I tried to, but you kept hollering and screaming at me to tell you the boy's name that made me bleed. I don't know anybody I like enough to let him do that to me. . . ."

Her last sentence made me feel so much better. "I'll pick up some pads," I told her.

I suddenly felt very *old*. Even though I was already well into middle age, I had never really felt truly old until now.

"You do know that if you do something nasty, you can get pregnant now," I mentioned, giving Charlotte a sharp look out of the corner of my eye.

She nodded. "Jade told me a long time ago that getting pregnant was no big deal. She told me about those abortions you made her get."

That Jade. I was convinced that there was no hope for her, or of the two of us ever restoring our relationship.

I spent the next few days concentrating on my job. The times that Pee Wee came to the house to see Charlotte, he said nothing about Lizzie's betrayal and departure, and I didn't ask. I decided that if and when he wanted to discuss it with me, he would.

Since none of my neighbors reported to me that they'd seen Jacob lurking around my house or car again, I assumed that he had gotten the message. The only relationship between the two of us now was the one that involved the legal issue regarding his mother's unpaid funeral bill. But he got the last laugh on me with that one, too.

Two weeks after I had his paycheck garnished, his employer notified me by certified mail that Jacob had quit his job. That same day, my mother called me up to tell me that Scary Mary had told her that Jacob had fled the country and moved to Montreal, where some of his relatives lived. "You won't have to worry about him bein' in the way no more," she told me with a chuckle. "And with that wench out of Pee Wee's hair, maybe you got a chance of getting him back. Get on it!"

"Who said I wanted Pee Wee back?" I asked, glad she was in her house so she couldn't see the look on my face. I was sick and tired of people trying to tell me how to live my life—even my parents. I didn't want to remind my mother that had it not been for her, Lizzie would never have entered my life in the first place!

"Why not? Other than him havin' a restless, wanderin' pecker, ain't nothin' else wrong with him. And how many times do I have to tell you that ALL men are dogs? But as long as you keep 'em on a tight enough leash, you can make 'em behave."

# CHAPTER 62

Jade was released from the hospital a week later. By then, Vernie had fled. I didn't get to see him in person before he boarded a plane for Alabama, but he called me up from the airport. Just like that sweet Mexican that Jade had tried to bully into marriage.

"Annette, I just wanted to let you know that I am sorry I didn't have a chance to get to know you better. Just from the few times I did see you, I could tell you are a good woman. I don't believe any of that stuff Jade told me about you," he said, his voice trembling.

"Vernie, I am really glad you called. I have always been on your side, and I am so sorry that you had to go through all that mess with Jade before you took action. I don't condone violence, but in this case, she had it coming."

"I'm glad she's going to be all right and I still love her. But . . . but I don't *like* her. Does that make sense to you?"

"It makes a lot of sense to me because I feel the same way. I don't like a lot of the people I love." We both laughed. "Do you think you'll ever come back to Ohio? Or do you think you will try to resume your relationship with Jade in Alabama?"

"HELL NO!" Vernie roared. "I'm sorry. I didn't mean to holler like that. But I wouldn't try to resume a relationship with Jade in heaven!"

"That's a very potent statement, Vernie, but I understand. You don't have to apologize for anything to me. I just wish you the best."

"I called up my mama the other day, and she's already got me an appointment with a lawyer when I get home."

"Oh? I am so sorry to hear that. Are you thinking about getting a divorce?"

"Annette, since the day I married Jade, that's all I've been thinking about! Before I left, I did hug her and I told her that I was sorry about hitting her with that lamp. She didn't even apologize for hitting me first, but she told me that she was glad nobody got killed. She also told me how upset she was about me making her break off her silk-wrapped nails when we were struggling over that lamp."

"That's Jade for you," I mumbled.

"Anyway, I'm sorry I hugged her now because I think she took it the wrong way."

"What do you mean by that? Does she think you're going back to Alabama just for some R and R?"

"I don't know what that damn girl thinks, and I don't care!" Vernie yelled. I was so glad to hear him being so much more assertive. I was sorry that he had not been that way sooner. Maybe his marriage would have had a chance.

"She kissed me on my jaw and told me to take care of myself. She also told me to 'stop being such a crybaby' and to get to know my Bible better so I could be a better husband."

I rolled my eyes and let out a heavy sigh. "And what did you tell her?"

"I don't even remember what rolled off my tongue. But I know I didn't say anything about being a better husband to *her*. All I want to do is get the hell out of this state!"

"Good luck, Vernie. You have my address and phone number, and whenever you want to communicate with me, do so."

I didn't tell Rhoda about my conversation with Vernie when I met her for lunch the following Friday. I was in a fairly good mood and I wanted to stay that way. I hadn't read the newspapers or listened to the news on the radio in the last few days so I didn't know about Mike Tyson biting off a piece of Evander Holyfield's ear during their fight a few days ago. I didn't think it was funny, but when Rhoda told me, I laughed with her. By the time we finished lunch, I felt like my old self. But I knew I wasn't . . .

Pee Wee had started coming to the house every day now, but he still had not said anything about the future of our relationship. He didn't bring up Lizzie's name, and I didn't either. One reason I didn't ask him his business was that I didn't want to know if he had another reason for not mentioning our future himself. And it was a reason that Rhoda had brought to my attention. "Maybe he's still out there because he's involved with somebody else now," she'd suggested.

That was one thing that I had not even thought about. And if that was the case, I didn't want to think about it.

I decided to work late that night. Rhoda collected Charlotte from school and dropped her off at my parents' house so she could spend the night there.

After work, I stopped by a nearby deli and ordered a chicken salad for dinner. I took my time eating it, half of which I left on the plate. When I left the deli, I stopped at the Grab and Go convenience store to pick up a few feminine products and had a chat with the long-winded cashier. It was around nine thirty by the time I made it to my side of town.

There was some construction going on along my usual route, so I had to drive down Rhoda's street to get to mine. There was an ambulance parked in her driveway again! It screamed out of the driveway before I could even park my car.

Bully was standing in the front doorway with his shirt hanging open and a dazed look on his face. "What the hell is going on this time?" I yelled. "Where's Rhoda? Where's Otis?"

"Otis had a union meeting tonight. Rhoda's in de ambulance with Jade," Bully told me with a weary voice, still looking dazed. I knew that Bully and Rhoda had been lovers for decades, and I knew they cared about one another. They were one of the most passionate couples I knew. But what I couldn't figure out was why a handsome man like Bully was so attracted to a woman—his best friend's wife at that—with as many problems as Rhoda. But what did I know? There were probably people thinking a lot worse things about me.

"Annette, thank de Lord you're here! She dood it again! She dood it again!" Bully chanted.

"What did Jade 'dood' this time?" I asked, following Bully into Rhoda's living room.

"Of course you must know by now!" Bully said, turning to face me with his hands up in the air and waving like he was directing traffic.

I gave him an impatient look before I let out a loud groan. "Bully, I do not know. If it's not too much trouble, please tell me what is going on."

"Sorry. I grovel in modification," he said, giving me a slight bow, then lifting my hand and kissing it. "Forgive me, please. I am so overwhelmed."

There were a lot of things I loved about Jamaican men. Like the level of sensitivity some of them possessed and displayed, their charm, and especially their sex appeal. Bully had all of those qualities, but he was also the most exasperating man I knew!

"Bully, who did what?" I removed my hand from his and glanced at my watch. "Has there been an accident or something worse? If you don't tell me within the next few minutes, I am going to leave."

He finally got to the point. Like Otis, when Bully got excited, his accent thickened and his English got more convoluted. I could barely understand what he was saying. "Let me tell you. De server come a little while ago with divorce papers from Vernie. Jade was in Red Rose with some girlfriends when he come. He go dere and serve she. Right in de public eye, Jade explode. She catch afire like de burning bush! I predict so much hell to pay soon, I can already smell de brimstone. Anyway, she get so upset she have panic attack, can't breathe. She makes it home in the nick of time, waving divorce document like it was a death notice. Lo and behold, she falls and hits her head on corner of de coffee table. Me and Rhoda think it's better she go back to hospital because she was bleeding like crazy. I hope she is not doing too badly. Losing her man the way she did, that's pretty bad." Bully paused and gave me a curious look. "Of course, you know what *that* feels like, huh?"

I ignored Bully's last comment. "Jade must not be doing too badly if she's going out to a bar," I quipped. I didn't mean to sound as harsh as I did, but it was hard not to when it involved Jade.

"Oh, she had to be at Red Rose tonight. Very big night dere tonight. She talked about it all day! Tonight was de monthly hot body contest night," Bully explained.

"She just got out of the hospital and she's out entering a wet T-shirt contest?"

"Not wet T-shirt," Bully said with a dismissive wave. "Jade say wet T-shirt contest is for ghetto crowd. Only hot body contest for her— and she always win at least first or second place. She's a tart, that one."

"She sure is, Bully. Listen, I'm not even going to bother going over to the hospital. I'm tired," I said, looking and feeling like I'd been up for the past two days. "When Rhoda gets home, tell her I stopped by, and tell her to call me if she feels like it." I started walking toward the door; then I stopped. "No, don't tell her to call me up tonight. You don't even need to let her know that I was here. I'll talk to her tomorrow."

I went home and went straight to bed, and I didn't open my eyes until the next morning. And as soon as I sat up in bed, Rhoda called.

"Annette, I'm losin' my mind. I'm losin' my child," she whimpered so softly I could barely hear her. A split second later, her voice rose like a phoenix. "How will I ever be able to show my face again in the Red Rose? Vernie had Jade served with divorce papers there last night! And in front of her friends!"

"While she was competing in the monthly hot body contest . . ."

Rhoda gasped, then lowered her voice to a roar. "How did you know that?"

"I was passing by your house on my way home when the ambulance was pulling away last night. Bully told me. I told him not to tell you I was there."

"Can you believe that Vernie can be so mean? She's in bed now, doing fine, but still upset. No woman in her right mind ever wants to go through a divorce! Look at you! If Pee Wee had done to me what he did to you, I'd have probably killed him before I let my marriage end in divorce. I'm so glad that you decided not to get a divorce."

"There are a lot worse things than divorce, Rhoda."

"Such as?"

"Well, there are too many for me to list. But divorce doesn't scare me."

"Humph! You must know somethin' the rest of us don't know."

"I wouldn't say that. But like I said, divorce doesn't scare me. As a matter of fact, it looks like I'll be getting one after all."

# CHAPTER 63

I was about to pour myself a large drink, but I changed my mind as soon as I plucked a glass out of my dishwasher. For once, I wanted to be stone-cold sober when I talked to Pee Wee about our marriage. He'd said that he'd see me in a few hours.

Since my last conversation with Rhoda, which had been three days ago, I had done a lot of thinking. For one thing, I was not going to let my decisions be influenced by anybody else's unsolicited input.

Muh'Dear had come by the house last night and bombarded me with comments like, "You'd better be tryin' to get your husband back before another woman grabs him up." She said a lot of things like that, but the one that hurt the most was, "You done ran off two men this year, and that should tell you that you don't have what it takes no more."

Daddy had come with her and all he'd said was, "Girl, you do what you think is right for you. Whomever you end up with, you'll be the one sleepin' with him, not us."

Scary Mary had left several messages on my answering machine, but I didn't have the strength to call her back and listen to more of what she had to say.

Charlotte was the only one who said something that didn't upset me. "Mama, I don't know why everybody is all upset. It ain't like my daddy moved to Mars or dropped dead. He's still in our lives."

Pee Wee didn't show up until after eleven. By then Charlotte was in bed and I had settled myself on the couch with a glass of tea.

"No wine tonight?" he asked, easing down into that old La-Z-Boy that he still had not removed from my presence.

I shook my head. "I was not up for that," I told him. "You want some tea?"

"I'm up for some wine, if you don't mind."

After I poured him a glass of wine and set the bottle next to his glass on the coffee table, I returned to the couch. I took another sip of my tea and looked him in the eye. "We need to make some decisions. When do you plan to pick up the rest of your stuff? That La-Z-Boy has been getting on my nerves for years. . . ."

He drank some wine before he replied. "I know. Just like I was."

I rolled my eyes, ignoring his remarks. "There are a bunch of old tools and fishin' poles in the basement, too. If you don't want it, I can call the junkman."

His eyes got big. "I paid a lot of money for them tools and fishin' gear! You know that! You would give all of my stuff away to the *junkman?*"

"I will if you don't want it. I have no use for it. We've talked about this before."

He set down his glass and rubbed the palms of his hands together. "Is there a reason why you want me to get all my stuff out of this house?"

My eyes got big this time. "A reason? The reason is that you don't live here anymore."

He shrugged and mumbled something unintelligible under his breath. "Maybe you don't want nothin' around here that will remind your new friend of me, huh? Is that what this is all about?"

"I don't have a new friend, and if I did, I wouldn't even think about moving him into my house," I declared, waving my hand and snapping my fingers.

I hadn't told Rhoda about Jacob hitting me in the restaurant, and decided that I wouldn't. That was one thing I didn't want Pee Wee to know about. After what he'd done to Louis Baines when he found out that he'd hit me, I knew that he would probably kill Jacob.

"I've had it up to my gums with all of that shit! All I want now is to be happy. And if being alone is the only way I can do that, well . . ."

"What happened between you and Jacob?" he asked sharply, giving me a suspicious look. "I heard he took off for Canada."

"That's not important. You didn't come over here to discuss Jacob." We stared at each other for a tense moment.

I didn't know what was going through his mind, and I didn't want him to know what was going through mine. I didn't want to think about Jade and Vernie, the sorry state of my marriage, my daughter's welfare, or much of anything else. My thoughts involved a lot of things, and the one that stood out the most right now was Jacob. He had terrorized me, but now that he was gone, I saw no reason for Pee Wee to know that. Besides, as long as Jacob didn't plan on paying his mother's funeral expenses, he would never work in Richland again. If he ever did, I would not hesitate to sick a process server on him. Then I'd haul him to small claims court and have his wages attached some more. I was confident that his moving back to Richland was unlikely. And with the top-notch security system Pee Wee had installed in my house, I was not worried about anybody else threatening my safety either.

"Well, he is part of the problem," Pee Wee insisted.

"Look, Jacob is no longer a friend of mine," I said. I made that statement with such a firm voice Pee Wee had to know that I was serious. "That relationship is over, too. . . ."

He rose and stood next to the chair, still staring at me. "I don't mind lettin' you know that I'm glad to hear that," he said with a sneer. "I always knew you could do better than him."

I chuckled. "He said the same thing about you."

"Whatever." He rubbed the palms of his hands together again. "Well, since we started out as friends, do you think we can ever be friends again?"

"As far as I'm concerned, you and I are still friends. And will continue to be. But the difference now is that we are just friends. That's all."

"We're still married. We're still man and wife."

"You left me for another woman!" I said hotly, waving my finger in his direction like a sword.

He shook his finger at me and gave me an incredulous look. No, it was more of a hostile look, and I didn't like that look at all. "So? You left me for another man!" he snapped. I narrowed my eyes and gritted my teeth so hard it made him flinch. "What's that mean look for, Annette? I'm tellin' the truth, and you know it!"

"I didn't *leave* you for Louis Baines! I . . . I slept with him, but I didn't leave you for him. I didn't flaunt him the way you did Lizzie for everybody in town to see and pity me! I at least cared enough about your feelings to try and hide my affair. You rubbed yours in my face!"

"What difference does it make who did what? The bottom line is, we both fucked up!"

I leaped up off the couch and lunged for the wine. I took a long drink straight from the bottle. It was enough for me to get an immediate buzz. I whirled around to face Pee Wee again. "Do you want a divorce or what?"

"I don't know what I want," he said in a weary voice. That was not what I wanted to hear.

I returned to my seat, still clutching the wine bottle. "Well, when will you know? I don't plan on spending the rest of my life tied up in a situation like this! I can't live not knowing something more definite about our future together. If I or if we both meet somebody else that we want to marry, I don't want us to have to wait for a divorce to be final."

"You're right." He shook his head and slid his hands into his pockets. Then he looked toward the door. "I guess I should be goin' so you can get some rest. You look tired."

"I am tired. But the thing I'm tired about the most is the way we keep going around in circles about what we are going to do. Now, there is no reason why we can't agree on something right here and now."

"You're right," he said again. "If you want to go ahead with the divorce, go ahead. I ain't goin' to stand in the way of you bein' happy. I've done that long enough. I'll come by in a couple of days to get the rest of my stuff."

"Wait a minute." I raised my hand. "I've been happy most of our marriage. You haven't been standing in the way of me being happy. I don't know where you got that idea from."

"You know what, I'm tired, too. I'm goin' to go back to my place. If you have them serve me the divorce papers, that's fine. I can live with it. If you don't, well, I can live with that, too. Right now, I'm goin' home." He looked toward the stairs. "Tell Charlotte I'll take her shoppin' this weekend, and she can spend the weekend with me if she still wants to." He didn't hug me or even say good-bye. He just turned and walked away.

I didn't even wait for him to pull out of the driveway before I called Rhoda. She sounded sleepy, but she started talking right away. "I'm glad you called. I'm bringin' you somethin' tomorrow that's goin' to make you very happy," she informed me.

"Good. Don't forget to bring some batteries with it," I chided.

"Get your mind out of the gutter, you nasty buzzard. I was talkin' about some tequila. I'm goin' to make you some killer margaritas."

"That's good to hear. We can celebrate."

"Celebrate? Celebrate what?"

"Pee Wee's coming home," I told her. "I think . . ."

I heard her suck in some air and then let out a disturbing gurgle.

"Rhoda, are you all right?" I asked with concern. "Can you still talk now?"

"Yeah, some air went down my windpipe the wrong way. What you just said shocked me, I guess. I mean, I'm glad to hear it all, but I'm surprised. I just saw Pee Wee a little while ago, and he didn't even mention a reconciliation. When is he movin' back in with you?"

"Um, we haven't decided on that yet." I crossed my fingers as I stood in the window with the curtains cracked open enough for me to see Pee Wee. There was enough light coming from the moon and the streetlights for me to see him sitting in his car with his head on the steering wheel. "There won't be a divorce . . . this time."

"I am so happy to hear that!" Rhoda squealed. She sounded wide awake now. "This news gives me so much hope! If you and Pee Wee can get back together after all you've put each other through these past few months, anything is possible. You agree?"

"I agree with that," I said.

"Now as soon as my daughter's husband comes to his senses and realizes how much he loves her, he'll come back."

Before I could leave the window, or hide my face behind the curtains, Pee Wee looked up. He smiled at me for the first time in weeks. I smiled back. We waved to each other; then he backed out of the driveway and drove down the street.

I returned to my seat on the couch. The phone was still up to my ear, and I was still listening to Rhoda as she babbled on and on about the possibility of Vernie coming back to Jade. But none of that bothered me. I felt better than I'd felt in a long time. It was a while before I could get another word in edgewise. And that was only because she had to pause to clear her throat. "Rhoda, you're right. Everything is going to work out all right for all of us."

"Even Vernie comin' back to Jade?" she asked, suddenly sounding as eager as a child on Christmas morning.

"Even Vernie coming back to Jade," I said. "If Pee Wee and I can get back together and go on like before, *anything is possible.*"

I didn't know for sure if my husband was coming back to me, but if he wanted to, well, he was still my husband.

# READING GROUP
# DISCUSSION QUESTIONS

1. For years, Annette accused Pee Wee of having an affair, even though it was not true. When he finally did get involved with another woman, were you as surprised as Annette was?

2. If Annette had not badgered Pee Wee, he would not have hired Lizzie Stovall to work in his barbershop in the first place. Was Annette responsible for Pee Wee and Lizzie falling in love and moving in together?

3. When Lizzie showed up at Annette's house and told her face-to-face that she was in love with Annette's husband, Annette reacted violently. Was she justified in physically attacking Lizzie and Pee Wee?

4. Speaking of violence, when Jade's meek husband, Vernie, finally fought back against her battering of him—and almost killed her—was *his* violent behavior justified? Are you glad he finally stood up to her and then deserted her?

5. Annette tolerated Jade because of her relationship with Jade's parents. Each time Jade insulted her, Annette responded in ways that usually made Jade feel more insulted than Annette. Do you approve of the way Annette handled Jade's hostility toward her, or do you think she should have "turned the other cheek" the way she used to?

6. Annette didn't want Pee Wee to think that she was sitting at home twiddling her thumbs and that no other man wanted her. That was one of the reasons she got involved with the first man who approached her after Pee Wee's departure— one of her "throwaway" former boyfriends, Jacob Brewster. The other reason she rekindled her relationship with Jacob was because she felt guilty about his son committing suicide after a misunderstanding with her. Do you think she resumed her relationship with Jacob for the wrong reasons?

7. If Jacob had been more responsible, would Annette have fallen in love with him again and eventually forgotten about Pee Wee? If yes, why? If no, why?

8. Annette's daughter, Charlotte, got attached to Jacob right away. But she got too close to him too soon, which made Annette uncomfortable. Do you think that because Annette had been sexually abused throughout her childhood she is too suspicious and hard on men when it comes to her child?

9. Whenever Annette faces a problem, she turns to Rhoda—who consistently gives her advice that usually leads to another problem! Do you think it's time for Annette to stop taking advice from Rhoda and try to solve her problems on her own?

10. It didn't take long for Pee Wee to realize what a big mistake he'd made by moving in with Lizzie. Compared with Annette, Lizzie was a lousy cook, a terrible housekeeper, slovenly behind closed doors, and a woman with a hidden agenda. Do you think Pee Wee got what he deserved when Lizzie dumped him, then went to work for his rival and moved in with his rival's uncle?

11. When Jacob started to mistreat Annette, were you glad she severed her relationship with him? Do you think she should have done it sooner than she did?

12. Do you think that the main reason Pee Wee had an affair was because Annette had had an affair a few months earlier?

13. Do you think Annette's marriage is worth salvaging? If so, why? Do *you* want to see Annette and Pee Wee back together again?